The Black Country' in the West Midlands of the UK. Taught that hard work is the only way to live, Robert made a career in the retail furniture trade, working his way up from warehouseman to store manager.

In 2014, his life took a drastic turn when his wife was diagnosed with a life-threatening illness. He began to ponder the many hours wasted when, on public holidays or at weekends, he was working, leaving his wife to fill her time visiting with family or meeting friends, by herself.

Always a keen reader, fascinated by fantasy and science fiction, he imagined how wonderful it would be if, when faced with adversity, one could simply wave a magic wand and make it all better. Create a new world: two moons and a pink sky. Why not?

This world is his first creation… enjoy.

A huge thank you to my wife Jane, whose tireless encouragement and confidence in my dream eventually made it a reality.

To my best friend Nick, whose larger-than-life personality was inspirational.

To Kenny and Lucy of The Studio Tettenhall, Wolverhampton for their diligent attention to detail when producing the cover for this book, thank you.

To Nick Berriman for somehow finding the time to be my test-pilot, I will be forever grateful.

Robert J Marsters

THE ASCENSION OF KARRAK

Copyright © Robert J. Marsters (2017)

The right of Robert J. Marsters to be identified as author of this work has been asserted by him in accordance with section 77 and 78 of the Copyright, Designs and Patents Act 1988.

All rights reserved. No part of this publication may be reproduced, stored in a retrieval system, or transmitted in any form or by any means, electronic, mechanical, photocopying, recording, or otherwise, without the prior permission of the publishers.

Any person who commits any unauthorized act in relation to this publication may be liable to criminal prosecution and civil claims for damages.

A CIP catalogue record for this title is available from the British Library.

ISBN 978-1-9996518-6-2 (Paperback)
ISBN 978-1-9996518-0-0 (EBook)

PROLOGUE

As Karrak stared into the eyes of the man who lay dead at his feet he felt no remorse. His days of feeling any hint of compassion were a distant memory. People were flawed and weak, something he had deduced after the slaughter of his first victim, a man whose name was, to this day, unknown to him. The only emotions to pass through him now were hatred and rage. As he continued to stare, he could hear the snarling of the hideous beasts scrambling around at the foot of the shallow ridge on which he stood. Placing his boot against the scorched, broken corpse, he pushed it over the ledge, much to the beasts' delight as they gnashed and snapped at one another in an attempt to be first to the kill.

"Feast my pretties," he muttered under his breath, but even if they could have heard, they would not have needed this instruction. Teeth and claws ripped and tore at the flesh, and within seconds the body was in pieces, being devoured by these ravenous beasts. Not a natural lifeform, these were the result of Karrak's tormented mind. He had realised that killing was not always the most fun he could have using sorcery, he could twist and warp the minds of people just as easily as he could twist a small twig. Once this was done, they became his 'pets'. All sentience had gone and they obeyed his every command, with no comprehension of fear. Occasionally, Karrak would torture one simply for his own amusement, the others oblivious to its pain. Only then would he destroy it, throwing its carcase to the rest of the pack.

He turned slowly and quietly walked back into his cave, this being his temporary home. This was no simple cave, the barren rock of the walls remained but the ground was covered with large rugs, not of the highest quality but more than fit for purpose and furnished in a sumptuous manner with large wing-backed chairs strategically placed. Many large tables sat against the walls but few chairs were around them as they were not for entertaining guests. They were covered with scrolls and tomes, mostly on the subject of sorcery save a few that were on necromancy, a subject in which he had not had much interest until quite recently. For these to be of any real use he would need 'The Elixian Soul'. His power over the mind was great indeed, but sapped his own strength and he could only affect one person at a time, but the magnification of his power by the Soul would allow him to bend the minds of numerous victims who foolishly drew too close. Then would come his revenge on his dear father and brother who had so cruelly banished him, and he would be king. His pets would do his bidding, pets to him but they were people, or at least, they had been.

Stranger still was the way he treated them. They did, after all, alert him of the intruder's presence, as was the norm when a visitor approached, snarling and growling, acting as his own personal guard dogs.

Karrak was an imposing figure, standing almost six foot six tall and of a heavy muscular build. Even before he realised his affinity with sorcery people would avoid him, stepping from his path, and if that was not possible, looking down at the floor hoping not to catch his eye. Occasionally there would be the unfortunate soul who could do neither.

***

Once, in a tavern within the city walls, the barkeep had suggested that maybe he had had enough to drink.

"Who are you to tell me when I have drunk enough?" Karrak roared, grabbing the man by his hair and pulling him over the bar. A look of terror came into the barkeep's eyes as he was hoisted onto tiptoes in order to face his abuser, a difficult task being almost a foot shorter.

"I meant no offence, Your Highness, I was merely thinking of your wellbeing," said the man, noticeably shaking. The whole kingdom had heard of Karrak's violent temper.

"My wellbeing should not be your concern, peasant," he hissed and, lifting the man clean off the ground, drew back and head-butted him in the face. There was a loud crack as his nose shattered, blood spattered across his face as he howled in pain, but this was not enough for Karrak who then hurled the barkeep through a table, smashing it to pieces.

Almost as a whisper and whilst drawing his sword, Karrak continued, "Do you think that I would be advised by a piece of filth like you? I have scraped better from my boots." He raised his sword above his head...

"Sire!" The word, loud and unexpected, came from behind him.

Karrak turned slowly. A member of the royal guard stood before him head bowed, "Please forgive me Your Royal Highness, but His Majesty will not be pleased and has vowed that the slaughter of innocents will no longer be tolerated, even by a member of the royal house."

An evil grin came across Karrak's face.

"Yes," he said slowly, "yes my father did say that," at this he began to laugh, a slow menacing laugh. "You don't think that that comment was directed at me do you? I mean solely for me, simply because I have been known to be a little tetchy now and then?"

The guard offered no reply to Karrak's rhetorical question.

"Can a man not just be allowed a little fun?" He turned again to the poor barkeep.

"Well," he said leaning over him, "you get to keep your pathetic life, peasant. Tell me, have you learned your lesson?" The barkeep tried his best to speak, his words incomprehensible, whilst nodding his head frantically. "I don't think you have, not yet anyway." His sadism unsatisfied, Karrak raised his foot and stamped on the man's already blood-soaked face, then twice more. He placed the tip of his sword against his helpless victim's shoulder and thrust it into the joint, holding it there for a second before twisting it, the barkeep now screaming for mercy.

"Now you'll remember your place my dear barkeep, somebody bring me more ale."

Naively, in his youth, it had never crossed his mind that the power of sorcery could aid him in his search of ways to inflict more, and greater suffering. But now he had a sinister synergy with magical forces, and the unspeakable torture it allowed him to perform.

Thus was the cruelty of the man.

CHAPTER 1

As Karrak studied his tomes he heard a faint hissing sound from outside the cave. *The cleansing rain*, he thought, *at least that will wash away the blood of that pious wizard.* The wizard, who was now no more than a pile of bones scattered by his pets.

How did the fool think he could possibly defeat a sorcerer as powerful as I?

The wizard had approached the cave quietly, not intentionally, it was just his way. The growling from the beasts was through fear, not as a warning, for they could sense magical power, possibly a symptom of the curse that was put upon them by Karrak. As the visitor approached they had backed away, most uncharacteristic of these savage, twisted lifeforms.

"I am Emnor," he announced, "I will speak with you, cave dweller."

"What would you say that could possibly interest me, old man?" came the reply from within the cave. "Be on your way, I prefer my own company, stranger."

Remaining polite, Emnor spoke again. "I would speak to you face to face, Sir, not to the entrance of your lair, or are you fearful of me?"

In his younger days Karrak would have been outraged by this question, but he was far different from that person now. He emerged from his home, amused by this confident interloper. He drew himself to his full height, his black robes immaculate from the hood to the ground, the edges embroidered with ancient runes of gold thread. Emnor was impressed at how impeccably attired he was for one living in such conditions.

"I face you now, old man, what is it that you want? I am very busy and your presence is unsettling to my pets."

"Your pets are of no importance to me, but I advise you to keep them at heel, if they misbehave I shall be forced to put them down."

"You would wish to destroy these noble creatures!" exclaimed Karrak, "They do no harm and surely you would not expect me to be unguarded in these harsh surroundings?"

"I hardly think a sorcerer as powerful as you would need protection, Karrak."

"Well, well, well aren't we the clever one? You know my name, but you are mistaken, friend. I am just a simple man who enjoys living amongst nature. The lakes, the forests and the mountains are all I have, I am no sorcerer," Karrak was enjoying this little game of words.

"You, Sir, are Prince Karrak Dunbar, son of Tamor, heir to the throne of Borell, second in line to your brother, Jared, whom you tried to murder."

"And would have succeeded but for the likes of you, wizard," Karrak snapped, a maniacal glint in his eye. He so wanted to destroy Emnor. For the old wizard to have the audacity to even face him was as much of an insult to his power as a mouse teasing a cat.

"So what now, wizard?" he continued, "Do you mean to evict me or are you simply here to bore me to death with your inane prattle?"

"Neither, I am here to give you notice. You have three days to remove yourself from these lands, you and these abominations," replied Emnor pointing at the beasts. "If you do not, you will be driven out, by order of your father, King Tamor." Having said his piece, Emnor turned and began to walk away.

The rage came upon Karrak in an instant. He roared and thrust his hands out in front of him. Emnor had anticipated a cowardly attack by Karrak and turning swiftly raised his hand. A bolt of flame that had leapt from Karrak's hands was deflected but just managed to catch the side of Emnor's face. He could smell his own burned flesh and the singed hair of his beard before hearing the explosion, as the tree behind him was engulfed. He thrust his own hands forward now, casting his own spell. Spears of ice flew straight at Karrak, who simply held up one hand. A sheet of flame appeared before him and easily melted the ice spears. Emnor had suspected that his first spell would be of no effect and had just used it as a ruse to play for time, for even as Karrak had defused it, Emnor had cast another. A wave of ice was already encircling Karrak and before he could react, Emnor's second spell was upon him. The ice wave struck him from behind wrapping itself around his body like a blanket, encasing him and throwing him to the ground.

Karrak began to laugh, "Had your fun, old man?" he asked, "Because now… it's my turn."

He began to mutter under his breath and the ice instantly melted from his body. He rose to his feet, his voice getting louder. Trees began to erupt around Emnor, splinters struck him from every direction, some piercing his skin. Everything around him was ablaze, an evil smile now on Karrak's face as he glared at the wizard. His own conjured flame was about him, but he remained unharmed. He raised his hand and Emnor was lifted off the ground. Karrak, simply by moving his index finger from side to side as if conducting an orchestra, caused Emnor to crash into tree after tree lacerating and burning him beyond recognition.

"You now see what true power is," stated Karrak. "Your party tricks are no match for me, old man."

Emnor, still in mid-air could not comprehend anything that was being said to him. The pain from the cuts, burns and broken bones were the only things on which his mind could focus.

Karrak waved his hand and the flames were immediately extinguished, as Emnor's life was about to be.

He looked into the old man's eyes, "Time to die," he said. "Now what was your name again? Oh never mind." He held up his hand, his palm facing the wreckage of the once-proud wizard and once again began to chant. Emnor floated toward Karrak and began to shake as Karrak slowly closed his hand. Emnor's head began to contort as if under immense pressure until, with a crunch, the back of his skull split open, blood spurting like spilt wine. Karrak dropped his arm to his side, and Emnor's lifeless body fell to the ground before him, eyes still open.

Why had this impudent upstart accepted such a suicidal mission? Karrak pondered. *Did he have such fealty for my father? Did King Tamor actually send him? Or had he hoped to gain the fountain of knowledge contained within my library for himself, and why now?*

Countless wizards, mages or sorcerers would do anything to possess such a collection. Some would use it for their own evil purpose while others would bury, hide or destroy it to keep its power hidden. *Or was it because he was closer to finding the location of the Elixian Soul than he had realised?* He dismissed that question immediately. He did not make mistakes and if the Soul had been in close proximity, he would have heard its call. To him this was not arrogance, he knew that he was the most powerful sorcerer that had, or would, ever exist.

CHAPTER 2

King Tamor stood atop the highest tower of his castle, surveying the countless leagues of his kingdom. As far as the eye could see and beyond belonged to House Dunbar. He and his ancestors had fought many wars across centuries, brother beside brother and father beside son, to protect these lands but Borell had now enjoyed peace for over fifty years. The land was fertile and green, every tree was abound with succulent fruit and the livestock was of the finest pedigree thus supplying copious amounts of meat and poultry. Life in Borell was good and King Tamor's subjects knew that this was because of him. He was as loyal to them as they were to him.

"Tell me, Father, what do you see when you look across your lands?"

The king was quick to reply and spinning on his heel, bellowed at the top of his voice, "How dare you address me so in front of others?" he said, glancing across at his royal guard. "I am your king and you will address me as such, Your Majesty, My Liege, King Tamor, any one of these would be suitable!"

Prince Jared's expression did not change as he looked into his father's eyes. There were a few moments of silence between them, as slowly the corners of the king's mouth began to curl upwards, before bursting into fits of laughter and throwing his arms around his son, who was now also laughing.

"What I haven't seen is you, my boy, and for far too long. Where have you been? What took you so long? I expected your return over a month ago, why did you send no word?"

"Please, Father, one question at a time," said Jared smiling at the king. "I am dishevelled and smell worse than my horse, I need to bathe, and then we shall talk."

"Yes, yes of course, my boy. Go, get yourself cleaned up, oh, and we have some very pretty young maids new to the castle, should you need any help."

Jared gave a sigh, "Father, will you never change?" he asked, smiling.

"Well," said the king holding his arms out from his sides, "I can't help it if they all love me."

Jared made his way toward the steps that lead to his chambers. Once inside, he closed the door and half leaned, half fell against it. The pain in his shoulder was worsening, but how could he visit the court physician without his father knowing? He had sworn his personal guards to secrecy and this promise they would uphold, not through fear of reprisal, but for the love and admiration they all had for him.

He had barely removed his gauntlets and greaves, preferring to do this himself and not instruct one of his soldiers to undress him as if he were a helpless child. As he struggled clumsily with the buckles he heard a knock at the door and a voice announced, "Sire, I bring refreshment should you feel the need."

Jared knew the voice, it was Hannock, a loyal friend to the prince. "And by whose order were you demoted to the position of chambermaid, my dear friend?" said Jared pulling open the door.

"Well I thought you wouldn't mind me earning a little extra coin, Sire," said Hannock with a huge grin on his face. He stood with a very large tray balanced on one arm, the other stretched out to his side so that his hand and forearm were obscured beyond the doorway.

"What are you up to, Hannock?" asked Jared.

"Me, Sire? Nothing at all, Sire," and with this statement gave a tug with his secreted arm. A small, wizened old man suddenly appeared before the prince, looking more than a little unnerved.

"Alfred!" exclaimed Jared, "well I'll be… I thought you'd retired, my dear fellow."

"So did I, Your Highness," replied the old man, "but your 'friend' persuaded me to come out of retirement, just on a temporary basis of course."

"Did he now? Well in that case don't dally on the doorstep dear fellow, come in."

Hannock placed the tray on the table in the middle of the room and steered the old man to a chair next to it, "Answer me a question, Alfred, how long were you court physician?"

"Ninety-eight years, Captain," came the reply.

"And in all those years your primary care was that of the royal family was it not?"

"Yes, Sir, and it was an honour to be chosen for that duty."

"Would you ever break a promise to, or a confidence of, a member of the royal household?"

"I would die first, Sir, on that you have my word."

"Good, I'm glad that's out of the way. Sire, let's get that armour and shirt off you, shall we?" With Hannock's help, Jared undressed. The wound on his shoulder had started to fester and the smell from it was enough to turn the strongest of stomachs.

"Magic!" exclaimed Alfred, "Damn them all and their accursed spells."

Jared raised his eyebrows, "My word you've not missed a step have you, old man! One look and a diagnosis in a second, very impressive. I take it you've seen this type of wound before?"

"Yes, Sir, I have, and it's most unpleasant, may I ask when this occurred?"

Jared and Hannock looked at one another, obviously each hoping that the other would have an exact answer, but neither did. "About five weeks?" Jared said, looking at Hannock for affirmation.

"That sounds about right, Sire," nodded Hannock.

"Good, your armour must have deflected most of the force of the spell. If it hadn't, you and I wouldn't be having this conversation, Sire, you'd have died instantly. Now all I have to do is amputate the arm, cauterise the wound with a branding iron and you'll be fine!"

A look of horror came across the faces of Jared and Hannock. Alfred looked at them both for a few moments and began to chuckle. The two men stared at him in disbelief as he sat there highly amused at his own 'little joke'.

Alfred glared at Hannock, "Drag an old man round by his arm will you, all you had to do was ask." He then looked to Jared, "Now let's see about preparing a poultice for that shoulder of yours shall we, Your Highness?"

With the wound now cleaned and dressed, Alfred bowed as low as he could, not the easiest of tasks for a man of one hundred and thirty-seven, "I shall return tomorrow, Your Highness, to redress the wound. However, should you be in discomfort or need my assistance, please send your 'errand boy'," and at this he gave a wry smile to Hannock, "and I shall come immediately."

Jared thanked Alfred and walked him to the door, at the same time shaking his hand and placing some gold coins into his palm. Alfred bowed again and left.

"I do like that man," said Hannock laughing quietly, "having the cheek to call me an errand boy, now that's courage."

"You do realise that your feelings toward Alfred are not reciprocated don't you, Hannock?" Jared asked, a smile appearing on his face.

"You can't be loved by everyone, Sire."

"According to my father, you can."

***

Now dressed in more suitable attire, Prince Jared made his way to the throne room in search of his father. Courtiers bowed and curtsied before him as he made his way through the halls of the castle. Huge tapestries covered every wall with strategic gaps to accommodate roaring log fires set in deep inglenook fireplaces. The heavy iron cartwheel chandeliers, suspended from beamed ceilings, each holding a hundred candles, were adorned with stones and the reflected light from the flames caused each one to sparkle like a red star, helping to illuminate the huge expanse of these great halls. Heavy woven rugs covered the floors, with only the edges bared to show the pure white marble beneath. No, this was no cold, damp stone fortress it was a palace residing within a castle, comfortable, and safe.

"Ah there you are, my boy," King Tamor called, raising his voice to ensure that all courtiers knew of Jared's presence. "A toast," he announced, "to the safe return of my son and heir, Prince Jared." The toast was echoed around the room as various glasses and goblets were raised into the air.

"Thank you friends. It is good to be back in the bosom of my people," said Jared, and gave a gracious bow to the room.

"Come, sit with me, Jared. Tell me of your adventures in the wilds beyond our kingdom," instructed Tamor.

Jared crossed the room slowly, nodding and smiling at the various lords and ladies as he went. All wished he would stop and chat with them thus somehow raising their social standing. He had, of course, no interest in conversing with any of them. They bored him. The women, regardless of age, were giggling imbeciles and the men, if they could be called that, wouldn't know the difference between a sword and a longbow let alone its use. Reaching his father, Jared sat at his right hand, the rightful place for the heir to the throne.

"Something troubling you, Jared?" asked Tamor.

"I always long to be home with you, Father, but once I am and I see these prattling peacocks, I wish I were back patrolling in the wilds," he replied with a heavy sigh.

"One day my son, you shall be king to these peacocks, so I suggest that you learn how they roost before that day comes."

"Perhaps, Father, but that's a long way off yet. Can I just get drunk and try to ignore them, if only for one night?"

Tamor laughed, another one of his belly laughs. "You, my son, can do whatever you want for now, for you are a Prince of Borell and House Dunbar." Tamor grabbed a jug from the maid beside him and sloshed wine into a jewel encrusted goblet. "Here, my boy, drink," he said.

Many guests attempted to entice Jared from his father's side. Jared would make the excuse of fatigue after a long journey and then shoo them away with a wave of his hand, who would be so bold as to be insistent with royalty and refuse to take no for an answer? The evening was becoming easier for Jared, the warmth of the fire and the wine were actually making it quite bearable. Occasionally, he would look around the room at the women present, pausing for a second on the most attractive, but only for a second, making eye contact may mean he'd have to speak to one of them, fat chance.

Now, it was customary to have the royal guard present at all times and this evening was no exception. It was deemed a great honour to join these ranks and only the absolute elite were accepted. Once enlisted, each member was presented with a royal blue velvet cloak, a badge of honour that stood out amongst the red cloaks of the regulars. The ultimate goal, however, was to earn the purple cloak, of which there was only one. The only person to have the honour of wearing this was the captain of the guard, an honour held by Hannock. He alone had passed every test put before him. From combat, armed or unarmed, to battle strategies, he had never been bested.

Hannock's rank also had its privileges, and not just the obvious ones such as money and respect, it also excused him from having to attend social gatherings, such as the one Jared was, by duty, attending this evening.

***

Hannock was no ordinary man. He and Jared were the same age and had, more or less, been raised together. Hannock's father had also been in the royal guard but, unlike his son, had never risen to the rank of captain. As boys, the two were inseparable and usually up to mischief, being discovered in places they should not have been, or interfering with things they ought not to. One such occasion resulted in the pronounced scar on Hannock's cheek.

Amongst their childhood escapades, or 'adventures' as they referred to them, was the time they decided to sneak into the armoury. By slipping past guards and dodging in and out of shadows, they had achieved their goal. Once there they stood in awe, eyes wide at the array of weapons before them. Swords, shields, pikestaffs, bows and armour, all highly polished and in pristine condition. They had approached these, slightly hesitant, but also full of excitement.

"When I'm older I shall be in the royal guard and fight for the kingdom," Hannock had said, "I'll protect your castle for you, Jared."

No formalities existed between the two boys as yet. They were far too young to be concerned with such nonsense, no, they were more interested in having adventures, imagined yes, but to them, no less exciting.

"Wow, look at that one, Hannock."

Jared was pointing at the far wall which Hannock now turned to face. Hanging on a golden plaque in its centre was a crossbow. Now the boys were no strangers to crossbows, they saw them every day, but none like this one. This one was magnificent. Not just dull clunky pieces of iron and wood, crude but effective, this weapon was made with a skill that was more love than craft. A solid piece of rosewood had been carved and polished to form the stock and was as smooth as glass. Runes were carved into it and every piece of metalwork, that would normally be iron, had instead been forged from pure gold that shimmered in the light of the torches that burned either side of it. Even the bowstring was wound from gold thread.

Jared reached for it.

"I don't think you should touch that," Hannock said giving his friend a slightly nervous look.

"I'm a prince, I can do what I like," whispered Jared, not forgetting that they were somewhere they shouldn't be. But as the boys looked at each other they had to stifle their giggles by putting their hands to their mouths. Again, Jared reached toward the crossbow, but this time he grasped it firmly and lifted it from its plaque. He was caught unawares, he had not realised just how heavy the weapon would be and barely caught himself, and the crossbow, before it hit the ground. A look of relief came across the boys' faces, if it had hit the ground they would have been surrounded by guards within seconds.

"That was a close one," Hannock said, "put it back before you damage it."

"In a minute, prince, remember?" Jared replied with a cheeky smile. He raised the crossbow and pointed it at Hannock.

"What are you doing, Jared? Put it down."

But the prince was having too much fun, for some reason he felt powerful, as if this weapon had projected him into premature adulthood. "Hold cur, you shall not invade my lands, I will defend them to my dying breath, if you and your…"

Jared never got to finish the sentence. Without realising, his index finger had moved to the trigger, the slightest pressure had released the golden bolt and it flew through the air, glancing across his friend's left cheek and embedding itself in the wall. Hannock spun and fell to the floor screaming, as any child would, his hands and face now covered in blood. As the boys had feared, it only took a few seconds before the guard appeared. Jared stood, petrified, not by the arrival of the guard but because he had wounded his best friend in the world.

Guards began calling for the court physician to be summoned and, worst of all, the king was informed of the incident.

Tamor swept into the room his golden robes flowing behind him. He quickened his pace to reach the wounded boy and, after exchanging a few words with the court physician who had arrived a few moments before, turned to face Jared.

Jared wanted to speak, wanted to explain, wanted to apologise, but found he could not utter a single word as he stood in his father's glare, a solitary tear running down his cheek.

Tamor stormed toward him, Jared never flinched. His father was a good man and had never beaten either of his sons, believing that words and common sense were far better tools of learning. Prevention rather than cure was his way and proved to be accurate, until now. The king grabbed Jared by the shoulder of his tunic and marched him from the room, not allowing him time to speak to his wounded friend.

***

A few days after the events in the armoury, both Jared and Hannock were summoned to appear before the king. They had not seen or spoken to one another since the accident, for they both knew that's all it had been, an unfortunate accident. How to explain it to the king, however, was something completely different. They also had to justify their presence in the armoury in the first place, which was off limits to all except military personnel and the king himself.

There was a knock at the door of Jared's chambers. Two guards entered, ready to escort the prince. Reaching the throne room the guards took their positions, one ahead of him the other behind, and marched him in. Jared tried his best to keep in step with the guard in front, but failed dismally as his legs were much shorter. He never saw it as a childish game, he was trying to show his father, the king, the utmost respect.

Hannock was already standing before the king. A large dressing was wrapped around his cheek and Jared could see slight traces of blood still showing on it, causing a pang of guilt to shoot through him. He was positioned beside his friend but neither dared look at the other, their

26

eyes focussed on Tamor. Jared bowed to his father without speaking.

"Well at least you have not forgotten your manners," said Tamor, "such a shame that your memory fails you when you need it most, Jared. Hannock, how is your health today? Are you feeling better?"

"Yes Your Majesty, much better thank you," replied Hannock, looking at the floor.

"Do you like the rug, Hannock? My eyes are in my head boy, not on the floor, look at me when you speak."

"Yes Your Majesty, my apologies Your Majesty," he replied and raised his head.

"And how is my firstborn today? Are you well today, Jared?"

"Thank you, Sir, I am quite well."

"Now," began Tamor, "this unfortunate incident in the armoury. It cannot be ignored or go unpunished. I understand from Hannock's statement that this was just a game, an accident. However, there are very few accidental trespasses into restricted areas that are patrolled by my guards, guards who have already been punished for dereliction of duty. Can you now see that the consequences of your actions are suffered not only by you, but also by others around you?"

The boys looked at each other for the first time, and then back to the king.

"Yes Your Majesty," they replied almost simultaneously.

"So, you like to play with weapons," said Tamor. "Well, who am I to stand in your way? Tomorrow you shall report to the Master at Arms at dawn where you shall begin your weapons training. Be under no illusion, you will be given no preferential treatment. No quarter shall be given, even if you are a prince of the realm or his best friend. You shall not complain and will be subject to the same punishment as any other should you disobey orders, do I make myself clear?"

"Yes, Sire."

"Oh and just a word of advice boys, you may want to steer clear of the guards you slipped past the other night, just for a few days. I heard that cleaning out the cesspits is not the most pleasant of duties," at this he gave a loud laugh. "Dismissed."

***

The friends, as instructed, reported for duty the following day. Standing in the courtyard, the pouring rain dripped from their noses as they faced the Master at Arms.

"Bloody hell, I know I'm good but what the hell am I supposed to do with you two? I don't think we have any dresses that need mending, and my men help themselves to ale so we don't need bar wenches either. Alright, I suppose you'd better follow me," he instructed. "Your word is my command, King Tamor," he muttered under his breath, shaking his head.

The boys were taken to a large hut in the corner of the courtyard. Here they were issued uniforms. Not an easy job, as even the smallest size was still far too big for them, but with pins and belts they were kitted out as a temporary measure.

Thus began their military education. The most amusing thing, more so than their ill-fitting uniforms, was the look on their faces when they were handed wooden swords with which to begin their fencing lessons.

"Don't want you little ladies cutting yourselves now do we?" said the Master at Arms. "Well not just yet anyway."

The training was much harder than the boys could have ever imagined. The king spoke the truth when he told them that they would be treated the same as all raw recruits in his army.

Days turned into weeks, weeks into months and things got easier for them as both their strength and stamina increased. Hannock however, had to suffer a little more than Jared, for even though the king had said otherwise, the disgruntled guards were a little wary of treating Jared too badly. He was, after all, a prince, and none would risk incurring the wrath of the king just to get a little payback. Poor Hannock received many a clip round the ear and kick in the backside, but was proving to be very resilient as he endured this punishment and persevered.

***

One morning they both reported for duty as usual.

"Time to step up the game a little today, ladies," said the sword master. "So far you've been pitted against other non-entities such as yourselves, today however, you'll be training with some of the regulars."

The boys' eyes grew wide at the thought. *Was this the vengeance that the guards had sought all along? Did they mean to kill them and make the excuse that it was an accident, as the one in the armoury had been?*

Before sheer panic could set in, and it was approaching rapidly, the sword master spoke again. "I think we'll start with you, Prince Jared."

Jared's heart sank. *Why him? Why not start with Hannock? He was the better swordsman, after all,* he thought.

Not giving him time to think, the sword master nodded toward one of the guards and raising his voice just slightly, instructed them to take their places.

Jared walked toward the arena, just a roped circle to one side of the courtyard. His legs felt like lead, his heart was racing and his head was swimming. Facing his opponent, he raised his sword in salute and the sparring began. Jared was, of course, no match for the guard. He parried as many blows as he could and occasionally even managed to attempt to strike a blow of his own, to no avail. The guard toyed with Jared for what seemed like an age, striking him with the flat of his own wooden sword time after time. The blows were not hard, his opponent not being a sadist, but they were enough to leave bruises and after all, Jared already had plenty of those. Having seen enough, the sword master caught the eye of the guard and gave the slightest of nods. The guard acknowledged it and a few seconds later in one swift movement Jared's sword was spun into the air. The guard raised his sword above his head and roared, this of course being only for effect as he never meant to harm the boy. Jared however, did not know this, and thrust both his hands out in front of him toward the guard. "No!" he screamed.

This is when there was a turn of events that no-one could have foreseen, especially Jared. As he had thrust his hands forward he had also turned his head and closed his eyes, waiting for the death blow, but he would not prove to be the victim today. His opponent was suddenly lifted from his feet, thrown ten feet in the air and propelled backwards at lightning speed. He cried out, in shock rather than in pain, and in a split second came back to earth some thirty feet away, crashing through a cart full of hay. This, luckily, braced his fall, for the ferocity of this unknown force could have quite possibly killed him, had he struck the castle wall. They all stood there aghast, mouths open unable to comprehend what they had just seen. The first to speak was the sword master, "What in the name of...?"

The guard was quickly taken to the court physician. He was fine, mostly, just a few minor cuts and bruises suffered, not due to his flight, but by his landing. The Master at Arms checked Jared for wounds, but gave him the all-clear and, unsure of exactly what to do, dismissed him and Hannock for the rest of the day. The boys were now in Jared's chambers cleaning off the mud, Jared dabbing gently at his bruises.

"How the hell did you do it?" asked Hannock.

"Do what? I didn't *do* anything, I thought he was going to kill me and I just put my hands up to protect myself."

"Oh no, no, no, you don't get off that lightly. It was as if you pushed him, really hard, but without touching him. But how?"

"I have no idea, Hannock, honestly I don't."

Their conversation was suddenly interrupted by a knock at the door. "Your Highness, I must speak with you at the behest of your father."

31

"Oh bugger, here we go again," whispered Jared so as not to be overheard by the unwelcome guest outside the door, "I never even did anything!"

Jared opened the door gingerly and looked at the old man who now faced him.

"Your Highness, His Majesty asked that I speak with you concerning events that occurred a short while ago in the courtyard during your, erm, training. Oh forgive me, where are my manners? I am Emnor."

"Please, come in," gestured Jared.

"That is most kind, Your Highness. Your father believes that it would be better if I were to speak with you... alone."

Jared glanced at Hannock, not really wanting him to leave.

"Right, sorry," said Hannock. Pulling his shirt over his head whilst trying to bow to Jared, a feeble attempt at a bow anyway, he hurried toward the door. "I'll see you later, at dinner perhaps, Your Highness," he said with a slight snigger and dashed through the door giggling to himself.

"Strange boy," said Emnor.

"He's my best friend," said Jared, not liking the old man's opinion of Hannock.

"My apologies, Your Highness, I meant no offence."

"Am I in trouble again?" asked Jared closing the door.

"I don't know, Your Highness, should you be?"

"Of course not, I've done nothing wrong."

Emnor said nothing and continued to gaze at the young prince.

"Look, I don't know what happened. I thought that man was going to kill me and the next thing I know, he's lying in a broken hay cart. I never even touched him."

"Tell me," began Emnor, "exactly what happened."

Jared began to relate the details of his sparring session earlier that morning. Emnor listened intently as Jared never missed out a single detail whilst giving his blow by blow explanation. Finishing his statement with, "So you see, I never actually did anything."

Emnor sat stroking his beard, "Interesting, very interesting," he said.

"What is?" asked Jared.

"You said that you put your hands up in front of you? Is that so, or did you actually thrust them forwards?" asked Emnor.

"Now you mention it, I think it was forwards," replied Jared.

"Good," said Emnor, "very good indeed."

Jared sat there with a confused look on his face, thinking that the old man was another one of his father's loonies. He had plenty of them. Soothsayers, astronomers and astrologers, or as the boys liked to call them, barmpots.

"Tell me, Jared, oh, you don't mind if I call you by name do you, Your Highness?"

"Not at all, it saves time," Jared replied.

"How much do you remember of your mother?"

"Nothing really, I was very young when she died. Sometimes I think I can remember her face but even then

I'm not sure whether it's her or somebody else. As I said, I was very young."

"Jared, I do believe, from your recollection of this morning, that you have a gift, a very special gift."

"What kind of gift?"

"I think that you have the power of magic within you, Jared, and this morning was the very first sign of it."

"How marvellous! I can do tricks to impress the guards then maybe they'll take it easy on me when we're sparring, and Hannock will think it's fun too."

"No, Jared, you do not understand. I do not speak of mere party tricks. The power you possess, if harnessed, could change your destiny forever, therefore we must begin your instruction very soon if we are to refine it. I shall speak with your father and together we shall draw up a schedule. Time is of the essence."

Before Emnor had finished his speech, Jared had come to a conclusion, the old man was just another barmpot.

Emnor bowed and bade farewell to Jared, then swept through the door much faster than Jared thought a man of his age possibly could. For to young eyes, he looked very, very old.

Jared flopped back onto his bed still more than a little confused. *Great*, he thought, *more blasted training*.

Hannock had hidden behind a large tapestry, waiting for Emnor's departure. He then raced back to Jared, so that he could learn of Jared's conversation with the old man.

"So what are you then? A mage, a wizard, or are you an evil sorcerer? Because if you're one of those I can cut your head off now, stops you turning me into a toad later, see!" At this he burst into hysterical laughter, rolling around on Jared's bed, holding his sides.

"Shut your face, Hannock, it's not funny. That barmpot might take me off to some damp old monastery in the mountains or something? You may never see me again."

Hannock stopped laughing and sat bolt upright, a frown appearing on his face. "Mmm hadn't thought of that," he said, "we'll have to put a stop to that."

"There's nothing we can do about it. I'm not saying that they will send me away, but there's always a chance."

"Yeah, and there's also a chance of you growing wings, a tail and sprouting horns now you're an evil sorcerer, but let's hope that doesn't happen either," said Hannock, as hysterics took hold of him again.

"There's just no talking to you when you're like this, Hannock?" Jared promptly began beating him with a pillow.

CHAPTER 3

The next few months went as all others had with very little alteration to their daily schedule. The wooden swords were a thing of the past and they had now learned skills with shields, pikestaffs, longbows and crossbows, the only weapon that Jared was reluctant to discuss. Hannock found this amusing. The accident had taken place over a year ago now and, although he never told anyone, he liked his scar and felt it gave him more character. The real change was Hannock's proficiency with a sword. He wielded it as if it were an extension of his own arm, impressing the best swordsmen in the guard as well as his father, and most of all, the captain. It was quite obvious to all that this boy was destined for great things.

When they sparred against one another, however, the boys were fiercely competitive and neither would give any quarter. Many a time they attracted an audience without meaning to and guards could be seen making wagers amongst themselves, betting on the outcome. Strange that they would do this, for the result was always the same - Hannock won. The friends would never fall out over it, they were far too close and just saw it as their own personal game. Although most games one would never walk away with a split lip or a black eye.

Once they had finished their session there were always the same comments from the guards: *You'll get*

36

him next time, Your Highness, I'll still bet on you Sire, or, *I can feel a big win coming my way.* This would never happen, both boys knew that. They had worked hard, never complained and now fought well and this earned them a lot of respect from their brothers in arms. They were no longer regarded as children, they were regulars. Admittedly, they had never been into battle, but they had proved their worth and would soon be men.

***

Winter had come to Borell once again. The landscape was covered with a thick blanket of snow and the air smelled fresh and clean. The memory of Emnor had left Jared and this morning, just like any other, he had breakfasted with his friend and they were now heading across the great hall to attend to their duties as fully-fledged members of the guard. As Jared walked, joking with Hannock, he felt small arms wrap around his leg.

"Can I come with you today, Jared? I promise I won't get in the way."

Jared leaned down and lifted the boy in his arms, being careful not to press him too hard against his chainmail. "And what could you do if I did take you with me, Karrak?" he asked.

"I could feed the horses... or sweep the stables... or polish your sword..."

"Those are not the duties of a royal prince, baby brother, and besides you aren't that tall yet, we might lose you in the snow, it is quite deep. You just find something to do indoors where it's nice and warm, I'll see you when we return."

"I'm not a baby, I'm ten now. I hate it here, it's so boring," Karrak whined. Sliding from Jared's arms, he stormed off in a huff.

"Please tell me we were never that bad," said Hannock.

"Oh no my friend, we were much worse." Laughing, they continued across the hall.

They never made it to the door. Looking up, they saw the king enter, strange in itself as Tamor never took breakfast before nine o clock and it was not yet even six.

They both bowed low.

"Good morning to you both, and how does this fine day find you?"

They replied in turn, eager to get on with their day but not daring to show it, one does not simply rebuff a king. As they stood exchanging pleasantries, another figure appeared to the side but slightly behind King Tamor.

"Ah there you are, Emnor," said the king, "I believe you have already met Emnor? He's a very old friend of mine, and a wise one at that." Jared and Hannock greeted Emnor. "Anyway, I'm glad I bumped into you both," continued Tamor.

"Emnor needs to speak with you Jared, and I need to have words with you, Hannock, and before you say anything, the guard have been informed that neither of you shall be reporting for duty today so don't worry, it's all been taken care of." With this he took Hannock by the arm and steered him away, his voice trailing into the distance.

Jared looked into the old man's eyes. *The barmpot*, as he had referred to him in conversation with Hannock many months before.

"Did you think that the old barmpot had forgotten you, Jared?" asked Emnor.

Jared was unsure how to react to the question and simply continued to look at him. *How the hell did he know?* He and Hannock had been alone when they had had that conversation, it was not possible that anyone could have heard them, let alone Emnor himself.

"Don't worry, I've been called a lot worse in my time, of that you can be sure," he said smiling, a warm smile that reached his eyes. "May we adjourn to somewhere a little more private? What I have to say is for your ears only."

The pair entered the library. Two young women sat together, working on their embroidery and seeing the handsome prince enter the room, began whispering to one another and giggling.

"Excuse me, ladies, but my friend and I require a little privacy. Is there another room in which you could, perchance, continue with your embroidery?" Jared had always been taught that good manners cost nothing.

The two women looked at one another for a moment but did not move, rather taken aback by the request of the young prince.

"Did you not hear, you gossiping harpies," bellowed Emnor, "the Royal Prince just told you to get out, now do so before I turn you into swine and have your bacon for breakfast." His bellowing scared the wits out of the poor women, who scampered through the doorway, Emnor slamming the door behind them. "Do you know," he said, "some days I do so love being me," and began to chuckle, "always gets a result that does."

Jared wiped his hand across his face, he was right, an absolute barmpot.

The discussion between the two lasted for most of the morning. Emnor explained that the magic he believed that Jared could command was from his mother's side of the family. There was a history of white witches and mages trailing back centuries if one only knew where to find the archives which, strangely enough, could only be revealed with the use of magic. The one thing that had intrigued Emnor, however, was that the power was usually only passed on from mother to daughter and father to son, very rarely mother to son.

"This is nonsense. I don't know anything about magic, I'm a prince, don't you think that's enough to deal with? Can't you pick on somebody else? I like my life the way it is, I'm not interested in your fantasies, old man," snapped Jared.

Jared's outburst was more surprising to himself than it would have been to anyone else, proving that he was rapidly approaching adulthood. Emnor however was not surprised at all. "That's it, my boy, get rid of the anger and confusion, it'll help with your studies."

Emnor walked to the window and flung it open. He stretched out his arm and whilst faintly mumbling to himself, began to move his hand in a circular motion. Jared, out of curiosity, moved forward until he was standing directly behind Emnor. Ice crystals had begun to form around his hand, but were not actually touching it. Within seconds the ball of ice was about six inches in diameter. Without warning, Emnor thrust his hand forward. The ice-ball seemed to launch itself and was heading toward a tree that was at least a hundred feet away, gaining velocity as it did so, until with a loud crash, it hit one of the boughs, cleaving it from the trunk.

Emnor turned to face Jared, "Fantasies?" he asked. Jared sat down slowly as Emnor closed the window, "So you see my dear Jared, this is what I offer you, but only if you are willing."

Jared nodded his head, "Well," he said, "now that you put it like that…"

It was agreed that Jared would continue to be a member of the guard and tend to his duties each morning. However, after lunch, he would report to Emnor for instruction in the ways of magic. True, his father did have reservations with Jared's education in such things, but understood that he must be taught how to control it. His power had manifested itself once, uncontrolled emotion being the cause. It would not pay to have a repeat of the courtyard incident. A guard had been injured, but it could have been much worse. Tamor also realised that if Jared could master his powers, one day, if needed, they may aid him in the defence of Borell.

Combining studies was not difficult for Jared. He was used to the way things worked as a member of the guard and dealt with them almost without thinking, but he adored his studies in magic. Emnor was impressed at how naturally magic came to Jared, he remembered everything he was told and could repeat it verbatim.

The practical side however, did get off to a slightly shaky start.

Emnor had decided that the theoretical side of things was falling into place very easily for Jared and that today would be his first practical test, but that they should ride a little way from the castle so as not to be interrupted. Being totally honest, he thought it would be safer.

They had ridden for about two miles when Emnor stopped. They were at the edge of the western forest, a perfect spot. The trees opened slightly and a natural horseshoe-shaped clearing was at the very edge. Whilst practising there, they could not be observed, or spied upon, his pupil had a right to privacy. To the side of the forest ran a small stream edged with large boulders. Emnor studied the scenery, pleased that he had discovered the perfect testing ground for Jared.

"Now remember what I said, Jared, you must clear your mind, focus only on the spell, let nothing interfere with that focus and you'll be fine."

Each member of the magical society had a particular affinity with one type of elemental magic. For some it was fire, others water, wind or lightning. Emnor's, for instance, was water, but used as ice to increase its force. As of yet, neither of them knew exactly what Jared's would be, but hopefully, they were about to find out.

"Right then, Jared, let's see what you're made of, what element will it be?"

"Well that's the one thing I'm not sure of. If you remember, I never actually used any of those when I hurt the guard, I just kind of pushed him."

"Just kind of pushed him?" Emnor echoed.

"Well that's what happened," shrugged Jared.

"Well in that case I'll leave it to you to decide." Emnor sat down on a boulder, folded his arms, raised his eyebrows and waited.

Come on Jared you can do this, he thought to himself. *Focus, but on what earth, fire, wind, or water?*

He closed his eyes. For a while nothing happened. There was a faint rumbling as the ground began to tremble, Emnor never spoke, not wanting to break his student's concentration, but smiled at the result. The ground began to shake more violently and the rumbling became a roar, when suddenly one of the trees was ripped from the ground as easily as one would pick a small flower. Some of the smaller boulders around Emnor started to float and lightning bolts were striking them, appearing out of thin air. They struck again and again until the boulders glowed red, the uprooted tree shot a hundred feet into the air and the boulders followed it like hounds after a hare causing it to erupt into flames. Even before it had time to hit the ground again the tree was turned to ash, but the flames had spread to the nearby trees which were now also ablaze. The small stream seemed to grow and a huge wave suddenly appeared. It washed across both Emnor and Jared but then, luckily, it crashed into the trees dousing every hint of flame, the water ebbed back into its natural stream and all was calm once more.

Emnor, still sat on his boulder was now soaking wet. He wiped the water from his eyes and blinked at Jared, the smile literally washed from his face. "Can't make your mind up eh?"

The commotion had spooked the horses causing them to bolt. Emnor rose from his rock, gave a slight chuckle and began the long walk back to the castle.

CHAPTER 4

Twenty years had passed since Jared's first practical lesson in magic. He had become very powerful, far beyond the measure that Emnor had seen at their first attempt and kept telling him that, in time, he could become one the greatest wizards that ever lived. Jared always stopped Emnor at this point for, although a prince, he was still a very modest man. As time had gone by, they had become firm friends. Jared still enjoyed calling him a 'barmpot' occasionally, but now he could call it him to his face, and always with a smile. Tamor's hair and beard were starting to show a little grey, Hannock and Jared still remained the best of friends and his baby brother, oh God above, his baby brother, who now stood three inches taller than him and was built like a barn, had become a pain in his royal backside. Jared had forgotten how many bribes he had given to cover for his brother, for if his father found out... Karrak had beaten men senseless, simply, it seemed, because he wanted to, and Jared had already paid two women to leave the kingdom and take Karrak's illegitimate offspring with them. It seemed so long ago when the annoying little brat was always hanging onto his leg. Except when Jared was taking secret instruction from Emnor, Karrak's face would often appear from a doorway, or peep through a window. Jared just wished that he would grow up, or bugger off, he really didn't care which.

"Hello, Brother."

Jared closed his eyes. He had his back to Karrak, but could tell from his voice that he was drunk, again. He should not have been surprised, as Karrak was drunk most of the time.

"What is it, Karrak? I'm very busy."

"You don't look busy; you look like you're standing there posing as usual."

"I must consult with the captain of the guard. I'm heading downstairs now as a matter of fact, do you need some help, or can you fall down on your own?" asked Jared, raising an eyebrow.

"Help? Help? Not from you I don't, you pompous prig, I mean look at you, you're not half the man I am. Just because you wear that fancy uniform and your shiny chainmail, I'll tell you now if I'd have been firstborn..."

Jared had heard enough. "Yes I know, Karrak, but you weren't. We've had this conversation a hundred times," he said having raised his voice to drown out his brother's drunken tirade of abuse.

"Guards." Two very large members of the guard appeared, though neither of them was as big as Karrak. "Please escort Prince Karrak to his chambers, make sure he gets there safely. Go and sleep it off, Brother," Jared's last word said through pursed lips.

Jared made his way to the courtyard. "Guardsman, where can I find the captain?" he asked.

"I think he's in the uniform hut, Sire, shall I fetch him for you?"

"That won't be necessary, I do know where it is. Let's just hope he is where you think he is, you prat." Jared would not normally insult a member of the palace guard, but today Karrak had managed to get under his skin a little more than usual. He entered the hut and did, in fact, find Hannock there. "Captain, I'd like to see you in your office, if it's convenient."

"But of course, Sire, after you," replied Hannock. Entering his office, Hannock closed the door behind them. "Jared, where have you been? I've not seen you for three days. Hang on, what's wrong, my friend? You look like somebody just spat in your pint."

"It's Karrak! I swear he'll drive me insane one of these days."

"What's he done this time?"

"Nothing, or nothing that I know of, yet. All he does every day is wander around the taverns, sleeps with anything that looks at him and harps on about how things would have been if he was firstborn. He doesn't even have the decency to do it behind my back so that I can hear it as rumour, the spoilt brat does it to my face. Honestly, Hannock, it's only a matter of time before he drinks himself to death, falls off a tower or gets a knife in the back."

"One can only live in hope, Your Highness," said Hannock raising his eyebrows.

If any other man had made this comment, they would have been in the dungeon faster than they could blink, but Jared laughed for he knew that Hannock would lay down his life to protect Karrak as quickly as he would for himself, or King Tamor.

"And where is your darling sibling now, Your Highness?"

"I instructed the guards to escort him to his chambers."

"Escort him, or take him?"

"Do me a favour, Hannock, send a runner to check on him would you?"

"Your wish is my command, Sire," replied Hannock, and bowed very low in jest, receiving a slap on the back of his head for his impertinence.

The runner returned after a few minutes and stood before Hannock. "Out like a light and snoring like a drain, Sir," he reported.

"Well done, corporal," said Jared, before Hannock had time to speak.

"Begging your pardon, Your Highness, but I'm not a corporal."

"Do you want to be one?"

"Yes, Your Highness," replied the guard, enthusiastically.

"Then shut your face and get out. Report to Captain Hannock tomorrow morning at ten sharp, he'll take care of the official paperwork and issue your colours. Dismissed."

"Thank you very much, Your Highness."

"I said, dismissed."

The guard saluted Hannock, bowed to Jared, and dashed out through the door.

"What was that all about?" asked Hannock.

"Never you mind, friend," replied Jared. The runner was the guardsman that he had rebuked so unnecessarily a short time before. "Come on, I need a drink. Join me in the tavern?"

Hannock shrugged, pulled down the front of his tunic, and they both marched through the door.

***

Entering The Weary Traveller tavern, both Jared and Hannock realised that all was not well. The various villagers and traders within stopped in mid-conversation and looked toward the door. Realising that it was Prince Jared, the normal respects were paid, with everyone bowing. Jared simply nodded and gave a brief smile as the pair made their way toward the bar.

The woman who now stood behind it gave it her best efforts to curtsey, much to Hannock's amusement, as she could only have been described politely as being of 'large proportion'. "Your Highness, Sir, how may I serve you today?"

Hannock's mind raced with so many answers, *pork, bacon, just something small or maybe, any pies left?* A smirk came across his face and sucking in his bottom lip, he looked at Jared.

"Give me an ale," Jared said, "Hannock?"

"Oh, erm, the same," he said, stifling his laughter. He really did have a childish sense of humour, as more cruel answers entered his mind. Jared just looked at him. He knew Hannock better than anyone and could almost read his mind.

"Don't you dare," he said gently kicking his friend's boot, Hannock now grinning from ear to ear.

They turned and leaned their backs against the bar. Furtive glances came their way. Something was definitely wrong. Both turned back to face the bar wench. "Did something happen here?" enquired Jared.

"No, Your Highness, nothing at all, everything's fine," she said, but her voice became a little shaky at the end of the reply.

"He should be locked up and the key thrown away." The statement was made by a woman's voice, but neither Jared nor Hannock had noticed who made it.

"Who said that?" Hannock said, standing away from the bar as if on parade. The room had gone deathly silent, every patron looking to the floor. Hannock spoke again, "I demand an answer, who said that?"

A small, middle-aged woman now rose and walked around a table to face him, but continued to look at the floor.

"What did you mean? Who should be locked up? Well, don't just stand there woman, answer me."

A man behind her reached forward and grabbed her hand, "Sit down, Beatrice, it doesn't matter, we'll all be thrown in gaol, sit down for heaven's sake," he pleaded. They could not actually see the man, as he was obscured by Beatrice, who now turned to face him.

"No it's not alright, look at the state of you, he's evil. I don't care if he is a prince, they can put me in gaol, but the truth's the truth." Beatrice marched back around the table and flopped down on the wooden bench with a thump.

This was the first opportunity they had been given to see the man's face, well at least what was left of it. Both eyes were black and swollen shut. Both of his eyebrows were split and oozing blood, his lips in the same sorry state. His whole face was purple with bruising and swollen to twice its normal size, and dressings had been applied to his shoulder to cover yet another wound.

"What in the name of All Wars happened to you?!" exclaimed Hannock, "Did somebody drive a cart over your face, man?"

George, for that was the barkeep's name, as badly wounded as he was managed a little chuckle, "No, Sir, it just feels like they did," he replied, his chuckle cut short by the pain in his ribs, which he was now gently rubbing.

"Prince Karrak did it," blurted out Beatrice, "my poor husband did nothing wrong. Your Highness, your brother just attacked him for no reason, he should be punished like anybody else."

"Hold your tongue, woman, you speak of a member of the Royal House of Dunbar," advised Hannock quietly.

Jared raised his hand and the room fell silent once more. He turned to Hannock, "Send a runner, no, on second thoughts, go yourself. Fetch Alfred and get him to bring all of his medical stuff with him, if he needs any supplies, buy them for him on the way back." Hannock nodded in acknowledgement and exited the tavern. "Don't worry, dear fellow, we'll get you patched up," Jared informed George.

As all was now calm, Jared could speak at length with Beatrice, who explained exactly what had happened. "I swear, Your Highness, if that there royal guard hadn't spoken up when he did, my poor George would have been done for, he saved his life he did."

A short while later Hannock returned, Alfred in tow. Alfred took care of George, cleaning and stitching his cuts then dressing them, applying a splint to a broken arm, that even George had not noticed, and placing poultices to his many bruises. Jared thought that the worst wound was the one in his shoulder, but unfortunately he was wrong. At one point Alfred asked to speak to him, "I'm afraid, Sir, that it is beyond my skill to save the sight in the left eye, it has been blinded," was all he said, before returning to the care of his patient.

As they were due to leave The Weary Traveller, Jared turned to Beatrice, "Come to the castle tomorrow, we shall make suitable compensation for your inconvenience madam, ten o' clock, please, do not be late." Although he pitied these poor innocents, he still had to maintain his position.

Taking Hannock's advice, they returned to his office. Angered by the events in the tavern, Jared had wanted to confront his brother immediately.

"You heard the runner, Jared, Karrak's out cold. Even if you manage to wake him, you won't get any sense out of him. Wait until he's sober and then you can have your say."

"I'll kill him, Hannock, I swear I'll kill him. This time he's gone too far, he must be stopped. I can keep his shenanigans from my father no longer."

***

Jared entered the throne room, closely followed by Hannock.

The king sat on his throne surrounded by many pretty girls who, as usual, were talking drivel. This not only amused Tamor, but had become his favourite pastime, for he knew that every one of them had delusions of becoming his next bride, and the Queen of Borell. Something that would never happen.

The two men bowed low. "Your Majesty," said Jared, "forgive this interruption, but I have urgent need of your counsel."

"Oh look, it's the twins," said Tamor. "Girls, toddle off now, but don't go too far, I'm sure this won't take long," and gave them a little wave by wiggling his fingers as they left. "I do hope this is important, Jared," he said lowering his head so that his chin touched his chest, "I was having so much fun."

"Father, I must speak to you about Karrak."

"Why, what's he been up to now?" asked Tamor with a sigh.

Jared related the tale of the incident in The Weary Traveller.

"So, he gets into a tavern brawl and you think he should be punished for it? There are drunken brawls in every tavern, every day my son. If I were to lock up everyone involved, every time, my gaol would be permanently full."

"It wasn't like that, Father. The man he attacked is quite elderly and half his size. It was savage and uncalled for…" he paused briefly, "… and he's not the first victim to fall foul of Karrak's bullying."

"Well you've never mentioned it before," said Tamor.

"No, Father, I haven't. In hindsight, perhaps I should have. But he is, after all, my brother. I thought he might change, that it was the impetuosity of youth but instead it's become more frequent, and each attack more vicious than the last."

The king's expression changed. A look of concern had come across his face. "There was no mention of 'magic' being used at all was there?" he asked slowly.

Jared shook his head, with a puzzled expression, "No, Father, why?"

"No real reason, just wondering that's all," replied Tamor, flapping his hands as if to dismiss his own last question. "I'll talk to him tomorrow, first thing in the morning, alright? Don't worry, I'll calm him down, now off you go," and he simply waved them away.

Jared suggested that maybe Hannock should return to his duties. Hannock agreed and the friends parted. As Jared crossed the courtyard, a part of the conversation with his father would not leave his mind. *Why had the king mentioned magic?* He had made no reference to it, and Hannock had remained silent during their conversation. *So where had it come from?* He had no answers, *I still need that drink* he thought, and headed toward his chambers.

***

Jared had always kept up with his combat training, and today, like most days, he headed to the courtyard. Maybe an opportunity would arise that would allow him to finally defeat Hannock, he thought with a smile. Reaching his destination he had a quick look around, yes there was Hannock as usual, in the arena, giving weapons training to his guardsmen.

"Good morning, Captain," Jared said as he approached.

"Good morning, Your Highness," came the reply as everyone, including Hannock, gave a bow.

"I was just wondering, Captain, if you'd care to join me in the arena, so that I can kick your backside?"

Hannock smiled at his friend, "Your Royal Highness, it would be my honour to join you in the arena, but with respect…" he said bowing again, "… were I to allow you to kick my backside, would I then not lose the respect of the king's guard?"

"Well, we shall soon find out, shan't we, Captain?"

Whether they were royal or palace guard, raw recruit or serf, everybody in the courtyard was laughing and most had seen this all before, a scenario that was played out regularly by the two best swords in the kingdom. The wagers still taking place, as they had for many years.

They both entered the arena. Chainmail and armour had been removed, even gauntlets left to one side. No accidental wounds would occur with such skill involved. They stood back to back for a second and then paced away, reaching the roped edge of it simultaneously. Each was handed a weapon. They now turned to face one another, moving in closer until they were only a yard apart, the steel showing in their eyes. They saluted one another, ready for battle and raised… their riding crops! The raucous laughter that came from the crowd was almost deafening as the duellists tried to outdo each other. Now and again you'd hear an 'ouch!', and they called one another names that one would never use in polite company.

The duel was going well, Jared and Hannock getting into the spirit of it. Jared was too indisposed to see what the crowd had seen, as the atmosphere changed and a hush came upon them. They all bowed their heads, Hannock included, and only then did Jared turn to see why... there stood Karrak.

"Good day, Brother..." Karrak almost spat the words out, "... still playing soldiers with your little friends, I see." Karrak's hostile tone spoke volumes.

"Hardly playing, Brother..." replied Jared, "... You should try it some time. You never know, you might find it quite 'therapeutic'."

"And how do you think I would fare in your little 'game'?" asked Karrak.

"I'm not sure. Why don't you test your mettle? How about now? Against me." The tension in the air was palpable. In his mind Hannock was willing Karrak to accept the challenge and all that Jared could picture was George's face, beaten to a pulp by this sadistic, privileged bully.

But what happened next shocked them all...

"Oh, alright then," replied Karrak. "Why not? But we aren't going to use crops are we? I mean, we can use swords? We are adults after all, and we shan't bother with the armour. I mean, who'd actually stab his own brother?"

The last comment sent a shiver down Hannock's spine. Did Karrak actually think he had a chance of beating Jared? To his knowledge Karrak had never even picked up a sword, let alone practised using one. This was a little perturbing.

Jared had stepped over the rope in order to face his brother, and now re-entered the arena, beckoning Karrak to do the same.

"My word, not a lot of room is there? Here's an idea," and grabbing a sword, Karrak slashed through the rope with one strike. "That's better, gives one a bit more breathing room, don't you think?"

Jared said nothing and, reaching across, picked up a sword of his own.

"Now, what do we do? What are the rules?"

"Firstly…" replied Jared, "… we face each other in the…"

But he never got to the end of his sentence. Karrak lunged forward, thrusting his sword at Jared, a wild strike full of venom, but no grace. Catching Jared off guard did not work however, and he managed to parry the blow. Jared, being off balance, allowed Karrak to strike again, this time from above and with full force. He did not care about stance or form, he was just slashing wildly, but the brute strength that he had was quite formidable. This went on for a few minutes, but now Jared had his footing and was coping quite easily with the onslaught, but his brother's strength, My God where was he getting it from? Karrak again lunged forward, but this time Jared was ready for him, and with an upward stroke, swept the sword cleanly from his hand. Relaxing slightly, Jared stepped back, away from his brother, but as he did so Karrak let out a roar. He thrust his hands out in front of him and sparks flew from them, Jared did his best to dodge them, turning this way and that as his shirt began to smoulder. The ever-present hay cart behind him started to smoke, and then burst into flame. This was something that Jared had not expected, but he was no fool. He thought of a spell and was about to cast it when there was a loud crack, and suddenly, a deathly silence.

Jared looked up. His brother's unconscious body lay on the floor ten feet in front of him, and standing over it was Hannock, broken pikestaff in hand, "You're not going to hang me are you?" he asked. "This could be classed as treason."

***

Jared gave orders for Karrak's hands to be bound behind him, even though he was still unconscious. He did not want to take the risk of his brother being able to cast another spell when he awoke and believed that this may prevent him from doing so.

He beckoned to Hannock. Bowing his head toward him slightly, he whispered, "Take him to his chambers. Once you are there, gag him and tie him to his bed, post two guards both inside the door and out, and under no circumstances allow him to speak. Once you are done, report to my chambers, we shall address the king together on this matter."

"And if he is roused before we reach our destination, Your Highness?" asked Hannock. Jared looked around him. Snatching a pikestaff from a weapons rack, he thrust it toward Hannock, who simply nodded. Four guards placed Karrak's body on a stretcher and raised it, and with Hannock leading the procession, they headed into the castle, leaving Jared to bring order to the courtyard.

"My brother can get carried away when we play our little games…" he said with a false smile, trying to make light of the situation, "… he hates losing." But the guards never believed a word of it, they knew Karrak was a bad seed. "Get this mess cleaned up, men. This place is a shambles," he said, heading off.

Hannock entered Jared's chambers and, closing the door, spoke freely. "Jared, it's worse than we feared. One of the royal guard has been found dead. His body had been concealed behind some barrels near the tavern, his neck was broken."

"We can deal with that later, Hannock, we need to focus on the matter in hand."

"I fear they are one and the same, Jared, he was the one who stopped Karrak from killing the barkeep. The rest of the guard were dismissed shortly after they left the tavern. Karrak made the excuse that he'd be fine with just one and sent them away."

"And you think that Karrak killed him, outraged by the interjection?"

"His head was on backwards, Jared, only someone with Karrak's strength could achieve something like that."

"But there is no proof, no witness?"

"Unfortunately not Jared, but it's too close to the mark to be a mere coincidence."

"That may be the case my friend, but you know what my father will say, '*No proof, no conviction*'."

They reached the throne room and, on entering, were surprised to see Emnor standing before the king. His visits to the castle had become very infrequent over the last few years, and neither could recall the last time they had seen him when they had been together. The customary bow was made to the king.

"Before you start, I've already heard..." he said, holding his hand out in front of him, "... so don't start baying for Karrak's blood over a singed shirt and an incinerated hay cart!"

The two friends exchanged puzzled glances. *How could he know already?* No guard had been sent, no report given, not a word.

Not wanting to be overheard, they adjourned to the library, by chance the same room in which Jared had first witnessed the destructive power of magic.

"Please forgive me, Sire," Emnor began, "I have said many times that today's events were inevitable."

"Yes, I know that," said the king, "I just prayed that maybe you were wrong. That maybe he hadn't inherited the same gift as Jared."

Emnor had a very pious look on his face as he looked across at Tamor. "Sire," he said, "I am seldom wrong, but the power he has is very different to that of Prince Jared."

"Yes alright, you've made your point, wizard. The question now is, what are we going to do with him? He's still my son, and I shall not allow any harm to be done to him. Jared, where is he now?"

Jared explained the course of action he had taken.

"Captain Hannock, what are your thoughts on this?" the king enquired, "You may speak freely."

"Sire, I fear for the lives of my men and the citizens of Borell. Prince Karrak is volatile at best and, now that we know he has been learning magic, he could become unstoppable."

Jared was the next to be consulted. "He's insane, Father. I hate to say it, but I saw the rage in his eyes today and it is something we must deal with now, before he does something dreadful." Jared now took the opportunity to inform the king of the guard's murder.

Finally, King Tamor turned to Emnor.

"Sire, you now know why I have always refused to mentor, or even speak with, your second son. The use of words such as 'uncontrollable' or 'insane' cannot sum up the magnitude of his illness. From a very early age, for I sensed it even then, an evil has been within your son, corrupting and consuming his very soul. No mortal shall ever contain or control him. If he gains his freedom after this day, he will commit atrocities worse than you can imagine. Now that he has realised his power, his hunger for more will not be satiated."

Between them, the four forged a plan. Karrak would be taken to Reiggan Fortress, high in the Muurkain Mountains. But this was no ordinary fortress, this was a Wizard's Retreat. At any given time, it was occupied by upwards of a hundred wizards, warlocks, mages and the like. Emnor explained that the magical forces contained within Reiggan Fortress would always be strong enough to not only contain Karrak, but also protect him, especially from himself. "He will be well taken care of, Sire, no harm shall befall him," Emnor promised.

"And shall you visit him from time to time for me, dear friend?" the king asked.

"Karrak and I shall have a meeting, of that I am sure, Your Majesty. However, that will not be for some time yet, at least I hope not anyway," replied Emnor.

"Very well," said the king, looking a little confused by Emnor's last statement. "Jared, you shall supervise the transportation of your brother to Reiggan. Captain

Hannock will accompany you, with a detachment of the guard."

Tamor paused and looked at Emnor, "Emnor?" he asked inquisitively.

"I regret, Sire, that I shall not be able to make the journey. I have pressing matters elsewhere. I shall, however, contact my colleagues in Reiggan and have them prepare for the royal guest, and I may join Jared occasionally, if I have time."

Their departure was set for the following morning, before daybreak, to prevent prying eyes. The king, obviously upset by the discussion of his youngest son's impending incarceration, made the excuse of his faith in Jared's capability and withdrew.

"Your Highness," said Emnor, "take these." Reaching into his robes he produced two small glass vials and handed them to Jared. "They will ensure that your journey is uneventful."

"How so?" asked Jared.

"The red fluid will keep your brother calm, and help him sleep," said Emnor.

"You mean it'll knock him out? Fantastic!" said Hannock with a grin.

Emnor rolled his eyes, "The clear fluid will revive him but keep him docile, providing you administer no more than two drops."

Jared raised his eyebrows, "Impressive, but why wake him at all before we reach Reiggan?"

"Do you want him to starve to death?" asked Emnor.

"Good point, never thought of that."

"To awaken him, two drops of clear liquid into his mouth, two drops of red mixed into food or wine and he'll sleep again," instructed Emnor.

"What if he won't eat or drink?" asked Jared.

Hannock, not being able to contain himself, "Pikestaff."

CHAPTER 5

The following morning, they set off before dawn, as planned, and by daybreak were obscured from view by the trees. Jared and Hannock were mounted on white stallions at the head of the procession. Following them was a covered cart, in which lay Prince Karrak, surrounded by sixteen royal guard, marching proudly, heads held high, their highly polished armour gleaming in the morning sun, and at the tail a smaller cart carrying provisions.

"We should make good time if this weather holds, Your Highness," said Hannock.

"No need to be so formal, Hannock, we're not in the castle now, relax a little."

"But, what about the men, Sir?"

"They can't hear us, and besides, they couldn't care less. Look at them, they're enjoying the fresh air and sunshine."

"How long do you think it will take to reach Reiggan Fortress?" asked Hannock.

"Well, if the weather does hold, about fourteen days to reach the Muurkain Mountains, from there it depends on what condition the pass is in. That could add anything between three and five days, if we have to start digging through snow," replied Jared.

"You really do know how to cheer a fellow up, don't you?" said Hannock.

"What can I say? It's a gift."

"More like a curse."

The first few days passed uneventfully. On the fourth day, at dusk, they set up camp in good cheer, having covered more ground than they had expected. Tents had been erected, a fire set, and a meal prepared. Sentries were posted and everything was quiet, save for the subdued banter amongst the guard, who had yet to take their turn on watch. Jared was the only one who was to have any contact with Karrak, the soldiers having been given orders not to so much as look inside the canvas of the cart. Jared had palmed the two vials given to him by Emnor, dished out some food and was now inside the cart, tending to his brother.

Hannock, now finding himself at a loose end, wandered about the camp. As captain of the guard he still had to make sure that standards were maintained, but much as he tried, could see no major issues and turned toward his tent. It was at this point however that he overheard some of his troop's conversation. His interest piqued, he slid into shadow and listened intently…

"Some kind of sleeping sickness I heard, just fell down like he was dead, apart from his snoring."

"No, it's some kind of leprosy apparently, half his face fell off, and the other half's all mangled and such, makes you feel sick just looking at him."

"Well you're both wrong see, it's some kind of magic spell. Sent him mad in his brain it has and all he does is talk in strange languages and try to bite people."

"I ain't wrong it's that leprosy thing, that's why they won't let us see him."

"No, it's in case he bites one of us."

Hannock had heard enough and quietly stepped out, now looking down at the surprised soldiers, who shot to attention and saluted.

"Did you know…" Hannock began, "… that there have been wolves sighted in this area?"

"No, Sir," came the chorused reply.

"Oh yes, and big, well when I say big, I mean huge. One took a man's head clean off with one bite, apparently." The guards' eyes grew wider with every word. Hannock continued, "And if I ever hear you tittle tattling or discussing the personal lives of a member of The House of Dunbar again…" at this point he leaned forward, nose to nose with one of them, "… I shall personally rip out your guts with my bare hands, dismember you and feed you to them. Do I make myself quite clear?" Hannock was very proud of being a friend to House Dunbar and would allow no slur to go unchecked, to insult it, was to insult him. He tugged down his tunic and marched away.

Entering his tent he found that Jared had returned. "That was quick, being a good boy then is he?" he asked.

"You should be a little more careful, Hannock, and I say that as a friend. He is my brother after all, you know… a royal."

Hannock's expression changed, "He tried to kill you. What would have happened if…"

"But he never succeeded did he?" said Jared, "Thanks to you my friend. It looked much worse than it actually

65

was Hannock, he just had a tantrum because my father had the audacity to question his behaviour."

"If you say so, Jared, anyway, how is he?"

"He seems in perfect health, but when he speaks it's as if he's in a dream. Just staring ahead of him, he never blinked once whilst awake."

"So the potions work then?" asked Hannock.

"Perfectly," replied Jared.

"At last…" said Hannock, "… something that works in our favour."

But their journey had only just begun and, unbeknownst to them, they were being watched.

***

The intruders were close enough to see, but not hear, the events that were taking place. They watched the camp for over an hour, their distance allowing them to converse unheard.

"Look at 'em, fancy armour and fancy ways. I hate Borellians, let's just attack 'em now and 'ave done with it."

"Patience, Klag, time is on our side and, we know, there's nothing for three days in any direction other than back the way they came."

"But they're sitting ducks, Ramah. We could 'ave 'em all dead before they know what's 'appenin'."

"Maybe, but they have posted sentries, and we don't know what's in that cart. No, we shall bide our time and ambush them later."

"Let's just kill 'em now, eh? I 'ate waitin', come on let's kill 'em now."

"How many times must I tell you, Klag? You are very brave, but when have you ever been right? Just leave the thinking to me. You don't want to hurt that delicate brain of yours by trying to use it too much now, do you?" Klag was confused. Was that concern for his health, or was he being mocked? Ramah knew Klag very well, act first, think, or at least try to, later. This had gotten him in many scrapes in the past, and Ramah was the one that usually had to get him out of them.

They were Dergon. A dying race that had been decimated over the years. Coerced to fight in fruitless battles and unwinnable wars with false promises of great wealth and power, the mercenaries of this world. A most impressive race physically, each standing around eight feet tall, with magnificent musculature and glistening pale green skin. They were, however, one of the ugliest, with facial deformities of various degrees, a result of interbreeding. Buck teeth, cross eyes, huge warts and hare lips to name but a few. Depleted almost to extinction, not because they were weak, not because they were fearful, but because they were not the most intelligent of beings, and believed the false promises.

They were now, however, being led by Ramah. He was far more intelligent than any Dergon that had ever lived. Much broader than the rest, and far more powerful, he had taken control of his band only a year before by challenging and killing their previous leader. The battle between them had taken less than thirty seconds, resulting in Ramah cleaving the head from his opponent and holding it high in the air, thus earning the allegiance of his inherited followers. Since then, adopting a nomadic existence, new clan members were recruited, raising their ranks from a mere twenty to almost a hundred as they travelled. During their travels Klag had proven to be the most reliable amongst the group and as their number increased, so did Klag's standing. He was not what one would class as intelligent, but he was true and loyal to Ramah, as he had been somewhat of a punch bag for the previous leader. Ramah had promised all others that this would never happen to Klag, or indeed, any of them, providing they followed his orders and they whooped and cheered when they were told by Klag that they would now be expected to refer to Ramah as their 'chief'.

"We'll be alright now, lads, we've got a chief, he'll look after us," were the type of comment to ring through Ramah's new band.

"Klag, rally the Dergon, I've seen enough," said Ramah.

They backed away into the darkness.

The Dergon camp had been set about a mile from the Borellians. Ramah and Klag now sat by the large campfire. There was no conversation to be heard amongst the Dergon warriors, they had no interest in banter and very little interaction took place between them, preferring action to word. They always listened intently when Ramah spoke, in awe of his intelligence, as they were doing now.

"We could've though, couldn't we, boss? We could've taken 'em easy," said Klag.

"Probably, Klag, but we were outnumbered and they were well armed, I shall not risk the life of any of my fellow Dergon unnecessarily."

"But they're only little, tiny, I could squash 'em wiv me bare 'ands I could."

"Maybe you could, but we were outnumbered three to one and it's always best to err on the side of caution. Had we had the rest of our forces with us, I may have considered an attack."

"Ooh I love it when you talk like that, boss, but that's 'cause you're clever innit? That's why you're the boss."

"No, Klag, I am your chief," said Ramah, gripping Klag gently, but firmly, by the back of his neck.

"Yes, Chief, sorry, Chief, won't 'appen again, Chief," said Klag looking slightly nervous.

"Now, we shall eat, what's on the menu?" said Ramah.

"Some kind of meat, Chief," said Klag, looking pleased with himself at remembering to call Ramah by his preferred title.

"What kind of meat?"

At this another Dergon chipped in, attempting to gain favour, "It's rabbit, Chief, and erm, wolf."

***

The following morning the Borellians had breakfasted and then broken camp. Jared had not, as yet, seen Hannock.

"Have you seen Captain Hannock this morning?" he asked of one of the guard, but before the guard had time to answer, heard his friend's voice shout.

"Over here, Your Highness." Hannock appeared from behind a bush, a slightly concerned look on his face.

"Everything alright, Captain?" asked Jared.

"We weren't alone out here last night, we had company," said Hannock.

"How do you know?"

"It's always been a habit of mine to inspect the surrounding area whenever I break camp, Your Highness, a habit taught by my father, and I'm glad he did," said Hannock.

"Why, what did you find?"

"Some kind of footprint. Far too big to be made by someone of our stature, but they weren't animal tracks either, and they were spying on us. The tracks lead toward Muurkain Mountains."

"The way we're headed," said Jared. "Show me."

Hannock lead Jared into the woods. They had travelled about fifty yards when he stopped and pointed at the ground, "Two of them stopped here for some time, they were crouched so as not to be seen."

"How do you know that?" asked Jared.

"If you study the 'footprint' I suppose you'd call it, the front part of the track is much deeper than the back which means they were leaning forwards to balance themselves. Compare those tracks to the ones just behind, made as they approached and you'll see that the back of the track is shallower than the approaching tracks made when they were sure-footed."

"How come you never taught me these skills, Hannock?"

"You have your magic, Jared…" said Hannock, "… and I have mine."

They ventured a little further, when Hannock once again pointed to the ground. "They headed off in this direction, see how the front part of the track is wider than the back? I counted five sets of tracks, the two that watched, and three that were placed as lookouts. I don't know what they wanted, Jared, but they were organised, and stealthy."

"But who are they? What are they? These tracks are huge," said Jared.

"Not sure, they're too small to be ogres or giants. Mind you, they don't use stealth anyway, they just charge in blindly and start smashing everything in sight."

"I think I'd rather have that scenario, at least we'd know what we were dealing with. This is a most perplexing situation," said Jared.

"What if it's something to do with Karrak, you know somebody who doesn't want to see him locked up?"

"No, it can't be that, his power is very weak. He wouldn't be of any use to anyone," said Jared shaking his head.

"Well, whatever the case my friend, we must take care. It may be nothing, but best be prepared," said Hannock.

"Indeed," said Jared. "Inform the men of the intrusion, Hannock. Leave out the details."

Hannock briefed his men, had the horses saddled, and they set off.

***

Two days passed. They had neither seen nor heard anything untoward, making and breaking camp without incident and no more tracks had been found. Karrak was cared for by his brother and remained in good health, but the mood of the troops was slightly subdued.

"Another fine day," said Hannock, a huge grin on his face.

"If you say so," replied Jared, looking up at the heavy cloud formation.

It had begun to rain during the night and this had dampened the spirits of the procession somewhat, except of course for Hannock, who, much to the annoyance of his men, kept making obvious comments such as, 'It's only water.'

They had reached the Hebbon Hills and were about to start making their way through a gulley between them. On one side there was a gentle, mossed slope that rose to about thirty feet, on the other, a sheer rock face of double the height.

"I don't like this, Jared," said Hannock. "Not one bit."

"Can we go around, or over?" Jared asked.

"Not around, that would add two days to the journey. We could go over, but we'd have to go back the way we came for about five miles. And then of course, there's the problem of the carts, and this rock would be treacherous to walk on when wet, we could end up falling and breaking our necks."

"How long is this gulley, Hannock?"

"Not too far, I'd say about a mile."

"That's settled then. We go through. But make sure your men are on alert, this is a perfect site for an ambush," said Jared.

They entered the gulley. Their progression was hindered by rocks and boulders that had tumbled from the rock face to their left, preventing the passage of the carts. They would travel a mere fifty feet and Hannock would give the order to halt. The guards would move forward, leaving the carts unguarded, to clear the debris, then fall back to their positions of protection. Another fifty feet and the exercise would be repeated. The gulley became more and more impassable until, halfway through, they came upon a pile of rocks that would have taken a whole army half a day to remove. Hannock turned his head to Jared, then to the rock pile and back again. Jared bowed his head and gave a gentle sigh. He knew that questioning look. Whenever there was no solution to be found, Hannock would use it, and it was always aimed at him. Hannock knew all too well the power that Jared possessed and, in normal circumstances, respected Jared's reluctance to use it.

"We shall have to turn back, Your Highness. It would take far too long to move the blockage; we shall have to go around."

Jared knew this was his cue to take action. "No, I'll deal with it," he sighed. He dismounted and, raising his voice slightly, announced, "Men, what you are about to witness you must never speak of, that is an order."

"Yes, Sir," they replied.

Removing his gauntlets, Jared moved closer to the rock pile. He stood for a while, studying its formation as if he were working out some strange form of puzzle.

Hannock had ushered his men back toward the carts and given orders for the horses to be tethered to them.

Jared began to chant. A gentle breeze picked up around him, ruffling his hair. The breeze rapidly turned to a strong wind that then became gale force as the volume of his voice increased, still chanting. The soldiers watched wide-eyed, their mouths open, amazed at what they were witnessing. Jared was now shouting and the howling wind had become a tornado. The horses seemed to be screaming in terror as the roaring increased, the entire scene had become as black as the darkest night until with a roar Jared thrust his hands forward. The rock pile exploded. Boulders were reduced to the size of pebbles. The guards feared they would be killed as every piece was whipped into the air like straw until, throwing his hands to his right, Jared roared again and every piece was scattered across the mossed bank settling like sand drifting through an hourglass. The wind subsided, the howling stopped and the light returned, as Jared fell heavily to his knees.

Not a word was spoken by his men, as Hannock walked forward, "As you were, men," he uttered as he passed, eager to check on his friend. Leaning down, he took Jared's arm, "Are you alright?" he asked, although it was quite obvious that he was not.

"Oh you know, Hannock, just another day in the service of His Majesty," replied Jared, exhausted by the exercise.

Hannock insisted that they take a short rest period and Jared was made to eat and drink, in the hope of his regaining a little energy. Out of earshot of the soldiers, Hannock looked into his friend's eyes. "Are you sure you're alright?"

"I'm fine my friend, it just saps my strength for a while. Emnor said the more I use magic, the less effect it will have on me."

"You've not used it much then, have you? You look done in."

"I told you, I'm fine. Now shut your face or I'll have you put in the stocks, I'm a prince you know?" Despite his fatigue, Jared had not lost his sense of humour.

After a brief rest, they set off once more, Hannock having persuaded Jared to ride in the cart with his brother until he had regained his strength. It was still hard going and the frequent stops to move obstructions had continued, but both Hannock and his men, having travelled three quarters of the way through the gulley, could now see the end of it and were feeling a little more positive.

"Halt," called Hannock.

The guard were a little confused at this as there were no visible restrictions directly ahead of them. "Is everything alright, Sir?"

"Step forward lieutenant." The soldier promptly obeyed.

"Send two men to scout ahead, about a hundred yards should do."

"Yes, Sir."

"Tread carefully, men…" Hannock advised, "… if you see or hear anything before you reach a hundred paces, return immediately."

The two scouts set off. Reaching the point that had been suggested, they turned to face Hannock, one raising his arms to his sides in a gesture that gave the 'all-clear'.

They turned again and faced away, scanning the terrain ahead.

Hannock had seen something, just the slightest movement, not the branch of a tree or even a leaf in the breeze, at the exit from the gulley. Something had moved from left to right low to the ground, something green, something shiny. *What the hell was that?* He thought to himself. Holding his ground, he waited. Two minutes went by and still nothing happened, *Hannock old boy,* he thought to himself, *you're losing it.* "Forward," he ordered.

The procession moved forward as instructed. The gulley was wider at this end and this meant there were no impediments. Suddenly, the two scouts cried out in panic and began to run toward them shouting, but could not be heard as yet. Hannock, spurring his mount, began to canter toward them, still unable to see anything. However at this point he heard them, "We're under attack, there's loads of them, take cover".

Hannock looked beyond them and his blood ran cold. In a cloud of dust they appeared. Like a stampede the creatures charged, except they had riders. *What were these beasts, and who were their riders?*

Hannock was facing the Dergon!

The mounts they rode were immense. As big as a rhinoceros with jet-black skin that was as thick as any armour worn by warriors, three horns across their heads and glowing red eyes. The Dergon were riding them at a gallop, beating them with clubs to maintain their speed.

Hannock turned his horse as quickly as he could and charged back to the carts, "Take cover," he shouted as he dismounted hurriedly and ran to the cart. Jared was already climbing out as he reached it. "Draw your sword, Jared, this is going to get nasty."

The two soldiers never had a chance, one was trampled underfoot by one of the Dergon mounts, the other struck in the back of the head with a Dergon axe that literally cleaved it in two. Jared had no time to think of his brother's safety lying comatose in the cart, he himself had to survive in order to be of any use to anyone else.

Within seconds, the Dergon were upon them.

They charged their steeds straight through the centre of Hannock's men. Luckily the soldiers dodged the lead beast, but it clipped the covered cart, spinning it flat against the rock face, putting it slightly out of harm's way. Still at a gallop, it crashed through the provisions cart, scattering the contents and crushing the guard attempting to shelter behind it. Hannock snatched a pikestaff from the ground and hurled it. As the Dergon turned his mount, the pikestaff struck him in the throat, and he fell to the ground. His steed, in the melee, began to buck and kick as if to throw an unwanted rider. This, in turn, felled two more of the beasts, causing their riders to crash to the ground. One glamoch kicked out wildly, smashing the leg of the rider who howled in pain, but not for long, as Hannock severed his head, splashing his dark green blood across the ground. The battle was not going well for the Borellians. Hannock saw two more of his men fall, one to an axe, the other set upon by three of the enemy, who were smashing his body with battle hammers. He could not help; he had barely blocked a strike from a huge scimitar wielded by another of their foe. Parrying a second blow, he ran it through with his sword and kicked it away from him, leaving even more green blood dripping from the blade. He felled another and another.

Jared, being almost as skilled with a blade as Hannock, had also felled three of the marauders, but he too had witnessed his comrades fall. Looking up, he saw a clutch of the enemy charging toward him at full pelt, and roared "Nooo…," his spell throwing them all into the air.

Two more of their kinsmen fell, would all now be lost? Lost to an unknown enemy?

Hannock and Jared were now standing back to back. A quick glance revealed survivors lying on the ground, still moving, but badly wounded, when suddenly they heard a whistle, then another, then a third and a fourth. Four of their attackers fell before them, arrows in their heads. The rest, startled by this, began to screech as they fled, their strange mounts following them as a loyal dog would follow its master. Jared quickly glanced at the cart, it was virtually untouched. Sure that his brother was fine, he, like Hannock, immediately began to tend to the wounded. It had not even crossed their mind to whom they owed their lives. Their hearts sank as they checked their comrades. After this brief, brutal battle, only two had survived.

CHAPTER 6

Watching them from the peak of the rock face, Faylore wondered why anyone would venture into these lands with so little protection. She knew that they were from Borell, but *what were they doing here? They're like defenceless children,* she thought. *Borell is only a few days away and most of them are dead already.* Intrigued however, as she always was by other species, she held her position and continued her study. She was very different from most Thedarians. They were not at all inquisitive and despised many other species, believing them to be inferior.

Hannock dressed the wounds of the two soldiers as Jared checked on Karrak. He was unhurt, still comatose and oblivious to the carnage that had just taken place. Hannock then assessed the remains of the provisions cart, salvaging what he could and hoping that their new found foe would not return. He placed the unspoiled remnants by the wheel of the cart for Jared to place inside, recalling the order to leave its occupant undisturbed.

One of the stallions had been killed in the attack and the carthorses, having been inadvertently freed during battle, had bolted. They now had one horse, one cart, one sedated prince and two badly wounded soldiers. Things were not looking good. They hitched the stallion to the cart, eager to leave this pit of death.

"What are they, Hannock?" asked Jared, kicking gently at the shoulder of one of them as if to check that it was dead.

"Ugly," replied Hannock, kicking it himself, but with full force.

"Have you ever heard of anything like them before though? You have been on patrol a lot more than I."

"Well that's because you're a prince. You shouldn't be out in the wilds at all, it's very dangerous you know," said Hannock with his very best ironic overtone.

"And those things they were riding," continued Jared, ignoring the sarcasm. "I've never seen anything like those either."

"If we keep our fingers crossed, hopefully we'll never see them again."

"Well, if we do, I don't think we'll survive. Fourteen of our best men cut down like wheat in a matter of minutes."

"And we were about to be, and would have been, if not for the mystery archer."

"Why would you save someone and then not even speak to them, Hannock?"

"All I can think is that they weren't saving us. Maybe they just have a grudge against these things."

"It'll be getting dark soon. We'd better make for the trees..." Jared suggested, "... we can set a camp there. It should shield us a little, in case they come back."

***

"What do you mean, *they had help*?" bellowed Ramah.

"It was them Thedarians, Chief. 'iding somewhere they was, using them fancy bows and arrows, loads of 'em there was."

"Klag," said Ramah, tapping a large knife against his palm, "how many were there?"

"Like I said, Chief, loads."

"How many?" shouted Ramah, placing the tip of his knife against Klag's nose.

"Well I, I, I ain't really sure, Chief, like I said they was 'iding. Four of our warriors, sorry, I mean your warriors was dead in seconds with arrows in their 'eads. I couldn't let any more die, please, Chief, I'm real sorry."

"Did you at least find out what was in the cart?"

"No, Chief, sorry, Chief."

"I should have put one of the glamoch in charge," grumbled Ramah.

"Yeah, but they couldn't tell you what 'appened could they, Chief, 'cause they can't talk, can they, Chief? That's why we only rides 'em."

Ramah put his head into his hands. "Give me strength," he muttered, pondering over his next move.

"Klag, have ten warriors prepare for a journey northward. I have heard that there are more of our kind there, and I mean to recruit them. We shall not allow this minor setback to dishearten us. There is strength in numbers and I must increase ours, we shall leave at daybreak tomorrow."

"Ten warriors, north, daybreak tomorrow, got it."

81

***

Having left the gulley, Jared and Hannock continued to follow a small track through sparse woodland. "Looks like it's not been used much recently, Jared. Should be safe enough, but we must be vigilant." They made camp, setting only a small fire, secreted behind a clump of trees. Hannock prepared a makeshift meal from what little provisions he had managed to salvage. The two soldiers seemed to be holding up well despite their wounds and Jared and Hannock were attempting to formulate a plan in order to continue their mission.

"We need to get those two settled somewhere. If we could find a village, perhaps we could also re-stock from the local traders. We may even find a stable willing to sell us fresh steeds," said Jared.

"And fourteen royal guard?" added Hannock.

"Sorry, friend, I don't mean to be insensitive, our main issue has to be a concern for the living. We cannot help the dead, but their families will be well taken care of when we return home."

"You mean *if* we return home?"

"Alright, if we return home. We're not falling at the first hurdle, Hannock, we must trust in ourselves."

"Sorry, Jared, I'm just a little tired. I'll be alright when I'm rested. Can't stand the thought of having to put up with my own cooking though."

"Now that's the Hannock I know," said Jared.

They decided that northwest would be their best option. Hannock had heard that a village by the name of Ferendon lay in that direction which, with an early start, they could reach by nightfall the following day.

Jared, remembering Hannock's earlier comments, volunteered for first watch, insisting that he wasn't tired having rested briefly prior to their unexpected battle. An offer Hannock gratefully accepted.

Jared stared into the campfire, watching as the tiny flames licked at the base of the fresh branches he had placed on it. The only sound to be heard was the hooting of an owl close by. This helped Jared relax as he knew that, if anything large stirred in the darkness, the owl would remain silent. The battle in the gulley, combined with his use of magic, had taken its toll on him far more than he had realised. He patrolled the camp, contemplating the day's events, pausing briefly to check on his wounded men, and Hannock. With each step his legs grew heavier. He slumped down, leaning against the trunk of a tree that, due to fatigue, felt as comfortable to him as any padded chair. His eyes grew heavy, and within seconds, he was asleep.

***

Jared woke with a start. Slightly confused, he blinked a few times, not sure whether he was actually awake or dreaming. No more than three feet in front of him, sat on the ground, was a beautiful woman. Her platinum blond hair cascaded around her shoulders and framed her slender face. Her pure-white skin glittered in the moonlight. Her head, now tilted to one side, revealed her pointed ears. *Hang on a minute,* he thought, *pointed ears!* He made a grab for his sword.

"Looking for this?" she asked, holding out her hand to show Jared his sword.

"Well I just…" he began.

"You'll end up as dead as your friends if you're not careful. Anybody could walk into your camp and cut your throats while you sleep. Well, here you are then, take it." She held out her hand to present him with his sword.

"Thank you," said Jared.

"What for? It is yours after all."

"Well I know that, but all the same."

"What strange creatures you are. Who are you? Why are you here? Are you looking for something?" she asked. The questions came all at once, not demanding, simply filled with curiosity.

Jared did not feel threatened by the questions; her tone was actually quite calming. He rose to his feet and with a shallow bow announced, "I am Prince Jared Dunbar of Borell, son of King Tamor."

"Have you hurt your back?" she asked.

"No, why do you ask?" asked Jared.

"Why did you bend forward like that? I thought you were stretching your back."

"No, it's a custom in my homeland and is considered good manners."

"How strange. Did you think I knew your father?"

"No, why would you?" asked Jared.

"Then why did you tell me his name, if not for recognition? You are very strange."

"Well..." but Jared gave in, this was becoming hard work.

"So tell me Gerald, why *are* you here?"

"It's Jared," he said with a sigh, "and I am escorting my brother, who is sick, in hope of finding a cure for his ailment."

"Sick you say, is he dying?"

"No, his sickness is one of the mind."

"Oh, you mean he's mad?"

"No, I mean…, do you have a name?"

"What sort of a question is that? Of course I have a name, doesn't everyone?"

Jared ran his hand through his hair in frustration. "May I enquire what it is?"

"If you must."

Jared looked at her, "Well?"

"Yes I am thank you," she replied.

"What is your name?"

"Faylore Fellentheen."

At last, a breakthrough, an actual answer, he thought. Jared had met some perplexing folk in his life, but this one had to be the worst.

Faylore had remained seated throughout their conversation, but was now strolling around, studying the trees intently, stroking the trunks, the branches and the leaves as if she had become bored and was looking for something else to pique her interest. Jared was transfixed by her beauty. She was taller than he, much taller, about seven feet at his estimate. She wore a sleeveless tunic and breeches of emerald green, made from a shimmering, exotic fabric and on her feet, slippers that seemed to be made from leaves. Around her waist was a thick, brown leather belt and secured to this, a beautiful, curved silver sword, etched with runes. This hung against her left thigh, on the right, a dagger of similar design, and strung on her back, a silver longbow.

"Forgive my ignorance, Faylore, but are you an elf?"

Faylore glared at him. "Well if you're going to insult me, I think I'd better leave!"

"No, please don't. I never meant to insult you. I apologise, it's just that I am not well travelled and unfamiliar with your race."

She had turned away, her last statement having been made quite seriously. She really had felt insulted by Jared's last question. She paused, looking over her shoulder at him. "Very well. It's obvious that you are somewhat primitive in your ways, so I'll accept your apology."

At first, Jared had felt a little intolerance with this unusual visitor, but he was now becoming fascinated. "So may I…, what race are you?" he asked, remembering falling into the 'may I' trap, earlier. He had realised that, to converse with Faylore, one must be direct, remain polite, and ask questions in an inquisitive manner rather than a demanding tone.

"I am a Thedarian," she replied.

"And where is your homeland, Faylore?"

"Well, Thedar, obviously!"

Jared decided not to pursue this particular line of questioning, feeling that it may become a little complicated. He also did not want to run the risk of inadvertently insulting his unexpected guest again, and politely changed the subject. "Faylore, my friends and I were attacked earlier today in a gulley not far from here. All would have been lost if not for the intervention of an unseen archer. Was that you by any chance?" Jared asked.

"It was," she sighed.

"Well, for that, Faylore, you have my gratitude."

"Do not thank me. It is quite obscene to excuse any killing, whatever the circumstance. All have a right to live in this world. But the battle was unfair, I will admit. You were outnumbered and the attack unprovoked, however, if the roles had been reversed, it would have been they who received our aid."

Jared was a little taken aback by Faylore's retort, and the fact that she had said 'our aid', not 'my aid'. "Would you care for some refreshment?" he asked, "We have wine or water, and biscuits."

Faylore's inquisitive nature got the better of her once more. "What are biscuits?" she asked.

Jared roused Hannock, but left the soldiers to their sleep. "Hannock, this is Faylore, Faylore this is Captain Hannock."

Hannock pushed himself up on one elbow as Faylore sat, cross-legged, on the ground in front of him. "Well hello," was his immediate response.

Faylore was given water, her choice, and some biscuits, with which she was not impressed, and the three continued with conversation. Hannock realised very quickly that Jared was choosing his words very carefully, deeming it prudent to speak only when spoken to and refrain from making off-handed comments, or offer opinion.

"So, what were those things that attacked us, Faylore?" asked Jared.

"They are the Dergon," she replied.

"Why would they attack us, I mean *us*, specifically?"

"It was nothing personal, they attack everybody."

"So this was not an attempt at robbery?"

"They would have taken your belongings, but that would not be their reason to attack. They are warriors, they live for battle."

"But they retreated when you shot those four. If they live for battle why did they suddenly flee?"

"There are very few Dergon left now, and those few have been scattered throughout the lands. They are fearless, but cannot afford the loss of too many of their number," she replied.

"And what were those things they were riding?" asked Hannock.

"They are glamoch. They roam the plains in herds. Wherever there are Dergon, one can usually find glamoch."

"Are there others of your kind in this region, Faylore?" asked Hannock.

"But of course there are," said Faylore with a matter of fact tone, "they are all around you, I would never travel alone, it is far too dangerous." Jared and Hannock looked around them, but saw no other Thedarians. "They will not show themselves just because you wish it. They are with me, but find you most uninteresting." She glanced over her shoulder. "Very well," she said, and held up her hand, positioning her fingers in a way that could have only been a kind of signal. One of her fellow Thedarians appeared, dropping silently from a tree a stone's throw from them, bow in hand, then another and another, until at least a score were facing the camp.

Hannock looked at Jared. "Impressive."

"My kin and I shall stay and protect you for this night and ensure your safe passage on the morrow, for now, however, you must rest. Your two friends are badly wounded and shall be cared for in the morning. We have more effective remedies than the wrapped rags with which you bound them."

"We are most grateful, Faylore. I must ask, why, if your people have no interest in us, do they help so freely?"

"We would see none suffer unnecessarily and my kin are loyal to me. They do it partly through duty, although I do prefer to believe that they do it through love. I am their queen, Faylore Fellentheen."

***

The two soldiers were discussing their predicament. The change in them was amazing. The Thedarians had given them cordials and applied poultices and dressings, made from various powders and leaves that they had taken from pouches they carried. They had been bathed, despite their protest, and now looked well enough to continue their journey. A male Thedarian had approached Jared and Hannock once the guards were taken care of.

Hannock tried to insist that he was fine but the Thedarian had ignored him and, grabbing his head, forcefully poured a cordial into his mouth, holding his nose until he swallowed. Then it was Jared's turn who, although a prince, received exactly the same treatment. Karrak, still inside the cart, had remained undisturbed.

A short while later Faylore approached, and faced Hannock. "Well?" she asked.

"Well what?" asked Hannock.

Jared began to laugh, "Come along my friend, we have a long journey ahead."

"Why are you laughing? What did I say? Am I missing something here?"

Hannock was completely confused.

CHAPTER 7

Barden stared at Emnor for what seemed like an age, disturbed by the news he had just received. "You not only know 'who' he is, Emnor, you know 'what' he is. You should have destroyed him when you had the chance, and to make matters worse, you now tell me you've known of his existence for years, since he was a child. What on earth were you thinking?"

"No, Barden, I do not know *what* he is, only what he could become, but if we act now there is very little chance of it happening," Emnor replied.

"And it could have happened with the brother, but you omitted to tell me about him either."

"The prophecy tells of the second born, not the first. But listen to us, that scroll is over a thousand years old, it's even older than we are. I'm sure it'll come to nothing," said Emnor.

"How many said that about the Elixian Soul, Emnor? The scroll in which it was mentioned was double the age. We have had that in our possession for over five hundred years, having sworn to protect it and prevent it from falling into the wrong hands."

"That's something completely different. Barden, that's an object. We are talking about a life; you can't just snuff out a life as if it were a candle."

"Why not? It would be a far better idea than to let events take place as they are described in the scroll."

"But it's all conjecture and hypotheses, Barden. I don't know about you but I, for one, cannot just murder someone based on those."

"Rather that, than the alternative, Emnor. One life… or tens of thousands?"

"You cannot condemn a man for something he *might* do, Barden."

"Once I would have agreed with you, Emnor, but not now, not after the actions of his, or should I say, *their* mother."

***

Tamor was a very happy man. He was king, his subjects loved him, his kingdom was bountiful and only two days prior he had married the kindest, most beautiful woman in Borell. Life, as far as he could see, could be no better. Utterly devoted to his wife, where she went, he followed.

A blissful year had passed when suddenly, showing no symptoms of illness, the queen collapsed. The court physicians were called, but on examination had diagnosed that it was nothing serious. Informing the king that his bride had just overtaxed herself and with a little rest would be fine in a few days, the queen had been settled into her bed. But they were wrong. Over the next few days her condition worsened until, apologetically, the same physicians reported that there was nothing more they could do. Distraught at the news, the king issued a notice to all stating that great wealth would be given to anyone that could save his dying love from her mysterious, seemingly-terminal sickness.

Without notice or prior appointment, a stranger had arrived at the castle, stating that if he could not save his king's love, not only would he not expect to be given any reward, he would forfeit his own life, in apology. In desperation, the king accepted his offer.

The stranger entered the queen's chambers, followed by guards, who now carried his numerous, intriguing, steel-banded chests. He instructed all to leave, insisting that under no circumstances must he be disturbed. Peculiar chantings were heard and foul emanations came from under the door as Tamor waited anxiously. Suddenly, there was a blinding flash, then silence. The door to the queen's chambers opened. The sweat-soaked stranger supported himself by leaning against the wall, and looked exhausted. King Tamor nervously entered the queen's chambers and was overjoyed to find his wife sitting up in bed, smiling weakly at him. By some miracle, she had survived. The king, taking his love by the hand, bowed his head and wept with joy.

The stranger had been shown to a room to allow him to bathe and refresh himself, and once rested, had been summoned by the king. Tamor had asked the man to name his price, offering gold and jewels, lands and titles, but the stranger had refused them all, asking simply for one thing. Once Tamor's marriage was blessed with children, the stranger would be given an audience with the queen, alone, simply to pay his respects and enquire after her health. The king was astounded by this simple request and granted it readily, the man still refusing to take as much as a single gold coin for his services. He then left the castle, and his existence faded in Tamor's memory.

***

Another ten years passed. Tamor was now the proud father of an heir four years of age and a newborn, barely a week old, when the stranger returned, unexpectedly. He was greeted with great enthusiasm by the king, who immediately sent word and then escorted the stranger, to the queen's chambers.

There was no sound from within, but less than ten minutes later the stranger emerged and, thanking the king, bowed and, once again, departed.

***

For a while, things in Borell remained unchanged until, one evening, as the king and queen were dining, one of the maids accidentally dropped a tray of food. Ordinarily not a word would have been said, but on this occasion the queen had risen from the table scolding her for her clumsiness. When the maid offered her apologies the queen slapped her across the face, shocking everyone with her uncharacteristic behaviour. The king had raised the subject later in the privacy of their quarters, his wife insisting it would be remiss of her not to keep the servants in their proper place. But this was only the beginning. Rumours of cruelty by the queen were rife. Maids being tortured by having their hair pulled until it came out by the roots, or having forks and knives driven into their hands at the dining table for the slightest excuse, or being beaten by the queen in her private chambers for no reason at all, were only some of them. Rumours to most but, unfortunately for the victims, horrifically real.

Unexplained absences by the queen began to occur. Her relationship with the king was in tatters, as they now barely spoke to one another. Then, the disappearances began. Maids, cooks and general staff would simply be missing, but any sinister motives were swept aside by the queen, making an excuse that she had dismissed them, or that they had run off, finding the work too hard for them, anything to cover the truth.

The once-happy atmosphere of the castle was transformed. Tamor usually dined alone, the queen saying she had better things to do. She had insisted that the children be with her at all times, loathed to trust the 'incompetent' staff. The king reluctantly agreed to this. Any time he suggested anything, other than following her wishes, resulted in the queen going into a rage. His main problem with his wife, despite her much-changed personality, was that he still loved her deeply, and would never believe that she could hurt her own children.

Partaking of lunch, Tamor was chatting to one of his personal guards, when the subject of incarceration came up. He had questioned how long it been since the dungeon had been used and asked if the guard had any idea, but he could not recall. "I wonder if it could be put to any other use?" asked Tamor. The guard had remained silent. "Come on let's go and have a look shall we?" When they reached the dungeon door however, they found it locked. Tamor looked at the guard manning the passageway. "Well don't just stand there, open up."

The guard was very nervous. "Sorry, Sire, I can't. I don't have the key."

"Well go and get it from whoever does have it, go on, I don't have all day," ordered Tamor.

"I can't, Sire."

"Why not?"

"Orders, Sire."

"Orders? From whom? I'm the King dammit."

"The Queen, Sire, she has the key."

"Why on earth would she want the key to the dungeon?" he asked himself. The king had the castle searched, but the queen was nowhere to be found.

Later that evening, as the king dined, the queen entered the banqueting hall. When questioned by Tamor, she made the excuse that, as the dungeon was unused, she utilised it to store a few of her private things. It allowed her a total escape from castle life, 'personal space' as she referred to it. The king never pressed the issue and allowed her to leave, but he doubted her, for the first time ever.

***

Tamor, flanked by four of his personal guard, turned the key in the dungeon door, but it remained locked. "Locksmith, open this door," he ordered. The locksmith stooped, fiddling with the lock until they all heard the distinct 'click' as he successfully unlocked it.

"There you go, Sire," he said.

The king reached for the handle, but even before he grasped it, there was another audible 'click'. Trying the door, Tamor found it to be locked once more. He turned to the sentry in the hallway. "Are you sure there is nobody within?" he asked.

"Quite sure, Your Majesty, the queen came out about an hour ago and it's been locked ever since."

Under instruction, the locksmith made a second attempt, with the same result.

Tamor growled. "Break it down," he ordered.

His guard stepped forward, and in a few seconds, the door was open, split completely in two.

They all reeled back from the door, the stench was dreadful. One of the guards put his hand to his mouth in a bid to stop himself from vomiting but, unfortunately, was unsuccessful.

They entered and began to descend the spiral stone staircase, the reek getting stronger as they did so, an acrid and putrefying smell. By the time they reached the bottom step they could barely breathe, but all concern of this was erased from their minds by the scene with which they were greeted. In each corner of the room a brazier cast an eerie glow across the dungeon, making the scene even more abhorrent. Chained to the longest wall, at equal distance, were the bodies of three young girls, the eldest one twenty at most. Their mouths were gagged. They had been stripped to the waist and their legs bared, wearing only the tattered remains of their petticoats. The torture that they had endured was easily apparent with, wield marks and brands from red hot irons all over their bodies. Their torturer had ended their suffering by slicing them open from stomach to throat and pulling out their innards so that they now hung down like a gruesome decoration. Another body lay on the ground; she too had undergone the same sadistic treatment. But the worst of all was the corpse on the torture rack in the centre of the room. As the

97

king moved toward it there was a gentle cough. Turning to face the corner of the room the king gave a gasp for there, lying on a small makeshift cot, was his son, Jared. Blood had been smeared on his body to form symbols, symbols that he did not recognise as a language. Jared opened his eyes. Looking directly at his father he smiled, unaffected, it seemed, by the horrors about him.

Tamor snatched up his firstborn and handed him to one of the guards, ordering him to cover the boy's eyes and then began to tread slowly toward the corpse lying on the rack. This was the most sickening of all. The same fate had befallen the victim, but this time the innards had been removed and dumped in a pail to the side and there, inside the eviscerated body... lay Karrak.

His second son had been nestled into the corpse as if it were a cocoon. The king began sobbing uncontrollably at this sight and, as he did so, Karrak opened his eyes. He seemed to glare at his father as if he had been disturbed from a heavenly slumber, then Tamor saw that his eyes were jet-black. Horrified, Tamor fell to his knees, grabbing the edge of the rack to save himself and placing his head against the back of his hands, praying that this was just a terrible nightmare.

Two guards ran forward and, raising the king to his feet, half walked, half dragged him to the foot of the staircase, whilst the last guard lifted Karrak from his sickening cradle.

As they climbed the stairs not a word was spoken, but at the top, having regained his composure a little, the king turned, a fiery rage in his eyes, "Nobody goes down there, take my boys to the nursery, have them bathed and dressed and find the queen. Bring her to me in the throne room, in shackles if you have to, find her, NOW," he bellowed.

The castle and grounds were searched thoroughly, but the queen still was nowhere to be found. The captain of the guard reported to the king. "Double the watch," shouted Tamor, "she *will* return, sooner or later, and when she does, I want her arrested and dragged before me." The captain bowed and hastened from the room.

The king's wait would not be long. His sons were brought, cleaned and dressed, and placed at his side, now sound asleep in cots that had been laid ready. The court physicians had examined them, in turn, declaring them to be unharmed. Tamor had asked for Karrak's eyes to be examined, but on lifting the lids they appeared to be their normal, brilliant blue and the king convinced himself that what he thought he had seen must have just been due to the gloom of the dungeon.

Exhausted by his ordeal, Tamor, not wanting to disturb his children, had settled back in his throne, cushions packed around him, and was in an uneasy sleep when suddenly the double doors were blasted open with great ferocity and standing in the doorway, was his queen.

Outside the doors, four guards lay on the floor, dead or alive, the king was unsure. An eerie black smoke surrounded the queen as she entered the room. Dressed in a long black gown, she approached the king, the lights seeming to dim as she passed them. Her question threw his mind into confusion. "Did you think I would allow you to take my son from me?"

Her voice had changed, it was much deeper than usual and had a rasp as if her throat was devoid of all moisture. She had said '*son*', not '*sons*', singular, *why? And which 'son' did she mean?*

"You shall not keep him from his destiny, mortal, he will be great. A worm like you could never comprehend the power that shall be his. He will erase you all from existence, with his mother by his side to ensure it," rasped the queen.

Tamor realised that these were not the ravings of a lunatic. His wife had, in some way, been bewitched and had to be stopped, before she took her favoured child.

"You have two children my dear, of which do you speak?"

"My second born and I shall rule this world, mortal, I have no need of the weak one."

"Oh, so you mean to take Karrak?" he asked.

"Do not toy with me, I may even allow you to live, to prolong your suffering as you witness the demise of your kingdom."

"How very kind of you."

With her back to the door, she had not seen the guards who were now sneaking up behind her.

"But tell me, WITCH," said Tamor, emphasising the word for his guard to hear, "do you believe that you alone, can conquer an entire kingdom?"

Realising his ruse the witch turned. Seeing the armed guards, she thrust her left hand forward. Immediately, one of the guards dropped his lance and clutched at his throat as if being strangled. His head suddenly snapped to the side, and with a loud crack he fell to the floor, dead. The witch was now using her right hand. Tamor watched as this time a guard erupted in flames, screaming in pain as he thrashed around hoping to somehow douse them. Now her left hand again, but this attack was to be her last. The captain of the guard had charged in amidst the confusion and paused, just briefly, waiting for his moment. Clasped in his right hand he held a crossbow, a solid gold crossbow. As the witch turned for her third attack he raised it and, taking a short breath, released the bolt. The witch's head was turned to the side as the bolt struck. Piercing her temple, the solid gold bolt travelled through, its tip now visible on the other side of her head. The noise that came from her was not a scream or a shriek nor even a roar, it seemed to be a mixture of all three. She stood stock still for a moment, but never fell. She began to shake violently, so violently that her features were distorted until, without uttering another sound, she exploded in flame, literally, her limbs strewn around the room. The king, the captain, and his remaining men, were felled by the blast, but unharmed.

Fortunately, the captain had entered the adjoining room as the king had announced, indirectly, that they were dealing with a witch and had charged to the armoury to get the crossbow. Because, everybody knows, that the only real way to kill a witch is to impale the head with pure gold.

Search parties were formed and rewards offered. The king was convinced that these events were linked to the mysterious stranger who had come forward so readily and cured the queen of her illness so many years before, snatching her from the jaws of death itself. Tamor had only realised since the dealings with the witch, that he had never even asked his name.

"But I'll find him one day, and when I do…"

CHAPTER 8

"I don't know what was in that stuff that fellow gave me this morning Jared, but I feel as if I could run all the way to Reiggan Fortress with Karrak on my back without stopping once. I feel absolutely marvellous."

"Me too, I wonder if they'll give us the recipe? If we ask nicely, of course."

"Somehow I don't think it's worth asking, I know Faylore's alright, but the others don't seem overly keen on befriending us."

"Whatever makes you think that, Hannock?"

"Try it, go on, speak to one of them and see what happens."

Jared waited for a short while, then, catching the eye of one of the Thedarians called out to her. "Beautiful morning isn't it?" She tilted her head to one side as if she were contemplating whether to answer but then, without a word, she looked up and jumped into the lower branches of a tree she was passing. Jared looked at Hannock, who burst out laughing.

"Nice to see you can still make an impression with the ladies, Your Highness."

Jared was astonished and shook his head, laughing.

They were now leaving the woodlands. Ahead of them were miles of sweeping plains. A small track trailed into the distance and would now be their obvious route as it would lead them to Ferendon village in which they would rest for the night. The soldiers would be provided with lodgings and ordered to wait until they were re-united on the return journey, as their wounds should be healed by then.

Keeping up with the Thedarians was not the easiest task. They were tall and had long legs, making their stride much greater, and every so often they would stop to allow Jared's procession to catch up. Jared offering apologies each time. They were a fascinating race to watch, graceful, with sparkling white skin and platinum hair blowing in the gentle breeze. Hannock fell in love at least five times that morning. Faylore called a halt, at about midday and Jared took this opportunity to speak with her again.

"Faylore, I was wondering if there was any way, if you're not busy of course, I wouldn't want to inconvenience you, erm would you be our guide?"

"No, that would be impossible. I told you, I am a queen."

"Yes, sorry, my mistake. What I meant to say was, would you consider accompanying us, it would allow you to study us in greater detail?"

"I might. You are a little tedious, but also intriguing, and I would like to see your mad brother safe."

Jared remained calm. "My thanks for your consideration I am highly honoured Your Majesty."

"Yes, you are," she replied.

***

It was nearing dusk as they approached the tavern in Ferendon. Faylore had agreed to accompany them for as long as she could and bade farewell to her fellow Thedarians. Hannock believed his eyes were playing tricks on him. He had looked away from the Thedarians for the briefest of moments, but on looking back, found they were already gone, as if they had simply vanished.

Jared had rented rooms for his party, all except Faylore of course, who said she would feel uneasy opening her eyes and not being able to see the stars. Jared and Hannock carried Karrak in through a back door to save people gawking and he now seemed comfortable, on a bed at the far end of the room. Hannock made himself scarce as Jared produced the two vials used for treating Karrak.

"I'll go and see what I can find in the way of supplies, Jared, meet you at the bar when you're done?" Jared raised his thumb.

Hannock did well on his 'shopping trip', managing to replace most of the foodstuffs and provisions they had lost, as well as a cart, not as big as their previous one but that was unimportant, as there were now only three of them. Finding good horses in this region was going to be difficult, he had been told, and he had to be content with the purchase of a pair of mules. *At least this would allow Jared to ride his own horse,* he had thought. Riding on the back of a cart would be good enough for him, but not for a member of House Dunbar. Faylore had followed him every step of the way, fascinated by the fact that he had to make purchases from others. Thedarians are completely self-sufficient. Questions were asked regarding almost every purchase, *What's that for? Why do you need that? Why do you need the beasts, is there something wrong with your legs, can't you walk? Why does he like those shiny pieces of metal, what will he do with them?* Her questions seemed endless.

Hannock was glad when they returned to the tavern. Bidding Faylore goodnight, he entered. *She's so exasperating*, he thought. The two soldiers were sitting at a table, a flagon of ale between them. Hannock walked to the bar and spoke to the barkeep. Taking two bottles of wine from him, he then walked over to the table, handed one to each soldier and pointed to the passageway that lead to their room. "Rest," he ordered. They rose from their seats and headed off.

Jared entered the barroom shortly after and sat down opposite his friend, "Any luck?" he asked.

"There's a man with a huge flying carpet and he said for twenty gold coins, he'll fly us directly to Reiggan in the morning."

Jared laughed.

Hannock informed him of his purchases and of Faylore's interjections, "I mean, Jared, how can you not know what money is?"

"They seem to have no need of it my friend, they must grow or make everything that they require."

"Even their weapons? Have you seen them? You have to have serious talent as a smith to produce something like that."

"From what I've witnessed so far, Hannock, I wouldn't think that there's anything a Thedarian couldn't do, if they put their mind to it."

"Do you think they're trustworthy?"

"Well they saved our lives, you can't get more trustworthy than that, *and* they could have killed us at any time, if they'd have been of a mind."

"Well that's a fact, Jared, I suppose I'm just not used to folk helping without wanting some kind of reward."

"I know, but it's nice to find the exception to the rule don't you agree?"

"Absolutely. We must study this, Faylore. I know, we'll get her a gift as a surprise."

"Just be careful, Hannock, have you noticed how touchy she can be?"

*****

Ramah had followed his plan. He headed north, Klag by his side with the ten selected Dergon following closely behind. They had covered quite a distance and had soon come upon three of their own kind, wandering aimlessly at the foot of some small hills. It took minutes for Ramah to convince these ragged, gormless individuals to join his group. "Here you are, here's some nice clean clothing for you. Put it on, put it on," he urged. The Dergon were not the most hygienic of species, but even Ramah had reeled at the smell. "Nice iron helmets, and a sword each, you can throw away those awful clubs now, go on, go on."

Ramah had realised some time ago that convincing his fellow Dergon was easy, although slightly wrong. You just had to treat them like children at first by using coercion or bribery. "Klag, get our new friends some meat. You would like some meat wouldn't you?" asked

Ramah. Once the new recruits were dressed, you could not tell them from the others.

"'ere, Chief," said Klag, "'ow come you talk to 'em like that?"

"Like what, my dear Klag?"

"Like they're your bestest mates 'n' that."

"One has to be gentle with them at first, Klag, to earn their trust. One must speak calmly. They don't know me as you do, they don't know how kind and fair a leader I am, and they're not as clever as you." He'd also learned that flattery worked just as well.

"Cor the Chief told me I was clever. Clever Klag, ooh I like that, clever Klag," he kept repeating to himself.

Ramah's recruitment campaign continued. More and more joined him. Slaying the current head of a group was a simple enough task and very few of them could think for themselves, always craving leadership. Within a few days, eighty-seven new 'volunteers' now followed him. "We shall give it another five days my General," he said to Klag, slapping him on the head, which was his idea of showing affection, "five more days and we shall have an army, my friend."

Klag's eyes grew wide. *General, friend,* clever General Klag the Chief's friend. He shivered with excitement.

Ramah was correct, recruitment became easier and easier. He hardly ever spoke now. Klag had taken the initiative and, with the help of his warriors, their number had tripled, with Dergon actually seeking them out, eager to join. Ramah sat at the top of the hill looking down at his warriors. A pride welling in his chest, he raised his voice and bellowed down to them, "The time of The

Dergon has come," causing his new followers to chant, 'Dergon, Dergon, Dergon.'

***

Faylore had taken the lead, her long legs striding easily across the grassy plains. She had spoken very little that morning, but had studied the two friends as they packed up the cart, hitched the mules and saddled the horse. Karrak had been lifted into the covered cart and made comfortable, and instructions were given to the two soldiers before they were ready to leave. Throughout their preparations, Faylore had paced, sighing occasionally, placing her hands on her hips and tapping her foot, not disguising her impatience. Although bemused, she had survived the wait until, eventually, they set off. Their progression would, of course, now be increased, with the acquisition of the mules. Mounted once more, Jared rode at the tail of the procession so that he could converse with Hannock, who sat on the back of the provisions cart, his legs dangling, swaying gently as it trundled across the uneven terrain.

"This is much better," said Hannock, "we should be able to make up for lost time, if we don't have rain and the ground remains firm and even."

"Our path is clear for miles, Hannock, so no nasty surprises, and best of all, we have Faylore now, her senses seem to be much keener than ours, you know!"

"I know; she is impressive isn't she?" Hannock had a dreamy look on his face like an enamoured schoolboy.

Jared laughed and, spurring his horse gently, rode ahead in order to speak to Faylore.

"I saw no bows, Gerald, what do you use to hunt?"

"We have bows and crossbows in the covered cart, and it's Jared."

"Why didn't you use them against the Dergon when they attacked?"

"We never had the chance, they were on us too quickly."

"It never looked that quick to me. How strange you are." She quickened her pace and marched ahead, seemingly losing interest in the conversation.

Two more days passed. The trio's time was taken up with Jared and Hannock reminiscing over childhood events, and Faylore's constant questioning. She was becoming used to the Borellians' ways and they hers as their friendship was beginning to form. Faylore, however, still regarded her new-found friends as very strange, but had also gleaned that they bore no malice to others.

They broke camp on the third day, the most unusual day to date. Faylore was attempting to supervise, in order to speed up the process, as impatient as ever, to continue their journey.

It was raining again. The Borellians took this in their stride, but Faylore produced a full length, hooded cloak of emerald green from her pack and wrapped it around her shoulders, drawing the hood over her platinum hair. Hannock gave a little sigh and the dreamy look returned to his face, as well as a stupid smile. This was wiped off with a whack around the back of his head, as Jared struck him with a leather glove. "Back with us, Captain?" he asked.

Faylore looked over her shoulder and smiled. Yes, a most unusual day.

The soggy ground hindered their progress, but only slightly, and by late afternoon they reached the foothills of Peralorn. Rising very gently, the grassy slopes, despite the rain, were easy to traverse with only sparse rock formations. As they started the ascent, Faylore suddenly signalled for them to hold. Her two friends looked at one another, their confusion obvious, as they could neither see nor hear any reason for this abrupt halt. Swiftly, Faylore armed herself. "We must help," she said.

Bow in hand, she sprinted away at such speed that her cloak was now blown horizontally behind her as she disappeared over the horizon. Hannock leapt into action, running to the cart and snatching up two bows and quivers of arrows. Jared spurred his horse and, grabbing Hannock by the arm, swung him so that he was now seated behind him. Turning, he charged after Faylore. Reaching the top of the ridge the pair could not believe their eyes. Faylore, now stood on top of a rock, was firing arrows at a herd of beasts that numbered at least fifty. Massive beasts with black skin and red eyes… glamoch.

The arrows bounced off the hides of the glamoch as if they were made of iron until, with a loud thump, one fell dead, an arrow through its eye. The others were now charging the rock on which Faylore stood, causing it to shake, shards breaking off as the beasts slammed head first into it. Faylore, her footing unsure, was struggling to aim.

The Borellians had now begun their own attack and managed to fell another glamoch, resulting in part of the herd turning and charging toward them. Hannock's eyes grew wide, "Oh bugger."

There was nowhere to shelter, the stampeding beasts were now a mere twenty feet from them. Hannock felt himself pulled backwards, violently. As Jared stepped

110

past him, he thrust his hands forwards and gigantic flames flew from them, not leaving them but from them as he moved them from side to side. The beasts reeled and bellowed in terror. Jared began walking forward the flames still roaring from his palms, herding the glamoch away until finally, they turned, and fled to escape their fiery fate.

Hannock, now seated on the grass, looked up at Faylore. "What was that all about?" he asked. Without a word, she jumped down and strolled around the rock on which she had been standing, then with lightning speed, made a grab for something behind it.

"Ow, ow, ow, that really hurts you know? It was an accident, I mean, I didn't do anything, it was somebody else and they ran away, please let go, that really hurts."

Faylore now dragged her captive from his hiding place by his ear, and what an ear, or indeed ears? Stood before them was the most peculiar creature that either Jared or Hannock had ever seen. He was about five feet tall, but two feet of them were his head, and his ears were nearly the full length of it. His body was dumpy but his sleeveless arms were huge with biceps as thick as tree trunks. He had enormous green eyes a small pointed nose and very rosy cheeks. One could actually describe it as cute but for his arms. On seeing the rest of the party, a beaming smile appeared on its face.

"Hello," he said, "I'm Lodren."

Slightly taken aback by this pleasant greeting, Jared stepped forward and offered his hand. "Jared Dunbar," he said, "This is Captain Hannock and Queen Faylore," he added, gesturing in turn to his two companions.

"Very pleased to make your acquaintance, can I have my ear back now please?" Faylore released her grip.

Lodren stood rubbing his ear as it turned bright red, a result of its harsh treatment by Faylore. "You've got a very good grip you know, for a queen?"

The impudence, Faylore thought, *for a queen, indeed.*

"Join us for a moment, Lodren," said Jared, as he headed back to the cart not waiting for a reply.

"If you insist," said Lodren, following him.

Jared wanted to return to the carts, he couldn't leave his brother unprotected.

"Nice horse by the way," said Lodren, then he pointed at the mules and added, "shame about them though."

"What are you doing out here, Lodren? And why are you alone?" asked Jared.

"I'm a Nibby," he answered holding his arms out from his sides as if the statement was the answer to everything.

"What does that mean?" Jared asked the question inquisitively.

"You don't know?"

"No, I'm afraid I don't," said Jared.

"Where are you from?" asked Lodren.

"We are from The Kingdom of Borell," replied Jared.

"So, what do you call yourselves?"

"We are Borellians."

"So, you're from Borell and you call yourself a Borellian. Well, I'm a Nibby because I'm from nowhere."

"That makes no sense," said Jared looking puzzled.

"Right, how can I put it?" Lodren paused for a second and raised his finger in a 'eureka' gesture. "A nomad, you'd call me a nomad. I am a Nibby and I'm a nomad."

Hannock had to chip in at this point, "Well at least you'll never get homesick."

"How did you manage to get yourself into that mess with those beasts?" asked Jared.

"Just hungry," replied Lodren.

"Just hungry?"

"Yes I thought I could bag a stray one, they taste lovely if you use the right herbs. Can't beat a nice glamoch steak. Mind you the shoulder's nice as well, but only if it's slow-roasted."

"Bag a stray one! No offence, but how on earth did you think you could bring down one of those things by yourself? I mean they are pretty big and…" Jared's voice tailed off. He might insult Lodren by mentioning his small stature, and that would simply be rude.

"Come on, I'll show you." Lodren started walking back up the hill. Reaching the point where the felled glamoch lay, he paused and looked down. "I'll be with you in a minute," he said, rubbing his hands together. He carried on, disappearing behind the rock where he had hidden earlier. Emerging a moment later he was holding a hammer, but what a hammer. It was as big as Lodren himself and he smiled at it as he raised it into the air. He now stood before the rock that Faylore had used for elevation. "Sorry about this," he said patting it gently and then, swinging the hammer as hard as he could, brought it down with an almighty crash and smashed it into pieces.

Hannock, as usual, "Stone me."

Leaving Lodren to his own devices, they returned to the carts, discussing what they had just seen. Lodren rejoined them a short while later with many leaf-wrapped parcels, obviously containing glamoch meat, and began to stow them away in a backpack he had secreted earlier, which had also explained the acquisition of the leaves. "Anybody hungry?" he asked.

They had decided to press on and invited Lodren to join them.

"Why not?" he said, "should be good for a laugh if nothing else."

Late that afternoon, they were fortunate enough to come across some old, disused stone cottages and the Borellians took advantage by settling in one of them for the night. Lodren, much like Faylore, preferred the outdoor life and they had left the two of them in order to discuss their progress and tend to Karrak's needs.

"Have you ever seen strength like that before, Hannock?" asked Jared.

"Well there was this one chap..." replied Hannock, glancing at Karrak.

"My brother is powerful I'll admit that, but this... Nibby, well, he's in a league of his own."

"He'd be a good asset to us on the rest of our journey Jared. If we could persuade him to stick with us, things could be a lot easier."

"I wonder. Do you think there's anything he might want or need, Hannock?"

"Well he says he's a nomad. I wonder if they use coin or just barter for anything they can't get in the wilds?"

"Well, the easiest thing would be to just ask him, that is of course if he's still here in the morning," suggested Jared.

Hannock began to laugh. "I wonder how those two are getting on? I bet the conversation's simply flowing." His manner changed, "And how are you? I mean you're not tired?"

"Well maybe a little, but no more than usual, why?" asked Jared.

"Jared, you cast that fire spell today and it never even affected you, you never even flinched," replied Hannock.

"I know, and unlike the last time, I actually felt stronger after."

"Good old Emnor was right then. Tell you what, you keep up with your magic and pretty soon we won't even need that magic carpet I mentioned, *you* can fly us to Reiggan."

***

They arose the following morning and were pleasantly surprised to find that, not only was Lodren still with them, but was eager to join them in their 'adventures' as he called them. A word that Faylore found to be most vulgar.

They travelled yet another day without incident and, once camp was set, Lodren had insisted that he would take care of the 'catering', another strange word that he had used. Jared and Hannock had their reservations, but as much as they protested, Lodren had said that it was only fair that he be allowed to 'do his bit'. The meal prepared, they sat around the campfire. Faylore attempted to leave but Lodren begged her to at least try some of the food he had prepared. "Your Majesty," he said most politely, "I do understand that your palate is far more refined than ours, therefore I have prepared dishes solely for your delicate taste buds."

Faylore, surprised at his wonderfully formal manner, accepted and took her place.

They raised their plates in unison, each taking tentative nibbles at the unknown cuisine. Their hesitation lasted but a few seconds as their taste buds were overwhelmed with the delicious flavours! They had made an unspoken pact to not ask what the ingredients were, but the meals produced from them were wonderful! Lodren was overjoyed by the response, cooking being his love, "I'm really going to enjoy cooking for you three."

***

"With the ones we've already got, Chief, and the ones what you've got 'ere, that means we've got, erm, how many is it, Chief, I ain't no good wiv numbers."

"No, now that you mention it, I had noticed that slight flaw in your character, Klag. Never mind, my plan is coming to fruition, and one such as yourself who has a bovine brain should be quite adequate."

Klag raised himself to his full height and pushed out his chest, taking it as a compliment.

"And in answer to your question, we are now over four hundred strong."

"Ok, Chief, what's the plan then? What we gonna do wiv our army, I mean your army, I mean, what you gonna do wiv *your* army?"

"For too long, Klag, the might of the Dergon has been used to win the wars of others. For too long we have been given the scraps from the tables of kings who keep the fortunes of war for themselves. It is time for the Dergon to have a kingdom of their own, and I shall sit upon its throne. We cannot win a war with so few warriors, however weak our enemy, for we would easily be outnumbered. The numbers we do have therefore must suffice to take our first steps. We shall raid villages and destroy townships. Word of our victories will spread far and wide and all others of our kind will join us until our number reaches thousands and, when that day comes, we shall take kingdoms for our own."

On reaching the rest of the horde, the Dergon began to make ready for the first stages of their planned uprising. Leather armour was made from glamoch hide and issued to all Dergon that were still without. Helmets, heavy swords and shields of iron were forged and Ramah himself taught his warriors fighting techniques, to aid them in their upcoming battles. Warriors would fall to their knees exhausted, only to be pulled back to their feet and forced to endure even more gruelling battle training. These were Dergon, they were not weak, each would fight to his dying breath and were convinced that soon, they would conquer the world.

***

The four companions had now reached the base of the Muurkain Mountains and set up camp and Lodren, as

117

agreed, was taking care of the catering. The air had become a little cooler and the travellers had changed into warmer attire, well not all, Lodren had pulled a light waistcoat from his backpack and insisted that this was all he needed, as the cold never really affected him.

At this point Hannock leaned across to Jared and whispered, "Where would you find a jacket with sleeves wide enough to fit those arms anyway?"

"Do you know the route at all, Faylore?" Jared asked.

"I can tell you the route as it has been explained to me in the past, but I have never actually taken it myself," she replied.

"I tried it once, but I was driven back by the snow," announced Lodren.

"Why didn't you tell us that before?" asked Hannock.

"I don't like to poke my nose in, and anyway you didn't ask me."

Hannock shook his head "Oh for f…"

"How far did you get, Lodren?" asked Jared loudly to drown out Hannock's foul language.

"Nearly half way. I never pushed myself, it was only a trail I hadn't used before and I just wondered what was up there."

Hannock was amazed, "You decided to climb a mountain, just because it was there?"

"Well yes, I suppose I did," replied Lodren.

"What a barmpot!" exclaimed Hannock.

"Good evening, how are you all?" They all jumped up, grabbing for weapons as they had not seen anyone approach. "Oh dear. My apologies, did I startle you?"

Before them stood Emnor, chuckling, having obviously amused himself.

Jared extended his arm and signalled for Faylore and Lodren to lower their weapons.

"You'll get yourself shot doing things like that, old man," Hannock said curtly.

"Maybe, but there'd have to be somebody fast enough first," replied Emnor, still chuckling.

Introductions were made and the camp settled. Emnor was given food, Lodren not taking *no thank you* for an answer. Tactics for their impending ascent were addressed as Emnor produced a scroll, on which a map was drawn, opening it for all to see. "Now this would be your best route," he began, "however, at this time of year the snow can make it impassable, so there are alternatives. Now if I were you, and the easiest route could not be followed..."

Hannock interrupted, "Hang on just a minute, you're a wizard, and a powerful one from what I'm told, can't you just..." and at this point he gave a high-pitched whistle and made a motion with his hands like a bird taking flight.

"Oh no, no, no, I'm not allowed to do anything like that. I'd be in a lot of trouble, we wizards can't do that to mortals, we might hurt you or even kill you and that simply would not do."

"Oh well, just a thought," said Hannock shrugging his shoulders.

The discussion continued as they studied the map. "Oh and by the way, you should be careful if you stray from the paths. There are many caves on the mountain, some hidden by snow and we can't really be sure what may be lurking in them," advised Emnor.

"Thanks for that, bundle of joy you are, hidden paths, avalanches and now monsters in caves, I really don't know why you bothered turning up here you…"

"Shut it, Hannock," said Jared.

Emnor, feeling that his errand was done, bade them all a fond farewell, turned and wandered off into the darkness.

"What a lovely wizard. He's great isn't he!" said Lodren, his frequent beaming smile showing in the light of the campfire.

***

After breakfast they set off, Faylore not in the best of moods as she had had no tree to sleep in the night before, but Lodren did his best to cheer her up. "Can I get you something Your Majesty? How about some of that nettle mint tea you like so much? Perhaps a honey biscuit, now I know you like those, won't take a minute, it's no trouble."

"I bless the day we met Lodren, I really do," said Jared.

***

Ramah, mounted on his huge glamoch lead the march, Klag, astride a slightly smaller beast at his side. His army, on foot, followed as he rode at a steady pace. There would be no marching done by these warriors. They were not soldiers, they had no grace or finesse. They were marauders, walking, breathing, killing machines bent on drawing blood with no care to whom it belonged. With them, they carried their weapons of war, large roughly forged swords and iron shields, all black in finish. No time would be wasted by Ramah's smiths in cleaning or polishing. The pace, set by Ramah, was for a reason.

The Dergon, engaged in wars waged by others had, on numerous occasions, been used to strike terror into the hearts and minds of whatever foe they had been set upon. Ordered to charge, they would mindlessly hurl themselves into battle, but this would never fare well for them. Used as a spearhead they would always attack when the enemy was at full strength and in good health, needlessly sacrificing their lives because of it. Inevitably, this selfless act would always leave their enemy severely weakened, allowing their employer's armies an easy victory, as they moved in only to strike the final blow.

Ramah was more bloodthirsty and ruthless than any of his warriors and longed for battle as much as they, but would not sacrifice a single life unnecessarily, for if his ultimate goal of complete domination over these, and other lands, was to succeed he needed as many as possible to survive. He explained his strategy to Klag who, in turn, passed this information down through the limited ranks of Ramah's army. No more would they charge blindly, they would use stealth, sneaking up on their enemies and striking before any defence could be mounted.

They had reached the village. Quietly, they moved to surround it, meeting a few unfortunate victims on the outskirts as they did so. These were dealt with swiftly by having their skulls split, their necks broken or their throats cut or torn out. Within minutes they were ready to strike. They moved in. Screams could be heard from the villagers as they came face to face with their attackers. Their screams did not last for long as the victims were butchered without mercy, every last man, woman and child. All were beheaded, the heads mounted on spikes and displayed in the centre of the village... the terror of the Dergon had begun. Ramah knew that this was no victory as such, just a crowd of defenceless villagers. He looked upon it as a training exercise for his warriors who, now they had tasted blood, would want more, and by the time a real battle came, they would be ready.

***

The ascent of Muurkain Mountain was going well, as there had been little snowfall. They had to stop occasionally to clear a drift or two but on the whole, they were pleasantly surprised by their easy progress. Hannock was not convinced as easily as the others and seemed very moody and ill-tempered. "You just give it half an hour and we'll be up to our blasted necks in it, you just watch, bloody snow."

Jared was a little concerned with Hannock's demeanour. This wasn't him. He never complained, ever, even as a child. He'd been shot in the face with a crossbow and hadn't even mentioned it since, other than in jest. Something was wrong, very wrong.

"We'll be alright, Mr Hannock," Lodren had tried to assure him, with his usual smile and 'can do' attitude.

"What do you know? It'll be over your head, smile about that then Stumpy."

Jared could see that these words hurt Lodren's feelings. "Take no notice of him, Lodren, he's just in a bad mood. Probably the cold getting to him," he said.

Faylore was watching closely by this time, but never uttered a word. She suspected what was wrong with Hannock but chose to keep it to herself for now, just in case she was mistaken. Although, in her heart, she knew that she wasn't.

They had now climbed roughly a third of the way up the mountain but as they rounded a bend, found their path completely blocked. Admittedly, the companions could have passed if they had been careful, but there was no way the animals, let alone the carts, were going this way. Jared contemplated using his magic, but decided against it. Spooking the animals on a precarious mountain pass could be disastrous.

"I told you, didn't I tell you?" moaned Hannock.

Jared for the first time in his life pulled rank on Hannock. "That's quite enough, Captain Hannock, we'll have a little less of that if you don't mind?"

Hannock was shocked, and it showed. "Yes, Sir, terribly sorry, Sir, won't happen again."

"Let's hope not. Now let's have another look at that map and see if we can figure a way around this mess." Studying the map, they saw that only a thousand yards back, there was actually another way around.

With a little pushing and pulling they managed to turn the carts and headed back the way they came. Reaching the point marked on the map, they found just another rock face. "But it's supposed to be here. Look, it's clearly marked on the map. Maybe there was a landslide and it got covered, I mean we have no idea how old the map is!" exclaimed Jared.

Nobody noticed Lodren approaching from behind. He had picked up his hammer and was creeping up behind

Hannock as he raised it in the air, then crash, down it came. The others jumped, this was the last thing they were expecting as they attempted to solve the riddle of the disappearing trail.

"What the hell?" cried Hannock.

Lodren smiled, "You might want to stand over here a bit," he said, gesturing for them to move toward him.

At first there was an eerie silence. This gradually gave way to a gentle crackling noise, like fresh ice stepped upon for the first time. Slowly, the volume increased and became a deep rumble like thunder as the ground began to shake, and then came the boom, like a thousand simultaneous explosions. The companions clasped their hands to their ears as the noise became almost unbearable, trying to balance themselves as the ground moved beneath their feet. They feared for their very lives and stood terrified, as the side of the mountain began to slip away before them, plumes of dust filling the air, blinding and choking them.

The noise ceased abruptly, the dust cleared and the trail they had sought had now been revealed. "There you go," Lodren continued, "one trail… thought it was there."

"How did you know?" asked Jared, still coughing from the inhaled dust.

"Oh you know," replied Lodren, "lucky guess."

"Lucky guess!" exclaimed Hannock.

"Do you like repeating what I say, Mr Hannock."

"Lucky guess. He brings down half a mountain and… lucky guess!" They all looked at Hannock, slightly amused at his disbelief.

The detour was adequate and their ascension continued fairly unimpeded. They still however, had not managed to reach the main trail, but luckily, as the daylight began to fail had discovered a cave set back slightly from their path. They entered cautiously, weapons drawn. An existing occupant may not offer a warm welcome to unexpected visitors. They found the cave to be of a medium size, very ordinary and unoccupied. The carts were brought inside. Lodren set a campfire and began his catering duties as the others tended the animals.

"Not a lot of room in here is there?" Hannock said, grumpily.

Lodren stepped forward. "Can I help?" he said picking up his hammer.

"NO! Thank you, we're fine as we are," said Jared, a slight panic in his tone.

Lodren returned to his campfire, sniggering.

They had eaten their fill and, as was the norm, Jared rose and removed the two vials from his tunic, turning toward the cart.

"Go on, off you go, take care of sleepy," said Hannock.

Jared turned to face him. "What do you mean by that, just what is your problem Hannock?"

Hannock went into a rage at this and jumped to his feet, facing Jared. "He's my problem," Hannock replied sharply, pointing at the wagon, "that beloved brother of yours. He tried to kill you, he murdered a guard, if he were anyone else he'd have been hung or burned at the stake for using magic but oh no Daddy has to take care of his baby boy and to top it all big brother holds his hand and feeds him just to make sure he's safe. Why don't we just cut his throat and throw him off a cliff? That's what you'd do with any other psychopath but instead we're half way up a freezing cold mountain with two freaks, babysitting him."

Jared was shocked at this outburst from Hannock, confusion stemming any words he might say. He dropped his head, "We'll talk about this later," he said quietly.

"We'll talk about this now. My whole life I've taken care of you, Your Highness and what do I get? Do this Hannock, do that Hannock. My name's *Charles*. Do you remember? When was the last time you used it, *Charles*, not difficult is it?" Not even realising it, his hand had reached toward his sword and was now resting on its hilt. "See? Not a word. You have no idea what I've had to put up with over the ye…"

There was a high-pitched, ever-so faint whistle. Hannock's tirade had stopped suddenly as he put his hand to his neck, a small green feathered dart protruding from it. A puzzled look came into his eyes, his lips moving but uttering no sound. His eyes closed and he collapsed in a heap at Jared's feet.

"I think that's quite enough of that," said Faylore with a sigh.

Jared turned to face her and saw in her hand what looked like a short, green straw. It was in fact, a blowpipe.

"You've killed him," shouted Jared, "you've killed my best friend."

"Don't be so melodramatic my dear Jared, he's not dead, just unconscious."

"What do you mean, *just unconscious*?"

126

"He would have carried on and gotten worse. He might have hurt himself, or you and we can't tolerate behaviour like that in front of royalty now can we?" She walked over to Hannock and stooped down, removing the dart from his neck. "He's going to wake up with a terrible headache, poor lamb," she said stroking his hair.

Jared was more surprised by this comment than he was by the dart.

Lodren had not been fazed by any of it and seemed completely oblivious to the whole situation. "I know you're a little busy but I'm packing everything away, so if you want any more, speak up now."

Faylore set out a bedroll and she and Jared lifted Hannock's limp body onto it. "There you are my sweet, sleep well," she said stroking Hannock's cheek. She rose and turned to Jared. "I must speak with you, Jared, this unfortunate situation must end." They sat by the campfire, Faylore beckoning Lodren to join them.

"What can I do for you, Your Majesty?" Lodren asked, smiling as always.

"I shall need your expertise my dear Nibby," she replied, "but firstly I shall explain to you both what is happening with dear Charles."

Dear Charles thought Jared. *Dear Charles, what's going on? Have I missed something?* But he said nothing, waiting in anticipation for Faylore's explanation.

"It seems as if," she began, "Charles is besotted with me."

"Well I'd figured that much out for myself, but why's he become so violently aggressive?" asked Jared.

"Because of the simbor," she answered, lowering her head in embarrassment.

"What's the simbor?"

"It is a pheromone Thedarian females produce when they reach what you would call their 'teenage years'. Our kind produce simbor as your kind would get, what do you call them? Oh yes… pimples, such a pretty word."

Jared sat open-mouthed. "Right, thank you for that image, but what the hell has that got to do with," he paused, "… Charles?" he said, struggling to get the final word out.

"The simbor can affect the males of certain species. Some just feel a sense of great joy and happiness." Jared cast a look at Lodren, who was still smiling.

"Oh no, that's nothing to do with me," said Faylore hurriedly, "that's natural in the Nibby."

"Really?" came Jared's reply in amazement, "Now what do we do about… Charles?"

"We make a serum. Don't worry I have all the ingredients we need, I'm just not very good at preparing them. Somebody always made them for me and I'm sure Lodren can help on this occasion, but we must do it soon. If Charles suffers the effects of the simbor for too long the rage can lead to insanity."

"Obviously," said Jared, but luckily, Faylore never noticed the sarcasm.

Lodren was handed the ingredients and he and Faylore began the complicated preparation of the cure for Hannock's affliction. After an addition was made to the potion, a strict time limit was adhered to before the next ingredient could be added, until at last, the serum was completed and poured into one of Lodren's spare jars.

"Before we go any further, Faylore," began Jared tentatively, "I've noticed that your feelings toward Charles, seem to have changed. Does the simbor affect you in a similar way?"

"Not in the slightest, I just think he's adorably cute," she replied as if it were perfectly normal. Jared had known Hannock his entire life and would never have referred to him as 'cute'.

The serum was administered to Hannock. Faylore assured Jared that Hannock would be fine when he awoke, although he would probably be suffering a little amnesia, and only of very recent events. A deliberate side effect of the serum to save any embarrassment by the afflicted. As had already been said, the Thedarians would allow no unnecessary suffering.

***

They awoke the following morning. Well most did. Hannock had to be roused from his very deep sleep and on sitting upright immediately grabbed his head. "Oh my… what the hell was I drinking last night? I can't remember a thing. I didn't do anything stupid did I?" The other companions could not help themselves and laughed out loud, much to Hannock's annoyance. "Come on now, what did I do, tell me dammit, ooh my head."

Jared couldn't resist. "Nothing, now come along we must make a move… Charles," and the laughter began again.

***

The Dergon were on the move. Their number had increased, only by a score but Ramah was feeling confident and had chosen his next target, a village half the size again to the last. Ramah studied the scene and spotted four guards armed with crossbows, a kind of militia, stationed in the village square, but considered them to be no threat. Returning to his warriors, he gave his orders. Their tactics would be identical to their last, using the element of surprise. Without a sound, they began to surround their prey.

"But remember, Klag, you must hold your position until I give the order," Ramah commanded. Klag was stationed on the eastern side with Ramah on the west. Ramah could already feel the elation from the easy victory that was about to be theirs. But, his confidence was premature.

Suddenly, his warriors on the eastern side of the village roared and charged. Ramah was aghast, what were they doing? This had not been the plan, he had not given the order to attack… *Klag, the fool*, he thought.

Klag, leading his band of warriors had approached as planned, but drawing nearer had begun to think, a thing he never did well. *I could impress Ramah to bits if I beat the village with just my 'alf of the army, he'd be dead chuffed and it'd save time.* His excitement, having gotten the better of him, caused his actions and suddenly, at the top of his voice he roared, "CHARGE."

The four militia members in the village reeled to face them and released their bolts, every one felling a Dergon.

What happened next, Ramah could not have foreseen. Located at the northern end of the village stood a large barn. He had paid it no mind, simply taking it to be no more than what it appeared, much to his regret, as suddenly, the doors flew open. Twenty or more militia charged through them. They too, carrying crossbows, opened fire upon the charging Dergon, five more fell, ten, fifteen, this would not be the easy massacre Ramah had envisaged.

Taken aback, he paused. There was only one course of action left open to him as, he too, gave the order to charge. Ramah witnessed his brave warriors fall. He and his warriors hacked and cleaved until as before, all life was extinguished. The battle was done. His army celebrated their victory but Ramah himself felt no joy, as to him this had been a disaster, having lost at least fifty of their own. He called his warriors to him and stood before them, holding out his arm for Klag to stand at his side. Klag stood proudly beside his Chief, a twisted smile showing his brown, rotting teeth.

Ramah addressed his army solemnly, "We have achieved another victory my Dergon, but we too have suffered losses this day, and far too many. I made you a promise that none of your lives would be lost needlessly and today I have broken that promise, not purposely, but by putting my faith in another, I have failed you. Had my orders been followed we would still have our fallen brothers."

Ramah's body jerked slightly and the twisted smile disappeared from Klag's face. "This will not happen again, pay heed to this lesson. Fail me and you *shall* suffer the consequences."

Klag, still standing during the final warning, dropped to his knees and fell face first into the dirt, a large knife embedded to the hilt, in his skull.

***

Jared could not resist, he kept on all morning. "After you, Charles, keep up, Charles, are you alright, Charles?"

Come lunchtime, *Charles,* had had enough. "What's with all this Charles business? It's Hannock. You never call me by my first name, ever, it's always been Hannock, even my own father calls me Hannock, so knock it on the head will you! No more *Charles.*"

"Alright, alright if you insist… Charles." Jared ran ahead as Hannock took a swipe at him.

Their mirth however was short-lived. They had thought that reaching the main path would take roughly an hour, but as they rounded the very next bend the trail they were on ended, smashed away by a landslide or storm, just the edge still attached to the cliff remaining. Hannock groaned, "Bugger."

"It's not that bad, it's only about a fifteen-foot gap," said Lodren cheerily, "we can manage that."

"We probably can my dear Nibby," said Faylore, "but what about those?" she asked, pointing to the carts.

"Oh I'll take care of those, Majesty."

"And the horse and the mules?" asked Jared.

"Easy, like I said, I'll take care of them," replied Lodren.

"And how do you intend to get those, over there?" asked Hannock pointing.

"Well, I'll throw the carts across and then carry the animals one at a time. I'm not stupid, Charles."

"Don't you start. I've got enough with him."

"But that's impossible" said Jared, "you can't throw a cart."

"No, Prince Jared, *you* can't throw a cart, but I can."

At Lodren's request, they unhitched the mule from the provisions cart. He stooped and shuffled between the wheels and without taking a breath, lifted it above his head. "See…" he said, "…easy."

Hannock's jaw dropped.

"You'll get used to him," smiled Faylore, "how many more times must you be told? *He's a Nibby.*"

Faylore crossed first as she was the lightest and very nimble. Jared and Hannock followed. Lodren came straight after them almost at a run, carrying Karrak over his shoulder. This was thought to be a better idea than him being tossed around like a ragdoll in the back of the cart when it was thrown. Lodren then returned to the carts. The animals had been blindfolded to save undue alarm and Lodren was now trying to assess the best way to lift a horse. "I could just knock him out for a while?" he said reaching for his hammer, "Only joking, only joking." He lifted it with its front legs over one shoulder and back legs over the other and began the crossing, but even though the horse tried to buck in protest, he never missed a step. He repeated the process with the mules and now had only the carts to deal with.

He took hold of the first, advising the others to stand well back, and then with a very slight grunt he launched it. Landing on the other side, its wheels already locked, it scraped to a halt. "One down, one to go," said Lodren, moving to the second cart. This was the covered cart, the larger of the two and considerably heavier.

"Do be careful, Lodren, we don't want you hurting yourself old chap," said Hannock, with genuine concern.

Lodren lifted the cart as easily as he had the first and approached the gap. He rocked back and forth slightly and as it moved forward for the third time, he gave a mighty push. The cart flew into the air, but all had not gone quite to plan. As Lodren had released his grip, his waistcoat had snagged and as the cart took flight, he went with it. It was halfway across, Lodren still attached, his arms flailing wildly in an attempt to grab hold of a lifeline that didn't exist. It seemed as if the cart would clear the gap quite easily but that the Nibby was in danger of being crushed as it landed. His companions gasped in shock, but the worst was yet to come. As they looked on in horror, Lodren's waistcoat tore, the cart continued its flight, but he did not, and plunged into the gap. The cart landed the same as the first, scraping to a halt. Faylore fell to her knees, her two companions aghast.

They heard a *thump*, then again, and again, realising that the noise was coming from the gap in the broken trail. They approached the edge, gingerly peering over to see Lodren hanging onto the sheer rock face, still smiling. "Don't worry, be with you in a minute," he called.

All three began to laugh and cheer.

As Lodren fell, he pulled back his huge arm and punched the rock face, creating a handhold and was now repeating the process enabling him to climb back up. His companions threw him a rope and, once he was safe, Faylore threw her arms around him. She had become very fond of the Nibby.

***

"They shall be here in a day or two, Barden. Have the preparations been made?" Emnor enquired.

"Yes of course, but I still think you're overreacting."

"One cannot argue with lore, Barden. The scroll warned of this and we must not take the matter lightly."

"One failed fire spell, Emnor, *one, failed.*"

"Yes, I admit that it could have been a lot worse. However, he did attempt it, which means he now realises he has the ability to perform magic and knowing him the way *I* do, Karrak will certainly endeavour to learn more," said Emnor.

"And that is why we are bringing him here. The power of the Administration could suppress the most powerful of magis," replied Barden.

"His power was borne of madness; unlike his brother whose power is natural. His was obtained by absorbing five souls tortured into that madness, exactly as it is stated in the scroll. We must take great care; preparations must be made to the letter."

"And they are, Emnor. I told you he should have been destroyed as an infant, but he wasn't, and now we have to deal with the situation as best we can. Personally, I find it difficult to believe that one mortal can consume the soul of another, but why doubt us so?" asked Barden.

"I am unsure, I just have a strange feeling of unease and if something goes wrong, I fear Karrak will be hard to contain."

"Emnor, listen. The columns have been placed and the runes carved into them. The markings from the scroll have been etched into the floor and ceiling. Spells have been cast on the only door, nobody can get in or out of the chamber without prior knowledge of the incantation and I alone know that, *plus* he'll be kept asleep most of the time."

"And what if Karrak somehow draws the incantation from your mind, what then?" asked Emnor.

"Impossible. I shall remain outside the doors at all times and Karrak will be attended to by another, and of course, I'll be wearing this." Barden raised a talisman secured by a thick gold chain around his neck. "The Order of Corrodin will not allow another to probe my mind."

Emnor glanced at the talisman. He was unsure, as was everyone, of its origin, or indeed of its properties. Barden had begun to wear it some years before and as far as he could remember, had not been without it since. Only Barden knew its true significance.

"Let's hope you're right, Barden, because if you're not… I dread to think what might happen."

***

Faylore remained silent as their journey continued, embarrassed at her show of affection toward Lodren and Hannock. Thedarians rarely showed emotion but the simbor had affected her as well as Hannock and she would never, ordinarily, have been so sentimental.

"We should reach Reiggan by tomorrow evening don't you think, Hannock?" asked Jared.

"What? You'll have to speak up. I can't hear you over this blasted wind," shouted Hannock.

"Never mind," said Jared, waving his hand to show his last comment was of no importance.

The weather had turned, the wind blasting the snow into their faces and spooking the animals. They ploughed on, but the weather seemed to worsen with every step. Jared abruptly called a halt. "We must find shelter; the snow is blinding." He too, was now having to shout.

They suspected that the map bore no relevance to the paths that they were now being forced to take. Without option, they continued. Discovering a cave and without thought or hesitation, they entered, throwing caution to the wind. Catching their breath, they stared, but try as they might, their eyesight could not penetrate the abyssal blackness of the cavernous expanse.

"Any chance, Your Highness?" asked Hannock.

"Oh yes, of course," replied Jared. A flame appeared, nestled in Jared's palm.

"Hang on just a sec, Mr Jared," said Lodren. Rummaging in the provisions cart, he produced three torches, lighting them before passing them to the others. "That's better," he said.

"Trust Lodren to always have what we need," said Faylore.

"Plenty room in this cave, Mr Hannock," said Lodren with a laugh.

"Indeed. I don't think you'll need your hammer this time."

"I think we should make as little noise as possible," suggested Faylore, tilting her head to listen, "we are not alone." They all stood stock still, watching Faylore intently.

"What can you hear?" whispered Jared.

"Somebody humming a tune," she replied, "it's coming from deep within the cave and whoever it is knows of our presence. Stay here, I'll take a look."

"But you can't see in the dark," said Jared.

Faylore looked across at him, "No, Jared, *you* can't see in the dark."

Jared remembered his conversation with Lodren regarding the cart. "I'll shut up shall I?" he suggested.

Venturing further into the gloom, Faylore saw the faint glow of a campfire. Sneaking closer she witnessed a tiny individual, no more than two feet tall, tending to a spit placed across the flames. He was wearing a brown leather jacket with trousers to match, sported a goatee beard and had a shock of red hair with two small horns poking out of it. "I ain't got nothin' worth stealing, so you might as well bugger off now," he said suddenly.

She was taken aback by this, not at what was said, but that she had been detected. "My intention was not robbery, friend, merely curiosity."

"Oh, so you're a nosey bugger? Well you've had yer look. Now sod off."

Faylore was unused to being spoken to in such a way, but realising her trespass, she remained polite. "My apologies, friend, we shall not disturb you again."

"We? What do you mean we? You're not alone?" he asked.

"There are five of us, but we mean you no harm."

"What are ye doing here, pokin' around?"

"We were caught in the storm and simply sought shelter," replied Faylore.

With hands on hips, he looked her up and down. "Bring 'em down here. I'd rather have 'em where I can keep me eye on 'em," he said gruffly.

Faylore returned to her companions and, with her assurances of safety, they all returned to the camp of the grumpy individual.

Entering the firelight, Jared prepared to make formal introductions.

"Don't think you're gettin' fed, this is my dinner. Ye can use the fire when I've finished with it and that's all, and keep them bloody animals away from me, horrible smelly things," snapped the stranger, before Jared could speak.

Lodren tried to break the ice as this strange individual tended his spit, "I have some very nice herbs that might improve the flavour of that, happy to share if you'd like some."

"This is why I prefer to be on me own. Ye haven't been here two minutes and yer already sayin' me food's no good. Did I ask fer ye herbs? I'm fine as I am, ye can stick ye herbs."

"Just a thought, we're all different I suppose. Could I make the campfire a little bigger when I prepare our meals, as there are five of us?" asked Lodren.

"And now me campfire's not big enough. Anythin' else ye'd like to insult while yer at it?"

Hannock spoke for the first time, "Look, it's obvious we're not welcome, we'll just go a bit deeper into the cavern and leave you in peace."

"What makes ye think you're not welcome? Was it something I said!?" exclaimed the stranger.

Hannock was flabbergasted and Jared started laughing. Holding out his hand he announced "Jared Dunbar, and you are?"

"Grubb. No first or last name, just Grubb."

Having eaten, they all settled by the now, large campfire.

"Has this been your home for long?" asked Faylore.

"I come and go, sometimes here, sometimes not," replied Grubb.

Faylore had the distinct impression that this was not going to be an easy conversation.

"Do you know the area well, Grubb?" Hannock enquired.

"Yes, and no. Some bits I do and some bits I don't."

Lodren realised what it was that the others were attempting to glean and felt inclined to speed up the process. "We're trying to get to Reiggan Fortress and we're lost, can you help us get there?" he asked. The rest of the companions stared at him in disbelief.

"Well normally I don't involve meself in other's affairs, but if it means getting rid of ye a bit quicker, then yes I can, and I will. We just have to follow the cavern to the other side and it's not far from there. It's too late in the day to start now so get some sleep and we'll go in the mornin'," replied Grubb.

Looking rather pleased with himself, Lodren pulled his trusty backpack closer to use as a pillow, and settled down for the night.

***

The last leg of their journey had begun, at least they hoped it had. They were now well past the halfway point through the labyrinthine cavern.

"Be quiet as ye can through this bit. Don't want to attract any unwanted attention," advised Grubb without elaboration. Unfortunately, it wasn't long before they found out what he meant.

They heard the snuffling first and then the patter of the paws… wolves!

Appearing from the darkness they stalked closer. They began growling and snarling, their breath showing as steam would from a half-boiled kettle. They edged closer and would surely have attacked, when suddenly there was a roaring howl that seemed to stop them in their tracks. In an instant it appeared, *it*, because none of the group knew exactly what *it* was. Ten feet tall, four arms with hands as big as spades, talons like an eagle and walking on two legs. It charged toward the wolves that yelped in fear. One wolf jumped at the creature but was caught mid-air and thrown against the cavern wall, killing it instantly. The pack circled the strange creature, still growling, hackles up. The creature slashed once. The wolves, realising that they were outmatched, turned tail and ran.

The companions drew their weapons, Jared nestling a fireball in one hand, ready for battle. Unsure of the best strategy, they watched the creature intently for a few moments, for although it had scattered the wolves, they were still wary of its intention towards them, but were astounded when, incredibly, it began to shrink, getting smaller and smaller until, there stood Grubb. The creature had been Grubb, or was Grubb the creature? "Damned wolves are a bloody nuisance!" he exclaimed.

"Well, there's something you don't see every day!" said Hannock.

***

Tamor sat on his throne, arms folded. Staring into the eyes of the soldier standing before him, he asked, "Not one survivor?"

"No Sire, and all were beheaded, even the children," he replied solemnly.

"Who would do such a thing, and why?"

"Forgive me, Majesty, but it is more of a 'what' than a 'who', and I am not sure what 'they' are."

"What do you mean? Make sense man," snapped Tamor.

The soldier turned to his side and was handed a grain sack. "It was done by these, Sire." Drawing his hand from the sack, he raised the head of one of the fallen Dergon.

"Dergon!" exclaimed Tamor, "But I thought they were all but extinct. There can be no more than a handful left, and what there are have been scattered far and wide."

"We counted over fifty dead, Sire, but by the tracks they left, they number hundreds."

"This makes no sense, these animals are mercenary. They fight for the highest bidder during open warfare, they do not simply attack innocent villagers. They must be in someone's employ, but who is commanding them?"

"Sire, the only tracks other than the ones of these *things*, were the tracks of beasts, but nothing I recognise."

"Glamoch probably, they use them as we would horses, but that still doesn't explain who they were fighting *for*. They live for battle, not lands or titles, only blood."

"What are your orders, Sire?"

Tamor sat silently for a few moments, contemplating what action to take. *Why had he suggested that Jared should oversee his brother's safe passage? Why had he allowed Hannock to accompany them?* It had barely been two weeks since their departure and could be twice that before their return. His mind was in turmoil at the loss of so many of his loyal subjects, but he knew he must act swiftly.

"Assemble a platoon. Return to the village and track this filth. Observe only, do not engage, I need to know who employed them. Be very careful, use stealth, you must not be detected."

***

"So what is he exactly?" asked Hannock.

"He's a Vikkery," replied Faylore.

"A what?" asked Hannock.

"A Vikkery. Now how would you put it? A shapeshifter."

"That explains a lot," said Jared, "I was wondering how somebody his size could defend himself in the wilds, but I never would have believed it if I hadn't seen it."

"They are a very peaceful race and prefer their own company, hence the frosty reception," said Faylore.

"Now we know what he is, I'm glad he didn't get too upset at our first meeting," said Hannock with a gentle laugh, "here he comes now."

"We'll be there in a couple of hours. Oh and by the way, we Vikkery also have excellent hearing, so next time ye want to know something ask *me*, not *her*." Grubb snorted and strutted off.

Hannock was fascinated by Grubb and wondered just how to approach him without being either obvious or offensive. "We appreciate your help a great deal, Grubb. I don't know what we'd have done without you when those wolves attacked."

"You have plenty weapons, and a magician, you'd have coped easily enough."

"Maybe, but you saw them off by yourself before we even had time to act."

"Enough of this crap. What do ye *really* want?" snapped Grubb.

Hannock immediately went on the defensive. "I don't know what you mean dear chap, just being friendly, you know."

"We aren't friends, ye don't even know me and I didn't help ye for the sake of it, I just don't like wolves. Devious sneaky creatures they are, talking about people behind their backs."

"Talking? Wolves? I don't understand. Wolves don't talk," said Hannock.

"Like I said, we Vikkery have excellent hearing. Just because your kind can't hear 'em, doesn't mean they can't speak."

"Fascinating. Please forgive me for asking, but do you hear other animals speak?" asked Hannock.

"A few. Most of 'em are as they appear, just dumb animals. It's the hunters ye have to be careful of ye know, wolves, bears and the like."

"What if you met with one of those, erm, things, like the one you changed into when you chased off the wolves?" asked Hannock, arriving at the subject he really wanted to discuss.

"My word, ye have no idea do ye'? That's just something I made up. There's no *real* beast like that, four arms! Ye aren't right in the head if ye believe in such things," he tutted.

Hannock realised that he was now being mocked by Grubb, but not in a facetious way, and decided to keep the conversation going as long as possible. "Are you able to change into many beings, or just imaginary ones, Master Grubb?"

"Firstly, I told ye it's just Grubb and secondly, why do ye want to know?"

"Idle curiosity, Grubb, nothing more," replied Hannock trying to look as innocent as possible, but at the same time, yearning to have his question answered.

"Well it's like this," said Grubb leaning forward, Hannock leaned closer, "mind your own bloody business."

Hannock laughed, bowed to Grubb, and moved a polite distance away from him.

Jared looked Hannock up and down as he approached. "You just can't leave things alone, can you, Hannock?"

"I have no idea to what you are referring, Your Highness."

"Don't, *Your Highness* me. Honestly, you're like a child with a scab, you just can't resist picking at it."

"I asked a few simple questions that's all, I meant no offence."

"And luckily he took none, but Faylore said that the Vikkery like their privacy, you could have really offended him."

"We've never met anyone like him before. I couldn't help myself, I mean, to be able to transform yourself like he does would be pretty useful at times. Do you know something? I think for the first time, I'm actually jealous. Is this how normal people feel when they meet me?" There was a huge grin on Hannock's face.

"Can you just bear with me a moment, Hannock? Only, I'm wondering how big the noose needs to be to get over that big fat head of yours."

"That's the exit from the cavern just up ahead. Turn to yer right as ye leave, follow the trail and it'll lead ye to the bridge, Reiggan is just the other side. Don't worry, ye can't miss it," called Grubb.

Jared turned to face him. "I rather hoped you'd join us, Grubb. You have been most helpful and I feel that you should receive some form of payment."

"Don't need anything, don't want anything, I belong here, not in some wizard fortress. They'll be worse than him with their questioning and prying," replied Grubb, pointing at Hannock. "No, I know me place, and it's not in there with them. Farewell, and try not to come back, well not too soon anyway." He turned and walked away, only taking a few steps before morphing into the huge, four-armed beast. "Goodbye, Captain," it growled, disappearing into the gloom.

***

The scouting party had climbed as high as possible on the rock face and were now looking down on the Dergon camp, that sprawled into the distance. The men were whispering to one another.

"This doesn't look good, corporal."

"No... no it doesn't, I'd say there's about five hundred of these things. It seems as if there's some sort of ranking system, but no difference in... well, *uniforms,* I suppose you'd call them."

"I've not seen any of them giving any orders. It's difficult to see who's in charge. Hang on, something's happening."

One of the Dergon had appeared, larger than the rest and far more imposing and as he did, a hush fell about him. It was Ramah. To the soldiers, he looked the same as the rest, but began to give a speech that seemed to rouse his followers, which was apparent by their cheers.

"I can't hear a word he's saying, corporal. Shall I try to get a bit closer?"

"No. You might give away our position and I don't fancy our chances if we are discovered."

"So what do we do then?"

"Exactly what the king told us to do. They aren't being manipulated by any lord or king, they have their own agenda, whatever that may be and the king must be told. We head back to Borell and report our findings," replied the corporal.

With this they slowly backed away.

CHAPTER 9

The companions had reached the bridge and now stared in awe at the fascia of Reiggan Fortress. Carved into the mountain itself, but with far more skill than any mason could have achieved, were four statues. Each was at least a hundred feet tall and contained such detail that it appeared as if any one of them could turn their head or blink at any moment. The hooded robes in which they were adorned looked as if the slightest breeze would cause the folds to flutter or reveal a chest swelling, with an intake of breath.

"To reveal such beauty from solid rock is a rare gift," said Faylore.

"I've never seen anything like it. I wish I'd have tried harder the first time I was headed here," added Lodren. "Oh well, we're here now. Shall we?" He held his hand out in a gesture for them to proceed.

"Well we didn't come all this way just to stand on the doorstep," said Hannock.

Jared said nothing. Yes, it was impressive but there was something inside him, in his very being that warned him not to enter this place. Convincing himself that it was merely a fear of the unknown, he moved forward. The doors to Reiggan stood before them, these too seemed to have been carved from pure rock. They hesitated for a moment, but before any could speak, there was a crack and then a rumble as the doors, parting in the centre, began to slide open. A large circular courtyard lay before them. The boundary wall was virtually hidden by life-size robed statues, carved from pure white marble, a burning torch placed between each one. The flagstone floor was black with red runes and a compass painted onto it, and on each point of the compass sat a large brazier that burned brightly.

"Your Royal Highness, may I introduce the Head of the Administration, Barden Oldman. Barden, His Royal Highness Prince Jared Dunbar of Borell," announced Emnor, who had awaited their arrival with eager anticipation.

The two shook hands, and with formalities addressed, Barden made no secret of the fact that he was eager to deal with the removal of Karrak to secure quarters. With a wave of his hand, six robed figures approached the covered cart. Reaching inside, they gently lifted Karrak onto a stretcher and swiftly bore him through a double doorway, immediately behind Barden.

"Should we not escort them?" asked Jared, a little concerned for his brother.

"He is quite safe here, Your Highness, of that I can assure you," replied Barden.

"My apologies, Barden, it's just that… oh never mind, and please, call me Jared."

"As you wish… Jared. We shall visit your brother presently, once he has been settled into his new residence. He must remain asleep for the time being, you understand?"

"No not really, I thought he'd be secure here, unable to harm anyone."

"And he will. His mind will be in a state of unrest for some weeks yet and this precaution is for his protection against himself, more so than others. Over time he will understand his position, and hopefully come to terms with it."

"And should he not come to terms with it, Master Barden. What then?" asked Jared.

"We have dealt with many cases such as his. Given time he will embrace his power and use it only for good. He is not evil, simply tormented by confusion."

"I applaud your confidence, but you don't know him as I do. Although I love him as my brother, I would fear him as an enemy even more," said Jared.

Emnor stepped forward. "Jared, you must trust us. Your brother could be in no better hands, now enough fretting, come with me, I'll take you to your rooms." Emnor escorted Jared and Hannock and, as he recalled his previous meeting with Lodren and Faylore, asked one of his colleagues to show them to the orchard, understanding their preference for the outdoor life.

Jared and Hannock accepted the hospitality of their hosts and dined and drank with them but would have preferred dining with Lodren, who had really spoiled them with his cooking. Lodren had been permitted to build a small campfire in the orchard, allowing him to tend to his and Faylore's needs. The four met a little later and decided it best to retire for the day. Jared could visit with his brother the following morning, feeling that they could both benefit from a good night's rest.

***

Karrak was awake. He had been given no tonic, draught or elixir, he had awoken naturally, but found that he could neither move any of his limbs nor open his eyes. He was not bound in any way, but somehow paralyzed. There was no panic in him, no rage, in fact no concern of any kind. He was warm and comfortable and felt very contented, more contented than he had been for many years. *How strange*, he thought.

He became aware of the voices around him as he was referred to in the third person. At first, only key phrases registered, 'dead to the world', 'out like a light', but behind the others there was one faint, high voice. Although faint, it seemed to transcend all others. It was the one he perceived most, but alas, the one he could not hear clearly. Neither could he decipher a single word, but it was quite obvious to Karrak that it was he with whom it desperately wished to communicate. Karrak tried to speak, tried to call to the voice, ask it what it wanted, what it needed, but could make no sound as he lay there, as helpless as a newborn child. The voice faded and he could hear it no more. There were garbled discussions he could not fathom, talk of potions, hexes and spells. Although he did not fully understand, he found himself spellbound in his safe and insular world. His world of one.

He actually began to enjoy this strange feeling, an invisible intruder in this secret world around him. Strangest of all was the feeling of power. He felt strong, healthy, invigorated, as if he could fight an army single-handed when in fact, he could not so much as twitch a finger. Flashes of light and images came to him, as if he were dreaming or could actually see through the eyes of another and then his realisation of the truth, this was no dream, this vision belonged to someone else.

He was looking down at his own face as the hand in front of him wiped his brow with a damp cloth, and then dried it with another. Many thoughts and questions ran through his mind. *Was this a dream? Had he gone insane? Was he dead? Maybe I'm a ghost. No, that doesn't make sense, a ghost doesn't wash people's faces.*

No, this was something quite spectacular. If he could see through someone else's eyes, perhaps he could also control their mind or body. Or, better still, both.

He felt elation, but at the same time, exhaustion. He could no longer see, he could no longer hear, as his fatigue caused him to slip back into serene slumber.

***

"Your Majesty, they were alone. However, they appear to have their own agenda and the big one seemed to be giving the orders," reported the corporal.

"But that's impossible, they're not capable of rallying themselves. They receive orders, they don't give them. *How can the Dergon raise their own army?"* Tamor asked himself.

"We estimate their number to be around five hundred, Sire. Surely so few cannot be a threat to us. We outnumber them two to one at least. We should quell this uprising now, before their number is increased."

"Do not take them so lightly, corporal. They are savage and bloodthirsty and when that bloodlust is upon them, they are not brought down so easily. A precision shot with an arrow or bolt is sufficient, but to face them on the battlefield is something entirely different. I know, because I have done so. I ran one clean through with my sword and it barely slowed it. Only beheading it did the trick, and that took all the strength I could muster, for their flesh is much tougher than ours. By the time we make ready their number *could* increase, and we shall not be caught off guard so easily. No, corporal, we must number at least twelve hundred before we attack. Make preparations. We shall leave in three days and eradicate this scourge for good."

Tamor dismissed his soldiers and advisors, still unsure of his decision. He had fought the Dergon in the past and knew their savagery, they cared not who they faced in battle and were willing to die without thought or hesitation. Tamor's other concern was the mention of the apparent leader. *Who was he? What was he? How was he managing to control, let alone lead, this rabble? If the Dergon were being led by one of their own, was there a possibility that they would fight harder than they would for a mere payday?* Whatever their agenda, it could not bode well for any. *Would it have been easier if his sons were with him, or better that they were out of harm's way?* If Jared were here he could use magic against their foe but if that were the case *would he then be the largest target?* No, better that he was with his brother, away from this madness.

***

The companions met in the courtyard of Reiggan the following morning, and for the first time in weeks, felt well rested and at ease now that Karrak was secure. Faylore and Lodren were bound by no oath but had

154

become loyal friends to both Jared and Hannock and showed no intent of leaving their company any time soon.

"Good morning to you all. Barden sends his apologies for his absence and will join us shortly. He thought it wiser to oversee Prince Karrak's care personally this morning," said Emnor.

"How tenacious of him," said Hannock, a slight hint of sarcasm in his voice.

"Quite," replied Emnor, not impressed by Hannock's attitude.

"Is my brother well, Emnor?"

"He's fine, Jared, perfectly fine. He's still resting. We do however, believe that it would be best if neither of you have any contact with him until well after his treatment has begun," replied Emnor, looking from Jared to Hannock.

"Why?" asked Jared.

"Your last encounter was a little fraught, best not run the risk of a repeat," replied Emnor.

"But I've been facing him every day since we left Borell. Why should this time be any different?" asked Jared.

"You woke him with a potion that deliberately causes amnesia. We shan't be using the same technique. We shall wake him naturally when the time comes. He needs to understand the error of his ways in order for him to repent."

"Well I hope you've got some strong chains on him before you do. He's not going to be happy when he wakes up in a cell, you might want to stand back a bit," advised Hannock.

"There will be no chains, Captain. Barden can cope with Karrak easily enough," stated Emnor.

"Especially with you helping him, eh, Emnor?" said Jared, a knowing smile on his face. He knew just how powerful Emnor actually was.

"Oh no, no, no, I shall have nothing to do with your brother's rehabilitation," replied Emnor.

"Why ever not? You know him much better than Barden does," said Jared.

"Yes that may be true, but he does not know me, and that's the way it must be kept for now."

"Emnor, I just feel…"

But Jared's feelings were not to be heard. Emnor waved his hand indicating that he would discuss the matter no further. He turned toward the double doors, through which the robed figures had carried Karrak, and beckoned the companions to follow him. The doors, unaided, swung open silently. They travelled through passageway after passageway until, reaching a double door, Emnor turned to face them. "Your brother is within. I shall not be joining you. Once you have said your goodbyes you will not see him for some time. Do not mention his misdeeds. This is the beginning of a healing process and you must forgive his past… indiscretions. I'll wait here. When you are ready, I shall escort you back to the courtyard so that you can make preparations for your departure." Stepping aside, Emnor leaned against the wall and waved Jared forward.

The companions entered the chamber. In its centre, Karrak lay on a sumptuous bed that was surrounded by pillars carved with runes. There were markings on the walls and floor that were incomprehensible to any of them and torches burned on the walls, adding to the eerie atmosphere. Jared approached the bed and, leaning forward, took Karrak's hand and began to whisper to him. The others could not hear what was being said and remained silent, showing the respect deserving of a royal.

Karrak heard every word, Jared's expression of brotherly love and patronising platitudes as well as Hannock, muttering under his breath. Karrak felt nothing. No love for his brother, no anger, nothing, just wishing Jared would leave.

Emnor lead them back to the courtyard, where they began preparing for their departure, which they felt should be swift. "The weather should hold, at least for a day or so, and the going should be good," Emnor offered, as good advice.

"We'll go back the way we came. It may be the longer route but we won't have to contend with any snow for a couple of days, and we won't get lost," replied Jared.

"Famous last words. We had a map on the way here and we still managed it," said Hannock, sceptically.

"But we're just retracing our steps this time aren't we?" stated Lodren, who still had his trademark smile.

"When we reach the foot of the mountain I must leave you, just for a while. My people may be concerned with my absence and I must put their minds at rest," announced Faylore.

"Well of course you must, Your Majesty," replied Hannock, giving his usual over-exaggerated bow.

***

Soon they were ready to depart. They had been given extra provisions and a horse and now faced Barden Oldman, who had attended to bid them farewell. "We shall contact you in due course to update you of your brother's wellbeing," he said.

"My thanks, Barden. Should you need anything, please feel free to contact me," said Jared.

"I will try to meet with you somewhere on your homeward journey, Jared, but I cannot promise," said Emnor.

The large stone gates parted once more and the companions departed in good spirits, minus one cart and one prince.

Jared and Hannock were now both on horseback and, although he had protested a little, Lodren sat astride the spare mule that had been used to pull Karrak's cart. Faylore announced that *her* legs were working perfectly and insisted on walking.

"Being without the large cart should allow us a faster pace and if we get stuck at any point, muscles here can stick the provisions cart on his back and carry it," said Hannock.

Lodren smiled at him, "Glad to be of service, Mr Captain."

***

They followed the trail and could now see the entrance to the cavern.

"And just where do ye think you're going?" asked a familiar voice.

"Grubb!" exclaimed Hannock.

"Heading back into my cavern are ye? Didn't ye cause enough upset last time?" asked Grubb.

"We thought it safer, and we promise not to cause any disturbances this time, to yourself or the wolves, dear Grubb," said Jared, placing his arm across his chest as if swearing an oath.

Grubb looked at them all in turn. He actually liked this eclectic mix of companions. "Well, the only way to be sure of that is for me to tag along I suppose. Just to keep an eye on ye of course," he said.

"Of course Master Vikkery, of course, wouldn't have it any other way. If you'd like to save your legs a little, you can either jump in the cart, or you could ride with Lodren, I'm sure he wouldn't mind," said Hannock trying not to laugh. "Just to save a little time," he added.

"Ride on a mule? With a Nibby? Now that would be interesting." Grubb was most intrigued by this proposal and without hesitation, offered his arm to Lodren, who obligingly pulled Grubb onto the mule's back.

"Comfortable?" asked Lodren.

"It'll do," replied Grubb, who was secretly, thoroughly enjoying this new experience.

"Right, here we go then," said Jared, and the four companions, along with their hitchhiker, headed into the cavern.

***

Ramah, convinced that all was going to plan, had now raided four villages, each bigger than the last. They had yielded very little of value. A few gold coins and some semi-precious stones were the sum of the loot so far. He had no real need of gold as he looted everything he needed, but he had become avaricious and was bewitched by the glint of gold. Studying his Dergon warriors, he had now selected a new second in command, having decided that Klag's successor should be more intelligent than he had been, a difficult achievement. The typical Dergon were far removed from a race of intellectuals. His new second should lack the aspirations that had been the obvious downfall of his predecessor. It had taken careful consideration, but eventually Ramah had made his decision. Korbah was a magnificent specimen. Almost as big as Ramah himself, but with only half the brains. Ramah had watched him in battle and was most impressed at his strategy of using his comrades to shield himself from bolts and arrows. He was not as mindless as the rest, he thought before he acted and if his brothers in arms could learn this from him, it would be a great benefit. Ramah had told Korbah of his promotion, causing his new second to simply nod once. Ramah knew that he had made the right decision.

Korbah now stood before him. "Not sure how many, but somebody was watching us, footprints on a patch of dirt," he said.

"I shall teach you how to read the tracks properly, Korbah, but at the moment it's not important. We were being watched and you have done well to discover the fact, obviously a scouting party, but from where?"

"The tracks were heading toward Borell I know that," continued Korbah, "they had horses waiting, won't take them very long to get back there."

"Borell eh? So, they're making their move. First they send a scouting party to assess our strength, then ready their army to mount their objective. Interesting. We still have time to mount our defences, three days to Borell, three days to make ready and three days back to us. Yes, we have plenty time. Assemble your lieutenants, Korbah, war is coming."

***

"The lore of the scroll has been accurate so far, Barden. What makes you think that you can control Karrak? He is destined to become the personification of pure evil, he cannot be cured with kind words or magic," snapped Emnor emphatically.

"But we must at least try. We cannot leave him to lie in his present state until the day he dies. If we do, we would be no less evil than you insist he is, perhaps even worse," calmly replied Barden.

"Leave him as he is. He is at peace, unaware, and no danger to those around him," pleaded Emnor.

"In his surroundings he can do no harm. There are spells and runes to protect all against harmful magic. Emnor, I must at least try to save him."

"I cannot understand why you have had such a change of heart, Barden. You were the one who said he should have been slain and now all I see is that your mind will

161

not be changed. Very well, but do not look to me for aid, I want no part of this foolishness," said Emnor.

"I'm sure we shall endure without your help," sneered Barden.

"Beware, Barden, do not believe a word he says, do not trust him," barked Emnor. Storming from the room, Emnor slammed the door behind him and, within the hour, departed Reiggan Fortress.

Barden retired to his own chambers and was pondering over various scrolls spread across his large ornate oak desk. Page after page on sicknesses of the mind, from nightmares to hallucinations and madness, fell under his gaze as he sat in complete silence for many hours, transfixed by their content.

He sat forward to closer inspect something of particular interest, but as he did so felt a sharp pain in his chest. He looked down and tutted. His talisman had become entangled in his robes. Without thought, he took The Order of Corrodin by the chain, lifted it over his head, and placed it on the desk in front of him.

"Don't really need that on in here," he said quietly. A mistake he would live to regret.

***

Karrak was awake once more, still immobile, eyes closed. At first it was as silent as it had been the first time, but gradually the gentle mumbling began, quiet at first then slowly increasing in volume until every spoken word was crystal clear. The conversation had many sources, but the topic was the same by all... magic. The discussion continued, but quickly became a debate on how best to use particular spells, and who would be the best candidate for their type. Karrak listened with fascination. He himself had only just discovered that he was able to use magic, rather unsuccessfully and not for the most honourable of reasons admittedly, but it had been his first intentional attempt. There was a faint light now visible to Karrak and, as with his hearing, his blurred vision began to clear as he saw through another's eyes. There were cloaked figures gathered around a large table. So these were the faces to whom the voices belonged. *Was he actually in the room with them?* Try as he might he could not affect this person's borrowed line of vision, yearning to see more.

Then the one transcending voice came again, but this time it was clear, and Karrak knew without doubt, that it was speaking directly to him. "I give you this gift Great One. Use it well, learn all that you can and, when the time is right, find me."

Who was this? What did they want? How could he find them, when he couldn't even move? Would he be able to somehow control the person whose sight he was using, in order to find the owner of the voice? Karrak concentrated, but try as he might, the voice would no longer communicate.

There would be no answers to his many questions as Karrak, resigned to this, continued to watch his unknown, ignorant teachers. He listened intently to every word and took in as much as he possibly could with his restricted vision, until his fatigue became too great and he once again fell back into a deep, dreamless sleep.

***

Barden approached Karrak's chamber door. "I take it all is well?" he asked of the two wizards on duty. They nodded in response. One wizard looked pale and drawn. Barden placed a hand on his shoulder. "Are you alright, my boy? You look exhausted."

"Now that you mention it, I *feel* exhausted. As if I've been awake for days, Master Barden."

"I suggest you take some rest. Here, drink this before you go to sleep, you'll feel better after." Barden handed the young wizard a small vial containing a green tincture.

"That is most kind, Sir, I will. Thank you."

"Make sure you are relieved of duty before you retire. This door must not be left unattended."

The wizard nodded, half in agreement, half as a kind of bow.

Barden entered the chamber and went straight to Karrak's side.

"You look remarkably well for one who has slept for almost a month," he said, knowing that Karrak could not actually hear him. Leaning forward, he held a small glass vial to Karrak's lips and allowed two drops of liquid to fall between them. Taking a few paces back and placing his right hand on The Order of Corrodin, Barden waited. Karrak opened his eyes.

"Good morning, Your Highness," said Barden, and bowed before the prince.

Karrak sat up slowly, undaunted by his surroundings. "Who are you?" he asked gruffly.

"Barden Oldman, Your Highness, Head of the Administration here in Reiggan Fortress."

"So this is my gaol cell is it? For one poxy spell I'm banished to a wizard prison?"

"Not a prison, Your Highness, more a sanatorium. An infirmary of sorts."

"If it's an infirmary I can leave whenever I like, is that the case?"

"The king feels that you might benefit from our care, for a little while, Your Highness."

"How long have I been asleep?" Karrak's manner became typically aggressive.

"Almost four weeks, Your Highness," replied Barden, now holding his talisman with a much firmer grip.

"How did I get here? Was it you? Who did this to me, you slimy little toad?"

"You were brought here by your brother, Your Highness. Prince Jared was…"

"Jared. I should've known. First chance he had to get me out of the castle. Father's favourite golden boy, I suppose he had that sword-swinging idiot Hannock holding his hand as well eh?" barked Karrak.

"The captain of the guard was with him, Your Highness, purely for your added protection of course."

Karrak was losing his temper. "Do you think me some kind of fool, wizard?" he bawled. Karrak raised his arm as if to strike Barden, but was hit by an unseen force as if he was caught in a sudden tornado and thrown backwards onto the floor, stunned, and shaking his head as if he had had a door slammed in his face.

"Now we cannot tolerate behaviour like that, Your Highness," Barden said, very calmly.

"This room is protected and if you attempt to harm others, your intention will be reflected fivefold, so please, do not try that again. We don't want you hurting yourself." Reaching down he helped Karrak to his feet.

"How did you do that? You never even moved!" exclaimed Karrak, dropping back heavily onto his bed.

"I didn't *do* anything, Your Highness, *you did*. The idea is that you understand how your victim would have felt had you been left to your own devices."

Karrak was bewildered by the events. "Can you teach me how to do that?" he asked.

"Your Highness, I can teach you much more than that, but you must first learn a little humility. To be granted a gift such as ours is a great honour, gratitude and respect must be its bedfellows."

***

Barden's visits to Karrak had now become part of his daily routine, increasing in duration however, over the following weeks. Each visit brought similar complaints by the guards of a severe, unexplained exhaustion, something with which Barden seemed unconcerned. He would always offer the same tincture as he had to the first victim, and send them on their way. Today was no exception as, once again, he visited the prince. "How are you today, Your Highness?" asked Barden.

"Very well, Master Barden," Karrak replied pleasantly.

"You seem far more at ease than you were when you first came to us, Your Highness. Your temperament is much improved."

"Well I hardly came to you, Barden, I was kidnapped. For my own good, of course." Ordinarily this would have been said by Karrak in a rage, but he remained quite calm.

"Yes, Your Highness, indeed you were, and not a moment too soon."

"I understand that now. My actions were deplorable. I now see that my father and brother had no other option. They could have locked me in the dungeon to rot or executed me, but instead, decided to place me in your care," said Karrak, sounding sincere.

The two spent hours discussing various magics, Barden knowing he was quite safe and Karrak in good spirits, polite and willing to listen to all that was said.

"I know you have no reason to trust me yet, Barden," said Karrak, "but is there any chance of me being allowed to go for a short walk? It has been such a long time since I have seen daylight and I would be most grateful."

"Your Highness," began Barden, "I understand your apprehension but must regretfully decline. I cannot allow that yet. This segregation is paramount to your recovery but hopefully, before long, I will allow myself to grant your every request."

It was as Karrak had thought, he was a prisoner, and although courteous and respectful, Barden was his gaoler. Karrak sighed. "I understand, Barden, completely."

***

Karrak no longer had to endure the administration of a sleeping tonic and was allowed to retire each night as any other, tonight being no different. He closed his eyes, and after a few minutes, was asleep.

He saw that he was in the same room as usual and the occupants conversed in a similar manner as always. His sight was clear. The eyes were perusing a tome before them. Karrak concentrated as hard as he could. The hand reached forward and turned the page… success. This was what Karrak was willing it to do as he watched, but was it coincidence, was it his will or was it actually the will of the person whose eyes he possessed? He focussed his mind once more, another page was turned, then another and another. Karrak could control this body. He compelled it to rise and look about it, seeing a doorway approached it. Turning the knob, it swung open and Karrak could see a long, torch-lit passage ahead of him. "Where are you going?" asked a voice.

He was turning away from the door, *No, no, walk through the door,* he thought. But it was no good, he had lost his control. The eyes turned back to the table and continued with their owner's studies.

Night after night, Karrak continued to inhabit the body of any unknown host, but now, to a degree, he could compel it to do his bidding. He would cease all activity of the host and study tomes of his own choosing, whilst being careful to avoid detection by any of his unsuspecting classmates. He would hide one tome inside another and if anyone came close, would hold the combined works up in front of him and wave away any questions, as if he were deep in thought. He had not yet ventured outside, that could wait. The knowledge contained within this room was far too intoxicating to

168

allow Karrak's mind to contemplate that anything beyond the door could be of greater interest.

***

After their reunion with Grubb, the companions had spent a little time in idle chat whilst they headed back into the cavern.

"So, you're headed back to Borell now then are ye?" asked Grubb.

"Indeed, Grubb, we must not tarry. We are over a week behind our estimated itinerary," replied Hannock.

"Then ye shouldn't hang about either," stated Grubb, with a smile on his face.

Hannock gave him a strange look, not sure if he had understood.

"Grubb?" said Jared enquiringly, "Should we just head back the way we came, or could you recommend a better alternative?"

"There is a shorter route through the cavern but it's also a much darker way and I'm not sure if anything lives down there. I don't usually have need to head that way ye see."

"Both you and Faylore have excellent hearing, Grubb. Surely you would know of any dangers well before we reached them?"

"Maybe so," replied Grubb, "but it helps to know what to do about a danger, should ye come across it."

"All we came across were wolves, and I'm sure we can handle those," said Hannock.

"Do not be so sure that there is nought else to fear, Captain," said Faylore, "that was all we saw, but what else saw us, and chose to remain hidden?"

"How much shorter is the route, Grubb? I mean, is it worth the risk?" asked Hannock.

"Two days, maybe two and a half now I'm up here," he said. Grubb looked down at the ground from his perch behind Lodren.

"Lodren, are you happy with taking a shortcut?" asked Hannock.

"You know me by now, Mr Captain, I don't care which way we go as long as I can cook at the end of each day."

"Splendid, then the short route it is. Shall we, Your Highness?" said Hannock, allowing Jared to take the lead, but following closely.

"What do you think Faylore meant? Do you think there could be monsters lurking in the shadows?"

"I'm not sure, Hannock, but her kind know these places far better than we do, and by the sound of it, I think Grubb's a little apprehensive about the route as well."

"Well, we'd better be on our guard. Keep your eyes peeled, Jared, we've lost one prince today, don't want to lose another one now do we?" he said sniggering.

"Shut it, Hannock."

Almost a complete day passed as they wound their way down much steeper routes than the ones they had travelled before. Torches had been produced from the cart and Jared, with a wave of his hand, had lit them.

"He's useful to have around at times isn't he!" Grubb said, now enjoying his unusual adventure.

Lodren looked back at him, "Be careful what you say, Grubb, he's a prince," he whispered.

"He ain't no prince of mine," said Grubb, "but I can't help liking him."

"He's really nice, they're all really nice."

"And do ye think I'm nice, Lodren?" asked Grubb.

"Of course I do, because you are, you didn't have to help us, but you did."

"This being nice to everybody, it's not contagious is it?"

"How do you mean?" asked Lodren.

"Never mind, just forget it," grunted Grubb.

Camp was set and Lodren was busying himself, as usual, asking if there were any special requests of his culinary delights. Of course the answer was 'no', as all but Grubb knew that whatever he produced would taste delicious.

"You're all so easy to look after." A slight frown appeared on Lodren's brow. "You're not just being kind are you? I mean, you would tell me if there was anything wrong with the food?" he asked.

His friends assured him that there was nothing wrong, pandering to his ego, which was slight, and only related to his 'catering'.

Grubb stared at the meal that had been placed before him by Lodren. "Don't much care for foreign food," he said curling his lip, "but I'll give it a go."

Lodren stood over him, beside himself with nervous anticipation of Grubb's verdict as he licked gingerly at the food, "It'll do. I've had better," said Grubb. But they all knew the truth, as he finished eating before they did and asked for more.

***

Following the steep, seemingly endless, winding tunnels, Faylore ran ahead of them, craning her neck, listening intently to something inaudible to the rest. "Wait here," she said, and disappeared into the darkness.

They waited, as instructed, with bated breath. Faylore had been gone for some time and they were becoming a little concerned. "We must go after her. What if she's hurt?" asked Hannock.

"How sweet, Charles. But I can assure you, I'm fine." It was Faylore's voice and it was close, too close for them not to be able to see her, but where was she?

"She's dead. She's a ghost, it's the only explanation," said Grubb.

"I am not dead, Grubb, and I am no ghost." As Faylore spoke she began to appear, not from the darkness but right in front of them. Materialising, as if she had been invisible.

"You're just full of tricks aren't you!?" exclaimed Hannock.

"We Thedarians can blend into any background so as not to be seen."

"Ah, so that's why we never saw you or your people in the forest. Or when you attacked the Dergon in the gulley," said Jared.

"That is correct, Jared, not a secret we share lightly. I'm sure I can count on your discretion." Jared knew that this was not a request, as did the others.

"Grubb, do you know what a zingaard is?" Faylore asked.

"Please tell me you're joking. Not in here. Are ye sure?"

Faylore raised her eyebrows.

"Rock me stones, of all the... I mean... Oh for the love of..." but he never attempted to finish his rant, even he would not curse in front of a lady.

"What's a zingaard?" asked Lodren.

"Big, hairy, smelly, bad tempered and vicious, and when I say big I mean, *really big*. Did I mention smelly?"

"Calm down, Grubb. We can just sneak around it. They have excellent eyesight but their hearing is poor, as long as we tread carefully it won't even know we're there," Faylore said, trying to calm him.

"I know that, Majesty, you and me will be fine," he replied, "but we'll have this lot stomping about as well," said Grubb, pointing over his shoulder with his thumb.

"Can't we just tell it we mean no harm and pass by quietly so we don't disturb it?" asked Lodren most innocently, "I find being polite usually works." His naivety astounded them all.

Grubb was the first to speak, and with an unnerving calmness. "It won't care if you're polite. It will only want to know one thing... how... you... taste."

"Oh," said Lodren, "it's that sort of beast is it?

Jared needed to know more and turned to face Faylore, feeling he would get more sense from her, than from Grubb. "Just how big is this thing?" he asked.

"About twelve feet tall, enormous hands, razor sharp claws, mouthful of huge pointed teeth, covered in hair so matted that it doesn't burn and afraid of nothing. Oh and very, very aggressive."

"Nothing to worry about then! Tell you what, Jared, you go and shoo it away and we'll catch up with you later," said Hannock in a sarcastic tone that others could only aspire to.

"I'm so glad I brought you along, Hannock, my friend, I knew you'd come in useful. While this beastie is busy chewing on you, the rest of us can just run straight past without being noticed," said Jared.

"Your wish is my command, Your Highness," replied Hannock, bowing gracefully.

"When you two have stopped mucking about, we still have to figure out how we're really going to get past the blasted thing," said Grubb, becoming a little agitated by their antics.

"I'll be a decoy," said Faylore adamantly.

"No you bally well won't," retorted Hannock, "not while I'm around."

"How chivalrous of you, Captain Hannock," said Jared smirking.

"I don't remember asking your permission, Captain," announced Faylore, "I can lure the beast away, which will allow you time to pass through its lair safely, then I can meet with you later."

"What if you can't lose the beastie?" Jared asked, "You can't run forever and it'll follow you back to us anyway. No, I say we just attack it. Catch it off guard and destroy it."

"No harm shall befall any if there is another way, Jared. I have informed you of that before," stated Faylore.

"I understand that, but putting your own life in danger, to protect that *thing*, makes no sense."

"Not to you, Jared, but all life is sacred to my kind. If my life is in danger and the beast must be destroyed then so be it, but until that time comes it must be allowed the chance to live," she said sternly.

The plan was set. Faylore, using her chameleonic ability, would sneak past the zingaard. From a vantage point, she would allow herself to be noticed by the beast and lead it away from the others, enabling them to sneak past undetected. Reaching a safe distance, she would once again use her ability to blend with her surroundings, circumvent the zingaard and rejoin them.

Nearing the zingaard's lair, Faylore held up her hand. As agreed, they extinguished their torches. Surprisingly, they were not in complete darkness. There was a faint light source from a strange bioluminescent fungus that grew on the walls of the cavern, something they had not noticed before, having never needed to be without the ever-present torchlight. Their eyes grew accustomed to the new pale blue hue and gradually they saw it… the zingaard.

The description that Faylore had given was precise, but she had not mentioned the bulk of the beast. Its shoulders were about nine feet wide and its arms hung by its sides, almost reaching the ground. 'Huge' was an understatement. Then there was the putrid stench. Rotting carcases of glamoch and other animals, that had strayed into the beast's domain, were strewn about the floor and there were bloodstains everywhere, including the lower part of the walls. This was not a beast one would escape, if trapped alone. Signalling to the others, Faylore made her move. Before their eyes, she faded, until only a shimmering figure, similar to watching the horizon on a hot day, could be seen and she moved away from them in order to pass the zingaard. They had lost sight of Faylore, which eased them a little, for if they could not see her, neither could the beast. All eyes were now focussed on the zingaard as they waited with trepidation. Each of them could hear their own heartbeat as loud as a drum in those tense few moments.

"My, my, aren't you the impressive one?" Faylore's shout startled them all as it broke the silence.

The zingaard had been sitting on a rock, leaning against the cave wall, but now rose to its feet as quickly as its enormous bulk would allow. "Who's there?" it roared.

It spoke. Faylore had omitted to mention that it could speak, but Grubb had told them '*it's the hunters you have to be careful of*', and how right he had been.

"I've seen your kind before zingaard. Not as big as you I admit, but then again, not as stupid either. Getting past you was far too easy. No fun at all actually."

"You enter my home and think you can mock me?" growled the zingaard. "Let's see how you feel when I tear

176

off your limbs and feast on them." It began to climb after Faylore, who vanished as she made her escape.

"Time to go," said Jared, and they all ran forward.

They had wrapped the wheels of the cart in blankets to muffle the noise of the iron-banded wooden wheels as it trundled forward and all seemed to be going perfectly to plan, when one of the wheels jammed in a crevice. The wheel split and the cart dropped to one side, spilling the contents onto the bare rock. This was not much of a problem as Lodren rushed forward and yanked it free. Then disaster, every one of Lodren's beloved pots and pans fell from the cart and clanked and clattered onto the cavern floor, ringing like an alarm bell. They all froze. At first there was no sound, but then they heard the roar of the zingaard getting closer. They had been discovered.

Their foe had realised the ruse and now looked down on its intended victims. "I shall eat well tonight," it growled.

"We have no quarrel with you, beast," shouted Jared. "Let us pass and we shall do you no harm." As he said this, he drew his sword with his right hand, whilst conjuring a fireball with his left.

Hannock had drawn his sword, Lodren nursed his hammer and Grubb had transformed into his four-armed alter-ego. All were ready to do battle with this titanic adversary. Faylore reappeared, realising that their plan had failed, and was now above the zingaard, an arrow already nestled on her bowstring.

The beast roared, but even as it began to charge, Faylore's first arrow found its mark, striking the zingaard in the eye. It yelped in pain but was now enraged. It turned and saw Faylore. Slashing wildly with its claws, Faylore was unable to avoid them as they sliced across her

177

stomach, the blow bringing her crashing to the ground, blood-soaked and struggling for breath. Jared released the firebolt, again, a perfect shot striking the beast in the face and blinding it temporarily. It made for Faylore and was trying to grab her. Grubb clamped his four arms onto the beast's one, twisting with all his might until it snapped, as Hannock chopped demonically at its wrist. Now blind in one eye, its vision impaired in the other and its arm broken and bleeding, it roared and fell to one knee, panting heavily, its remaining arm helping to support it. The armed companions now began to hack at it. The zingaard pulled it clear and fell face first, the friends diving clear to avoid being crushed.

Lodren had been biding his time but now marched forward to face the beast, raising his hammer above his head. Glancing across at the wounded, bleeding Faylore, his heart skipped a beat. "You hurt Faylore," he roared, and with all his might, brought the hammer down, slaughtering the titan by crushing its skull.

The companions rushed to Faylore as she lay on the cold rock, mortally wounded. She smiled at them. "Oh good," she breathed, "you are unhurt."

Neither Jared nor Hannock could speak and Lodren had huge tears in his saucer-like eyes. It seemed there was nothing they could do to save her.

"Get out me blasted way," bellowed Grubb. They were all shocked by the now diminutive Grubb shouting at such a solemn moment. "Do you want her to die or what? Get out of me blasted way," he repeated. Grubb barged his way through and knelt beside Faylore. "I know it stings a bit, Your Majesty, but you'll be alright in a minute."

He placed his hands above the gaping wounds on Faylore's midriff. A faint glow came from Grubb's hands and Faylore arched as if she were being lifted by invisible arms in the small of her back. The light was getting brighter, accompanied by a gentle humming sound and as they all watched in amazement, Faylore's wounds began to close, and heal. The few minutes that passed felt like an age, before Grubb spoke again. "There you go, Your Majesty, you'll be fine in a couple of days, just try to take it easy," he said, and strutted away. "Oh, by the way," he called, "your dress is buggered."

Lodren strolled across to the body of the zingaard. Looking it up and down he scratched his head, *I wonder what it tastes like?* he thought.

***

Tamor sat astride a magnificent white stallion, surveying his army. "They will be aware of our approach," he announced, turning to his lieutenants.

"Providing they have not changed position, Your Majesty," one of them suggested.

"No, I know this scum. If they had half as many brains as they have muscles, we'd be in trouble. They'll hold their position in the belief they can overpower us with strength alone, but with our archers we can cut them down in no time. They use no ranged weapons, that is our strength and their weakness," replied Tamor.

The battle commenced. It was as Tamor had foreseen, at least a quarter of the Dergon horde was felled before any crossed swords with the Borellians on the battlefield. Ramah and Korbah tried in vain to control the actions of their warriors to no avail as, giving in to their primal instincts, they charged headlong into the fray with no concern for their own safety. Tamor watched from a vantage point as his resplendent army slaughtered this marauding, mindless enemy.

Less than an hour after the first bolt had been fired, all but a few dozen of the Dergon remained.

"Retreat," roared Ramah, realising the futility of a battle that was already lost. "Retreat."

His remaining warriors began to flee and Tamor, having had his fill of war many decades before, allowed their escape.

***

Karrak closed his eyes. Time to rest, time to learn. He was becoming more powerful by the day. How could he test his own abilities away from the confines of this accursed room? He had tried whilst in possession of one of his unsuspecting, oblivious hosts, but without success. Try as he might, he could not perform even the simplest of spells. Feeling his power grow, he then attempted the same during his waking hours within his chamber, still without result.

The transcendent voice was ever-present during his nocturnal activities, but he was still no nearer to discovering its source. How he yearned for this discovery, feeling that it may allow him to escape his tedious incarceration. 'Great one', it had called him, *did the owner of the voice revere him in some way?*

He drifted into sleep and the voice began, calling to him, begging to be found. Karrak's sight became clear, but there was no other sound to be heard, he was alone. His surroundings were unfamiliar to him. *Where was he? Who was he?* Looking around, he saw no clue, until he looked down at the ornate oak desk before him. The talisman, he recognised it, it was the one that Barden always wore. He put his hands to his face to feel if it was familiar to him in any way. He felt a leathery, wrinkled face with deep lines that were embedded into the skin, caused by the passage of time… Karrak had possessed Barden. It must have been the talisman that had prevented him from having this opportunity before. Now this was a body that could prove to be most useful. He turned to face the far wall of Barden's office. It was completely obscured by bookshelves, filled with ancient tomes unlike any he had seen during the study periods with his fellow students. Karrak grabbed one at random and began thumbing through it eagerly. The spells seemed to be far more powerful than any he had seen so far, for none of his previous literary encounters had instruction for dealing death. This was a library with which Karrak relished becoming well versed, for his nature had not changed. He longed to tear Barden and his minions apart, to see the blood dripping from their mangled corpses and with the tools before him, this was now a distinct possibility. He pored over tome after tome, drinking in the knowledge with fervour, relishing every word as combined, they detailed various methods for ending life. He lingered as long as he could, making sure to replace each tome to its original position, for if anyone would notice an anomaly, it would be Barden, and it would not pay Karrak to reveal his secret just yet. But when his opportunity arose, he would have his revenge on both Barden's Administration, and the royal house that had so readily taken his freedom.

***

Barden entered Karrak's chamber. He greeted him with his usual pleasant manner, but seemed different in some way, tired, weary and a little preoccupied.

"My dear, Barden, are you alright?" asked Karrak, playing his part of the concerned friend perfectly.

"Fine, I'm fine, Your Highness. Just an old man's fatigue."

"You should be resting. Burning the candle at both ends are we?" asked Karrak, with an inquisitive smile. Karrak's real intention was to see if Barden remembered any of the previous night. He couldn't care less about his health or wellbeing.

"I think it may be a sickness. Many Administration members have been suffering with it of late. A little rest seems to do the trick, but I am always guilty of not following my own advice."

"Which is…?"

"A tincture and plenty of sleep," said Barden, with a weak smile.

"Sounds like good advice to me. You should listen to yourself. Go on, get some rest. Come back when you're well enough, I can wait. After all, I don't want to catch whatever ailment you have."

"You're right of course, I should not risk infecting you. Please forgive me."

"Nothing to forgive, Barden. Now go, before I catch your lurgy and you do have something to apologise for."

Barden bowed and took his leave.

Karrak was almost beside himself with excitement and anticipation. The more Barden slept, the more he could possess him, and the more he possessed him, the more he could study his fascinating, gruesome library.

***

Pacing impatiently, Karrak became lightheaded for the briefest of moments. Steadying himself against the table, he seemed to know instinctively, that Barden had taken his advice and was sleeping, without the protection of his beloved talisman.

Loathe to waste a single moment, he made his way to the bed, lay down and closed his eyes. The connection was immediate, no waiting for his sight to clear. He held up his hand, or Barden's as it was, and clicked his fingers, perfect auditory response. He rose from the bed and headed for the bookshelves. Selecting volumes carefully, he studied the subjects he desired most, how to kill, maim and disfigure. Karrak was ecstatic at being offered so many ways to execute his favourite pleasures. He sat for hours, safe in the knowledge that his own body would not be disturbed, as his carers had already tended to his needs for the day. More and more he read until at last, the information he needed most was discovered, runes of protection, the keys to his gaol cell. If Karrak knew how they were applied, their removal would be simple. Each book now replaced in its original position, Karrak lay down, his liberty was at hand.

Seconds later, he opened his eyes, looking directly at the runes carved on the pillars, "You'll have to go," he said quietly.

Using a knife from a tray that had been left earlier, he began to alter them, only slightly, but enough to make them ineffective. He was a little annoyed with himself. *How could he have been so naïve?* It would have been obvious to any mere novice that they were there for a reason, as were the symbols on the floor. Nothing within this cell would be purely decorative.

Now to test his theory. He replaced the knife, then deliberately swept the water pitcher from the table. It smashed noisily on the flagstone floor. He knew the guards would ignore the noise, as he had had many tantrums during the early days of his imprisonment. Various broken pots, pitchers and sundry furniture items had been the result, and now his captors were impervious to such commotion. Karrak rapped gently on the door. "Excuse me," he called, "I've had a slight mishap, be a good fellow and fetch me some fresh water, would you?"

The door opened slowly. A young wizard stood there, surveying the scene. "Be with you in a few minutes, Your Highness," he said. They were his gaolers but had been instructed to be courteous. He was, after all, a prince.

Almost immediately, fresh water was brought to Karrak. "Close the door would you, there's a bit of a draught," he instructed.

The wizard did as he was asked and approached to place the pitcher on the table.

"Oh another thing," began Karrak, "stand on one leg."

This was the first test. No sooner had the words left Karrak's lips than the wizard raised one foot from the ground.

"Now hop up and down," and the wizard again, did as commanded.

"What's your name... wizard?" asked Karrak.

"Edward, Your Highness," replied the guard.

"No, try again. Your name's Mabel. So, what's your name?"

"Mabel, Your Highness."

It worked, Karrak was now able to control a conscious mind.

"Right, Mabel, this is what I need you to do. Go outside, close the door, turn to your little friend and slap him in the face, is that clear?"

The wizard nodded, a vacant expression on his face. "Yes, Your Highness," he replied.

"Well, off you go then, Mabel."

The wizard turned and walked through the door, closing it behind him. Karrak hurried forward and placed his ear against it, waiting for the ruckus that would hopefully ensue, but heard nothing. He hesitated for a moment, then rapped his knuckles against the door. The wizard outside obligingly opened it.

"Something else, Your Highness?" he asked.

Karrak looked at him and then at his colleague, who was evidently completely oblivious of Karrak's intentions. "I didn't get your name?"

"Edward, Your Highness."

"On second thoughts, Edward, I'm fine," he said, closing the door in the wizard's face.

Damn it. What use is it if I have to be able to see the puppet to make it perform? he thought.

It was obvious that this subject required further investigation for it to prove useful.

***

Ramah watched what remained of his fellow Dergon. Less than fifty had survived the encounter with Tamor's elite, and of those at least half were nursing severe wounds, incurred during battle.

"You'd have to tell them if they were on fire," he ranted, "over four hundred lost in one battle, why did I believe I could turn these fools into an army?"

Korbah sat in silence, offering no reply. More intelligent than most of his race, he was deep in thought, wondering how he had managed to escape unscathed from a battlefield that was more like an abattoir, where the Dergon were the cattle. The first rain of arrows and bolts had missed him completely and, admittedly, he had shielded himself with an ally as the second fell, but he had fought the soldiers bravely before being given the order to retreat. Only when he had cleared the field did he realise just how many of his fellow warriors had fallen, and how swift and absolute their defeat had been.

"I need others like myself to control them," Ramah continued, "others who show leadership and courage, on the battlefield and off."

"I tried my best, Ramah, but they wouldn't listen to me, they just charged forward. If you're going to kill me like you did Klag, can you do it now, while I'm facing you."

"Making an example doesn't seem to work, Korbah, your death would serve no purpose. I saw your attempt to bring them back in line. The bloodlust took hold of them again, you could not have stopped them."

"So what do we do now? What if they come after us?"

"They have no intention of following us, we wouldn't be here if they had. There's hope for you yet, Korbah, think ahead, that's what you need to do as a leader. We'll head into the hills once the wounded have patched themselves up, lay low for a while and figure out our next step. I'll think of something." Leaning across, Ramah slapped Korbah reassuringly on the shoulder. "We're not dead yet, Korbah."

***

The companions, having made their way through the lower caverns, were reliably informed by Grubb that they would reach the exit by that afternoon. They had all banded together to dissuade Lodren from sampling roast zingaard, despite his protestations that they might enjoy it. However, the overriding subject of the smell was the deciding factor. Unhindered, they continued, despite a brief encounter with wolves who, on seeing their intended prey, turned and ran into the darkness, growling.

Faylore had asked Grubb to translate what the wolves had said, but Grubb was still reluctant to use foul language in front of a lady.

"Grubb," began Faylore, "I owe you my life. Is there anything you desire that I could offer you in payment of such a debt?"

"There might be. I'll tell ye what, next time it looks like I'm going to die, I'll let ye save me, how's that?" he said.

Jared attempted to lighten their mood. "Lady and Gentlemen," he announced, "you are cordially invited to a banquet in your honour for the heroic deeds you have performed in the aid of House Dunbar, to be set for…" Jared held his hands in the air and shrugged. Ordinarily a date would have been set for such an invitation, but not knowing who could attend or when, ruined Jared's presentation somewhat.

"Good start to that speech, Your Highness," announced Hannock, "just kind of lost the flow at the end though, don't you think?"

After much discussion, to the point of pleading at one stage, Faylore, Lodren and even Grubb agreed to accompany Jared and Hannock back to Borell. Faylore explained that she may have to leave them, just for a day or two, to visit her kin, but that it was of no urgency at the moment. Jared empathised, being of royal birth himself. All three insisted however, that whilst in Borell, even as guests of the royal family, they would not sleep indoors.

"You shall have a temporary camp in the castle grounds. Faylore, you may choose whichever tree you wish to sleep in. Lodren, the campfire will be refuelled at regular intervals and you may ask for any ingredients you require for your 'catering' and, Grubb… well you can just do, whatever it is you like doing." Grubb, after all, was still a bit of a mystery to Jared.

***

Karrak, occupying Barden's body, was once again, taking advantage of his personal, extensive library. The old wizard's health had now become a major concern for the Administration. Suffering from permanent fatigue and unsteady on his feet, many feared that his ailment was perhaps a disease of the mind rather than a sickness of the body, as many tinctures and potions had been prescribed by the healers in Reiggan, without success. Devoid of any further inspiration it was deemed that they should simply allow him to rest and hope that this would result in his recuperation. If not, at least he would be comfortable in his last days, as nature took its course and his life slipped away. For Karrak, their decision proved ideal and he relished the fact that he would not be disturbed during his clandestine escapades. The extended nocturnal time periods allowed him to lay out many volumes at one time, in order to compare and cross-reference one to another. A far more effective and thorough process. He had already discovered all he needed to know on the subject of mind control and how to make the effects last longer, even if one lost sight of one's subject.

He flicked through page after page finding nothing of interest for some time before he eventually came across something unrelated, but most intriguing. "Well, well, well, Barden, aren't we the dark horse?" he mumbled, "the '*Elixian Soul*.' Now that's something that could be of great benefit to an ambitious man such as I." He paced back and forth, engrossed by the text before him. Looking up from the book, he spoke again, his voice developing a sinister air. "I think a slight change of plan is in order, old man. Time to allow you some proper rest, just for a few days, and then you and I shall have a little chat."

The days passed quickly, but not quickly enough for Karrak, who was reduced to providing his own amusement. Firstly, a tasteless puppet show, the puppet being the unfortunate attendant that brought his meals, regardless of who it may be. They would be instructed to perform a handstand, cartwheel or simple pirouette, allowing Karrak to hone his skills in mind control. Secondly, experiments in the art of torture. Causing a subject to obey a simple command was easy enough, but could he actually harm them without making physical contact, as it had been described in one of Barden's many tomes?

He had taken the first opportunity to test this ability. An attendant had placed a tray on the table when Karrak seized his moment. Standing behind the wizard, Karrak held out his hand, his palm facing forward toward his victim, and glared at him. His test subject fell to his knees instantaneously, holding his head in his hands as if a spike was being driven through it, his face contorted but making no sound. Karrak smiled, success yet again.

Timescale was also of importance to Karrak. How long would it take for the effects of mind control to wear off once a victim was no longer in his presence? Would they wear off immediately or not at all? He turned to the wizard, still writhing on the ground, apparently in agony. "Do stop fussing, you're fine now. Your pain has ended," said Karrak.

The wizard instantly rose to his feet, seemingly having suffered no long term effects from Karrak's sadistic trial. Karrak studied the attendant briefly. He needed to test the longevity of his control over his puppet. "Listen to me carefully, boy," he began. "Once you depart this chamber you will obey the following instructions implicitly; do you understand?"

The young wizard nodded his head.

"Good," continued Karrak, "in one hour from now you will return to me. Bring me… a dagger, with a ribbon tied around the hilt. Tell no one. Now leave."

Without comment, the young wizard left the chamber. An hour later he returned and presented the dagger to Karrak, ribbon attached. Karrak dismissed him and poured some wine into a goblet.

"Now all there is to do is wait. You will be here soon, Barden. I want the Elixian Soul and you're going to deliver it to me," he hissed.

***

"I'm fine, stop fussing. There's nothing wrong with me," barked Barden.

"But, Master Barden, you have been ill. You should take things slowly until you regain your strength," advised the young wizard.

"How many more times? I'm fine, now get out before I turn you into a frog or something," and clamping his hand on the shoulder of the young wizard, Barden promptly steered him to the door.

He dressed and glanced around the room. "Looks like they've all had a good rummage through my books while I've been asleep," he chuntered, "that won't happen again. Now where's the Order of Corrodin?" But, search as he might, he could not find it and merely believed that it had been put away for safe keeping. *I'll find it later,* he thought.

He busied himself that morning by catching up on recent events, which didn't take long as hardly anything ever happened in Reiggan Fortress that any number of wizards could not contend with. Enquiry after enquiry however, still left him no wiser as to the whereabouts of his sacred talisman. He could not bring himself to believe it to be stolen and deduced that, in his delirium, he had inadvertently secreted it himself.

"Do you have any idea what happened to my talisman, Jacob?"

"I am afraid I have no idea, Barden," replied his friend.

"How's our young prince doing?" asked Barden.

"He is quite well behaved and courteous. He asked after you every day during your illness. I think his rehabilitation is going splendidly, only due to your supervision of course."

Barden raised his eyebrows, he hated backscratchers. "Well in that case, I think it only polite to pay our guest a visit," he said.

"Are you sure that's wise, Master Barden. I mean without the Order of Corrodin? We still don't know Karrak's true frame of mind or intentions."

"Oh I'm sure he'll be fine… under my supervision of course," he replied, sarcastically.

***

Barden entered Karrak's chamber. "Good afternoon, Your Highness, so good to see you again."

"Good afternoon, Master Barden. I see your health has much improved."

Barden turned and closed the door behind him. "It has, I'm pleased to say. My legs are a little shaky, but there's no need for anyone but us to know that," he said with a brief smile.

"Come, Master Barden, be seated. We can forget protocol as there's just the two of us, no need to stand on ceremony," said Karrak, sitting on his bed.

"You are most kind, Your Highness, thank you, I think I'll accept your gracious offer," replied Barden, taking a seat at Karrak's table.

"I'm glad you dropped by," Karrak said with a smile, "there's something I need to ask you about."

"Please feel free, Your Highness. Ask away."

"Just a minor thing really... the Elixian Soul. What is it and what does it do?" A look of horror came upon Barden's face. He attempted to rise from the chair but Karrak was too quick for him and thrust out his arm, his fist half clenched. Barden felt himself pushed by an invisible force back into the chair.

"We'll have none of that, Barden. I have questions and I want answers. You have those answers, and you're going to give them to me, one way or another." Karrak had not yet possessed Barden's mind, he was simply controlling his body. "I don't want to hurt you, old man. Well that's a lie really, I want to tear your arms out of the sockets and your head off that scrawny neck of yours, but if you co-operate, I might just offer a little leniency, and kill you quickly."

"You can kill me if you wish, but if you do, you'll never get the Soul."

"Why ever not? Surely you don't believe an old duffer like you can stop me. I mean, I've been possessing your body for weeks, you couldn't even stop that. Oh, and you really should learn to bathe more often," said Karrak, wrinkling his nose as if there was suddenly a bad smell under it. "But I digress, tell me about the Soul."

He blinked slowly and glared at Barden. "What is *the Elixian Soul*?"

Barden spoke in a monotone voice. "It is an enhancement for black magic," he replied.

"What do you mean by BLACK magic?" asked Karrak.

"Magic that is used solely for destruction or death," replied Barden.

"How much does it enhance the effectiveness of spells?"

"It is said to increase one's natural power ten-fold."

Karrak leapt from the bed. "Where is this Soul, old man?" he barked.

"Entombed, deep in the bowels of Reiggan Fortress," replied Barden mindlessly.

"Can you get it, by yourself, I mean?" asked Karrak.

"I am unable to obtain it alone. The spell to release it from its solitude can only be performed with the combined power of five."

So you need four other wizards to help you, Karrak thought. "You're the chief of the Administration, they have to follow your orders, don't they? Get me the Soul, Barden. Don't draw any attention to yourself, or to me... but get me the Soul."

"Yes, Your Highness," replied Barden.

Karrak stood back and lowered his arm and Barden's head fell forward to his chest. A second later he looked up, blinking and slightly confused. "Please forgive me, Your Highness. Did I doze off?"

"Don't worry, Barden. Our little secret," Karrak smiled.

"I must leave you now, Your Highness. I have just remembered a very important matter that I must attend to."

"Don't let me keep you, Barden, you go about your business... don't be a stranger, see you very soon." It had worked perfectly. Barden would acquire the Elixian Soul.

Karrak's vengeance was at hand, and wreaking havoc as he sought it, would make it all the sweeter. He placed his hand inside his tunic, clasped his hand around the gold talisman and drew it out. Holding it in the palm of his hand he looked down at it.

"So you're The Order of Corrodin, a pleasure to make your acquaintance."

CHAPTER 10

Barden closed the door to Karrak's chamber as he left but had taken no more than a dozen steps before he lost his footing and fell heavily to the floor. The two wizards guarding Karrak ran over to offer aid.

"I'm fine thank you. I just went a little lightheaded that's all. A breath of fresh air and a drink of water and I'll be fine," protested Barden.

More wizards appeared and escorted him to the courtyard, where he was given water, and a chair brought to allow him to sit for a while. He kept insisting that he was fine and eventually persuaded the gathering to disperse, allowing him some privacy.

The last of the crowd had disappeared from view. Barden stood and walked across the courtyard so that he now stood between two of the marble statues. He held his arms out to the sides, placing a hand against each, and closed his eyes. A gentle breeze blew the fallen leaves around his feet as the statues started to tremble gently. The statues began to shake more violently now as the breeze became stronger, causing Barden's robes to flutter. Exactly what he was trying to do was unclear, but whatever it was, it had been unsuccessful. After a minute or so, he dropped his arms back down to his sides, glaring at one statue, then the other. He paused for a moment as if deep in thought then, turning swiftly, stormed across the courtyard.

***

Karrak had had no contact with Barden. *Could he glean anything regarding the old wizard's progress should he possess his body? Surely the Head of the Administration would leave no obvious clue of his intentions toward the Soul?*

He decided on the traditional approach of simply sending a messenger, seeking an audience with Barden who promptly arrived within minutes. "You sent for me, Your Highness?"

Karrak raised his hand, immediately all expression left Barden's face. "What's going on, Barden? Why don't I have the Soul? Why am I still sitting in this cell?"

"The Soul can only be retrieved by the Five, Your Highness, and as yet, we are only four."

"Make sense, Barden. Surely you can find another wizard. There are more than five of you here."

"No, Your Highness, there is only one Fifth. He is the only one who has the remainder of the release spell."

"Why didn't you tell me that before?"

"I apologise, Your Highness. He will return presently, then I shall retrieve the Elixian Soul for you."

Karrak was bored and angry. He instructed Barden to sit so that he could release his mind and torment him, just to pass the time.

"So, can you remember what you've been doing for the last couple of days you horrible little wizard?" he asked.

A look of confusion swept across Barden's face. "I have no memory. Karrak, what have you done?"

"What… no, 'Your Highness'?"

"Why have you done this? What do you want?"

"The Elixian Soul, don't you remember?"

"Well let me get it for you. I was going to give it to you anyway, at the earliest opportunity."

"Of course you were, Barden. The Soul that can only be used to enhance BLACK magic, and *you* were going to give it to *me*?"

"Why wouldn't I? After all, I made you what you are."

A frown appeared on Karrak's face. "What do you mean… you made me?"

"Didn't your father ever mention your mother's sickness? That she was a white witch? How she made a miraculous recovery after the visit by a stranger? How that stranger returned years later and had a private meeting with her? How she started practising black magic and sacrificed five young girls? I was the stranger. Your mother was nearly dead when I first saw her, I just finished the job and then raised her from that death. The second time I saw her was simply to make the corruption of her soul absolute. Necromancy is a fine art, but every soul resurrected is also tainted. You could only be born from a tainted soul. Your coming has been prophesied for over a thousand years, Karrak, but it had to begin with the unnatural death of your mother… and I was the one who caused it. I am here to serve you, willingly." The look in Barden's eyes was enough to convince Karrak that he was telling the truth.

"So you created me? You created the monster that is Karrak Dunbar? Do you expect my thanks?" asked Karrak.

"I wish only to serve you, Your Highness. Command me and I shall do your bidding."

"My dear Barden, you're doing that anyway. Do you think that I would ever trust a slimy underhanded little weasel like you, without control? A wizard who murders ailing women in their sickbeds," he screamed.

Barden was terrified, and Karrak could see his terror.

"You will follow my commands, weasel, and do my bidding, right up until I tear your puny little body apart with my bare hands," he said, raising his hand above Barden's head.

Barden, once again, looked calm. He would carry out all of the tasks Karrak had set him whilst in his oblivious trance... then he would die by Karrak's hand, slowly, and painfully.

***

In due course, Barden arranged a meeting with his four colleagues and they had joined him in the circular courtyard, eager for an explanation. Barden faced them, ready to announce his reasons. "My friends, it has come to my ears that all is not as it seems here in Reiggan Fortress. Certain members of our institution are plotting, as we speak, to steal the Elixian Soul," he announced. There were murmurings between his fellow wizards.

Barden continued. "I cannot name names, for I have no real evidence, but I do have my suspicions. A few that are loyal to myself and the Administration have come forward and voiced their concerns. I therefore believe that it would be prudent to remove the Soul from Reiggan and I, solely, shall be responsible for its relocation. We shall remove it from its hiding place together, as was always the agreement, but you four must then leave me to bear the burden alone, thus setting you free from the dangers of persecution for information regarding its whereabouts."

"But, Barden," began one of the wizards, "it was always deemed that no solitary wizard should have possession of the Elixian Soul, for fear that the temptation to use it would be too potent to resist."

"Do you question my authority, Master Fellox?" Barden asked the wizard calmly. "I have served Reiggan Fortress and protected its secrets since before you were born. Surely you cannot believe that I, Barden Oldman, Head of the Administration would be so easily tempted?"

The wizard shuffled his feet uneasily. Lowering his head, he looked down at the ground.

"Not tempted, Master Barden, but the carriage of the Soul by oneself could be most perilous and I am only concerned for your safety," he replied.

"That is most considerate of you, Fellox, but I think I am a powerful enough wizard to protect myself should the need arise."

"But you could be outnumbered, overwhelmed before you have a chance to act in your own defence," continued Fellox.

"That is why it must be done now. Only we Five will know of its removal. I trust you all implicitly, and that trust, ensures my safety."

His four colleagues huddled together in muttered conversation. Barden was not insulted by his exclusion from the brief debate and stood, calmly waiting for their decision.

"Very well, Master Barden, if you feel that it is for the best, we shall support your decision," announced Fellox.

Barden approached the two statues he had originally faced alone. Two wizards stood either side of him and they all raised their hands to face the statues. As they concentrated, the two figures turned ninety degrees and glided away from one another, revealing a wide stone staircase. The Five stepped forward and began their descent into the darkness. The gloom lasted just a few seconds, for as they walked torches on the wall ignited spontaneously. Deeper and deeper they went until, reaching the foot of the staircase, they faced a huge manmade cave, hewed from the solid rock of the mountain. To the side of the cave stood a double door, seemingly made from solid gold and, as with everything else in their world, embossed with strange, mystical runes. The wizards stood before the doors and repeated their earlier process, causing the doors to swing open outwardly. Barden proceeded through them unaccompanied.

He stood in a room similar in design to the courtyard, but without the statues. In its centre stood a pedestal and placed upon it, a small golden chest. Barden stepped forward and slowly opened it. There was a sudden blaze of light from within that caused Barden to shield his eyes with his hand.

Reaching inside, Barden removed the light's source and held it aloft, in awe of its splendour. A blood red ruby as large as a man's fist, that pulsated as if it contained a heart, lay in the palm of his hand. Crimson droplets fell from it as if it were haemorrhaging, dissipating as they fell, never reaching the ground. By order of Karrak, Barden had retrieved the Elixian Soul.

Gazing upon its beauty, none would have believed that this treasure could hold a power so sinister and evil, but throughout the ages, it had destroyed entire civilizations.

Carefully, Barden returned the Soul to its gilded cage, and gently closed the lid.

He must raise no suspicion if he was to deliver it successfully to, who he believed to be, its rightful owner. Bearing the chest, Barden returned to his unsuspecting colleagues. "You must escort me to my chambers," he ordered.

Dismissing his entourage, Barden entered his chambers alone. Placing the chest on his desk he stared at it at length. It would be unwise to attempt its presentation to Karrak immediately, he must bide his time. He could not risk detection when his task was so close to completion.

***

The companions grew closer to one another with each passing day. Jared and Hannock had become accustomed to Lodren's ever pleasant, happy attitude to life, Grubb's equally grumpy one and Faylore's sometimes aloof but also inquisitive nature and the three in turn had embraced

Jared's regal steadfastness and Hannock's childish, sarcastic, but inoffensive, sense of humour.

Faylore had parted from them for two days, believing them to be safe, but had rejoined them along with a few other Thedarians who, it was quite obvious, quickly became bored with their company and departed again.

Lodren approached Jared. "Mr Jared," he said inquisitively, "where do you do your cooking in your castle? Well not you, obviously, but the people who cook for you."

"Why is it obvious that someone cooks for me, dear Lodren?" asked Jared, "Maybe I cook for myself."

"Well, no offence, Mr Jared, but your cooking's horrible!"

"How do you know? You've never tasted my cooking."

"Mr Captain told me. He said you couldn't even boil an egg without burning the water."

"Oh did he now!" exclaimed Jared looking across at Hannock who immediately threw up his hands in mock defence.

"You wouldn't expect me to lie would you, Your Highness? Not a good example of Borellians is it, lying to our new friends?"

"On a more serious note," said Jared turning to address the group, "when we arrive in Borell you must show Hannock the proper respect due to his position. He is the captain of the guard, and as such, is in command of our entire army. Please do not mock him in the presence of anyone other than present company."

"But I can call him a prat until then, eh?" Grubb's timing was, as always, impeccable.

"By all means, help yourself, don't mind me!" exclaimed Hannock feigning indignation.

"Mr Jared, *where is the cooking done*?" asked Lodren again.

"Sorry, Lodren, how rude of me. In the kitchen," replied Jared.

"What's a kitchen?"

Jared explained how the castle had an entire room with ovens and burners, used solely for the preparation of food. Lodren was beside himself with glee. "Can I have a go in it? Can I have a go in your kitchen, Mr Jared? I won't make a mess, promise."

"Lodren, my dear friend, you can do whatever you want. Within reason of course."

Lodren, without a word ran off toward the cart. He wanted his pots and pans in perfect order when they arrived in Borell so had decided to give them another wash, just in case.

***

Later that day they approached Ferendon Village. Their jovial banter ceased as they drew nearer, for the sight they beheld was horrific. Every building had been destroyed and there were still bloodstains on the ground. The bodies and severed heads that had caused them had been removed by one of the king's patrols, but this of course was unknown to the companions. The soil in the centre of the village stood proud of the surrounding area, a banner of remembrance mounted at the northern end of the strange excavation. It was a mass grave. The soldiers who buried them had not known the names of the villagers and the banner had been placed as a mark of respect. This was the only trace of civilization having ever existed in Ferendon.

To the eastern side of where the village had stood, there was a pile of ash and bones. Faylore, now standing at its edge, flicked a skull with her foot. "Dergon," she announced.

This was the site of the second Dergon attack. This was the village where, in its defence, the people had fought bravely and claimed the lives of more than fifty of their foe. The two guards would ever be unsung heroes, for as their health had increased they had set an arena similar to the one in which they had trained in Borell. Their practise sessions had piqued the interest of many villagers who came to the guardsmen with offers of free ale, wine and food in exchange for tuition in combat techniques. To the villagers it was just a game, something different, but they were taught in the same way as any raw recruit and although none had survived the Dergon, it had prolonged their lives, if only by a matter of minutes, allowing them to despatch so many of their enemies.

"Dergon. You mean those things that attacked us in the gulley?" asked Hannock.

"The same," replied Faylore.

"Why would they attack a village?" asked Jared.

"I have no idea. This makes no sense," replied Faylore.

"Well somebody knows. They didn't bury themselves, this is the work of one of our patrols, the flag signifies that. We'll find out when we get home, then we will make them pay for this," it seemed that Hannock sought a bloody revenge.

***

Barden was single-minded as he headed through the passageways of Reiggan Fortress. He must deliver the Elixian Soul to his master, nothing else mattered. Many wizards attempted to engage him in conversation, but he would permit no delay, indicating that he was far too busy to speak with them. Greetings by others were received with a simple nod and a false smile. Eventually, he approached Karrak's chambers.

"Master Barden."

The voice came from behind him. Barden knew the voice. The two wizards guarding the door sidestepped, covering the entrance. Barden was furious, but turned around calmly. "Can I help you in some way?"

He was approached by Dane Fellox, who was flanked by at least ten other Administration members. "We do not believe it to be in your best interest to face Prince Karrak whilst in possession of the Elixian Soul, especially as you no longer wear The Order of Corrodin," said Fellox.

"Do you think that I would be so naïve as to carry the Soul with me, whatever my destination?" asked Barden.

"Ordinarily, no, Master Barden. But you have been quite ill recently and may be carrying it, inadvertently."

"So now I'm a forgetful old fool?" Barden remained outwardly serene but was filled with rage at the intervention of, what he believed to be, irritating, second-rate conjurers.

"My comments were not meant as an insult, Master Barden," began Fellox, "but we at the Administration must be mindful of our charges, living, or inanimate."

"We... what do you mean, we?" Barden shouted, "How dare you? I am the Head of the Administration; I *am* the Administration. You worms wouldn't have the power to light a candle if not for my teachings you pathetic upstart."

"Maybe we should continue our discussion elsewhere, Master Barden. Your chambers perhaps?"

Fellox knew the danger was imminent, but could think of no recourse. Barden was old, that could not be denied, but he was also the most powerful wizard in Reiggan, if not the world.

"Why don't you continue your wittering... in your grave." Barden's eyes blackened and, without warning, he cast a lightning spell that hit Fellox full in the chest, completely disintegrating him.

The doors to Karrak's chambers flew open. Karrak glared at the first wizard he saw, which happened to be poor Edward, the puppet with which had already had so much fun.

"Defend me," he bellowed, and Edward immediately began casting fire spells at the remainder of Fellox's party.

Barden drew the Elixian Soul from his robes. Turning to face Karrak he stretched out his arm but, just before Karrak could grab it, an ice spell hit his shoulder and the

Soul flew through the air, and landed, skimming across the stone floor until it hit the wall. The wizard that cast the spell watched its trajectory and now cast another identical spell encasing the Soul in a block of ice that fused it where it lay. Fire, lightning and ice spells filled the air, Edward was killed within seconds by a fire spell that hit him full in the face. Karrak saw the Elixian Soul glowing in its icy tomb, he could hear it calling to him, *find me, find me*, repeating over and over. He cast a fire spell in an attempt to release it, but realising his intent, two wizards cast ice spells, making it even more inaccessible.

Karrak was under direct attack, feeling that at any moment he would be destroyed, for he and Barden were hopelessly outnumbered. One of the senior wizards, now facing Karrak, was nursing a fireball in both hands. Karrak thrust his hands forward creating an ice wall that only just prevented his incineration. His mind raced, what to do next? Before he could decide a hand grasped his shoulder. He suddenly felt an incredible force, that seemed as if it were inside him, tear him backwards, as the scene before him shimmered, and then was gone.

He was dizzy and fell to his knees, his eyes closed. He rubbed his face trying to regain his composure. Opening his eyes, he found that he was surrounded by trees, he was in a forest. Struggling to his feet he looked about him, he was not alone, Barden lay on the ground motionless and silent, his robes singed and torn as a result of their close call with death at the hands of the Administration. Karrak never gave him a second glance, he didn't care. "Well, what do you know? The old coot saved me! He was telling the truth, he does want to serve me. Well, why not… for now anyway."

He checked himself for wounds, there were none. Karrak began to laugh. True, he hadn't obtained the Soul, but at least *he was free.*

CHAPTER 11

King Tamor, having been informed of Jared's return, hurried to the castle gates to greet him personally. Climbing down from his horse wearily, Jared smiled at his father and they embraced one another as they always did.

"Heard you had a bit of a run in with those blasted Dergon, Jared," said Tamor.

Jared lowered his head, "Yes… and lost most of our escort. We would have fallen too if not for the Thedarians."

"Who are the Thedarians?" asked Tamor.

Jared turned to face Faylore. "Please forgive me, Queen Faylore, this is my father, King Tamor Dunbar," then turning to his father, "King Tamor, Queen Faylore of Thedar."

"Very pleased to meet you, Your Majesty," said Tamor taking Faylore's hand in an attempt to kiss it.

Faylore snatched her hand away. "What are you doing? Jared, what's he doing?" she asked.

"The king was merely going to kiss the back of your hand as a mark of respect."

"Why?"

"It's just a polite greeting," said Jared, now feeling a little awkward.

"You never had a kiss on *your* hand," said Faylore.

"Well no, you see…"

Jared gave up on his attempted explanation, once Faylore reached this stage of awkwardness the questions would keep coming. Waving his hands dismissively he continued with his introductions. "Lodren, Grubb, meet…"

They approached the castle. Jared imparted the tale of their journey to Tamor, including their rescue by Faylore in the gulley and the heroic deeds of both Lodren and Grubb within the caverns of the Muurkain Mountains.

As they entered the throne room, Tamor felt that he and Faylore had started off on the wrong foot and decided to try again. "It seems as if I owe you my son's life," he said with a light-hearted smile.

"No thank you," she said adamantly, "you can keep it, I don't want it."

Tamor was now completely confused. *Did this strange queen actually think that he was offering her Jared's life?*

Jared had heard the brief exchange between them and thought it best to intervene. Taking Tamor to one side, he offered him some gentle advice. "Say what you mean Father. They don't use pleasantries as we do, it may seem a little rude to you, but to her it's fine. Just speak to her plainly."

"I *am* speaking plainly, she's just weird," blurted Tamor.

"And how do you think *we* appear to her?"

"Normal?" asked Tamor.

"We're not normal to her, she thinks we're the weird ones, Father!"

"Really? Fancy that," said Tamor.

Grubb was his usual self. Not one for conversation, he milled about the room, picking up anything he found vaguely interesting, tutting, shaking his head and then putting it back down again. Lodren, on the other hand, seemed fascinated as he stood open-mouthed at the splendour of the castle. He followed Jared at a polite distance, looking like an excited child, desperate for answers to a myriad of questions. Jared sensed that the Nibby could wait no longer and turned to face him. "Was there something you wanted, Lodren?"

"Well, I was just wondering, Mr Jared, could I see your cooking room, please, if you're not too busy?"

"It's called a kitchen, and yes, of course you can. I'll have someone show you the way."

The head cook was summoned and after a brief introduction, Lodren headed off with him, the two talking as if they had known each other for years due to their mutual affinity with the preparation of food. Their discussion covered so many culinary intricacies that it was hours before the others saw him again, "Lost track of the time," he said.

Hannock asked that he be excused. There was nothing that he could add to the conversation, that would not be covered by one of the others. His request was denied, by the king himself. "I know you are not my son, Charles…" began Tamor. Jared smiled as he remembered the simbor incident. "… But you have been with Jared his entire life, and I do think of you as one."

Hannock bowed respectfully. "You are most kind, Your Majesty." He was waiting for Faylore to ask if he had a bad back again, but fortunately, she remained silent.

They were all seated and the conversation became more intense as the subject of the Dergon was raised.

"Four villages completely erased from existence," Tamor informed them.

"Four!?" exclaimed Jared.

"Yes, four, all the same, every head severed and put on a spike," said Tamor.

"What did they want?" asked Hannock.

"We have no idea. They were acting alone apparently, following one of their own. Big blighter, intelligent too. We burned the bodies of all we killed, at the village and the battleground but we never found him, he must have been one of those that escaped."

"How did he manage to escape, Father, how did *any* of them manage to escape?"

"I let them go. I won't kill indiscriminately as they do. They were beaten, hardly a handful of them left. There'd been enough slaughter already, so when they ran, we never gave chase."

"Father, how did you know that we had been attacked by the Dergon?"

"An old friend of yours told me."

"Who?" asked Jared.

"Emnor," replied Tamor.

"Emnor has been here? But I thought he was going to help take care of Karrak."

"Emnor wants nothing to do with Karrak, never has. Reckons he's a bad seed."

"Can't disagree with him there." Hannock had a look on his face that seemed to say, *'did I say that out loud?'* Hannock had proven his loyalty to the royal family countless times and, understanding that there was no love lost between Karrak and Hannock, Tamor ignored the comment.

"So what will be Karrak's fate, without Emnor to guide him?" asked Jared.

"The Head of the Administration, Barden Oldman has taken that responsibility," replied Tamor.

"We met him in Reiggan," Jared informed him.

"What's he like?" asked Tamor.

"Old, wrinkled, grey beard, grey robes, a typical wizard really," replied Jared.

"Emnor seems to rate him. Says he's possibly the most powerful wizard on the planet," said Tamor.

"He'll need to be. We all know how… difficult, my brother can be."

The day wore on and the trail weary companions were showing some slight indications of their fatigue. Tamor called for attendants to show their guests to a campsite that had been prepared for them in the castle grounds. Lodren bowed graciously before the king, Grubb simply nodded and Faylore, being royalty herself, thanked him for his hospitality before departing.

Tamor shuffled forward on his seat and leaned toward Jared. "Beautiful woman that Faylore, is she married?"

"She's too tall for you, Father," replied Jared. "Goodnight."

***

The weeks passed and Jared and Hannock had resumed their normal palace duties. Lodren had made himself quite at home, enjoying the hustle and bustle of the busy castle kitchen, whilst becoming firm friends with Raymond, the head cook. Grubb was the most unlikely visitor of all, not seeming in any rush to depart Borell. Exactly what he did most days was a mystery, so he was just left to his own devices. Faylore came and went freely. Her people would appear, usually on a weekly basis, and she would leave with them to attend to matters that, obviously, were only of concern to the Thedarians.

All was peaceful, too peaceful for Hannock after their mission to deliver Karrak and, as time went, by he became increasingly bored. For this reason he had approached Jared. "I thought it might be an idea to accompany one of the patrols soon, Jared," he said.

Jared looked at him knowingly. "As bored as I am, Hannock?" he asked.

"Oh no, not at all. Just like to stretch my legs a bit, make sure everything's alright in the villages. Protect the borders, that kind of thing."

"You're a terrible liar, Hannock, just admit it, you're bored."

"Alright, I'm bored. There, I've said it, so what's your answer?"

"Next patrol leaves in two days, we'll be leading it," said Jared.

"Marvellous," said Hannock, rubbing his hands together.

***

The morning of the patrol's departure had arrived. Jared and Hannock neared the stables to collect their horses and were not surprised to see Lodren, complete with laden cart and Grubb, waiting for them.

"Good morning, Mr Jared, Mr Captain. Are we off on another adventure then?" asked Lodren.

"Well, we're off on patrol," said Hannock, "but there's no need for you to go, unless you want to of course?"

"No need, Mr Captain! And who's going to make sure you're fed properly if I stay here?" exclaimed Lodren.

Hannock now turned to Grubb. "And your reason?" he asked.

"Keep an eye on ye. Don't want ye getting into any trouble. I'd probably get the blame for not being there to help," mumbled Grubb.

"Your concern is most reassuring my dear Vikkery," said Hannock with a slight smile, and a hint of irony.

Grubb gave him a blank look, ignoring the irony and glanced around him before offering a reply. "Bog off."

Faylore was not present. She had joined her kin a few days prior and it was agreed that if she wished to join them, she would easily catch up later. They proceeded through the castle gates, to begin their patrol.

***

Faylore, as anticipated, had found them as they set their camp one evening. The four, accompanied by twenty royal guard were quite safe, but for some reason, felt incomplete without her presence.

The following morning they entered one of the many villages scattered along their route. Jared, as always, along with Hannock, joined the village elders for an ale in the small, makeshift tavern.

"Your arrival is most timely, Your Highness."

"What is your name, Sir?" Jared asked, offering the man respect.

"Godfrey, Your Highness, Godfrey Rannul."

"So why is our arrival so timely, Godfrey?"

"Well you *are* here to deal with that young wizard I presume, Your Highness?"

"What young wizard? I have received no reports of a wizard. Tell me more."

"Well, he turned up here a couple of weeks ago. Three times more since. Comes into the village, uses the tavern, gets drunk and threatens people. Stung poor Jimmy over there with his magic 'cause he wouldn't give him free ale. Then started waving a stick around. Called it his 'wand', saying as he could turn people into all sorts o' nasty things if we didn't give 'im what 'e wanted, and when 'e went, 'e took all Jimmy's coin with 'im."

"What do you mean, he stung him?" asked Hannock.

Godfrey turned to face Jimmy. "Go on. Show 'im."

Jimmy began removing a swathe of bandages from the side of his face. He turned his head for them to see. The wound was hideous. The lower half of his ear was missing and from there to his neck was badly infected, almost gangrenous.

Hannock never hesitated, crooking his finger at Jimmy in order for him to follow. He took him outside, leaving Jared to his meeting with the elders.

Hannock ordered one of the guard to take care of Jimmy's fetid wound.

"Stone me!" exclaimed the guard as he fumbled through the abundance of medical supplies whilst studying the festering injury, "What did this?"

"Poxy wizard," Jimmy replied.

***

They received a similar tale from another village, visited two days later and another the day after that. Each time the description of the wizard was the same, small, skinny, and always pointing his wand at people. His actions, according to witnesses, were becoming more aggressive. More victims with similar wounds to Jimmy were treated by Jared's guard and the wizard had now also taken to incinerating buildings and livestock if his demands were not met. Jared, after hearing of the Dergon attacks, had sworn that he would never allow the king's subjects to be terrorised and was convinced that they were now closing in on this heinous, rogue wizard. Acting on information given by the villagers, they began their manhunt, and it was not long before Hannock found his trail. Two days of pursuit passed, until at midday on the third, Hannock stood scratching his head. "Lost him. The ground's far too rocky, I'll never find him now," he said.

Faylore stepped forward, studying the ground. "Perhaps I can help," she offered. Leaning toward the ground, she placed her hand on a flat boulder, then another and another, until she had touched around a dozen. Standing, she pointed her finger, "He went that way."

"How do you know?" asked Hannock.

"The stones he stepped on are warmer than the others, but we are still a day and a half behind him."

"The stones are warmer!" Hannock was flabbergasted.

"Are there any villages nearby?" asked Jared.

"No, Your Highness," replied Hannock.

"Good, at least there'll be no one in danger before we catch up to him."

"He might have a camp somewhere near here. If only we could travel faster," said Jared, his frustration showing.

"I could go and have a look for ye, if ye want me to that is," said Grubb. Even though he said it as if it would be a great inconvenience, his offer was sincere.

"Even as your alter-ego, I doubt you'd be that much quicker, Grubb, best stay together for safety's sake."

"Fella with the four arms is not all I can do," said Grubb.

"What else can you do?" asked Lodren, at last finding something interesting about their conversation.

Grubb spread out his arms and started to shake himself. Before their eyes he was sprouting feathers. His face stretched forward, his nose became a beak, his arms became wings and his booted feet splayed into talons until, within seconds, he had transformed into a golden hawk.

"That's fantastic, Mr Grubb. Isn't he good, Mr Jared!?"

Grubb, the hawk, soared into the air and flew off into the distance. Hannock turned to Jared. "He's just full of surprises, isn't he?"

Grubb returned some time later and, landing in front of Jared, turned back into the grumpy Vikkery they all knew. "We won't catch him for at least two days. He's way ahead of us at some kind of camp he's set up at the top of a hill. He'll see us half a day before we get to him," he reported.

"Not if we catch up to him at night," said Hannock.

"There's twenty-five of us, horses and a cart. Do ye think he's blind and stupid?" asked Grubb.

"Well we won't all go, just a few of us," suggested Jared.

The companions had every intention of it being them.

Grubb continued his reconnaissance flights every couple of hours over the next day and a half and they were now close enough for Jared to order the guard to set camp and hold their position. The protests from the guard concerning Jared's safety were duly noted, but still rejected by the prince. "Hold your position. Do not break camp until we return," Jared ordered.

The companions moved out, eager to ensnare the wizard.

A little closer than Grubb's estimate, they reached the foot of the hill two hours later and were now strategizing their attack. Faylore, within reason, could move stealthily into position, using her unique chameleonic skill to flank the wizard. Grubb, disguised as a hawk, could fly above him and swoop in at the last second. The others however would crawl as closely as they dare and mount a surprise frontal attack, panicking the wizard and allowing them the opportunity to apprehend him swiftly, before he had time to resist them.

No bravado would be attempted by any member of the group. This was no armed felon, this was a wizard and as such, a dangerous adversary.

Grubb circled high above the scene. Ordinarily he would not have been able to see Faylore, but with his raptor eyes, he could clearly see her shimmering outline merely yards from the unsuspecting wizard. Jared, Hannock and Lodren had managed to ascend the gentle slope and were now at the camp's edge, when the wizard spoke. "If you wish to survive this night I suggest you step into the light before I judge you an enemy, sight unseen." This was something they had not envisaged.

"You have committed crimes against the people of Borell and must answer for them. Do not resist and no harm shall come to you, you have my word," called Jared.

"And who are you, that skulks in the darkness, to offer me your word?" asked the wizard.

"I am Prince Jared Dunbar of House Dunbar; my word is law."

"Why, Jared Dunbar, should I obey your laws?"

Hannock could contain himself no longer. "Listen you scrawny little runt, give up or I'll come in there and cut your bloody head off."

"Put your dog on a leash, Dunbar, before he gets you both killed, or are there more than just the two of you?"

"Try to hurt my friends and I'll smash your head in," shouted Lodren.

"That's three, or are there even more of you?"

Hannock turned his head and whispered to Jared. "Likes the sound of his own voice this one."

"I think they all do. Remember Reiggan?" replied Jared.

"Can I just go and bash him now, Mr Jared?" asked Lodren.

The wizard was now on his guard, pointing his wand in front of him.

"You'll be dead before you even get close, Prince."

Grubb, seeing an opening, seized his chance. Closing his wings to his sides he dove down toward the wizard's hand as he brandished his chosen weapon. The three friends charged into the camp, but not quickly enough, the wizard cast a spell. A green mist shot from the end of the wand as quickly as a firebolt and hit Jared in the shoulder, spinning him round in mid-air and taking Hannock down with him as he hit the ground. Lodren, seeing his friends fall, wanted revenge and resumed his charge, hammer held aloft. Grubb had reached his mark and snatched the wizard's wand cleanly from his grasp with razor sharp talons as Faylore appeared right behind the deranged warlock. Lodren stopped dead in his tracks. A look of confusion had come across the wizard's face, *how had this happened? Where had she come from?* He did not know the answers as he looked down at the curved, runed sword that now protruded from his chest, the hilt unseen, as it was pressed firmly against his spine. Slowly, he sank to his knees. "Do you think you've won? There are others like me, it is our time. We have protected fools like you for far too long. We shall burn your kingdoms, kill your families…"

Faylore placed her foot against his shoulder and pushed, withdrawing her sword. The wizard was dead.

He had been the result of Karrak's twisted experiments, driven mad by prolonged periods of possession combined with the resulting fatigue and amnesia. But of this, the companions were oblivious.

Jared was now their priority. Stripping his armour from him they inspected his wound that somehow, already seemed infected.

"Same as the villagers," said Grubb. "Out of the way." He held his hands above the wound in the same way as he had when Faylore was on death's doorstep, but after a few minutes realised that it was having no effect. "I don't understand, it's not working. Why isn't it working?" he asked.

"It's not a wound that can be healed so easily, Grubb," said Faylore, "The treatment of hexes and curses is always difficult, he'll be fine. It's just going to take time."

Grubb transformed into a hawk once more and flew to inform the guard to meet them as quickly as they could. The same guard who had treated Jimmy now attended to

Jared's shoulder and, within the hour, Jared, although a little disoriented, was awake. "Did we get him, Hannock?" he asked as soon as his eyes opened.

"Yes, Jared, we got him," replied Hannock. Hannock had heard the death speech of the wizard, but held his tongue. He would discuss it with Jared later when he had rested and was a little more coherent. Two of the guard placed Jared gently onto Lodren's cart and covered him, allowing him to rest.

Hannock, as a military man was used to hiding his emotions but now, as he stood before Faylore he took her hand. "You saved our lives tonight. Faylore, Jared means more to me than any brother could, if I lost him…"

Faylore gazed into his eyes. "What a strange race you are. You embrace life but risk it for one another so readily, at any moment it could be snatched from you. Why lose that life when it is so obvious that it would be a heartbreak to those near to you?"

Hannock smiled. "The most powerful magic in the world, Your Majesty… Love."

***

Jared awoke, slightly delirious. "Hannock," he groaned. Hannock rushed to his side. "What happened?"

"You were wounded by a nasty spell, similar to the villagers, it's your shoulder…"

"*Oh really!* I hadn't noticed," snapped Jared, wincing in pain as he attempted to move his arm.

"It happened so fast, Jared, I couldn't…"

"No, no. I'm sorry, Hannock, I never meant to snap at you. It just that… it's agony."

"That poultice should ease the pain until we can get you back to Borell. Once you're settled, I'll bring a fresh patrol and continue the search."

"Continue? But you said you got him."

Hannock explained what the wizard had said before he died. "I need to check the other villages to make sure there aren't any more of these wizards troubling them, then I can rest."

"Well you can think again, Captain. We're not going home until *we* check the villages, and that's an order. Get my armour and my horse, we have work to do."

Hannock begged and pleaded with Jared to return to the castle in order for his wound to be attended to, but Jared would not hear of it. "Once we have checked the villages we'll go home, and inform the men that if they blab about this to anyone, I'll have them put in the stocks."

"You mean apart from the king of course?"

"I said *anyone*, Hannock, *especially* the king."

***

Day by day and village by village, their mission continued. They entered each one with trepidation and spoke with the village elders, fearing the worst. Luckily, their fears proved to be unfounded as the list of remaining outposts grew shorter, and reaching the last village, Jared, exhausted due to his own stubbornness, met with the elders. They had neither seen nor heard anything untoward and were more concerned with the prince's health than their safety. It was thought that a brief respite and a night at the inn would help and, too tired to argue, Jared had relented. The idea, of course, had been Hannock's and the following morning, much to his relief, they turned and headed home.

"When we get home, Hannock, I'm going to sleep for a week."

"How's the shoulder, Jared? Does the dressing need changing yet?"

"Changed this morning when you were getting the men ready," said Jared.

"We'll get it looked at properly when we arrive home."

"Can't do that, the court physician will go straight to my father. It's his sworn duty to inform the king of any wound or minor injury incurred by a member of the royal family."

"Don't worry, I've got it covered," said Hannock, winking at him.

"What are you up to now?" asked Jared.

"We'll be back in Borell soon. Fear not, Your Highness, you're in safe hands."

***

Barden opened his eyes. Lying on the ground in complete darkness and unsure of his surroundings, his first attempt to rise was halted by the aches and pains across, it seemed, his entire body. His wounds, of which there were many, were superficial but to one of his advanced years, very painful. He glanced around in a bid to get his bearings, he was in a cave, alone, or so he thought.

"Sleep well?"

"Karrak? Is that you?" asked Barden, peering at the silhouette.

"Of course it's me you fool, who else would have kept watch over you as long as I?"

"How long have I been asleep?"

"Two days. I had to keep checking to make sure you weren't dead."

"Not yet, but it was close I fear, very close, too close."

"Yes, we need to talk about that, Barden. Glad you brought it up."

Barden's mind began to race as he recalled the turn of events that had placed them both here. He had failed to deliver the Elixian Soul as he had promised. A look of dread came upon his face as it dawned on him that he would now have to face the wrath of Karrak for that failure.

"Prince Karrak, I must…"

"Don't call me that," bellowed Karrak.

"I am no longer a member of the festering House Dunbar. My heritage was destroyed the moment I was incarcerated by you and your turnkeys. I am Lord Karrak from this day forward, understand?"

"Yes, my Lord."

"Now, the Elixian Soul, how are you going to get it for me?"

Barden was expecting the question but was hesitant to reply. Whatever he said would not be received with understanding.

"It is doubtful that the Soul still resides within Reiggan, Lord Karrak. It will have been relocated within moments of our attempt to acquire it."

"Don't you mean *your* attempt, Barden? You were the one who allowed them to follow you. You are the one who lost his grip and dropped it. You are the one who allowed it to be frozen in a block of ice and you are the one who, rather than fight for it, ran away with his tail between his legs."

"We would have been killed, Lord Karrak. I feared not for my own life, but for yours. You do not know how to transport yourself. If I had been killed, you would have been next."

Karrak, now sitting on a rock, drummed his fingers against his thigh as he stared at Barden. "Alright, Barden, I'll give you that. Now where would they have taken the Soul?" he asked.

"It will be in a location that is unknown to me," replied Barden nervously.

"That's the problem. You don't know, and they're not stupid enough to put it somewhere you might suspect. Well, I'll get it eventually, but patience is not my greatest virtue. You will aid me to hone my skills, I will not be caught off guard again."

"It would be my honour, my Lord."

Barden rose from the ground and stepped toward Karrak but then whirled around, a firebolt appearing in his hand. He had heard a cough, and began to look for the person responsible.

"Oh don't mind him, Barden," said Karrak, beckoning toward the darkness. A man appeared, at least Barden believed it to be a man. He lurched toward them, deformities of his spine and legs preventing him from walking properly. "I haven't named him yet," Karrak informed Barden, "I know, I'll call him... 'Barden'."

"My Lord, where did you find him? What happened to him?"

"Two days Barden, *two days*. I had to find something to amuse myself with."

The wreckage of a man that now stood before them was an innocent passerby, a victim of his own good intention. He had discovered Karrak as he lay unconscious, outside the cave. He had given him water and enquired after his health. His reward was to be tortured, thus providing Karrak's *amusement*.

***

Karrak's instruction in magic covered many subjects. He seemed to have a penchant for fire spells, but this paled into insignificance as soon as mind control was introduced. He continued to practise on the poor stranger he had taken as his pet until one day he went a little too far, and the poor soul perished, his body twisted beyond recognition. Karrak showed no remorse at his death, merely mentioning that he would need another test subject as he dragged the corpse from the cave. Even Barden, his greatest advocate, was shocked by his callous demeanour.

Karrak walked, as he did regularly, through the forest and happened upon another stranger who was attempting to repair the broken wheel on his cart.

"Having a spot of bother?" asked Karrak.

The stranger turned slowly.

"What's it to do with you? Sling your hook before I break your face."

He was almost the size of Karrak, the tell-tale scars on his face revealing that he was a ruffian.

"Now that's not very nice is it? I merely asked you a question." Karrak had a huge smile on his face, thoroughly amused that this vagabond thought that, in some way, he could bring harm to him.

"Second time, piss off. I won't warn you again."

"I think you need a lesson in manners," sneered Karrak.

The traveller stood and stormed toward Karrak, fists clenched. He was within arm's length before Karrak held out his hand. The stranger stopped abruptly as if he had been struck in the chest and fell to his knees. This was, after all, self-defence and enough of a motive for Karrak to practise his art of mutilation. How easy it had been to goad the fool into action. Karrak turned his wrist back and forth and with each movement a part of his victim was affected. First his face, which looked as if someone was pulling at his cheeks, stretching the flesh so far that it looked as if it would tear open. His jawbone stretched outward, crunching and cracking as it contorted under Karrak's magical manipulation. His arms and legs twisted, the joints bending the wrong way. His would-be attacker was attempting to beg for mercy but all that came from his contorted lips were incoherent whimpers. Karrak continued with his experiment for over half an hour as tears ran down the bleeding cheeks of his prey until, with a spin of Karrak's wrist, there was a loud crunch, and the victim fell to the ground dead, Karrak had deliberately broken his neck.

Karrak rubbed his hands together, pleased with his results. "Interesting" he said and, without a second glance, headed back toward his cave.

Karrak became more powerful with Barden's instruction. His ventures into the forest continued and many bandits, and innocents alike, suffered the same fate as the first. Time after time he would kidnap unsuspecting strays, sometimes bringing them to the cave, others tortured where they were discovered, but always with the same inevitable conclusion... their death.

CHAPTER 12

Jared was comfortable next to his father, as the goblet of wine that Tamor had poured, had been the first of many. The pain in his shoulder had now subsided, a combination of the skilful application of the poultice by Alfred, and alcohol. He glanced around the room once more, still careful not to make eye contact with the peacocks. His brow furrowed suddenly, maybe he had over-indulged a little. Shaking his head, he realised that his eyes were not playing tricks on him. At the far end of the hall, obviously trying to get his attention, was Hannock. Jared rose and unsteadily approached his best friend.

"I'm so glad you're here, Hannock," slurred Jared. "These people are so boring. See him over there…"

"I need to speak to you, outside." Hannock, grabbing him by the elbow, marched Jared from the room.

"What on earth's wrong, Hannock?"

Hannock gave Jared a look of disapproval. "How much have you had to drink tonight? You're wobbling all over the place."

"Probably more than is good for me. But those people, really, Hannock, you have no idea…"

"Well I've got something that'll sober you up."

"I don't want to sober up, I've got to go back in there and…"

"Karrak's escaped!" Blurted out Hannock.

"What!? What do you mean, he's escaped?" asked Jared, closing one eye in an attempt to focus.

"Barden helped him escape. Attacked the guards, killed one of them, and escaped."

Jared shook his head, trying to make sense of the devastating news. "Does my father know yet?" he asked.

"You're the first," replied Hannock.

"How did you find out?" asked Jared, still swaying.

"One of the senior wizards from Reiggan Fortress. He's already gone, said it was most important that he return immediately."

Jared, bleary-eyed, looked at Hannock. "I think I'd better be the one to tell my father."

"I agree entirely, but not yet. You need to sober up, then we'll see him together," said Hannock dragging Jared toward his office.

Jared was plied with medicinal beverages, supplied by Alfred, and had done something nobody should witness a prince doing, before, sometime later, the friends headed back toward the throne room.

Jared approached the musicians. Holding out his hand for them to cease playing, he turned to address the room. "Ladies and gentlemen, forgive my intrusion, you must all leave." No apology was offered to the guests as, with Hannock's instruction, the guards escorted everyone from the room. King Tamor had not questioned his son's decision to end the gathering so abruptly and sat patiently, awaiting his explanation. Jared ordered the guards from the room, Hannock being the only exception, and approached his father.

Their conversation had barely begun when there was a bang on the door and a guard announced, "The wizard Emnor seeks an audience, Your Majesty. He informs me that it is of great import, Sire."

With the king's permission, Hannock opened the door, allowing Emnor to enter. "Forgive me, Your Majesty, I came as soon as I heard the news."

"I've only just heard myself, Emnor, how did you get here so quickly?"

"That is of no importance, Tamor, finding Karrak however, is."

"He'll just find a tavern somewhere, get drunk and probably beat up some poor barkeep. Don't you think you're overreacting a little?" asked Tamor.

"Sire, he has departed Reiggan with Barden, the Head of the Administration as his accomplice. He could show up here at any moment, seeking revenge."

"Revenge? For what?" asked Tamor, "For wanting him to be well?"

"He does not see it so. He feels that he was imprisoned as a punishment for his actions within your kingdom. He will return, Tamor, and when he does, he'll be looking to vent his frustrations on all who had a hand in his incarceration."

***

"Lord Karrak, enough, please." Barden begged as he lay on the ground panting.

"But I must practise, Barden. On your feet, once more."

"I cannot, my Lord. Your fire spells are the most powerful I have ever known; I cannot defend against another one."

"Hopeless. It just begins to feel right and now you need to rest. If only you were younger."

"If I were younger I would not have been able to help with your understanding of the immense power at your command, my Lord," said Barden, lowering his head so as not to appear impertinent.

"Don't grovel, Barden. You'll want me to feel sorry for you next, and we both know that won't happen. After all, *you* made *me* what I *am*, remember?"

"Yes, my Lord. But you already have more power than I could ever aspire to command."

"Really? Not surprising. After all, you are a puny little sprat aren't you?"

Barden resented the comment, but, remaining subservient, simply replied, "Yes, my Lord."

"It's about time I paid a visit to my family, don't you think?" asked Karrak.

"It may not be wise, my Lord, they may be expecting you."

"What! Surely my father and brother will welcome me with open arms?"

"They imprisoned you for the death of a mere guard, without evidence, my Lord. What would they do given the events that took place in Reiggan? They may seek to hang you," replied Barden.

"Then best not to give them that chance... I'll kill them both."

A sinister smile appeared on Barden's face. "And the kingdom will be yours, my Lord."

"Yes, it will. But I am not naïve enough to think I could sack a castle by myself. I shall need help."

"There is *one,* that would come to your aid, my Lord."

"Why would I trust you, Barden? After all you failed me last time."

"I apologise once more, my Lord. There is another that would be a willing ally, and he has warriors at his command."

"And who is this leader of warriors?"

"His name is Ramah, my Lord. A Dergon Chief."

"And just *what* is a Dergon?"

Barden explained, at length and with much detail, the heritage of the Dergon. From their fighting for the highest bidder in many wars, right up to their last battle, with King Tamor.

"So he has no love for my father, or Borell? He could prove useful."

"I am led to believe that he still leads a band of at least a hundred, my Lord."

"Where do I find this Ramah?" asked Karrak.

"He has made camp in the hills not far from here, two days' ride at most."

"I won't be riding though will I?"

"I suggest, my Lord, that we make our approach obvious. They are beasts and we do not wish to appear hostile if we mean to recruit them as our allies."

"I notice you're using the word 'we' a lot, Barden. Don't start getting ideas above your station will you? After all, I am the one to whom your sacred scroll refers am I not?"

"You are indeed, my Lord, forgive me. I wish only to serve," replied Barden, bowing to his master.

***

The companions sat around the campfire in the castle grounds. Jared had requested their presence, and all were eager to know the reason for the gathering.

"It's about my brother," began Jared.

"The mad one?" asked Faylore.

"Yes... no" how should he answer? Karrak was showing signs of madness but he could not bring himself to say it aloud, at least, not in front of others.

Hannock intervened, "He's not mad, Faylore," he said calmly.

Jared was glad that his friend had spoken as he was unsure of what to say next.

Hannock continued, "He's insane."

"Hannock!" exclaimed Jared.

"These are our friends, Jared. We must tell them the truth, however much it hurts to say it."

Jared, of course, knew that Hannock was right and held up his hands in submission, "Carry on, Hannock," he said, "you tell them."

"He was always a spoiled brat, but as he got older his temper got worse. He's a mountain of a man and enjoyed bullying people, until one night he went too far and killed a guard in a fit of rage. That's why we were taking him to Reiggan, when we met you three. Now, apparently, not only has he escaped, Barden aided his escape, and one of the young wizards was killed in the process."

"Didn't like that Barden. Soon as I clapped eyes on him, I knew he was a wrong 'un," said Grubb, being as outspoken as ever.

"Such a shame. He seemed so nice," said Lodren.

"My dear Lodren," said Hannock, "to you, an axe wielding maniac would seem nice."

"Thank you, Mr Captain, kind of you to say so."

Hannock had a look of disbelief on his face, but said nothing.

"Does anyone have any idea where they could have gone? If they do, I could have my people search the area," Faylore offered.

"Not a clue," said Hannock.

"Well, I'll have them report any strange events that may prove useful," she added.

"Urge them not to approach him, Faylore. By the sound of things his magic is very powerful. Your kin should not be placed in a perilous situation, I won't accept that," said Jared.

"Neither will I, Jared, but you know of our ability to blend. It worked against one wizard, it should work against another."

"I'm not so sure, it seems the young wizard we faced was a novice. It may not work against one more experienced. Better not take the risk, Faylore."

"Why don't we go and have a look for them, Mr Jared. We might have a bit of luck, and he's not going to attack his own brother is he?" asked Lodren.

"That's where you're wrong my dear Nibby," said Hannock. "He already tried to kill him once, and now he has grown stronger, he's more dangerous than ever."

Faylore placed her hand on Jared's. "Your brother tried to kill you?" she asked.

"Yes, and if he'd known more about his prowess with magic sooner, he would have succeeded. That's the only thing that saved me, that and having a pikestaff rapped round the back of his skull."

Hannock held up his hand. "Guilty."

***

Karrak approached the Dergon camp, his steps were light, but stealth was not his objective. He was almost at the campfire before one of the Dergon let out a howl. A dozen or so of his fellow warriors rushed forward, their intent, to slaughter the intruder. Karrak threw up his arm and there were shrieks of shock as they all flew into the air untouched, then landing heavily on the ground, all bar one, who landed in the centre of the campfire itself. Karrak turned to the side and held out his arm. The camp fell silent, bar the yelps of the Dergon who was attempting to douse the flames that had engulfed his legs.

"Bring me the one you call Ramah," Karrak said calmly. The Dergon, unsure how to react to the stranger's order, stood looking at one another. "Are you all deaf?" bellowed Karrak, "Bring me the one you call Ramah, NOW."

"You are either very brave, or very stupid," said Ramah sidling from between his warriors, "which is it?"

"Well I'm not stupid, and looking at this lot, there's nothing to be afraid of either."

"What do you want, magician?" asked Ramah, "There's nothing for you here."

"On the contrary, I think I've found exactly what I was looking for."

"Which is?" asked Ramah.

"Brave warriors, my dear Ramah, with a braver leader of course."

"Forget your flattery stranger, it does not work on me. We are proud warriors but have renounced our mercenary ways. You cannot employ us to fight your battles."

"Such big words, but you misunderstand me, I'm not here to employ you, I'm here to help you."

"Do we look helpless to you? We need no help stranger, now leave," said Ramah calmly.

"You mean you don't want revenge on Tamor Dunbar, or Borell? I heard that your last encounter with them was slightly embarrassing, to say the least. Got your backside well and truly kicked, by all accounts."

"He slaughtered four hundred of my warriors." Ramah was becoming slightly annoyed, which was exactly what Karrak needed.

"That's what I heard, and I'm here to offer my help. Don't tell me you don't want to do the same to him."

"I want to kill every last Borellian I find and rip their king's head off with my bare hands."

"But of course you do, what true leader wouldn't? Be honest, it's just a dream. With the aid of my sorcery, Ramah, it could become a reality."

Ramah lowered his head, eyeing Karrak carefully. "Just how powerful do you believe your sorcery to be?" he asked.

"Ask these," Karrak replied, pointing at the Dergon he had sent soaring into the air.

"With one hand, Ramah, just one hand, and no real effort."

Ramah gestured for Karrak to sit by what remained of the campfire, most of it having been extinguished by the falling Dergon warrior. "Why do you wish to help us, sorcerer?"

"I am Karrak Dunbar, second son of Tamor. My father, the old goat, had me gaoled simply because I tried to kill my brother."

The reaction from Ramah was again, as Karrak expected. He began to laugh, a deep laugh, echoed around the camp by his army. "Ambition, I like that. Simply tried to kill your brother," Ramah's expression changed, "but what if we defeat your father? What then? You turn on us once he has been usurped and slaughter us as your enemies. Do you think me so foolish?"

"If I thought you were a fool, Ramah, we wouldn't be having this conversation, you'd all be dead now."

Karrak said this in a very matter of fact way, and Ramah believed him. "If your sorcery is so powerful… Karrak? Why do you need us?"

"If I were to approach the castle they would simply bar the gates. They are too cowardly to face me. If you were to lure them out, I could destroy them all, leaving you and your army to spill through the gates and exact your revenge."

"Why would you do this for us? What do you get, Karrak?"

"I get my home back. With the king and my brother dead, the castle would be mine."

"And where do we go once you have your fine castle, back to these hills?" asked Ramah.

"You can stay in Borell, come back to the hills or have another castle built wherever you want, Ramah. My gratitude shall afford you whatever remuneration you see fit."

Ramah was still dubious. His thirst for revenge was great, but as he conspired with Karrak, the doubt in his mind was soon erased with Karrak's skilful manipulation. It was agreed between the two that soon, Karrak would revisit the campsite in order to make their final preparations for the attack on Borell, allowing Ramah the time to make ready, what remained of his glorious, Dergon horde.

***

Karrak, having returned to his cave, now stood at the entrance. He pondered over recent events, his unexpected incarceration; the aid of Barden in his escape; his experiments with the manipulation of the form or mind of a random individual; but most of all, the revenge he sought on all that had, in his mind, betrayed him.

Barden, his usual fawning self, hurried over to greet his new master. "I trust all went well, my Lord?" he asked tentatively.

"As well as it could when one is dealing with animals," sneered Karrak.

"Ramah has agreed to an alliance then, my Lord?" asked Barden.

"He believes he has. That's all I need."

"I do not understand, I thought we wanted the Dergon as our allies, my Lord."

"Now that's the problem, Barden, you think too much. You may have been a bigwig with the Administration, but you're nothing now, a nobody."

Barden lowered his head. "No, my Lord, forgive me my Lord."

"That's the other thing, Barden, you're always apologising. If you kept your mouth shut and just did as I ask, you wouldn't have to, would you?" Barden shook his head, not wanting to antagonise Karrak. "I've been thinking Barden, and I have a question for you."

Barden looked up at Karrak. Questions directed at him were usually a forerunner to some sort of abuse by Karrak, mental or physical, depending on his master's mood.

"Why do I suffer you so, Barden? I mean, you've shown me all you can regarding sorcery, so you're no use for that any more. You use the term 'we', when it's quite obvious that you don't have a useful idea in that grey, matted head of yours."

"My Lord, I shall try harder to please you, any command you give…"

"I hadn't finished! See? You interrupted me, again. Now where was I? Oh yes, I almost forgot…" and with this Karrak sneered and lowered his voice, "You… Murdered... My... Mother."

Panic had set in and Barden began to babble. "My Lord, please, I did it for you, so that you would become…"

These were the last words that Barden would ever speak. Karrak held out his hand. Barden fell to the floor, screaming in agony, as his body began to warp and twist with his torturer's manipulation, his face contorting and his bones cracking.

"Did you think I'd forgotten? Did you think that I would ever trust you? Don't worry, old man, I'm not going to kill you, just neuter you a little. You need to be kept on a very, tight leash."

Barden's screams grew louder as Karrak's metamorphosing intensified, for the more Barden screamed, the more the sadistic nature of Karrak's soul demanded. Barden was now unrecognisable. No more was he a wizened old man, he was some sort of beast, unlike anything seen before. He had a muzzle, a mouth full of canine teeth and four legs similar to a wolf. The screaming ceased, and now, cowering with fear at his feet, was Karrak's new pet. "Now that wasn't too bad, was it?" asked Karrak.

He had twisted Barden's body with less effort than an artist moulding a lump of clay. The cruellest torture for Barden however, was that his consciousness had been left intact, allowing him to realise the true horror of his predicament. Any who saw him would shy away from his hideous form and without the power of speech, he could not beg for help or mercy.

Not done with Barden's humiliation, Karrak approached the beast and reaching inside his cloak, removed a collar. "I have a gift for you," he said, fastening it around Barden's neck and roaring with laughter, a maniacal laugh, proof to anyone that would have witnessed his actions, that Karrak was now completely insane. He looked down at his pet, "Now don't go running off, Barden. I'll find you and bring you back and then you'll have to be punished, and remember this... pets, sleep outside." He kicked Barden as hard as he could, flinging him into the air. The beast yelped and scampered out of the cave. "Don't worry," Karrak shouted after it, "you'll have some new friends to play with soon."

***

Emnor, after his fleeting visit to Borell Castle, had returned to Reiggan Fortress and was now frantically searching what had been Barden's chambers. Tomes and scrolls were laid out on the desk in an order that only Emnor understood, and he moved from one to another, searching their content. A young wizard stood a few feet away watching with puzzled interest.

"What exactly are you looking for, Master Emnor?"

"Any clue as to where Barden may have taken, Karrak," Emnor replied.

"Forgive me, Master Emnor, but there are scores of us. Surely Master Barden, as powerful as he is, and Prince Karrak, pose no threat to Reiggan?"

"I have known Barden since before you were born, Harley. He is a danger with which you would not want to contend, my young friend. He has turned to black magic, the proof is in these scriptures. He believes that Karrak is some sort of saviour who will rid the earth of menial lifeforms, such as you or I, as if we were a plague."

"But that is insanity! He would aid him in an attempted genocide? Master Barden!"

"Oh yes. He believes that Karrak is destined to rule the world."

***

Emnor, despite his polite objections, had been named as Barden's successor as Head of the Administration. He was the most experienced member, not to mention the oldest and wisest. Put to a vote, the decision by his colleagues, was unanimous. "Very well," said Emnor, "if that is your wish, I accept the post, *temporarily*. Once this business with Barden is concluded, however, we shall reconvene to discuss a more permanent solution to Reiggan's leadership." He felt honoured that his colleagues held him in such high esteem, but at the same time, did not want to be restricted by his new post. To him, his freedom to come and go as he pleased, was paramount.

Time passed with no word of Barden or Karrak reaching Emnor's ears until, eventually, there were whispers of strange beasts and disappearances in the south. Emnor felt he must investigate. Administration members protested, saying that he should send one of them, but his reply was that he would not ask anyone to do something he was not willing to do himself. "After all," he had said, "they *are* only rumours."

So much fuss had been made, regarding Emnor's safety, that he had been forced to formulate a plan and had begun to make the strangest of requests of his young, intended apprentice.

"Harley, fetch me a pig. Not a piglet, a fully-grown pig. Take it to the chamber that Karrak occupied during his... visit."

"A pig, Master Emnor?" asked Harley.

"Yes, Harley, a pig, hurry now, I don't have all day. Oh and, Harley, don't keep calling me Master, it makes me sound so old."

Harley raised his finger as if he were about to speak, but looking into Emnor's eyes, thought it wiser not to mention his senior's age.

"A pig, right, Emnor, a pig," and he wandered off, muttering to himself.

Harley returned a while later. A scruffy-looking yokel followed him, a large man, leading a pig by a rope. Emnor stared at the man but said nothing and kept a straight face despite the fact that the similarity in appearance between the pig and its owner, amused him greatly.

Reaching into his robes, he passed Harley some coin which Harley, in turn, gave to the pig-faced man.

"Thank you, Sir, if you need anything else…"

Harley ushered him from the room, where another wizard took the duty of escorting the man from the premises.

"Where did you find him?" asked Emnor.

"One of the villages down on the plains. I had to transport him and the pig. He didn't trust me to take him the coin later."

"Well done, Harley, that will be all for now," said Emnor dismissing the young wizard.

Harley nodded and headed for the door. He longed to ask Emnor why he needed a pig but held his tongue understanding that, if he needed to know, Emnor would have told him. He closed the door behind him.

Emnor approached the pig, "Well at least *you're* clean," he said smiling. He held out his hand, palm facing the pig. It began to twitch and shake and then wobbled as it began to grow taller and stood up on its hind legs. The snout drew in and the ears became smaller, its hind legs grew longer and straightened and its front legs stretched out, its trotters becoming feet and hands on its new limbs. Its face, now flatter, transformed, sprouting new features as it grew a long, grey beard. All of the transformations took only a minute until, Emnor lowered his hand, and was now looking… at himself. "Not bad at all," he said quietly, "but we can't have you naked can we?"

He took a few minutes to place robes on his doppelganger and tidy its beard. He now stood, admiring his work. The 'pig' just stood there motionless. There was no consciousness present in this created lifeform. Emnor took no pleasure in erasing the mind of a dumb animal but realised that it would be kinder than the poor beast suffering the agonising pain of the transformation.

Satisfied with his results, Emnor lay on the bed and closed his eyes. A second later the doppelganger held up his hands to study them.

"Not bad," it said, "not bad at all," it repeated.

Emnor had, of course, possessed the perfect replica of himself. The concern from his fellow wizards had given him the idea. If the fake Emnor was destroyed, admittedly a shame for the pig, he, at least, would survive. His intention was to eventually face Karrak, and the destruction of this body was indeed, a distinct possibility if Karrak's powers, with the aid of Barden, had grown significantly.

A simple test was needed. Poking his head through the door he asked a passing wizard to summon Harley to the chambers. Harley, arriving a short while later and, after knocking politely and entering, stood before Emnor who had carefully covered his real body.

"You summoned me, Emnor?" he asked, as he quickly glanced around the room, wondering what had happened to the pig.

"Did I?" Emnor asked, feigning a cross between ignorance and amnesia, "Can't remember what I wanted you for now, too much on my mind. So sorry, dear boy, it'll come to me later no doubt."

"Is there anything else?" Harley asked, now completely confused.

"No thank you, sorry to waste your time. You carry on with whatever you were doing."

Harley wasn't stupid, far from it in fact. Emnor had summoned him for a reason and his reason had been achieved. He was ambitious and tenacious, but knew when to keep his mouth shut so, with a slight nod, he left the room.

Emnor rubbed his hands together, perfect. Not only had his puppet worked, he had found a worthy apprentice along the way.

Harley was not completely sure what the test had been, but he had realised that this had been one.

As the new Head of the Administration, Emnor attended many meetings over the following weeks. The Elixian Soul had been secreted once more and security measures at Reiggan had also been addressed, but in the back of Emnor's mind was still the worry of Karrak's possible attempt to gain revenge on the Borellians. "We must aid them should they need it," he said during one such meeting.

"Why would Prince Karrak risk exposure by doing exactly what we think he will?" asked one of the seniors.

"His need for revenge will eat away at his very being. It will consume him and drive him insane, if it has not already done so. Mark my words, Karrak will try to kill his own family."

***

Ramah sat, honing the edge of his black sword, glancing up as Karrak neared him. "What's your plan then, sorcerer?" he asked.

Karrak raised his eyebrows at the insolent tone used by Ramah. "Watch your tongue, Dergon," he snarled. Korbah, still loyal to his leader, stepped forward. "And what are you going to do, dog? One more step and I'll roast you where you stand," snapped Karrak.

Ramah held up his hand and Korbah took a step back.

"That's better. Keep your distance," Karrak sneered at him.

"Are we going into battle today, sorcerer, or are you just here to insult us?" asked Ramah.

Karrak looked around at the Dergon warriors, repulsed by their appearance. He wanted nothing more than to take pleasure by butchering every single one of them himself, but had to face a solitary fact, he needed them... for now. Turning back to Ramah he spoke again, "Are they ready?" he asked.

"They *are*, but what are *your* intentions, sorcerer?" Ramah asked, still a hint of doubt in his voice.

"A simple plan. One that even *your* followers can understand," replied Karrak.

Korbah growled at the slur, but remained stationary. Karrak glanced at him and laughed. "As I was saying. Lead your warriors in a frontal attack, make as much noise as you can to get their full attention. The arrogance of the Borellians will get the better of them, causing them to open the gates and charge directly at you. You however, must hold your position until they reach the halfway point between you and the castle. Then, and only then, divide your forces equally to each side. I shall pass between you and destroy every last one of them, leaving you only open ground to cover before you enter the gates. You may lose a few warriors to arrows, but once inside, you can exact your revenge quite easily against such a diminished force. I will follow once the castle is taken, then we can discuss the well-earned compensation for your endeavours. An easy victory, wouldn't you agree?"

"We shall see, Lord Karrak, but trust me, any hint of deception and I'll kill you myself," answered Ramah.

Karrak stayed calm, he had a loathing of the Dergon. Their green skin, their deformed faces and most of all, their stupidity, disgusted him. The sooner they were eradicated, the better. "Why would I deceive you, Ramah? We *are* friends after all."

***

The Dergon moved stealthily into position. If they were spied too soon, the plan would fail, and this was a risk that Ramah was not willing to take. Reaching their position, they were now set.

"Just picture your hands around King Tamor's throat," Karrak had said.

"CHARGE!" Roared Ramah.

The Dergon, following his orders, flew headlong toward the castle gates.

In the distance, a horn sounded and the gates sprang open. The mounted Borellians charged through, bearing down on their targets. Reaching the halfway point they saw the Dergon part, but could see no reason for them to do so, only making them easier prey for their spears. The enemies clashed, screams and roars were heard as the battle commenced. Ramah spun around and around. *Where was Karrak? Where was the sorcery that had been*

252

promised to aid them with their victory? Dergon warriors, one after another, fell to axe, spear and sword.

For the briefest of moments, Ramah saw Karrak. He had not moved, not a single step as he laughed out loud, whilst witnessing the slaughter of the Dergon, before vanishing.

In the blink of an eye, he re-appeared between the castle gates, pausing momentarily to salute Ramah before turning away and walking through them. With a wave of his hand, the gates closed behind him. "Now where's the old goat hiding?" he asked himself.

"Welcome home, Brother," Jared shouted from high on the ramparts.

Karrak looked up, shielding his eyes from the sun. His arrival had not, as he believed, been undetected.

"Well, well, if it's not big brother. Where's your sidekick, Hannock? Are his lips not firmly on your backside as usual?"

"Not today, Karrak," shouted Hannock, "but you know me, never far away from defending the royal house."

"There he is. Your little toy soldier. You should be a little more courteous to me after what you said in Reiggan, Captain. Who knows, I might allow you to live so that you can serve *me*, not torture you like I'm going to do to my obnoxious brother and traitorous father."

Jared looked across at Hannock. "But you never *said* anything in Reiggan."

Hannock racked his brains, trying to recall the events at Reiggan. Suddenly it dawned on him. How could he have heard, he was asleep? The realisation on his face was obvious.

"Hannock, *what did you say*?" demanded Jared.

"I said it so quietly, how did he hear?"

"Said what?" asked Jared with an urgent frustration.

Hannock was now glaring at Karrak. "Let me just cut his throat and have rid of him. And I meant it."

"You coward. You would have murdered me in my sleep. Not even the courage to face me like a man," said Karrak mockingly.

"I'll face you now, Karrak. Just you and me, any weapon you choose."

Hannock was headed toward the steps that lead down from the ramparts.

"Hannock, no!" shouted Jared.

The only way to hurt Hannock was to attack his pride and Karrak knew this.

Now halfway down the steps, Hannock drew his sword. "I'm going to take your bloody head off, Karrak."

Karrak pouted. "Oh the poor soldier's all upset, come here…" his tone changed to a growl "…and I'll make the pain go away."

Jared knew that Karrak was enjoying this game and that no good would come of it, especially for Hannock.

Karrak thrust his hands out in front of him as Hannock reached the foot of the steps. Hannock, being a seasoned military man, had expected this and dodged to the side, but not quite far enough, as the firebolt glanced off the side of his breastplate, mostly going under his arm but searing his exposed bicep. Jared was almost as quick to respond and in turn had thrust his hands forward. Nothing could be seen, no fire, no water, no ice, but Karrak was suddenly blasted backwards by the invisible force and he crashed into the gates behind him.

Hannock, driven by rage, was attempting to get to his feet but was hit by another firebolt, this time in the back, throwing him to the ground where he remained, motionless. There was a boom like thunder as the ground split open before Karrak, who fell forward into the crevice that had appeared, confusion on his face.

"Sorry, Mr Jared. I missed him." It was Lodren.

An arrow whistled past Karrak's head, missing him by an inch, then another and another.

Karrak threw up a fire wall that turned the following arrows to ash before they reached him, but he did not block the talons that ripped a piece of flesh from his cheek. He was dazed, he could not focus, as hard as he tried. Karrak struggled to his feet. "I'll kill you all," he roared and threw up his hands once more.

"Not today ye won't." A large creature had appeared immediately in front of him. He hesitated momentarily, he had never seen the likes of it before. His confusion grew as he studied its form, about ten feet tall and with... four arms? It punched him full in the face with two of its fists, launching him into the air. He landed in a heap. The rain of arrows had resumed, the four-armed beast was charging at him and the ground beside him split once more. Realising his defeat, he closed his eyes... and vanished.

***

Faylore reached Hannock first. He was badly burned. Tears welled in her eyes as she turned to Grubb, who had now squatted beside them. "Can you help him?" she begged.

"He's pretty bad, Your Majesty, but I'll do me best."

Jared and Lodren were now with them and Jared took a knee beside his dearest friend. "I'll give you anything, Grubb, anything, just save him."

Grubb rubbed his hands together as the others turned Hannock over. Faylore gasped at the sight of his wounds. One side of his face was almost gone, literally melted. The flesh had been seared from his bicep and the bone could be seen beneath, and on removing his armour, three of his ribs were visible.

"He's going to be fine, Mr Jared, you'll see," said Lodren, openly crying.

Grubb spent half an hour taking care of their wounded friend before turning to the rest of the companions. "I've done as much as I can, his arm will be fine and his back. His face doesn't look that bad now, and it'll look better with time. There's nothing I can do about his eye, Jared, it's gone, nothing left to heal I'm afraid. I'm really sorry."

Jared's mind flashed back to his conversation with Alfred in The Weary Traveller, when George was the first to suffer such a wound. "Don't you dare apologise, Grubb," he said, "Hannock's alive, alive because of you."

They had survived their encounter with Karrak, but at great expense, having nearly lost their friend. Worst of all, was that it had been for nought... once again Karrak had escaped.

***

Karrak re-appeared on the outskirts of Barnford, one of the smaller villages in Tamor's kingdom. His wounds were minor, despite the attempts of the companions to make them more severe. He leaned against a fencepost in order to catch his breath. *How had he failed?* he thought. *Who had come to Jared's aid? The unseen bowman, the being with the hammer, the four-armed creature. Who were they?*

At least he had managed to kill Jared's lapdog, Hannock, or so he thought.

Venturing into the village, he stumbled through the open doorway of the tavern. A young girl rushed from behind the bar and grabbed his arm. "What happened to you? Here, sit down," she said.

"Bandits," replied Karrak, "a few miles from here…"

"Alright," continued the girl, "that can wait, let's get you cleaned up first." She cleaned and dressed his wounds with surprising ease and Karrak was intrigued by her skill.

"You have a healer's touch, my dear lady. Are you a physician?" he asked, smiling.

"No, Sir, my father was a soldier. I learned how to patch up his wounds from a young age, it comes as second-nature now, second to running the tavern," she laughed, "It comes in handy when the customers start brawling after too much ale!"

"This is your tavern then?" asked Karrak.

"Yes," she replied, "left to me by my father."

"But you said your father was a soldier?"

257

"He was," she replied, "but he was not the sort of man who wasted his money on ale and gambling. He saved his pay for many years and bought the inn as an investment for his retirement."

"And your mother?" asked Karrak.

"She died when I was a child. I barely remember her."

"What a tragedy, my dear, you are still so young and already an orphan. Your father died in battle I presume?"

"No, Sir, he was murdered."

"Murdered?!" exclaimed Karrak.

"Yes. His body was discovered, hidden behind some barrels, in the grounds of Borell Castle. His neck was broken."

"How terrible for you, but it must have given you some satisfaction to see the murderer hanged?"

"No, Sir, he was never caught!"

Karrak remembered grabbing the girl's father, squeezing with all his might and then twisting until he heard the crunch as he crushed the life out of him. "I feel I must apologise my dear. You have been so kind and I have no means with which to pay you. I am a humble merchant and the bandits, they took my wares as well as my coin." His act was working perfectly.

The girl took his hand. "Don't worry about that," she said, "my father always taught me that we should help a person in need. There may be a day when I need *your* help," she smiled.

"And if that day comes, you shall receive more than you deserve, dear lady, far more."

The girl held out her hand. "My name's Maria, by the way."

***

Karrak spent the next few days recuperating with the help of Maria, who waited on him, bringing food and drink at regular intervals, glad of the interruption to her fairly mundane life. Various villagers came and went, each attempting to engage Karrak in idle conversation but instead receiving a frosty reception as he showed his true colours. They were of no use to him, there was no need for civility toward them.

Karrak, sat at a table in the tavern, glared at the two locals who had dared to enter the now, hostile atmosphere of the tavern, an atmosphere that was felt by all except the hostess, who had become besotted with the handsome stranger.

The patrons sat at the bar on tall stools and occasionally one would look in Karrak's direction during their mumbled conversation. Karrak suffered their impertinence for a short while but, as was always the case, his temper got the better of him. "Something to say to me?" he asked. "Come on, out with it." The locals said nothing, pretending that it was not they who were being addressed. "I'm talking to you. Answer me." Still they said nothing. "As I thought, children in a classroom. Telling tales and making up stories."

Karrak could contain his true nature no longer. Turning to the girl he smiled, a fake smile that, for the first time, unnerved her. "Do you like animals, Maria?" he asked.

"Yes, Sir, I do," she replied.

"Oh good," he said, "you'll like this then," Karrak held out his hand.

The hospitality that was given to Karrak, the free board and lodging and the tending of his wounds meant nothing to him. His paranoia, aroused by the unexpected patrons, caused his actions. Believing he had been recognised by either one, or both, prompted his decision to ensure that his anonymity remained intact. Standing in front of the door he prevented their departure as, one by one, they were all morphed into beasts that resembled Barden's new form. His payment for the kindness shown to him was to enslave them all.

Once darkness fell, he vacated the village, heading toward his cave, escorted by his three new pets, the third being poor Maria.

***

Hannock was inspecting his troops as he always had, his unusually large, solid gold eye-patch, glinting in the morning sunlight.

"Not good enough," he bellowed, "rust on swords, dull armour, pathetic. There'll be another inspection in three hours and if I find as much as one speck of rust on a weapon or one smudge on any armour, you're all on report, and the first duty will be to scrub the cesspit. Dismissed."

Jared strolled casually toward his captain.

"Good morning, Your Highness," said Hannock, bowing slightly.

Jared spoke quietly. "What rust? What smudged armour? They were immaculate."

Hannock looked at Jared and raised his eyebrows, "You know that, and I know that, but they don't know that."

"Of course they do, so why?" asked Jared.

"They all think that since I lost my eye I've become a little… eccentric, so if that's what they think, who am I to disappoint them?" Hannock really was milking the subject of his battle scars.

"I think you suffered more damage *inside* your head than outside," said Jared.

"What! How dare you, Sir?"

They both began to laugh.

"What do you think of the new patch, Jared?" Hannock turned his head to the side, to allow Jared a better look at his newly acquired adornment. "The king presented me with it."

"I know, Hannock, I was there," said Jared with a sigh.

"Bravest soldier that ever served the crown he said, saved his son's life, he said."

"I know," and looking again he added, "Shut it Hannock."

Hannock had not gone mad, well no worse than he always had been, he was just teasing his best friend, as he always did.

"Don't you think it's a bit big though?" asked Jared.

"King Tamor said I should wear it as one would a medal. Show it as a badge of honour, awarded for bravery, above and beyond the call of duty."

They were joined shortly after by their three loyal companions. Lodren stood, pushing his stomach forward, to allow everyone the best possible view of a magnificent belt buckle he now wore, solid gold of course. "Look at this," he said proudly, "King Tamor gave it to me for helping out with your *brother* problem, even though I made a bit of a mess of his courtyard."

"I think you did a bit more than help out, Lodren," said Jared, "and the courtyard has been repaired now," he added looking around.

Hannock turned to Grubb. "And what was your award, Master Grubb?" he asked.

"Didn't want anything. Not too keen on gold, bit too glinty for my liking."

"But the king must have given you something?" asked Jared.

"Well of course he did," said Grubb, slightly embarrassed as he looked across the courtyard. Tethered to a post at the far end, was a pure white pony. "His name's Buster."

Ever since the day he first climbed on the back of Lodren's mule, he had secretly wanted a steed of his own. A horse would have been far too big for him, but Buster was perfect.

"You're a very nice Vikkery, Mr Grubb. He couldn't have a better master," said Lodren.

"Alright, alright so I got a pony, it's only to help me carry stuff, didn't really want it but the king insisted." Nobody was fooled by Grubb's grumpy attitude.

Jared looked into Faylore's eyes. "And you, my dear Lady?" he asked as he bowed.

"Nothing," she replied calmly, "I have no need of anything. You are all safe, that is reward enough for me."

Jared stepped forward and embraced her. "You really are the most benevolent person I have ever had the privilege to meet, Faylore."

Faylore was beginning to understand the ways that Borellians showed their affection toward one another, and allowed Jared his moment. "Thank you," she said, feeling slightly uncomfortable as she pushed him away gently. She was a kind person, but not a tactile one.

A guard approached the gathering and, bowing firstly to Jared and then Faylore, announced, "The king requests your presence, Your Highness, all five of you, in the throne room, at your earliest convenience." Bowing again, he marched away.

Speculation over the reason why was not entered into as Hannock, standing bolt upright and pulling down the front of his tunic, spoke for them all, "No time like the present."

Entering the throne room, the usual etiquette was followed. King Tamor sat on his throne and six chairs had been arranged in a semi-circle facing him, one already occupied by Emnor.

Tamor spoke first. "Emnor and I have been discussing the situation with Karrak."

"Chop his bloody head off!" Unusually, it was not Hannock who offered this suggestion but Grubb who, on this occasion, had beaten him to it. "Sorry, Majesty, but he's a wrong 'un. You can see it in his eyes, he's barkin' mad."

Tamor closed his eyes and, placing his hand across his face, gave a loud sigh. If this was the general feeling of his subjects, it appeared that his youngest son was, in fact, doomed. "I understand your feelings, Master Grubb, but surely there must be some other course of action. He is, after all, my son, and I would prefer something a little less harsh than decapitation."

"My people are greatly skilled in healing the sick, Tamor, but I fear that your son is beyond our help. His sickness is of the mind and what Grubb is trying to say, although rather crudely, is what we all believe," Faylore lowered her head apologetically.

"He's not very nice. He hurt Captain Hannock and he tried to kill Mr Jared, I mean, the prince." This was just about as harsh as Lodren could be, when speaking ill of anyone.

Tamor looked at Hannock. "I know your feelings toward Karrak. The others have had their say and it is only fair that you be allowed to speak your mind, Captain, and please, speak freely."

Hannock took a deep breath and composed himself. His hatred of Karrak was immeasurable, but he understood that a torrent of verbal abuse would serve no purpose. Pausing for a moment, he spoke slowly. "Your Majesty. I have seen your son raised in these very halls since the day he was born. I have witnessed his cruelty to your subjects. He delights in the fear and pain of others and he will not stop. Even if we discover his location, capturing him will be difficult, we have already had a demonstration of his power," he placed his fingertips against his eye-patch, emphasising his meaning, and continued, "it took the five of us combined to stop him last time, and even then we could not apprehend him. But, if we succeed next time he should be buried deep in the dungeon, chained, gagged and blindfolded for the rest of his natural life at the very least. If, that is, you cannot bring it upon yourself to have him executed for treason."

Tamor sat back in his throne. The condemning statements from the four had horrified him, *would no-one come to the defence of his son?* He now gave Jared a pleading look. *Surely his brother did not want him to die, or to be caged like an animal for life?*

"Father, if we do find him, he will not surrender. He will fight and if we do not kill him during that fight, he should be executed on arrival back in Borell."

"But he's your brother!" implored Tamor.

"No, Father, he *was* my brother. He is now a murderer and a traitor. He would slaughter you and I, given the slightest opportunity, just to gain your throne, and after that, every loyal subject in the kingdom would suffer his tyranny. No, Father, I can protect him no longer... he must die."

Emnor rose from his chair and approached the king, offering what little comfort he could. "I am sorry, my liege, but I warned you many years ago that this was inevitable."

Tamor, although silent, had begun to cry, tears streaming down his chubby cheeks. Despite Karrak's abhorrent behaviour he was still Tamor's son, and Tamor loved him. Wracked with guilt, he excused himself and left their company.

Emnor now faced the companions. "There is something that I must discuss with you all, a secret that has been kept by the Administration for many years. It is called the Elixian Soul." He regaled the tale of the Elixian Soul to the companions, who all now sat open-mouthed, unsure of what to say next.

Hannock spoke first, "So what you're saying is, that not only does Karrak *want* to find the Soul, but that he is actually *destined* to find it?"

"That is the prophecy of the scroll, yes," replied Emnor.

"If you were to destroy the scroll, would it destroy the prophecy?" asked Faylore.

"If one destroys a map does it mean that the buried treasure will not exist?" Emnor asked in return.

"Well, you say you're the only one who knows where the Soul is, so if we lock you away, he'll never get it?" offered Grubb.

"Hadn't thought of that," replied Emnor, smiling at him.

"You can't lock up Mr Emnor!" exclaimed Lodren.

"I'm sure he didn't mean it like that," said Hannock, but looking across at Grubb added, "then again."

After some time, with many ideas falling flat, Emnor admitted that he intended to face Karrak alone once he was discovered.

"He'll kill you!" exclaimed Jared.

"Thank you for the vote of confidence, Your Highness. I do have powers of my own you know."

"I understand that, Emnor, but you don't have the same violent nature. You use your magic for defence, he uses his for attack. He likes to maim and wound, torture and victimise in the most sadistic way."

"You can go off people you know, Jared," Emnor said with a frown on his face.

"But you know I'm right, Emnor, facing him alone would be madness. Emnor, you can't…"

"I'm not going to stand there and simply let him destroy me, just test his strength a little."

"Roast 'is nuts, Emnor. Just *roast* 'em." Grubb had such a way with words.

CHAPTER 13

Months passed and quickly turned into years. Promises of great riches and reward brought no information to the kingdom regarding the whereabouts of the fugitive Karrak. Signs had been posted in every village warning that, if seen, villagers should avoid any contact with him and report it to the guard immediately. But those signs had now faded and become worn by the elements. Peace was upon Borell once more, not even reports of bandits on the roads reached the kingdom which, although good news, concerned both Tamor and Jared alike.

Emnor's visits continued. He too had nothing to report on the subject of Karrak, but feared that this would not be the case forever.

Lodren and Grubb had made their home in Borell. Lodren had proved invaluable in the castle kitchen and Grubb was still doing… something. Nobody seemed to know exactly what he got up to day after day.

Combat training had commenced one morning and one of the guards had received a nasty wound to his forearm. Hannock, inspecting the wound, summoned the court physician.

"No, Sir, I'll be fine. Give me an hour to get it cleaned up and I'll be back."

268

"A big man like you! Afraid of the court physician are we?" asked Hannock.

"Not at all, Sir, but it'll heal quicker if I..." he stopped, obviously not wanting to finish the sentence.

"If you what?" asked Hannock.

"Nothing, Sir. Look, it's not going to stop bleeding by itself. May I take that hour?"

Hannock, intrigued by the guard's reluctance to divulge any information, dismissed him.

Wrapping a cloth around his own arm, the guard hurried off and on rounding a corner, was rapidly pursued by Hannock. He tailed the man through the grounds and out of the gates, pausing occasionally to secrete himself behind various obstacles. Five minutes later the soldier, hesitating for a moment and furtively glancing around him, dashed between the flaps of a large tent.

Hannock marched after him. He didn't like mysteries and, on reaching the tent, yanked the flap to one side. Pausing briefly, he placed his other hand on his hip, amazed at what he was witnessing. The guard was sitting cross-legged on the floor, his arm outstretched, and in front of him, his hands pressed firmly against his patient's wound, was Grubb. "Grubb! What are you doing?" exclaimed Hannock.

Grubb gave Hannock a filthy look, "Mind your own bloody business, go on, sod off!" he snapped.

Grubb, as miserable and grouchy as he was, had set up a kind of hospital. Managing to keep the secret, he had treated many cuts, gashes and various other wounds and abrasions, not solely for soldiers, but all residents of Borell. It was his way of feeling useful. He never sought praise or monetary compensation for his actions and most times, even grumbled if offered thanks or a gift. The smallest, grumpiest member of the companions had the biggest heart and most generous nature of them all.

Faylore's absences had become longer and more frequent. The companions understood that, as Queen of the Thedarians, her time with them was precious, but missed her greatly whenever she had to leave their company. Little did they know that the graceful, sometimes aloof queen, missed them all just as much, but had vowed to bring the ingrate Karrak, to justice. She had given instructions to her people that they, whilst being covert, should seek out the sorcerer, but never approach him and should notify her upon his discovery.

***

Faylore was strolling along one of the many trails with a few of her folk, calmly watching the sun set, when they heard a voice, sobbing in the distance. Without hesitation, they rushed to investigate. Parting the long grass, they discovered a man lying on the ground, slashed and bleeding, his wife crouched over him in a fervent attempt to stem the flow of blood from his fresh wounds. She gave a start at the appearance of Faylore and her kin.

"Please, we have nothing," she cried, terrified at the presence of the strangers.

"We are not here to harm you, my dear lady," Faylore assured her.

Looking across at one of her fellow Thedarians, Faylore nodded. His reaction was immediate and he stooped down to offer aid to the wounded villager. Two others took his wife gently by the arms and moved her to one side, allowing the first to work unimpeded. Faylore stepped forward and embraced her gently. This was most unusual, her fellow Thedarians confused by her actions. Faylore had studied the Borellians intently, and knew this to be a fitting gesture with which to instill trust. "What happened, were you attacked?" she asked.

"Yes, my lady," the woman replied, sobbing uncontrollably.

"Who did this to you?" asked Faylore.

"Some kind of beasts, my lady. We have no idea what they were, we've never seen anything like them before. A bit like wolves but not as big, and with no fur. We'd be dead if they hadn't been more interested in the mules. They tore them to shreds, ripping lumps of flesh from them while they were still alive. We just ran, but one of them swiped at my husband before we got away and did that to him," she pointed at her husband.

Faylore continued with her line of questioning. "How many were there?" she asked.

"Five, six, seven, I'm not sure my lady, it all happened so fast." She was now shaking.

Faylore reached into a pack and, removing a shimmering shawl, wrapped it around the woman's shoulders as she asked her next question. "Where did this happen?"

"About a mile to the south, my lady."

"Did you see where they came from?"

The villager's wife glanced from one Thedarian to the next, eyeing the weapons that they all carried. "No, you mustn't go after them. They're vicious, you'll get hurt, or worse. Loads of people have gone missing from the villages around these parts, now we know why. These things have been killing them."

"Do not worry about us, first we must get you to the safety of your village. That *is* where you were headed isn't it?"

The woman nodded.

The Thedarians tended to the villager's wounds, applying various pastes and poultices, before wrapping them in bandages, from yet another of their packs. Two now carried him between them, following Faylore. Returning their temporary wards to the relative safety of their village, the Thedarians headed back to the site of the attack. Very few words were spoken. They knew one another's thoughts on the matter, they were about to investigate the attack by these unknown, savage beasts. The return to the site had been much swifter without the burden of the wounded man and they now studied the tracks on the ground that had been left by the beasts. Faylore ran her fingers across one of the tracks. "I do not recognise these prints, do any of you?" she asked.

All shook their heads apart from one. He stepped forward, slightly unsure of what he was about to say. "I believe, Your Majesty, that these beasts were *created* rather than born. They have five pads, unlike a wolf, which as you know, has only four. I think that they were people, somehow changed into whatever they are now."

Faylore, despite how fanciful her kinsman's explanation sounded, was inclined to agree. Five fingers would become five toes, each toe becoming a pad.

"We shall follow the tracks," she said, and began to track them, with the aid of the others. After a few miles the tracks stopped. There were no trees, no hills, caves or tunnels, they simply ceased. "Impossible!" exclaimed

Faylore, "they can't have just disappeared." She continued in the direction the tracks were leading when suddenly the rest of her people gasped. She turned to look at them. "What is it?" she asked.

"You are invisible, Your Majesty, and not through the use of our ability," explained one of the Thedarians.

Faylore retraced her steps, and became visible to them again. "And now?" she asked.

"Visible, Your Majesty."

"Magic," Faylore deduced. "The whole area is hidden by magic. If we follow the direction of the tracks I am sure they will resume a little further on."

With this, they followed her as she ventured forth once more. Ten yards further on, the tracks resumed. Simultaneously, they all took the initiative to use their chameleonic ability, becoming just a shimmering hue in the darkness whilst tracking their prey. A cave was now visible and so, at the foot of the ridge in which it was set, were the beasts. They were patient as they watched the beasts that now scrabbled around in the dirt, growling and snapping at one another.

Hours passed until, at last, Faylore saw what she had so desperately wanted... Karrak strolled out of the cave. She longed to draw her bow and put an arrow between his eyes or charge and run him through with her silver, curved sword, in revenge for the harm he had done to her friends. It was rare for a Thedarian to feel such intense emotion and for a few moments she was overwhelmed. Regaining her composure, she gestured toward the others, and they all retreated silently.

Passing beyond the border of Karrak's magical shield, one of the group spoke. "Your Majesty, my understanding is that this Karrak and his animals are evil. Why do we not simply execute them?"

"It is not our place to condemn this sorcerer, regardless of his crimes," Faylore replied. "We must make haste to Borell. Their king has a decision to make."

They entered the gates of Borell Castle. As always, the reception committee consisted of her four companions, whose smiles quickly dissipated at the sight of Faylore's serious expression. They stood, hesitant, awaiting the bad news.

"Faylore?" said Jared questioningly.

"I've found him… I've found Karrak."

Hannock spun around, pointing at one of the guards, "You, ready my horse," and turning to another guard, "you fetch my armour," then to Faylore, "where is he?"

Jared grabbed Hannock by the arm, "Hannock, calm down, you can't go alone. Faylore hasn't even told us where he is yet."

Hannock was close to rage, "I don't care how far it is. He can be at the end of the world, it ends now. He took my eye, and now *I'm* going to take his life."

"My, dear Captain, five of you could not beat him last time. Honestly, what chance do you think you would have alone?" The companions turned to face the voice, it was Emnor.

"Keep your nose out of this, wizard, this is none of your affair," Hannock bellowed, "Trying to protect one of your own are you?"

Jared understood Hannock's frustration, but felt that it was time to save him from himself. "That's enough

Captain," he roared, "one more word from you and you'll be cooling off in a cell, do I make myself clear?"

Hannock screamed at the top of his voice, took a deep breath and kicked the ground. "Sorry, Jared," he said quietly. Looking at Emnor he bowed slightly, "My apologies, Master Emnor."

Emnor had not risen to the insult. The scars on Hannock's face and the loss of his eye meant that, Emnor felt, he need not apologise. Waving his hand in dismissal of the situation he merely said, "Stressful times, Hannock, we all need to blow off a little steam occasionally."

Hannock was mortified that he had allowed himself to erupt in such a way, and felt ashamed at his unwarranted insult of the honourable Emnor.

Emnor spoke again, "Maybe we should adjourn to the throne room, Jared, I'm sure your father will want to hear the news." Turning to the guards who, by order, had brought Hannock's horse and armour, he dismissed them, "He won't be needing those. Not yet anyway."

As they entered the throne room, the king rose from his seat. "This can't be good," he said, "especially if the twins are here," He looked between Jared and Hannock with an affectionate smile.

"It depends on your point of view, Father," said Jared, "Faylore has discovered Karrak's location."

The king flopped back heavily onto his throne. "Well, he had to surface sooner or later I suppose," he sighed.

Faylore explained how the discovery had been made, describing at length the presence of the transformed beasts, to make a point of Karrak's unyielding sadism.

"So what now?" asked the king, "Send an army after him to ensure his death?"

Emnor, trying to be sympathetic to Tamor's plight offered a suggestion. "Your Majesty, allow me to visit with Karrak alone. Perhaps I can reason with him. I know that neither I, nor anyone else, can turn him into the innocent he once was, but if we agree not to hunt him, on cessation of his practises, you could simply banish him?"

Tamor, slumped in his throne with his chin on his chest, raised his eyes to look at Emnor. "Banish? Simply? Do you think it so easy for a father to condemn his son?" he asked.

"I know it is not, Your Majesty, but it is better than the alternative."

"And what is the alternative, Master Emnor?"

"Chop his bloody head off, like I said before," Grubb answered, saving Emnor the trouble.

Jared stepped forward and took his father's hand, "I know this is difficult for you, Father, but Grubb is right, if he can't be stopped... he must be destroyed. Let Emnor try it his way and if he's unsuccessful..."

"We can bury him and then execute the sorcerer that notched up another murder." Grubb, although outspoken and abrupt was, of course, correct. The gathering turned to face Grubb. "If ye don't like what I have to say, don't ask me," said Grubb.

"Nobody asked you anyway!" exclaimed Lodren. So far he had had nothing to offer the conversation, but Lodren had timed his comment perfectly. Grubb simply shrugged his shoulders.

"You do realise, Emnor, Karrak won't like being threatened?" said Jared.

"Of course I do," Emnor replied.

"But you're still willing to face him, alone?" asked Hannock.

"He feels that his power is infinite and that a single wizard will not be a threat. If an army turns up to face him there can only be one of two results, one, he escapes again, or two, a lot of people die," Emnor folded his arms as if to rest his case.

"Well let's just hope he chooses to bugger off then," and Grubb, mimicking Emnor, also folded his arms.

***

Harley was dismayed. Reiggan Fortress, the place he had called home for the last four years, had changed, and not for the better. The once-sedate and relaxing atmosphere in which to dwell, had become one of suspicion and rumour that seemed to physically darken the halls and passageways of the formerly, much revered institution. Unfortunately, now every member of their secretive community was perceived with doubt as to their motives, by all outsiders. Each day he recalled the escape of the prince, and Master Barden's betrayal of the Administration.

Leaving his room, he headed along the passageways, nodding in acknowledgement as he passed others on the way to his destination. Looking furtively around, he quickly entered a room that was quite unremarkable. Dimly lit, Harley paused for a moment, to allow his sight to adjust. Approaching a bookcase at the far end, he glanced over his shoulder before reaching for a large tome and drawing it forward on the shelf by just a couple of inches. Suddenly there was a gentle scratching as the bookcase seemed to sink into the wall, before sliding to one side, revealing a narrow, dark passage. Stepping into the gloom, the bookcase slid back into place behind him, leaving Harley in pitch-black darkness. There was a click as, one by one, torches burst into flame along the walls as he walked along until he reached another door. Opening it, he blinked a few times, the light flooding the passageway as he entered the room. Benches were placed against the walls. Burners were placed on them, over which multi-coloured potions bubbled and steamed, producing incredible results. The steam from one potion became crystalline as it left the flask, turning to ice; another produced sparks that crackled faintly; and a third produced a small, but intense, green flame.

"You're late, Harley. You should have been here an hour ago."

"Had a few tasks to complete, for Emnor," Harley replied.

"That's Master Emnor to you, Harley."

Harley just looked at the young wizard, who had only meant it as a joke. Harley's sense of humour wasn't what it used to be, and he offered no response to the comment.

There were three young wizards present in the room, Harley being the fourth.

"So, have you made any progress?" asked Harley solemnly.

"Of course we have. We have gold, silver, platinum or copper."

"Who in their right mind would use copper?" Harley asked.

"Apparently it's the best thing to use if you're dedicated to fire spells," answered one of his fellow conspirators, a young wizard by the name of Xarran Althor, who also happened to be Harley's closest friend.

The discussion they were having was, of course, regarding the most suitable metal from which to make a wand. Frowned upon by the senior wizards as being unnecessary, the younger generation had discovered that, with the right wand, one could concentrate a spell. Rather than blowing up a whole tree with a fire spell it was possible to direct a flame at a single bough and sever it as cleanly as one would with a blade, only much faster, and with even greater precision. Many experiments had been carried out by the four, even to the point of trying to make a wand from various woods, which was preposterous, as the minute one tried to use a fire spell, the wand would be incinerated.

The manufacture of the individual wand was more a love than an art. These were not just metal rods, but intricate filigrees of the purest of metals. Imbued with magic and encrusted with semi-precious stones they were not only beautiful, they were also virtually indestructible.

"The old fellows won't like the idea of us making these you know. They'll probably ban us from ever using them," continued Xarran.

"You can't refer to them as 'the old boys', Xarran. They are learned, senior wizards and have been perfecting their skills since long before we were born, don't forget that," snapped Harley.

"Don't get me wrong, Harley, I have the utmost respect for our tutors, but they are so opposed to change that it just becomes a little frustrating at times. I tried to broach the subject of wands with Gambillon last week and he cut me dead, said they were for amateurs."

"Do you realise how old he is, Xarran?" asked Harley.

"I'd say a little older than the mountain this fortress is set in, about half a million."

Harley shook his head. He knew how talented a wizard Xarran was, and that one day he would be great, but he also knew how stubborn and dismissive he could be when the mood took him. As much so as the seniors he was denouncing, without him realising his own hypocrisy. To avoid what could become an unnecessarily lengthy debate, Harley returned to the subject of the manufacturing of wands and turned to the third attendee, a quiet, almost withdrawn individual, by the name of Alexander Hardman, a name that really didn't suit his diminutive stature and submissive nature. He was though, in fact, the most intellectual of the group and his thoughts and ideas on the improvements that could be made to enhance the use of magic were revolutionary, it being his idea to investigate the use of wands and the materials that should be used in their manufacture. "So what's your latest discovery, Alex?" he asked.

"It's Alexander, not Alex," he replied without looking up from his work, "And in answer to your question, I've deduced that gold is the best for earthbound spells, I should have realised that sooner."

He gave no explanation for his deduction, and no-one ever questioned his reasoning. He was fairly touchy when it came to questions that delved too deeply, or criticism, his usual response being to simply leave the room and not come back for hours or sometimes days. However, when he was in attendance, he made a huge difference to their discoveries.

The fourth of the group was Maddleton Drake. At first, not appearing to be the brightest of students, Drake was with them for one simple reason. Known as Mad Drake, his name suited him perfectly. He would try anything, no test or dare was too great for him and he had the scars to prove it. As soon as a new wand was fashioned, Drake would be there, hand outstretched, ready for its inaugural test. One could say he was the stupid one of the four but compared to you or I he was still a borderline genius when it came to magic.

"How did you make your discovery then, Alexander?" Harley asked.

"That would be me," said Drake, looking a little sheepish.

"Why, what happened?"

"Well, I was supposed to just move a stone across the room, and it went a little bit wrong."

Xarran leaned against a bench and folded his arms. "Went a bit wrong? You took half the floor *up* and half the wall *down*, Drake."

Drake smiled, seeing the funny side. "I can't help being such a powerful wizard, can I?"

"But…" interrupted Alexander, "… it did prove that I was correct."

"Oh it did that alright," said Xarran, "I'm just amazed that nobody heard it, I was waiting for half of the Administration to come bursting through the door."

Harley's role within the group was not only to organise their dubious experiments but to offer security.

He spent more and more prolonged periods in the company of Emnor, and although he would never divulge any sensitive or privileged information to his friends, it did allow them a little breathing room knowing who would be where, and when.

"I'll leave you to it, I have to meet with Master Emnor," said Harley "Make sure you're out of here in the next hour."

The others nodded, and Harley headed back down the dark passageway.

***

Reaching Emnor's chambers, Harley knocked gently on the door, and entered when instructed to.

"Always prompt, Harley, I do so like that in a person," said Emnor.

Harley nodded his head once in acknowledgement of Emnor's admiration, but said nothing.

"I'll get straight to the point, Harley. I think it time to take an apprentice, and I'd like it to be you." Harley was surprised by this, and it showed in his face. "It's not as bad as you think," continued Emnor, "Your duties would be much the same as they are now, but I see great potential in you and after all, we old ones can't live forever however good our longevity is. We need young blood in the Administration." He sat forward and raised his eyebrows, waiting for Harley's response.

"I really don't know what to say, Master Emnor... yes?"

"Yes will do nicely for now. But as you've accepted, I hope your conversational skills increase dramatically in the future," he smiled.

Harley relaxed a little and returned the smile. "Of course, Master Emnor."

"Just one thing, Harley, before we go any further… you won't be needing the Order of Corrodin anymore. I'll take that from you now shall I?"

Harley's heart began to pound, *how did Emnor know?* "I beg your pardon, Master Emnor?"

"The Order of Corrodin. It's on a chain around your neck under your robes and has been for months, oh, and how are the wand-making sessions going, made any progress?" Harley's mouth was moving but making no sound. "Are you alright, Harley? Why don't you sit down? Oh don't tell me you're having second thoughts, you really would make a first class apprentice," Emnor's smile widened.

Harley, almost without thinking, placed his hand inside his robes. Removing the chain on which the Order of Corrodin was secured, he handed it to Emnor without saying a word.

"You see, after a while, Harley, you won't always need to be able to read someone's mind to know what's going on in their head, and you definitely won't need an amulet to stop others reading yours. Feeling better?"

"I never stole it, Master Emnor. At first I just put it on to keep it safe and then never thought to take it off again."

"It's a magic amulet, dear boy, makes you think you need to wear it to keep yourself safe from prying eyes and ears, it's not your fault. You had a secret, or at least you thought you had, so it just fed on it."

"About that, Master Emnor, it was all my idea, the others…" Harley began hurriedly.

"Calm down, Harley, I don't care about your wand experiments, as a matter of fact I'm quite intrigued. I'd like to see how you're progressing, I mean you've been at it for months now, you and your three friends that is."

Harley was stumped. Emnor knew everything, but he had no idea how, as he sat there staring blankly into the eyes of the old wizard who was still smiling at him.

"Still interested in being my apprentice?" asked Emnor.

"Of course, Master Emnor, it would be an honour," Harley was slightly shaken with how transparent he was to Emnor but had managed to compose himself just enough, in order to reply.

"Excellent," said Emnor clapping his hands together.

"When will my instruction begin, Master?" asked Harley.

"Begin? Begin! We started months ago, Harley. I've drawn up the contract, you just need to sign it." Emnor unrolled a scroll that was lying on his desk and, turning it toward Harley, handed him a quill. "Just sign it at the bottom, dear boy, administration rules, makes it official, just there above my own signature," he said wagging his finger in the general direction of the scroll.

"Forgive me, Master… but, a contract?"

"Of course, stops all the nonsense at a later date should you get, oh I don't know, incinerated, dismembered, crushed, that sort of thing."

Dismembered… incinerated? thought Harley.

"Don't look so concerned, Harley, just sign it... it's been weeks since anyone's been dismembered."

A look of alarm came across Harley's face as his eyes shot from the contract to Emnor, who now had a smirk on his face. Brilliant? Yes. Wise? Yes, but with a wicked sense of humour embroiled within his genius. Emnor did like to tease his pupils.

Harley, realising that he had walked into Emnor's joviality trap, sighed, and signing the contract, handed it to Emnor.

"Perfect," stated Emnor and, levitating it before him, promptly turned the scroll into ash in mid-air.

The look of confusion on Harley's face was a sight to behold as he sat there open-mouthed, trying to work out the relevance of the scroll's incineration. Emnor, placing his hand on the corner of his desk, leaned forward. "Claptrap," he said.

"Sorry," said Harley, more confused than ever.

"Absolute claptrap. As if signing a piece of parchment is going to make you any more loyal. It's the symbolism, dear boy. You thought it would prove your loyalty, and it did, but your *word* is good enough for me, will you give me that?"

"But of course, Master," replied Harley, nodding fervently.

"Good, let us begin."

"What... now?" asked Harley.

"Indeed now, that's why I brought you here. There is a task you must perform for me immediately."

Harley, without realising, sat forward. Apprehensive yes, but also with an unexpected yearning for his task to be revealed.

"Now this is a secret that only you and I must share, Harley. You must not divulge anything you see or hear within my chambers, is that understood?"

"Of course, Master Emnor," replied Harley rising from his chair as if to attention.

Emnor strode across the large office and took hold of a screen, close to the wall at the far end. Behind it there was a bench, but whatever was on it, had been covered with two large horse-blankets. Emnor took hold of the corner of one of them and turning to Harley, quietly uttered, "Remember your oath, *not a word to anyone.*" Drawing back the blankets, he revealed his doppelganger. Harley's eyes widened as he looked from it, to Emnor and back again rather nervously. "Don't worry, Harley, it's just a copy. I have a mission on which to embark, a very dangerous mission and by using this extension I mean to survive it."

"I don't understand, Master."

"Good. If you did it would mean that you had been dabbling with arcane magic... or even necromancy."

"Master Emnor, I would never..."

Emnor waved his hand to dismiss Harley's protests of innocence.

"I know, I know. Calm down, Harley, I wasn't accusing you, *I need your help.*"

"Anything, Master Emnor, just ask."

"I cannot tell you the details of my mission at the moment, but I will tell you this, if you fail in this task… my life will be forfeit."

Harley looked aghast at Emnor's statement. He had been an apprentice for barely ten minutes and now the Head of the Administration was about to put his life in his hands.

"But, Master, what if I don't, I mean, what if I can't…" A slight panic had taken Harley, but it was nothing that Emnor had not been expecting.

"Calm down, Harley," he said in a serene, but also stern tone. "The task is simple enough, but your concentration must be unwaning if I am to live to tell you the tale of my adventures when I return."

Harley took a deep breath that swelled his chest, held it for a moment, and looking at Emnor breathed out slowly and audibly for his benefit. "What will you have me do, Master?" he asked, suddenly sounding very mature and official.

"That's my boy," said Emnor and patted Harley gently on the shoulder. Opening his desk drawer, Emnor took out a velvet pouch and placed it on the desktop. "This, Harley, is the Heart of Ziniphar," and removing it from the pouch Emnor held, in the palm of his hand, the largest ruby that Harley had ever seen.

"Master, it's magnificent… what is it? I mean, Sir, other than a ruby?"

"Very astute, Harley, to realise that it is more than it at first appears. This gem, when placed directly above the heart, binds the soul to the body, keeping it pure, and for a while can actually protect one from death itself."

"How, Master?"

"Forgive me, Harley, time is pressing. We shall have to save that discussion for another day."

"As you wish, Master, but it is mesmerising, it must be unique?"

"No, it has a twin… but its twin's purpose is the complete opposite of this, it loves nothing more than to cause suffering and death. As I said… another day."

Harley, struggling to take his eyes from the Heart of Ziniphar, looked at Emnor. "How are we going to use it, Master?"

"Sharp as a knife. I knew you were, that's why I chose you."

Harley tilted his head slightly to one side, waiting for Emnor's answer.

"I'm going to lie on the bed. Once I am asleep I can take control of my double, then *you* must place the Heart of Ziniphar above the heart of my real body.

"But, Master, you could have done that yourself."

"Oh no, no, no, the gem might try to bind my soul to that fake body and that would be disastrous. Last time I controlled it I kept getting yearnings for rotting cabbage and turnips. I can't live my life like that, and every now and then I kept rubbing mud on my face, well when I say mud…"

"Why on earth would you want to rub mud on your face?"

"Never mind, just trust me when I say it's not the worst thing that happened," he said, inadvertently rubbing his buttocks.

Emnor crossed the room lay on the bed and closed his eyes. Harley felt a little awkward. *Should he leave and come back later once Emnor was asleep, or should he just keep quiet and wait?* Barely a minute had passed before the question was answered for him... *neither*. Harley started a little as the fake Emnor suddenly sat up in his peripheral vision.

"That didn't take too long did it, Harley? Take the Heart of Ziniphar and place it on my chest, my real chest that is, well my own chest... you know what I mean."

Harley placed the ruby on the chest of the reposed Emnor and turned to face... the other one.

"Now, once I depart, Harley, you must watch the Heart of Ziniphar as a hawk watches its prey, never take your eyes from it. Now it may darken slightly but don't worry too much, that's to be expected, but if it darkens to virtual blackness it means that I am in great danger. Take this parchment Harley." Reaching inside his robes, Emnor produced a small pre-prepared scroll and handed it to his apprentice. "Should the gem reach the point of only showing the slightest hue of red, you must recite the incantation on that scroll immediately, thrice, no less, do you understand?"

"Yes, Master Emnor... but what if it turns black?"

"Please do not allow that to happen, Harley... that will mean that I am dead." Pulling a chair across to his unconscious body, he steered Harley toward it. "Remember, Harley, under no circumstances must you avert your eyes from the Heart of Ziniphar."

With that said, there was a shimmer of light, a slight wisp of smoke, and Emnor vanished.

***

The old man shuffled through the village undetected. He was not trying to avoid the gaze of anyone in particular he was just such a pitiful sight that nobody turned a hair as he passed them in the rain. Dressed in a hessian cloak, that was not far from being a rag, he made his way along the muddy main road, his head bowed to the ground, his cloak raised slightly above the mire revealing his unshod feet. The villagers simply took him for a beggar, and begging was frowned upon by the locals, even the poorest of them. Pausing for a moment, the old man turned to a woman who was deep in conversation with another. Without raising his head he spoke. Surprisingly, he had a deep clear voice that took the woman by surprise, as she had not noticed his approach. "Forgive my interruption, madam," he said politely.

At this, the woman turned to face him and immediately recoiled with obvious repulsion, drawing her shawl tightly around her shoulders as if to shield herself from this bedraggled vagabond. "What do you want? Go away, you'll get no handouts here, beggar!" she snapped.

"Rightly so, madam, it would be most distasteful for anyone to disturb an upstanding citizen such as yourself, but I am afraid I must. However, I would not beg, I merely need the location of your local tavern, as I am a stranger in these parts," said the old man.

"Why am I not surprised? Another grog-swilling old layabout. Find work, clean yourself up. You never know, you might like being clean and wearing boots to keep your feet warm," she sneered. There was no need for the woman's tirade of verbal abuse toward the old man, after all, he had simply asked directions.

"My apologies, madam, I meant no offence, good day to you." The old man resumed his shuffling through the mud, but had taken just a few steps when he waved his hand gently from side to side beneath his cloak, a motion that was undetected by any prying eyes. The woman behind him immediately placed her hand flat against her chest and gasped as if fighting for breath. Her eyes widened as she grabbed at the friend before her. She began to cough uncontrollably as she slowly sank to her knees, the whites of her eyes turning red due to her sudden asphyxiation, then with a final gurgling rasp, she fell back onto the ground, stone dead. The old man snorted and continued on his way.

After a few minutes he entered the shoddy-looking inn, 'The Hangman's Noose' it was named, a name that suited the dank atmosphere with which he was greeted. The barkeep leaned forward and placed his elbows on the bar. "What do you want?" he asked. He was not being rude, this was his way of asking his patrons what they would like to drink. There was no such thing as polite conversation or etiquette in this establishment, or even indeed, the village.

"Port, best you have," replied the old man, throwing a gold coin on the bar in front of his host.

On seeing the coin, the barkeep's attitude changed. "Of course, Sir, take a seat I'll bring it over, anything else?" he asked, lifting a goblet from under the bar and wiping it with the cleanest rag he could lay his hands on, before reaching for a bottle behind him.

"Yes. Information," was the reply.

"Oh well now you see, Sir, information costs a bit more than port around here, dangerous, if you know what I mean?"

The old man once again reached inside his cloak and gently withdrew a coin purse that appeared to be well stocked. He placed it on the table in front of him and patted it gently.

"Danger is immaterial. What is your price, innkeeper?" he asked, gesturing for his host to take the seat directly opposite his.

As he sat, the innkeeper tried in vain to get a glimpse of the stranger's features. He thought it was an old man, but his face was obscured by the hood of the tattered cloak, and had been, since he had first entered. Unnerving to most, but not to the barkeep, who was used to dealing with 'dubious' characters. "Now what would you like to know, Sir?" he asked, reaching toward the coin purse. In the blink of an eye, a dagger slammed into the table between it, and his hand. He snatched his hand away, but it was quite obvious that if the hand had been the old man's target, he would not have missed.

"I think that it is only fair, barkeep, that the information should come before the payment, do you not agree?" he asked. The barkeep nodded nervously.

"I wish to know the whereabouts of one Thadius Dethmold, also referred to as Mr Death."

"Never heard of him, sorry, friend, you've got the wrong village. Enjoy your port, Sir!" The barkeep had jumped up from his chair the instant the name had been spoken, obviously startled by the old man's enquiry.

"Sit down," said the old man sternly, "I'm not finished with you yet."

"I can't help you, Sir. I'm really sorry but I can't, you must have heard wrong."

He was desperately trying to stop the old man talking and held out his hands, making patting gestures as if to shush him, now almost in a panic, his head wheeling from side to side to make sure they were not being spied upon.

"You know the man, and you know where I can find him... and you *are* going to tell me."

"And what exactly, do you want of this... Mr Death?" The voice had come from the other side of the room. It was calm, but somehow, intimidating.

The old man however, was not intimidated. "That is my own business, Sir... and his, should I make his acquaintance," he replied.

The stranger rose from his seat and strolled across the inn. The barkeep, seizing his chance, made himself scarce, all thought of remuneration forgotten.

A tall man of slim build, the stranger took what had been the barkeep's seat and, reclining slightly, placed his feet on the table. "Thadius Dethmold, at your service," he said with a hiss in his voice. As he spoke a second man appeared behind him and, pulling across a chair, sat next to Dethmold. "Choose your next words very carefully, old man, they could be your last," said Dethmold. The old man never spoke. His face still hidden by his hood, he sat silently, waiting to see how this game would play out. "Now I'll be asking the questions, and you'll be answering them, alright, old man? Firstly, give me your name."

"Who I am, at present, is unimportant. What I want however, is vital to your wellbeing," replied the old man.

The thug who had joined Dethmold at the table grabbed the dagger that was still embedded in the table top. "When the boss asks you a question, you answer it or

I'll open your throat and get the words out myself, understand?" he growled.

The old man held the palm of his hand toward Dethmold's henchman, who began to shake violently. He clasped his hands to the side of his head and screamed in pain as blood began to seep from his eyes and nose. Dethmold tried to move, but found that some unseen force was pinning him to his chair, painlessly, but firmly.

The thug shook violently, the blood now streaming from all facial orifices until, with a loud crack, the shaking stopped, as did the man's heart.

Dethmold was a thief, a torturer and a murderer who did not scare easily, until now. Now, he was terrified.

***

The old man stood up and arched his back, as if he were stretching after a long slumber. A black smoke started to emanate from his body and after a few seconds, enveloped him until he was completely obscured. The longest ten seconds of Dethmold's life passed as he watched the smoke dissipate, but now the old man was gone. Before him stood a giant of a man dressed in immaculate black robes embroidered with runes of gold thread, his eyes were closed. As his eyes opened he began to speak. "I am Lord Karrak... from this day forward, *you*, will serve *me*."

With the slightest of hand gestures, Dethmold, chair included, was levitated by Karrak to eye level. Karrak stepped forward and leaned in order to be nose to nose with his captive. "I hear that you can find things, Dethmold, that you can procure that which is unobtainable. I do hope these rumours are true as I have travelled a considerable distance and would hate to have had a wasted journey… time is so precious after all; don't you agree?"

Dethmold did not answer, he couldn't answer. Still pinned to the chair, his mind was racing. *Who was this sorcerer? What did he want,* and most of all, *what did he want from him?*

Karrak held out his hand and wiggled his finger in front of Dethmold's face. "Well answer me, dog, cat got your tongue?" Karrak chuckled at his own, unintentional witticism. "Oh that was quite amusing, dog, cat, got your…"

Turning away, he waved his hand, and the chair, complete with occupant came crashing to the floor, breaking the legs and spilling Dethmold onto the floor. Regaining the use of his limbs, Dethmold rose to his feet and glanced at the door. Karrak still had his back to him, *maybe he could make his escape before the sorcerer had time to react, but what would be the consequences should he not make that escape?*

"You won't even make it to the door," Karrak said quietly. Turning to face Dethmold, he pointed at the corpse slumped on the table. "That's your alternative, Thadius, now choose. *Serve me,* or *die.*" His immense stature and calculated speech, made the sorcerer all the more menacing.

Dethmold, not taking his eyes from Karrak, dropped to his knees and put his hands together as if about to pray. He took a deep breath. "What do you wish of me? My Lord," he added to the question.

"Wise decision, Dethmold, very wise indeed, but don't patronise me and do not try to sound intellectual, we both know that you're as educated as a slug and let's face it, only half as attractive."

Dethmold was unused to fear, well, not his own anyway. Fear and intimidation were the tools of his profession, a profession he found to be not only very lucrative, but with which he had a great affinity. Now however, he was at the point of someone else's figurative blade, and for the first time in his wretched life, he understood the terror that he had driven into the hearts of his own victims for so many years. A terror that diminished into insignificance, any of the few emotions he had ever felt. These thoughts took mere seconds as Karrak retook his seat before him and leaned forward, his elbows resting on his knees.

"I seek allies, Dethmold. Not mere scum such as you obviously. I seek the company of others like myself, those with a proficiency with magic. Yes, I could find them myself, but I am only one man and as I have already explained, my time is precious, I can spare none for reconnaissance. That's why I need you, or at least someone like you. Do not be fooled, Dethmold, betray or fail me and your passing will not be as quick as your little friend here. There are far worse things than death, of that I can assure you, and you can be replaced, should the need arise."

Dethmold turned his head. The dead man's blood had oozed into a pool on the table top and was now beginning to drip onto the floor beside him. He closed his eyes and bowed his head to his new master, resigned to his unwilling servitude.

Thus was the first alliance formed, decided by a single party, not by mutual agreement. During those few short moments, Dethmold could see no benefit toward himself. Now, as he grovelled at the feet of his new master, he realised that as long as Karrak lived, the future would be gilded to *his* advantage.

***

Days turned into weeks as Dethmold's venturing took him far and wide in his attempt to hear even the faintest of whispers concerning mages, wizards or the like. Under instruction from his new master, he would make no attempt to contact or even venture near, any area, in which such a person may dwell. Firstly, it may antagonise them and, secondly, should Dethmold be killed, Karrak would have to recruit another suitable candidate for the position and, despite his boast, knew that there were actually very few that possessed the knowledge or guile to perform the duties he had laid at the feet of the now, subservient Dethmold.

With each report, Karrak would once more disguise himself as the old man and immediately depart The Hangman's Noose, having made it a sort of base from which to oversee any progress that was made by Dethmold or his lackeys. The conversations held within the walls of the inn were always guarded, as Karrak's occupation was not a permanent one. Two or three days a week, the old man would shuffle through the door and study his surroundings for a moment, before transforming into his true form. The innkeeper proved to be of no inconvenience as, strangely enough, he had mysteriously disappeared on the day of Karrak's very first visit. Very rarely did Karrak return to the inn on the same day that he received new information regarding 'one of his own'. Dethmold had found five who may be of interest to his master, but Karrak was impatient for news of more, many more. Frequently, due to lack of information, Dethmold had been flung across the room, either with the use magic, or by brutal, physical attacks by Karrak, infuriated by his ineptitude.

Once a bully and tormentor, the now nervous shell of the one referred to as 'Mr Death' so many times in the past, approached his master, head bowed facing the ground, too fearful to look him in the eye. "Lord Karrak..." he began, "I have word of one of your kind camped near Barnetts Hill about twenty miles from here."

Karrak was studying parchments that he had laid out on the table, and without even glancing up, he replied, "Oh really? Well I hope you are more reliably informed than you were the last time Thadius. My time was wasted discovering nothing more than an old tramp living a squalid existence, in a hole excavated beneath a tree. Not his fault that my time was wasted I took pity on him. Death was a release for him, he'd suffered long enough."

"You killed him, my Lord?" asked Dethmold.

"As I said, Thadius, I released him from his painful existence. Take care, for if this is another waste of my time..." He grabbed Dethmold by the hair and pulled his head down, slamming his face into the table, "... you may be next."

Karrak rose from his chair. The familiar black smoke enveloped his body and after a few seconds, there stood the bedraggled old man. Not as impressive in stature as Karrak's true form, but just as imposing when one looked into his cold, grey eyes. "Barnetts Hill you say?"

"Yes, my Lord, just east of the nearby wood." Dethmold still, did not look up.

Karrak lowered his voice to a deep menacing whisper and spoke slowly, "Hope that you do not see me again this day, Thadius. If this is another fool's errand it will prove unpleasant for you." The old man turned and headed through the door.

Stepping outside he surveyed the village with which he had been so disgusted on his first visit, it had changed dramatically. No more were its inhabitants standing on the street gossiping about one another, blood could be seen in puddles on the ground and the facades of many of the remaining buildings were blackened and charred. Very few had escaped the carnage that had befallen Cheadleford. Karrak had attacked the village simply as a statement. Question his power or authority and pay with your life. Dethmold had been forced to witness the slaughter, lest he forget to whom he was now enslaved.

Despite the atrocities that Dethmold had witnessed, one confusion remained in his mind. Not once, since his first appearance in Cheadleford, had Karrak left The Hangman's Noose as himself, always choosing to disguise himself as the old man, prior to his departure. Dethmold never mentioned it to any of his gang of ruffians. They were mercenaries after all, and he was sure that any one of them would try to curry favour with Karrak, given half a chance.

Karrak strode along the lane for a short distance, glancing around occasionally to ensure he was not being watched, before waving his hand in a circular motion, and vanishing.

***

Having attended to his sinister, sordid business, Karrak, later that day, returned to his cave.

He removed parchments and scrolls from his robes, not the tattered robes of the old man but his own, and placed them on one of the tables laid out within the cave. His pets were still outside snarling and yelping at one another, much to his annoyance. The wildlife was beginning to avoid the area, detecting the danger from these carnivorous predators. Karrak deduced that the fuss was due to hunger and, as he had made them, felt a warped responsibility to feed them. He stepped from his cave, causing most of the beasts to back away from him but a few remained and slinked around his feet. He leaned down and slapped one, the only one that wore a collar, as if petting it. "What's the matter, Barden, hungry?" he asked. He grabbed another that had just leaned against his leg. "And who were you?" he asked, "Who cares anyway?"

As the words left his lips, he drew out a large dagger and drove it through the top of the beast's skull, killing it instantly. Its body went limp, and Karrak threw it down the gentle slope, with a little laugh. Holding his arms out to his sides, he bowed and whispered, "Dinner is served."

Over the next few hours, Karrak studied the abundance of literature with which he had returned. All was quiet for some time, until the familiar growls and snarls of his pets met his ears once more. *What was disturbing them this time?* The answer came without his investigation, as suddenly from outside he heard the voice of a man announcing.

"I am Emnor, I will speak with you cave dweller."

***

300

King Tamor paced back and forth. "But why? Why now? It makes no sense."

Hannock stood before the king, a blank expression on his face. "Personal reasons, Your Majesty," he replied.

"Personal reasons my backside, Hannock, spit it out man, explain your insanity dammit."

Hannock offered no reply.

Jared had heard the commotion in the throne room, as had Lodren and Grubb who entered, bowing to the king as they did so. Jared immediately approached King Tamor. "What's wrong, Father?" he asked.

Tamor's voice was raised in frustration. "He's gone mad," he replied, pointing at Hannock, "you talk to him, see if you can make any sense of it because I'm damned if I can."

Jared turned to his friend, a puzzled look on his face. "Hannock?"

Hannock took a deep breath and looked to the floor, shuffling his feet slightly, knowing that his reply would not be received favourably. "I wish to resign my commission as captain of the guard," he stated.

"What? Why? It was all you ever wanted."

"And I have served loyally for many years, Your Highness, but I feel that now is the time for me to *step down*, as it were."

"See what I mean, there's no talking sense to him. We've been going around in circles for the last half an hour and all I can get from him, as a reason, is that it's for personal reasons, and that's no reason, Jared. He worked himself half to death and now he just wants to throw it all away, not to mention the fact that there's not one single soldier amongst the regiments who could do the job half as well as he does," bellowed Tamor.

Most unexpectedly, Grubb stepped forward. Making eye contact with the king, he bowed again, in apology for his interruption. "Your Majesty, I'm not one for fancy words, that I'm sure you're aware of, so I'll come right out with it… let me talk to him, I think it might help."

Tamor waved his hand, allowing them leave to adjourn to the far end of the room.

The four drew up chairs and sat huddled together.

"What are you doing you prat? You can't just resign as captain of the guard," said Jared.

"Well that's what I'm doing, Jared, I have things I need to do and being stuck here for the rest of my life will not allow me to achieve personal goals."

"Such as?" asked Jared.

"Oh that's an easy one to answer," chipped in Grubb, "Like killing your brother, without you getting in the way and trying to save him."

Jared leaned forward. "Is that really what you are doing here, Hannock, throwing away your whole life for revenge?"

Hannock did not reply, it seemed that Grubb's deduction was absolutely correct, and the look on Hannock's face confirmed it.

Grubb spoke again. "You are forgetting one thing though, Captain."

Hannock raised his eyebrows as he looked across at Grubb questioningly. He had planned his revenge down to the last letter as far as he was aware.

"If," Grubb began, "the captain of the guard of Borell were to battle with a prince of the realm, and had no other option than to kill him in self-defence, surely no crime would have been committed and no recourse needed? However, should a citizen of Borell knowingly seek a prince of the realm in order to murder him, that would be seen as assassination, therefore that person could be charged with treason and, if found guilty, hanged for his crime." Grubb could be a grouchy, cantankerous, annoying individual at times as he always spoke his mind, but on this occasion, no-one could argue with his logic.

Jared smiled, folded his arms and put his feet up on the chair against Hannock's legs.

"Argue with that then, barmpot. Is Karrak's death worth sacrificing your own life for?" he asked.

Hannock was consumed with hatred for Karrak and his thoughts of revenge but he had no intention of dying to achieve his aforementioned, personal goals.

For the first time, Lodren spoke. "You are amongst friends here, Mr Captain, Sir, and we will stand by you through thick and thin. But what Grubb said is right, with us by your side, you'll get what you want. We can help a captain see, but we can't help an assassin, even if he is owed an eye."

Hannock sighed, a deep sigh of resignation, understanding and gratitude that he had such friends. He rose from his chair and approached King Tamor slowly. "Your Majesty, I wish to withdraw my resignation," he announced.

303

"I should bloody well think so," shouted Tamor, "Jared, get him out of here before I have him flogged for wasting my time."

"Thank you, Your Majesty," said Hannock, smiling at the king.

Tamor simply gave a brief smile, shook his head and waved him away. His love for Hannock was not far removed from that of his eldest son.

CHAPTER 14

Jared had to consider many things during preparations for their mission. To capture Karrak, if at all possible, was of course, his main objective. But other considerations troubled him. *Should the companions go alone? Should they take an escort? If so, how many? How long would their journey take? What provisions would they need? Would there be game if they ran short?* These questions ran through his head and, as decisions were made, the necessary steps taken.

A week later the companions had decided to go alone, it was thought that a smaller number would draw less attention.

The four sat around a table in The Weary Traveller on the eve of their departure, going over the last details of their mission.

"It's a shame Queen Faylore isn't coming with us, I think she's lovely," said Lodren.

"Don't you worry, I'll be there. I'm lovely," laughed Hannock.

"No Mr, Captain, you're just nice, you're all nice, but she's lovely."

"Not getting a crush on the Queen of the Thedarians are you, Lodren?" asked Jared.

Lodren blushed, "Of course not, Mr Jared, I love her, but not like that. She's a real lady, and beautiful."

Hannock was still laughing. "And tall and blonde and fair skinned…"

"Don't make fun, Mr Captain, it's not nice."

"Quite right, Lodren. My apologies dear friend," said Hannock, now reducing his mirth to a boyish grin, "here have another drink" and leaning forward, he poured more wine for everyone.

"Are all your weapons ready then?" asked Grubb.

"Everything's ready. That reminds me, I got you this…" Hannock reached down to the small pack on the floor beside him and lifted it onto the table, "…you never know," he added, placing a linen-wrapped parcel in front of Grubb.

The only gift that the little Vikkery had ever received was his beloved pony, Buster, and he was still finding it hard to understand why people just gave things away willy nilly. "What is it?" he asked.

"Open it and you'll find out," replied Hannock.

Grubb removed the linen wrappings to discover a beautiful dagger. The hilt was fashioned from pure silver and encrusted with jade and pearls that shimmered in the light as he inspected the razor sharp edge of the blade.

"Just in case you need a little self-defence," said Hannock.

Grubb was lost for words. A dagger it was, but to someone only two feet tall it was more like a sword. He raised his hand in front of him, watching it as it transformed, a razor sharp talon appearing on each finger, comparing them to the single blade of the dagger. "It might come in handy for something," he said shrugging his shoulders.

***

Dawn came and the companions busied themselves in the courtyard, making final additions to the two provisions carts. Three horses were saddled and ready as Grubb appeared leading Buster with a great pride that swelled his chest. They were ready to leave when suddenly, Lodren slid from his horse and ran off in the direction of the castle kitchen. "Cheese," he shouted as he ran. Two minutes later he returned carrying a whole block of cheese, "I know this is your favourite Mr Jared and I nearly forgot." The others just shook their heads as he climbed back into the saddle. They had barely covered five yards before he dismounted yet again. "Spring onions," he yelled, as he ran off to the kitchen.

"Anything else?" asked Hannock as he returned, "Maybe a sheep or two? Half a cow? An apple tree?"

"Bless me, Mr Hannock you're right, apples," and off he ran again.

Before his return the other three dismounted and leaned against the well, arms folded, waiting. He appeared once more, this time with a basket of apples in each arm.

"Are we leaving today or not, Master Lodren?" asked Jared.

"Of course we are, Mr Jared, but we can't have you going hungry."

"If you pack any more food we'll need another cart, *no more*!"

Lodren chuntered under his breath as he packed away the apples in the nearest cart. Eventually, with no more interruptions from the panicking Lodren, they passed through the portcullis to begin their mission.

***

Harley sat for what seemed like an age, staring at the Heart of Ziniphar. Nothing happened, no change of colour, no movement from Emnor, nothing. He strolled across the room, stopping occasionally by various artefacts, but not daring to touch them. Leaning down he would peer at them whilst closing one eye, hoping that maybe a secret would reveal itself, but none did. He wandered back to Emnor's side and again checked the gem that lay on his chest, still nothing. Opening the scroll, he read the words on the parchment. Three times he read them to himself, but it was no good, they still made no sense to him as they were in a language he had never seen before.

What seemed like an age had only been an hour, but this turned into two and then three. Harley, now having retaken his seat, once again stared into the Heart. Resting his elbows on the bed he placed his head in his hands and, bored witless by this most tedious of tasks, he gave into the inevitable.

He opened his eyes, annoyed with himself at having dozed off. *Oh well, no harm done* he thought.

Rubbing his eyes, he turned to look at the Heart, and went into a total panic… it had turned black. For the first time, he noticed the slight trickle of blood coming from Emnor's nose.

308

I've killed him, he thought, this time holding his head in his hands for an entirely different reason and pulling at his hair, but suddenly he saw a glimmer of hope. Frantically inspecting the Heart, he was convinced that he could see the slightest hint of red deep within. Fumbling in his robes he tore out the scroll, opened it, and began reading aloud:

Reditus Meus Anima, Meus Essentia, Nos Necessum est Reconcilio

Reditus Meus Anima, Meus Essentia, Nos Necessum est Reconcilio

Reditus Meus Anima, Meus Essentia, Nos Necessum est Reconcilio.

Harley held his breath, staring at Emnor, hoping to glimpse the merest spark of life, but also dreading that he was too late. He flopped down into the chair and leaned forward, wrapping his arms around his head. Emnor had entrusted him with his life. *How could he have been so careless?*

Sitting bolt upright suddenly, Emnor bellowed, "***by all that's sacred,***" and promptly dropped straight back down again, rubbing his face as if he had just been slapped.

Scared out of his wits, Harley had jumped sideways spilling onto the floor, along with the chair, that slid half way across the room. "Master Emnor, you're alive!" exclaimed Harley, rushing to his master's side, or at least trying to, as his feet had become entangled in his robes, causing him to fall flat on his face. Regaining his footing Harley grabbed Emnor's hand. "Are you alright, Sir, can I get you anything?" he asked hurriedly.

Emnor blinked a few times and was obviously short of breath, "Water," he hissed, "water."

Harley grabbed the pitcher from the desk and attempted to pour some into a wooden cup but Emnor, in dire need to quench his thirst, snatched the pitcher from Harley's grip and began to pour the water into his mouth. He drank heavily but in his haste, not surprisingly, also poured a great deal of it over himself.

Emnor had the reputation of being an absolute gentleman with impeccable manners and never cursed or swore, but on this occasion, the only *ever* occasion, he did let his true feelings be known. "***Bugger me 'til doomsday, that bloody hurt!***"

Harley now stood, mouth open, speechless. A few minutes passed as Emnor regained his composure, with the occasional 'ouch', sharp intake of breath or the rubbing of a particularly sore spot on his body. Now breathing normally, he looked across at Harley, who had a look of dread on his face. Emnor swung his legs around and sat on the side of the bed.

"Master Emnor, I'm so sorry, it was only for a moment, well I think it was only a moment…"

"Be quiet, Harley, you're babbling again," said Emnor calmly.

"But you've been hurt, and it's all my fault," blurted Harley becoming agitated again.

"I'm fine, Harley, honestly. My mind witnessed the destruction of that other body and believes that I am hurt, therefore it is linking its pain to me, but that is already beginning to ease. No harm has been done and, after all, I am still alive, thanks to you, dear boy."

This was not the reaction that Harley had been expecting. Being turned into a frog or blasted across the room by his mentor would have been something that he could understand but he was completely confused by Emnor's 'there, there never mind' approach.

"Master, what exactly happened to you? You were in a right state when you woke up."

"Got my backside kicked," announced Emnor, starting to laugh.

Harley still didn't understand and now looked more confused than ever. Emnor offered no more information but Harley could not help himself. He was a young man and very inquisitive and his next question left his lips before he even realised he wanted to ask it.

"By who, Master Emnor?"

"That's whom, Harley, don't be lazy when it comes to speech, dear boy, gives people the wrong impression, and in answer to your question, Prince Karrak Dunbar, second in line to the throne of Borell."

"But, Sir, wasn't he the lunatic we had imprisoned here, the one who kidnapped Master Barden when he escaped?"

"Oh dear, is that what you think happened? Take a seat, Harley, we have things to discuss. On second thoughts, give me a minute to change my robes, these are soaking wet. Wonder how that happened."

***

The companions had begun to set up camp. A fire had been set, Hannock had surveyed the surrounding area for animal tracks or footprints, but found the ground devoid of either, Jared was studying his maps and Lodren was busy with his catering.

"Right, anybody fancy anything in particular?" Lodren asked. The others shook their heads, happy for him to make the decision. Hannock ventured a little closer to Lodren's pots and pans, something that one had to do carefully, for the Nibby was most protective when it came to his kitchen equipment. "What are you doing, Mr Captain?" asked Lodren, a very faint snarl in his voice.

"Not touching, Lodren, wouldn't dream of it, dear friend," answered Hannock retreating a few steps and holding his hands in the air just to prove the point.

"Good. I don't mess with your soldiering, so don't mess with my catering." Lodren was looking up at Hannock with a determined scowl on his face.

"Never entered my mind, Lodren, just noticed that you're cooking quite a lot, considering there's only the four of us."

"Mind your own business," snapped Lodren and, turning his back, continued with his preparations.

Hannock sat down on a log and leaned across to Grubb. "Have you been giving him lessons?" he asked.

Without even looking, Grubb replied. "Get stuffed."

"Obviously not then, he's still far too polite."

Jared was always amused by the banter that was exchanged between Hannock and Grubb. It reminded him of when he and Hannock were carefree children. He could still hear his best friend's childish voice threatening to cut off his head if he was a sorcerer. But that was a long time ago. Both now secretly wished that their adventures were over, and that peace would return to Borell.

Once the meal was prepared they all sat down to eat. It was usual for Lodren to potter around and join them a few minutes after they had begun, but not so on this occasion. He had traditionally returned to his campfire after serving the others, but after a few moments returned carrying a large wooden tray covered with various dishes.

"Back in a minute," he said, and promptly disappeared into the darkness.

The others cast each other questioning glances but before they had time to speak, Lodren returned, empty handed.

"What was that all about?" asked Hannock, as Lodren made himself comfortable next to them, his own supper in hand.

"Thought they might like something," said Lodren quite relaxed.

"Who might like something?" asked Jared.

"Them out there," answered Lodren, pointing away from the camp.

"Who's out there, Lodren? Do you know them?" asked Hannock.

"No." Lodren said nothing more, finding his supper far more interesting than the conversation.

"So where are they exactly, can you see them?" asked Jared.

Lodren sighed. "I don't know who they are, where they are or what they want, Mr Jared, I just know they're out there. I thought giving them a bit of supper would show them that we're friendly so they won't attack us while we're asleep."

"As if we can sleep, now we know that we're being watched!" exclaimed Hannock.

"Not everybody is bad, Mr Hannock, sometimes you've just got to trust people."

"Lodren, they may not even be people. They could be three-headed monsters and their idea of supper, might be us."

"Well we'll just have to wait and see then won't we!" But not once did Lodren look up from his supper during the entire conversation.

They took it in turns to stand watch and the night passed peacefully. As dawn broke, Lodren headed out to collect his tray and returned a few moments later. "I thought they might at least try it," he said grumpily, staring at the untouched dishes.

"Let me see that, Lodren, if you would," said Hannock. Hannock shuffled the bowls around the tray as Lodren held it.

"What are you looking for, Mr Captain?" asked Lodren after a few seconds.

"I don't know how to say this, Jared, but he was right. We *were* being watched," said Hannock.

"Of course we were, *I told you that!*" exclaimed Lodren.

"Lodren, I have even worse news for you, they didn't like your cooking."

"Nonsense, they never even tried it, the bowls are still full, look," chirped Lodren, aghast at the possibility that someone existed who did not adore his lovingly prepared dishes.

314

"See here, Lodren, the drag mark across the top of this stew?" continued Hannock. "Someone, or something, licked it and the small dip on the side of that puree, caused by a tongue being dipped into it. Oh yes, these have been tasted, and whoever did the tasting, didn't like it!"

Lodren went into a real strop and stormed away, ranting as he went. "You're making it up because I warned you away from my pots and pans. How could you be so cruel when all I want to do is feed you and look after you? I mean... *really*!"

The next couple of days were a little tense, with Lodren hardly saying a word and riding at a distance behind them as they travelled, apparently mortally wounded by the unseen presence that had spurned his delicious cuisine. He was as polite as always, but seemed to find things to do each time one of the others attempted to strike up a conversation with him. Well, to be honest, not so much things to do, more excuses, to prevent any such conversation from taking place.

The end of another day, another camp set, another fire burning brightly in the darkness and Lodren busying himself around it. Hannock sat close to Jared and nudged his arm, nodding toward the oblivious Nibby. A similar scenario was unfolding with, what seemed to be, far too much food being prepared for it to be for just the four of them. Not daring to say a word for fear of upsetting him again his companions carried out their own tasks and duties. "Five minutes," he announced, prompting the others to lay down whatever they were doing, for Lodren accepted no tardiness when it came to meal times.

Each was served in turn as usual and Lodren approached them with a small tray in hand set with a small selection of dishes, but he did not take his place, neither did he venture out into the darkness to offer it to the still, unseen strangers. A few seconds passed and Lodren turned away from them and bowed.

"Oh dear," said Hannock, "he's gone mad, now he's giving food to imaginary friends."

"I'm only invisible if I choose to be, Charles, you should know that." The voice was familiar to them all and with a shimmering glow, Faylore appeared before them.

"Dinner is served, Your Majesty," announced Lodren, leaning forward to present her with the tray.

The companions spent the next few minutes exchanging pleasantries and catching up with one another's recent exploits. Faylore had intended to visit them in Borell but, having been informed by King Tamor of their mission, had pursued them, tracking their progress easily, with the aid of a few of her more mature, experienced kin.

"So, Lodren, you *were* correct when you said we were being followed," said Hannock, at last having a good reason with which to cheer up the uncharacteristically depressed Nibby.

"I wasn't talking about the Thedarians," answered Lodren.

Jared took the opportunity to inform Faylore of the encounter and the snubbing of the food that had so upset Lodren. "They never ate a bite of it, Faylore, I mean, how rude can you be?"

Faylore noticed the glum look on Lodren's face and smiled. His wounds could not have been deeper if he had been hit with a blade or arrow. "What exactly did you prepare for your unseen guests, Lodren?"

"There was stew, sausages, oh, and some meat pies. All sorts of stuff," he replied.

"But you never saw them when you took the food from the camp?" she asked.

"No, they stayed in the darkness. But I know they were there, like I knew *you* were there."

Faylore cast glances at her kin and, without a word being spoken, they nodded at each other, as if in agreement.

"Every dish contained some form of meat then, Lodren?" asked Faylore.

"Yes, like I said, there was a stew and… oh dear," he replied.

"Do you think that maybe, whoever they are, aren't meat eaters?"

Lodren now had a beaming smile on his face. There was nothing wrong with his cooking after all, the unseen guests were simply vegetarian. He began jigging up and down on the spot. "So if I cook them a vegetable broth, they'll eat that?" he asked.

Hannock could contain himself no longer. "Just a minute, bird-brain, we're not here to feed anyone who feels like dropping in unannounced. You'll be laying out tables and polishing the silverware next!"

"Thank you, Charles, we'll remember next time," said Faylore.

"Present company excepted of course, Your Majesty," added Hannock, bowing slightly but remaining seated.

Jared was witnessing, as he had done so many times, Faylore using her royal standing to make Hannock squirm, an art she had perfected some time ago. He decided to intervene and leaned forward. "So who are they, Faylore?" he asked.

"Well, from the information you have so far, I'd say it's the Gerrowliens."

"Oh not them!" exclaimed Grubb suddenly.

"You suspected it all along, Grubb, don't deny it," said Faylore.

"Maybe I did, maybe I didn't, I just hoped it wasn't," said Grubb in his usual grumpy manner.

"You knew all along, Grubb?" asked Lodren, "You let me think there was somebody who didn't like my cooking all this time, when you could have just told me? What a horrible thing to do." Lodren snatched the dishes from the companions, but not from the Thedarians, and stormed away to his campfire.

Grubb shrugged his shoulders. "You can't please some people," he said.

"The Gerrowliens. Who are they, Faylore?" asked Hannock.

"A warrior race, native to these lands, beautiful too, in their own way," she replied.

"Another warrior race, perfect, just like the Dergon I suppose? So will they ambush us or just come charging into the camp when they're ready?"

"Neither, Charles, they are a very honourable race. I hope they never heard you comparing them to Dergon, they'll be most insulted if they did."

"Well they should just introduce themselves properly then instead of skulking around in the dark," stated Hannock.

"You seem to forget, Charles, this is their home, you are the trespasser. If anyone should be introducing themselves, it is you, to them."

"Well if we knew where they were, we would!" exclaimed Hannock.

Grubb spoke again, "You say that, but trust me, it's not that easy."

"What's easier than saying hello, Grubb? You just walk up to someone and say hello, pleased to meet you," said Hannock.

"You know when somebody gets on your nerves, Hannock, and you get all sarcastic and impatient with 'em?" asked Grubb.

"I do not 'get sarcastic', Grubb, impatient maybe, but never sarcastic."

"Oh no, *never* sarcastic, Hannock," stated Jared.

Hannock tried his best to ignore the last statement and pulled down the front of his tunic, a habit he had formed whenever unable to think of a suitable response, especially if it was close to the mark.

Grubb continued. "Well these fellas could teach you a thing or two about sarcasm. They're so far up 'emselves you wouldn't believe it. They think they're better than everybody. Stronger, faster, more intelligent, you just can't talk sense to 'em once they decide on something. Even if they're wrong, and they know they're wrong, they won't admit it. It's infuriating."

Jared leaned across and placed his hand on Hannock's arm. "Sounds like a match made in the heavens, you might even be related," and he burst out laughing, much to Hannock's annoyance.

Lodren had been listening intently to the conversation as, one by one, he had relieved their guests of dishes and bowls without comment. He rejoined the gathering taking a seat next to Faylore, whom he adored. "Queen Faylore, what do they look like?" he asked.

Faylore placed her arm around his shoulders, well as far as she could considering the width of them, for she, in return, had a great fondness for the Nibby.

"As I said, they are a beautiful race, almost as tall as we Thedarians but much broader and then of course there is the fur."

"Fur!?" exclaimed Hannock.

"Yes, Charles, fur. Gold and black striped fur across their faces, large pointed teeth, and hands with razor sharp claws, for they are descended from wild cats."

"You *are* sure that they don't eat meat… or people?" asked Hannock, his hand moving to the hilt of his sword.

"Quite sure, Charles, and they don't attack either. They defend themselves if necessary, but otherwise, would make no threat toward another, well other than the Hissthaar that is."

"And just who are the Hissthaar?" asked Hannock. He knew that he would probably regret asking the question, folding his arms and preparing for the worst.

"Do not concern yourself, Charles, we shall travel with you and the Hissthaar would never attempt to harass *us*, you will be quite safe." Faylore had said this in a way that meant that she was not prepared to discuss the matter further.

***

"I say we just attack them, kill them all and have done with it. Let's face it, they kill other lifeforms and eat them, they might try to eat us."

"Poom, I'm sure they would not try to kill or eat us. The meat that is in their food comes from dumb animals, sheep, glamoch, not intelligent races such as ours." Lawton looked Poom up and down. "However, they may make an exception in your case," he added.

"Let them try, I'll take the lot of them by myself, I'll beat them to a pulp, they wouldn't have a chance. Did I tell you about the time those four…"

"Yes, Poom, you did, and about the time you got ambushed, and the time there was a gang of Hissthaar and you beat the one to death with his own arm, and every other fight you've ever had, and won."

"Sorry, Lawton, I just get a bit carried away."

"Some days, Poom, I wish you would."

"That's nice isn't it, you'll need me one day and I'll be there to help, if anyone tries to hurt you I'll knock them clean out. Did I tell you about the time I was…"

Lawton ran his hand across his face and sighed, he loved Poom more than a brother. They were alike in so many ways that it was difficult to separate the minds of the pair, apart from one thing. They were a warrior race, that was undeniable, but, as with any fighting force, there were differences of opinion when it came to the strategy of a battle. Lawton would plan to the last detail, Poom would grab the nearest weapon, if there was one, and charge in, throwing caution to the wind. Lawton was a huge being, a little portly, but powerful with it. Poom on the other hand was not much to look at. Almost as tall as Lawton and only half the build, when it came to fighting, he was a demon, who could, and had, bested foes twice his size. Peace had reigned over their lands for many years now. Lawton was content to live a calm existence and, although he had a love of life that kept him far younger than his actual years, was prepared to live out his life without pointless wars. Poom however, could not forget his glory days and loved nothing more than to regale his past battles to any younger member of the clan who was willing to listen, never omitting a single, gory detail. Most times, whilst in Lawton's company, Poom would avoid the subject, slipping very occasionally into the '*Did I tell you…*' scenarios.

Unfortunately for Lawton, he had heard the tales many times over and on occasion, unable to curb his friend's enthusiasm, would make an excuse to escape his repetitive, inexhaustible supply of tales regarding his acts of carnage and heroics. Despite this, neither would prefer to be in any other company and were now watching the camp with interest.

"What are they doing here, Lawton? There's nothing for days in any direction and, by the looks of things, they're headed straight for Shaleford Forest, our forest."

"Well I'd be inclined to agree with you on their direction, but I have no idea as to their intention, Poom."

"Well they'll reach the forest by tomorrow night as they're so slow, so I say we go ahead, get some rest and wait for them to catch up. Once they reach the forest we'll question them and find out what they want."

"You see, Poom, you can think when you have to, not once did you say ambush or attack."

"I'll attack you if you're not careful."

"Of course you will, of course you will," replied Lawton wrapping his arm around his friend and rubbing the top of his head, "Wouldn't have it any other way, need a spear?"

***

"What do you mean *he knows*?!" exclaimed Xarran.

"Exactly what I said. He knows," replied Harley.

"But how does he know, you told him didn't you? To get into his good books," said Drake.

"I never told him anything, Mad, he already knew. He's known for months."

"Don't call me Mad. It's Drake. Just call me Drake."

"It makes sense though, I mean that he already knew. We couldn't have gotten away with this unless they had left us alone, we would've been discovered by now, surely?"

"Thank you, Alexander. At last, somebody can see sense," said Harley.

"So are they going to let us carry on then?" asked Xarran.

"Yes," replied Harley, "but Master Emnor has insisted that he be present before we conduct any tests in future, to make sure that it's safe."

"We always make sure that it's safe," stated Alex.

"Oh really?" asked Harley, "How long did you say it took you to repair the wall and the floor?"

"He's got a point I suppose," muttered Drake.

The door opened and the boys stood to attention as Emnor entered, what they thought, was their secret room. "Morning, boys, how are you getting on. Anything exciting?" he asked.

They cast furtive glances at one another, unsure of how to answer. Emnor looked from one to another, eyebrows raised in anticipation of some sort of response.

Harley, now used to Emnor's ways, stepped forward. "We have been experimenting with the suitability of different metals for certain spells, Master Emnor. Would you like to see?"

"Indeed I would, but first I have a question. Would your research stretch to the imbuing of a staff as easily as it is to a wand?"

The four conspirators grinned at one another. It seemed as if they were going to enjoy the involvement of Master Emnor in their research, for the grin on his face was as big, if not bigger, than theirs.

Emnor said very little as the enthusiastic band turned their explanation into a full blown presentation of their achievements, even dodging searching questions as they attempted to receive any sign of approval he may have. He would simply nod or stroke his beard and fix one of them with a gaze as a sign for them to continue, which they did with fervour, their energy seemingly inexhaustible.

Two hours passed fleetingly and Emnor had deduced that these mere novices possessed more magical knowledge than some wizards that were closer to his age. He had seen and heard enough. "Gentlemen…" he began, "…it is obvious that your research has gleaned many possibilities, and the demonstrations you have performed with your wands is most impressive, but in order for you to progress even further, your ideas must be bigger." Holding out his hand, palm facing upwards he closed his eyes and mumbled a few words. A wooden staff appeared, perfectly balanced across his hand. Thrusting the staff toward Drake he bluntly asked, "What can you do with that?"

Without hesitation Drake grabbed the staff and held it high in the air. "Easy," he announced, and instantly turned it to ash.

The others never flinched, much to Emnor's surprise.

"I meant something constructive," sighed Emnor.

"Not possible with wood I'm afraid, Master Emnor," said Alexander, "far too brittle you see?"

"Well you could have mentioned that earlier."

"We did, Master Emnor, different metals, different spells, remember?" Xarran pointed out, regretting his attitude almost immediately.

"Mind your manners, Xarran." But the reprimand had come not from Emnor, but from Harley, who had the utmost respect for his mentor.

Xarran dropped his head forward, "My apologies, Master."

"No harm done, Xarran, we all get a little carried away at times," said Emnor, patting Xarran on the shoulder, "So what material *would* be suitable?" he asked.

"That depends on what your primary magic will be, Master," answered Alexander.

"Let's just say it must be suitable for *all* types of elemental magic."

The young mens' eyes grew wide with excitement. This was something that they had discussed many times, but had not dared to attempt. A wand would not withstand the imbuing of more than one type of magic, but a staff? That idea had not entered their minds. They began to babble at one another, "*Gold, platinum, brass, silver, pewter, copper*," all suggestions relevant to a particular type of magic.

Emnor held up his hand and a hush fell upon the group. "If each metal were to be set as a layer in order to construct the staff, would that work?" he asked.

"Too heavy," answered Alexander.

"A central core of one metal, enhanced with stones and surrounded by the other metals, as filigrees could sustain the staff's integrity," suggested Harley.

"What length would it need to be, Master Emnor?" asked Drake.

Emnor hadn't given this any thought and stood up, arms outstretched. "Six feet?" he asked, raising his eyebrows inquisitively.

His pupils looked at one another, nodding in agreement.

"I'll leave it in your capable hands then," said Emnor. "Oh, just one more thing, I need you to make a setting for this." Reaching inside his robes he drew out a small velvet pouch and placed it on the table in front of him. "It needs to be fastened to a chain about eighteen inches long, gold preferably. Take care of it for me would you, and look after it, it is quite valuable." Slipping his fingers into the pouch he removed the Heart of Ziniphar. Emnor winked at Harley, turned quickly, and left the room.

***

The roar of the wind was almost deafening. Tree boughs bent, dust blew around them and even the water in the nearby river flowed in an unnatural direction, away from its banks.

"For House Dunbar," roared Jared, as the boulder before him exploded into tiny, gravel-sized pieces that were strewn in a twenty-foot radius.

"He's getting really good at this boulder smashing, don't you think, Grubb?" said Lodren.

"Yeah I suppose so. If any boulders, rocks or stones attack us, they won't know what hit 'em," answered Grubb.

"Why does he shout at them before he blows them up?" asked Faylore.

"I believe it helps him focus his energy," answered Hannock.

"How strange… does he not like boulders, only he seems to destroy quite a few of them?"

"Can't stand them, Your Majesty, stubbed his toe as a child you see and has never forgiven them since," replied

Hannock. Faylore was used to him now and just raised her eyebrows in response. "Well done, your Highness, another one bites the dust, or should I say, becomes dust?" called Hannock, chuckling at his own witticism.

Jared approached them, brushing the dust from his tunic. "How long before we eat, Lodren?" he asked.

"Half an hour or so, Mr Jared," answered Lodren "but as you're obviously hungry, have this to keep you going," and handed him a platter with sliced apples and cheese.

"I swear you're a mind reader, my dear Nibby, thank you."

"Well that's why I'm here, to look after you lot."

"Didn't offer me any apples and cheese," mumbled Grubb under his breath, forgetting how acute Lodren's hearing was.

"Well if you'd said you were hungry, I would have. I'm not really a mind reader you know," snapped Lodren. Turning to the provisions wagon, he grabbed a platter and slapped a lump of cheese on it, along with an apple. "Here," he said, thrusting it toward Grubb, "now stop moaning."

Grubb took the platter, head lowered, "Thank you, Sir, much obliged Sir," he chuntered.

Hannock, watching the scene, was highly amused and had to stop himself from asking where his cheese and apples were, fearing that this would put poor Lodren back into his depressive state of a few days prior.

"You are becoming most proficient with your magic, Jared," said Faylore.

"I wish I had no need of it, unfortunately something tells me that it must serve its purpose, when the time is right."

"And what would that purpose be?" she asked.

"I wish I knew, Your Majesty, I wish I knew," he replied.

"Well, we've been fortunate so far. On the road for a week and nobody has attacked us yet," said Hannock.

"That's a blessing I suppose," replied Jared.

"What about the Gerrowliens, Faylore, do you think they'll attack at some point?" asked Hannock.

"Oh no, they are far too civilised, they would never ambush anyone. They always have the decency to tell you they're going to kill you before they do so," she replied.

"How polite of them!" exclaimed Hannock.

"Don't worry, Charles, we may not even meet them if we behave respectfully in their lands."

"I'll believe that when I see it, or don't. You know that as soon as we get near Shaleford Forest, they'll show up, bein' all pompous and arrogant, bloody Growlies." Grubb was making it quite clear that he was not a fan of this, as yet, elusive race.

"You must not call them that, Grubb, you know they don't like it," advised Faylore.

"Don't care what they like or don't like," said Grubb gruffly and snorted.

"We will be entering their homelands and you must show them the same respect that we showed you when we first met in your cavern," said Faylore.

"S'pose you're right," Grubb could not argue with Faylore's logic.

"So when will we reach Shaleford Forest?"

"Before nightfall, Mr Jared, you don't want to get there after dark... that's when the Hissthaar come out. As long as your campfire is set before that, they won't come near."

"Who are the Hissthaar, Lodren?"

"I'll tell you later, Mr Jared, lunch is nearly ready, don't want it to spoil do we?" answered Lodren, noticeably unnerved by the subject.

Repacking the carts with the few items that Lodren had needed, they resumed their journey until, well before dusk, they could see in the distance, the edge of the treeline that was Shaleford Forest.

"This is where the fun starts," said Grubb, stroking Buster's neck as if the pony understood him.

CHAPTER 15

Karrak stood at the entrance of his cave. As usual his pets slinked around, but had become wary of getting too close for fear of ending up as a meal for the others. The only one to venture near was Barden. Was there still a trace of his consciousness present within the twisted body of the grotesque beast? Karrak had toyed with the idea of attempting a reversal spell, but only in order for him to further torture Barden. *How much more pain could he inflict without killing either the beast or the wizard should the reversal be successful before, once again, twisting him to his animalistic state.*

His thoughts were soon interrupted. A few yards from his cave there was a crackling noise and then, what appeared to be, a small storm cloud appeared with mini lightning bolts striking within it. It grew larger until, with a loud crack, a cowled figure stood calmly before him. As this was happening there were other strange events, clouds of smoke of red, green or black, shimmering as if the light were bending and apparitions, ghosts or spectres that one could see through, but all with the same result. Wherever an anomaly had occurred, a cloaked figure now stood, twenty in total. These were to be Karrak's allies, his *disciples*.

Karrak gestured toward the cave entrance. His guests remained stationary for a time, unnerved by the strange pack of beasts between themselves and their suggested destination. "My friends, I thank you for attending, shall we step inside? Trust me it is far more than at first it appears. Do not worry about them, just my guards, an alarm call of sorts," he assured. He waved his hand gently toward his pets and they scampered away knowing what came next should they not. His guests entered the cave at a leisurely pace, their host following closely behind.

Karrak had met them all in turn, relating his personal tale of banishment from his homeland for simply not accepting another's rules. Playing on the feelings of the assembly, not looking for sympathy, but making it appear that he was persecuted merely because his powers were misunderstood, as were theirs, had enticed them to the gathering. Now, before these likeminded individuals he could finally begin to put his plans in motion.

He began his rehearsed speech. "We are more powerful than they, my friends. Why should we be governed and made to serve them? We should be the ones who are to govern and they should be the ones to serve us. Not because we can, but because we should. Their pointless wars not only cost countless lives, it costs far too much coin. Paying smiths, armourers and fletchers obscene amounts of gold in order to settle some petty squabble over lands or pride is arrogant and unnecessary. We could rule not only these lands, but the entire world, putting an end to war, making fortunes for ourselves and living by our own rules, the rules befitting the most powerful sorcerers in the world."

"Lord Karrak. It is a grand scheme indeed but there are very few of us, how are we to defeat armies?" asked one of the gathering.

"I can understand your concerns, my friend, but we need only to achieve one goal, in order for any one of us

332

to stand against one hundred, however well-armed they may be."

"And that goal would be…?"

"The acquisition of the Elixian Soul. If I have that, we shall be unstoppable."

"If *you* have it?"

"I am, my friend, the only one who can wield the power of the Soul."

"Where do we find this Soul?"

"*That,* my friend, is the answer I do not have."

"And, if we were to make this discovery. What then, would prevent one of us from taking this *Soul* for ourselves?"

Karrak paused. Running his fingers through his hair, he raised himself to his full height and spoke slowly, to ensure that they heed his warning. "Trust me when I say this. You would be destroyed by its properties. Join me and I shall share its power with you. No more would you answer to any mere mortal. Your path shall be of your own choosing, forged as one would forge the links of a chain, and as short, or long, as you wish it to be."

The questioning sorcerer stared at Karrak briefly before he spoke. "My name is Darooq, and I shall join you, Lord Karrak."

Karrak held up his hand. "In order for this to be successful, Darooq, nobody shall *join* me. They must *serve* me."

Darooq tilted his head to one side for a moment and studied the impressive Karrak. "In that case, Lord Karrak,

I am at your service," and taking a knee, he bowed to his new master.

In turn, all present, followed suit.

***

Emnor studied the setting in which the Heart of Ziniphar had been placed. Solid gold with a chain to match, it was a most beautiful piece of craftsmanship.

"We didn't think you'd want it too fancy, Master Emnor, your robes are fairly plain and we thought a more subdued look would be far better.

"What? Oh no, no it's not for me... but it is perfect," he replied.

"Not for you? Master Emnor, do you realise how much that thing's worth?" asked Drake.

"More than you can imagine, dear boy, far more in fact," Emnor replied, still examining the jewel and its new setting.

Harley, far more used to his mentor's ways gave Drake a gentle kick under the bench. Drake looked up and mouthed 'What?' not understanding what he had done wrong. Harley rolled his eyes and shook his head.

"Tell me, gentlemen, how are you faring with that staff I suggested?"

Xarran became a little excited and hurried to the cupboard in the corner of the room. "It's not quite finished, Master Emnor, but we're more than half way," he said. Removing an oilcloth-wrapped object and placing it on the bench, he gingerly revealed their creation.

Exactly six feet in length, the core of the staff was a slender platinum rod, inset with topaz and amber. Gold filigrees had been fused along the entire length, filigrees so fine that they looked as frail as a spider's web despite the jewels that they housed. Emnor, unable to contain himself, immediately reached out to take the staff.

Alexander grabbed his wrist before he could clasp his hand around it. "No, Sir, it's not finished. We're still working on its construction and it's not imbued with any magics yet so is still very fragile. Grip it too hard and the outer layers could shatter. Once it's completed however, you'll be able to smash through doors, without using magic if you need to."

"But how is that possible if its construction is so delicate?" asked Emnor.

"The whole becomes greater than the sum of its parts, Master. You must have heard of that?" said Xarran smugly.

"Well, yes, I suppose so, but I never believed that rule could apply to the manufacture of a staff," answered Emnor.

They had had their glory and Harley decided that it was time for him to step in. "Master Emnor, there is still much to be done, other metals to add and maybe a few different gems before it can be imbued... and then of course, it will need to be tested."

"But of course, my dear Harley. Will you require me for the testing?"

Drake looked a little worried at this point, he had always tested the wands and would have felt most aggrieved should he be ousted when it came to testing their most adventurous creation to date, but his fears were soon allayed.

"No, Master Emnor. Mad... erm, I mean Drake, knows the testing process. He's done it countless times, so better that he does it, you know, until we know it's safe for you to use," replied Harley.

Drake's expression now changed. This thing was much bigger than any wand he had tested and he had temporarily forgotten the destruction of the floor, and the wall... *oh bugger*, he thought, *maybe he should let the Head of the Administration test his own staff*. But it was too late, he had already been 'volunteered'.

***

Lodren had the campfire roaring in no time. The weather had remained dry and so had the wood that they had collected from the edge of the forest, found lying on the ground. "We made good time today, Mr Hannock. We've still got a good hour of daylight left and I'm already set to make a nice big meal for us all."

"Yes, not too bad, and it'll give the horses a chance for a good rest as well. Oh my word, just look at him!" Hannock pointed across at Grubb who was with Buster, stroking his mane and kissing his nose. "When's the wedding then, Grubb," he asked laughing.

Grubb gave one of his best scowls. "Get stuffed, Hannock."

"You shouldn't tease him, Charles, it's not polite. Have you never had a pet?" Faylore asked.

"I had a chicken once," answered Hannock.

"You had it for two days, Hannock, two days… and then you ate it!" said Jared.

"Oh yes, yes I did. It really was a delicious pet," said Hannock, his eyes glazed in reminiscence.

Jared made his way toward Lodren. Stopping in front of him, he folded his arms. "Tell me about the Hissthaar, Lodren, and no dodging the question this time. Who are they?"

"Oh you really should stay away from them, nasty creatures, not a nice one amongst them."

Hannock drew his sword instinctively. The question had been answered, not by Lodren or any other of the companions but by a deep growling voice somewhere outside the camp. "Show yourself. I am captain of the guard of Borell. If you have any ill intent I promise I shall cut you down faster than you can blink," shouted Hannock.

"Oh really?" came the reply, "Just how fast are you then, Captain?"

"Show yourself and you'll find out," answered Hannock.

"Bloody growlies, I told ye, didn't I tell ye?" hissed Grubb.

The voice spoke again, but this time the words were not directed at them. "Did you hear that, Poom, he thinks he's fast."

"Yes, but they all do don't they, when they don't even know what fast is, Lawton."

"I have an idea, Poom. Why don't *you* show this captain fellow what fast is? Then he might just have a bit

337

of a rethink… Poom, put the spear down you won't be needing that."

"But, Lawton, I just thought that maybe…"

"There you go again, Poom, trying to think. It's just a demonstration, you don't need to kill anyone… well not yet anyway."

"Why is it that whenever I begin to enjoy myself, you stop me? I'm not that old yet."

"Yes you are, but you're the only one that doesn't realise it. At least be mature about this."

"Alright, alright, what do you want me to do?"

"Just go into the camp, say hello, and come straight back."

The fact that they hadn't even lowered their voices had concerned Hannock slightly and he now stood, heel dug firmly into the ground, ready to strike anything that approached aggressively. Scanning the trees before him he saw nothing move. He had lost one eye, but the other still worked perfectly, but as he blinked there was a slight breath of wind. As he opened his eye, no more than three inches from his face was something he was not expecting. A head much larger than his with yellow catlike eyes and gold and black striped fur surrounding a mouth full of razor sharp teeth with canines that were at least three inches long. Before he could react it gave a roar so deep and loud that he felt it reverberate in his chest. He swung his sword as hard as he could but all that the blade cut was thin air.

"Where did it go? Did you see it!?" asked Hannock.

"I saw something. Well I think I saw something," answered Jared.

"I thought he said he was fast, Lawton."

"He did, Poom, I heard it distinctly, he said he was fast."

"He didn't seem very fast to me. If I'd wanted to, I could have killed him, even without a spear."

"Oh I believe you, Poom, I saw it with my own eyes."

"He didn't. He's only got one."

"The other one probably got bored with going so slowly and moved out for a faster life."

"What, like in a snail perhaps?" There was a strange noise coming from where the voices were, not snarling or growling nor even snorting but a mixture of all three. What the companions never realised at the time, was that they were actually being laughed at.

"Now, we've assessed that old one-eye is no threat, but what about the others, Lawton?"

"Well there's the one who shouts at rocks and then blows them up. I like him, he's hilarious."

"Yes, but I don't think he wants to do it, his house tells him to do it."

"Oh yes, dumdum wasn't it, remember him shouting 'for my house dumdum'."

"He's cracked in the head that one, but I think he's harmless, Lawton."

"He does blow things up, Poom, but it takes him ages to do it. You'd be behind him well before he could blow *you* up."

"I know, about five miles behind him." And the strange laughter began again.

"We understand that we are in your lands, but is there really any need to be so rude and insulting?" asked Faylore.

The unknown comedian's laughter ceased abruptly. Slowly they turned to see Faylore standing right behind them, arms folded, eyebrows raised. The two Gerrowliens, for that is what they were, looked at one another. Poom slapped Lawton on the shoulder. "Now this one…" he said, "… I like."

"Would you care to join us? Food is being prepared as we speak, and you would be more than welcome," offered Faylore.

"No thank you," replied Poom abruptly. "You are meat eaters, and we do not eat the flesh of other beings."

"I believe you to be Gerrowliens and have heard it said that you do not have an aversion to the consumption of fish," said Faylore.

Her assumption was perfectly correct. It was a fact she knew to be certain, and the other fact she knew was that, being a feline race, Gerrowliens hated getting wet, therefore fishing would never be on their agenda. To them, fish was a delicacy they rarely had the opportunity to enjoy.

"Well maybe as a gesture, and to show that we bear you no ill will…" began Lawton, noticing that Poom had already started drooling at the thought of fresh fish, the saliva dripping from his chin, "we may…" he said now wiping his own large jowls, "be persuaded to join you, I feel it would be most impolite not to, please, lead on."

Faylore walked ahead of the two guests, a large grin on her face. She knew that once they tasted Lodren's cooking, she would almost be able to feed them from her hand.

They headed into camp. The atmosphere was a little tense at first as Lawton gave Poom a 'don't you dare start anything' look, and Jared did exactly the same to Hannock.

Lodren was awestruck as soon as he saw the two Gerrowliens. "Bless me aren't you handsome," he said.

Poom held his head high and tilted slightly to one side, then unashamedly replied "Yes… yes we are!"

Grubb however could not take their vanity and stormed off, making the excuse that he needed to feed Buster.

"But you've already fed him," said Jared.

"He's had a long day so he can have extra, that okay with you, Your Highness?" He could be heard chuntering away to himself for the next few minutes as formal introductions were made, and Hannock distinctly heard, 'bloody growlies' at least twice during Grubb's rant.

"I don't think the little one likes us," said Lawton.

"Oh dear, what a shame, I doubt I'll sleep a wink tonight through worrying," replied Poom, pretending to brush a tear from his eye, "someone half the size of my leg doesn't like me."

Hannock had perfected sarcasm and Jared would never have believed that there would ever be anyone better, but these two were absolute masters of it and had no hesitation when it came to showing it. Unfortunately, they were also very amusing when they did so and with the exception of Grubb, the companions began to warm to them within minutes.

"Don't you worry about it, the only one that Grubb likes is his pony, Buster," said Lodren, trying to lighten the mood.

Lawton gave Poom a knowing look. "Oh dear," he said, "he'll like us even less then when we eat it, then." They were of course, joking, and knew how Grubb would react. Yes, he was away from the group, trying to make it seem that he had no interest, but they all knew he was listening to every word.

He stormed toward the campfire. "Nobody is eating Buster, come on see if you can get past me. I'll tear you apart, both of ye, with one hand." Now, if it had been the two-foot tall grumpy Vikkery that had stormed toward them that would have been one thing, but within his first two steps he had transformed into his ten-foot, four-armed roaring alter-ego.

The reaction from the Gerrowliens was not what any of them expected. They fell backwards in absolute fits of laughter as soon as Grubb morphed, laughing so hard that Grubb stopped dead in his tracks.

Poom could barely speak, but somehow blurted out. "Is he always this touchy?" before his next bout of hysterical laughter.

Faylore had been the first to react, closely followed by Jared and Hannock, each with their arms stretched out in front of them, in attempt to calm Grubb.

"They're joking, Grubb, just joking, they don't even eat meat," said Jared hurriedly.

"They only have fish very occasionally," added Faylore.

The two Gerrowliens laughter stopped abruptly and they looked at one another.

"Oh yes… FISH. How long before it's ready? I'm starving," said Lawton, looking expectantly at Lodren.

"It'll be ready when it's ready, just have some tea or a biscuit or something to keep you going, shouldn't be too long," answered Lodren.

"Yes we know that. But how *long* is *long*?" asked Poom.

Lodren put his hands across his face. "It's like having two Mr Hannocks at the same time. I don't think even I can take that."

Sometime later, after their hearty meal, the conversation had become a little more civilised.

"So what are you actually doing here, Prince Jared?" asked Lawton.

"We're searching for my brother," answered Jared, slightly reluctant to go into too much detail as to why.

"Oh, did he run away from home?" asked Poom, with only the slightest hint of sarcasm.

"No, he escaped… again," snapped Hannock.

Poom's expression changed. "I take it he's not your favourite person then Captain?"

"No, Poom, he is not, but he will be when he's on the end of my sword."

"That's enough, Hannock, more than enough," said Jared quietly.

"I can see that this is affecting you more than you would have others believe, Your Highness. Your own captain threatens the life of your brother, yet you do not defend your own blood against that threat. Your brother's crimes must be great indeed but your friendship with

343

Hannock even greater. If we are to be of any help to you, then maybe a little more detail would allow us to judge the extent of our aid," suggested Lawton.

Jared explained the sordid details of Karrak's betrayal of everything that he and his father held dear. The Gerrowliens listened intently. The tale of Karrak's horrific deeds caused Poom to inadvertently growl quietly, but deeply at times, as Lawton patted his arm to calm him.

When the tale was done, Poom sat bolt upright. "This man should die, either at the end of your sword, or the point of my spear, Hannock, driven straight through his black heart."

"Tell me, Poom, why do you volunteer so readily, when after all, this is not your fight?" asked Jared.

Poom leaned forward. "I don't like bullies," he snarled.

"And to be totally honest, any excuse for a fight and Poom will usually be right in the middle of it," added Lawton.

"That may be the case…" began Poom in his defence "…but I never actually start any trouble do I? I just kind of… finish it, and I'm always on the side of the weak."

"Most folk stay out of others business and at your age you should have learnt that by now," said Lawton.

"At my age, that's choice coming from a relic like you. At least I'm not fat."

"Very true, Poom, very true. I may have gained a little weight, but at least I don't have bald patches in my fur, unlike certain Gerrowliens."

"They're scars. They aren't bald patches, they're scars."

"More like mange if you ask me," said Lawton.

"Charming, you're supposed to be my best friend and you say something like that."

The pair continued to jibe at one another for the next hour or so, the others just watching in amazement at their most amusing, harmless banter. It was obvious to all that they were the closest of friends.

Lodren persisted with his pampering of their guests until, even Lawton, who had a very healthy appetite, held up his hands in submission at the offer of even more food.

"No thank you, Master Lodren, couldn't take another bite. Poom, take care of that would you."

The companions looked at one another, a little bemused. Lawton had made the slightest of gestures with his hand and the faintest of nods toward the edge of the treeline.

"Can't you do it? I've eaten just as much as you have," pleaded Poom.

"No you haven't. Just do it, for me... please," begged Lawton.

Poom sighed and rubbed his stomach. Slowly he reached to his side, wrapping his hand around the shaft of his spear. A strange silence had fallen on them as they had all sensed that something was awry, but what, they knew not.

In the blink of an eye, Poom was on his feet and had launched the spear so quickly that nobody actually saw it leave his hand. There was a high pitched, hissing screech from somewhere just inside the edge of the forest and two seconds later, Poom was gone.

"Should we go after him?" asked Jared.

"What? Oh no leave him to it, he'll be fine, he loves it to be quite honest. Tries to make out he doesn't, but he's a warrior, it's in his blood and nothing will change him. But he has a good heart, and a more loyal and honourable friend you could never find," said Lawton.

"I know exactly what you mean," replied Jared, smiling at Hannock.

Poom returned a few minutes later, wiping his spear on some large leaves he had collected. Checking it in the firelight, he decided his trusty weapon was suitably clean and cast the leaves into the flames.

"How many?" asked Lawton.

"Only four. Got the first one with my spear and took care of the others by hand."

With this comment he held up the aforementioned hand and, splaying his fingers, revealed his razor sharp claws. Not one member of the companions could help remembering Grubb's similar display in the inn, on the eve of their departure.

"Four what?" asked Hannock.

"Hissthaar," replied Poom. "Horrible, nasty, slimy deceitful scumbuckets."

"Not your favourites then?" asked Hannock, a smirk sneaking across his lips.

Poom had no hesitation in teasing anyone if he was of a mind, but was never comfortable when the roles were reversed, and the look on his face made this very obvious. "No, far from it," he replied.

"How did you know they were there?" asked Faylore, "We Thedarians have both excellent hearing and sight, but I did not detect them."

"The smell of them, dear lady, I could smell them a mile away and so could Poom. We thought they might just slink away once they saw us here, but they had other ideas," answered Lawton.

"What other ideas?" asked Lodren nervously.

"They were waiting for us to leave. Once we had, they would have attacked."

"We have nothing of value, as such. Why would they attack?" asked Faylore.

"Food, madam, food," replied Lawton.

"Well we'd have shared with them, if they just asked," said Lodren.

Poom began one of his distinctive laughs, "You don't understand..." he said, "...they didn't want you to give them food, *you were* the food!"

A look of dread came upon Lodren's face as the realisation dawned on him. "They wanted to eat... *us?!*"

"Are you kidding?" asked Poom "With those arms? One of those would keep a Hissthaar going for a fortnight."

"Oh dear, oh dear, oh dear," was all Lodren could think of to say, inadvertently picking up his hammer.

Lawton rose from his seat and stretched. "We'll stay with you tonight and keep guard. We can discuss how best to continue in the morning. You lot just get some sleep, we'll keep you safe, don't worry."

Lodren gulped. "I don't think I'll sleep soundly again until I'm safely back in Borell."

The companions placed their bedrolls on the ground as Faylore, typically, leapt into a tree, followed by the

347

Gerrowliens. Grubb however, had no intention of sleeping. Transforming into the four-armed beast he strode forward, positioning himself at the edge of the camp, staring into the blackness of the forest. "I'll be buggered if I'm putting my friend's lives in the hands of a pair of bloody Growlies," he snarled.

True to his word, Grubb did not stray from his post until dawn broke.

***

"Why don't you just tell me what I need to know? Join me, Derrin, we need not be enemies."

"You're a deranged, sadistic lunatic, Karrak. I'd kill myself rather than join your squalid ranks. Go on, kill me, finish this, you'll learn nothing from me."

Blood ran from Derrin's eyes and nose. As it reached his swollen lips he spat at Karrak in blatant defiance. Kidnapped two days prior, he had been subjected to torment and torture persistently by Karrak and his followers. When it was thought he could take no more they would allow him time to regain his strength and composure, even administering aid to prevent his inconvenient, untimely death.

"Dead men tell no tales," Karrak had advised, knowing that if anyone had the information he sought, it would be Derrin.

So far, only physical torture had been used, in a vain attempt to loosen Derrin's tongue. Karrak and the others knew that it would be impossible to read his mind. He was, after all, a senior wizard with the Administration and far too powerful for this to be effective. Contemplation of such actions had given rise to the fear that it would be he who would control the mind of anyone attempting to invade his own.

Dethmold watched from the shadows. Many times he and his cohorts had beaten men in order to achieve their goals, but this, this even he found obscene and felt physically sick, bearing witness to such barbarity. Even before the man was strapped to the chair, Dethmold had attempted to leave, only to be stopped by Karrak before he could make good his escape from The Hangman's Noose. "And just where do you think you're going, Thadius?" Karrak asked quietly.

"Don't want to be in your way, my Lord, that's all," he had answered nervously.

"Don't be preposterous. You may be able to give me some pointers, this is after all, how you used to make a living is it not?"

Dethmold shuffled back into the room. Nobody could give Karrak any advice on how to inflict pain, and of that, they were both certain.

Darooq entered the room and, heading straight for Karrak, presented him with a large wooden case.

"Well done, Darooq. Did everything go to plan?"

"Not exactly, my Lord, one of our new order was killed, but I managed to bring him back in time, he won't be as useful as he was, but at least he's alive. Well, sort of."

Karrak held the case up in front of him, pondering over it. "Yes, they can be nasty little buggers when they're cornered."

Derrin, strapped to the chair, was beginning to look slightly alarmed as he suspected that the contents of the case were directly linked to him and unfortunately, he was correct.

"Now, we'll try again shall we?" asked Karrak, smashing the side of the case into his captive's face. "Where have you hidden the Elixian Soul?" he screamed.

The man coughed and spluttered, again spitting blood from his badly swollen lips.

"I've told you already, you can torture me, do your worst, kill me, I have nothing to say to the likes of you, maggot," he breathed.

"There are *worse* things than death you know. Like my little friend here." Karrak forcefully pressed the case against the side of Derrin's head and smiled, the familiar maniacal gleam in his eyes. "Can you guess what it is? Can you hear anything scurrying around in there?" he asked.

Derrin said nothing as he glared at his captor.

"It's a Globbiran spider, do you know what one of those is?" asked Karrak. Derrin's glare continued, but still, he did not speak. "No? Well let me tell you. You see they are most unusual. Normally a spider gives birth to hundreds of live young, and *their* first act is to eat the mother. I know, repulsive isn't it? Now the Globbiran however doesn't want to be devoured by its offspring, so it lays its eggs in the ear of a host, you, not to put too fine a point on it. Now when the little buggers hatch, they have a voracious appetite and the first thing they'll find is your brain, only a light snack in your case, admittedly, but that's not the worst part. You see, they don't eat all of it, only certain parts. I don't know how it works, *exactly* but I do know this, once they leave your body, you will tell me all I need to know and more. But you, you won't know a thing about it. You will simply be a talking shell, for about four hours anyway, and then you'll die. So what do you say, co-operate, or spider dinnertime?"

The screams could be heard half a mile away. Dethmold curled into a ball in the corner of the room. Rocking back and forth and shaking uncontrollably, he began to laugh, but not in amusement. Witnessing the huge spider attaching itself to the side of Derrin's head as he screamed and begged for mercy was just too much for him, Dethmold had lost his grip on reality.

"Three or four days I'd say," said Karrak, "then I find out *exactly* where my prize is."

CHAPTER 16

Emnor flicked the various parchments and scrolls around on his desk. He truly believed in the Administration and what it stood for, and had felt highly honoured when his colleagues had deemed him the most suitable candidate to be made the new Head. The novelty however, had worn off far too quickly, and he was finding the position mundane and quite frankly, boring. The only escape he had was his new connection with Harley and his friends. Their enthusiasm and tenacity reminded him of his own youth so many decades before, when even the simplest of magic was frowned upon. It was more traditional for a young man to find a trade such as a smith or a farrier, not to have fanciful ideas of magic spells and incantations. This resulted in him being labelled as 'workshy' by his fellow villagers.

'If you don't have callouses or blisters by the end of each day, you haven't earnt your corn', was one comment that had been made to him. Strangely enough, the man who made said comment, couldn't understand how he had managed to catch a cold in the middle of summer. Emnor had known it was wrong to wish it on his neighbour, but he was a bit of a rebel, and deeply insulted by such a slanderous remark.

A knock came at the door and Emnor, without looking up, bade his visitor enter. It was Harley. Emnor's sullen look was suddenly transformed into a beaming smile.

"Harley, my dear boy, what can I do for you today?" he asked.

"I think it's more about what I can do for you, Master... Your staff is complete."

Emnor leapt up from his seat. "Excellent, excellent, lead the way then."

"But don't you have other things to do, Master, it *can* wait... if you're busy?"

"Busy? Of course I'm busy. Can't you see? Look at all those pieces of parchment. Harley, by all that's sacred, get me out of here!"

Harley couldn't help himself. In his years at Reiggan he had never met anyone as mischievous as Emnor, well, not someone of his age anyway. He began to laugh and bowed to his Master. "Master Emnor, if you would care to follow me."

Hurrying through the familiar passageways, they reached the not-so secret room just a few minutes later, to be greeted by Alexander, Xarran and Drake.

"So where is it then, let's have a look at what you've come up with," said Emnor excitedly.

Xarran opened the cupboard, removed the familiar oil-cloth parcel and placed it on the bench. Taking a pair of tongs, he carefully removed the coverings from the staff. Emnor gasped, because what he saw was indeed, breathtaking. When he had first seen the staff it was impressive, but now it glistened like fresh snow in the morning sunlight. More gems had been added and slim shards of gold had been inlaid between tiny diamonds along its length.

"May I?" asked Emnor holding out his hands as if he were asking to coddle a mother's newborn.

"But of course, Master. It is yours," replied Harley.

"Pass it here, Drake, there's a good fellow," said Emnor.

Drake smiled at him. "Ooh, please, Master Emnor. Don't tempt me... don't tempt me."

Emnor looked a little confused. "Sorry, what did I say?"

"It's been imbued now, Master Emnor," said Xarran.

"What difference does that make?" asked Emnor, completely unaware of the significance.

All eyes turned to Harley. "When a wand, or in this case a staff, is being made, anyone can handle it without repercussions. Once it has been imbued however, it will attach itself to the first person who touches it. From that day, it will be useless to anyone but its master."

"So what you're saying is that if Drake were to pick it up...?"

"It would be mine, all mine," said Drake with a pretend, sinister laugh.

"Well I never," said Emnor, "You boys really know your stuff don't you."

"We try our best, Master Emnor," said Alexander, "It's just that our best is better than everyone else's."

"That's it, Alex..." said Xarran with a sigh, "... nice and modest as usual."

Alexander shrugged his shoulders and held out his arms. "Why be the best if you can't say it yourself?"

"Quite right, Alexander," said Emnor, "Right, here we go." Emnor gently placed one hand on the staff, nothing happened. He placed his other hand further down and lifted it from the bench. He was surprised at how lightweight it was, considering the amount of platinum, gold and silver that went into its manufacture. "Gentlemen, it is magnificent, the detail, the craftsmanship, I'll say this…"

But his speech tailed off as the staff began to hiss very gently. Within seconds the hiss turned into a crackling and sparks began to fly along the entire length of the staff. Simultaneously it started to glow as flames, intertwined with the sparks, licked not only around *it*, but Emnor's hands as well, and all were now encompassed by what appeared to be a mini snowstorm in mid-air. Nobody panicked, they were awestruck at the spectacle before them. The four young wizards had created many wands in the past, but this had surpassed any of their previous endeavours by a hundred fold at least. After a few minutes, that seemed to last an eternity, the light show gently eased and the staff, still in Emnor's firm grip, simply emitted a calming, pale white glow.

"Do it again!" exclaimed Drake, "That was fantastic!"

Having calmed Drake down it was decided that it was time for Emnor to test his new staff. "What would you suggest, Harley?" he asked.

"Nothing too powerful, Master. Whatever you choose, the staff will enhance it, so the slightest spell will be far more concentrated than even you, Sir, will expect."

"An ice spell to start then, you can't blow anything up with ice can you?"

Harley raised his eyebrows and he, along with his friends retreated gracefully to what they thought would be a safe distance. Drake with a wand was one thing, but a Master with a staff could prove to be something completely different. The safe distance was at the other end of the room, by the door, just in case.

Emnor held the staff in one hand and pointed it at the far wall. "Just a small ice patch on the wall, just as a test," he said, trying to convince himself, let alone the others. A few seconds later the staff gave the slightest twitch and BLAM. The entire wall was covered, ten feet high, twenty feet wide and two feet thick, not so much of an ice patch, more of an entire glacier. Emnor shook himself and pouted.

"I think, for now… I'll practise outside."

∗∗∗

"Have you any leads as to where your brother is, Prince Jared?" asked Lawton.

"Apparently, he has occupied a cave some distance from here. It is thanks to Faylore and her kin that we now have a definite destination," answered Jared.

"But what if he is no longer there, where to then?"

"We have considered that possibility. Faylore and Hannock are both excellent trackers and if indeed he has moved on I'm sure we'll still be able to locate him."

"Excellent trackers," laughed Poom, "I've heard that one before. You come out into the wilds looking for footprints and broken twigs and you think you're an expert, HAH. But what if there are no such signs, what then, is my question."

"I happen to be the best in the kingdom when it comes to finding a fugitive, Master Poom. Nobody has ever evaded *my* detection," boasted Hannock.

"Is that a fact? Tell me, can you smell a tree and know that a passerby placed his hand against it to steady himself three days ago? Can you feel the heat from the ground where the same person slept even though he has been gone a week and it has rained heavily every day since? No? Not exactly an expert then are you?"

Hannock snorted and marched ahead, closely followed by his companions. Poom stood his ground looking rather proud of himself and Lawton stood beside him. A knowing glance passed between them.

"You can't *actually* do any of those things either, Poom."

Poom turned to his friend with a toothy grin on his face. "Well, Lawton, you know that, and I know that, but they don't know that, and after all, this is our land. Best to let them know who is in charge around here, before they start thinking they can order us around."

"Do you actually like *anybody*, Poom?"

"No not really, apart from you of course. But I am becoming quite fond of one of them," he said pointing at the companions.

"Oh, you mean the female?" said Lawton.

"My word not at all, oh what's his name now? Oh yes, Grubb, nice and grumpy, doesn't mince his words."

There was a look of disbelief on Lawton's face as he turned to his friend and sighed, "I have come to the conclusion that there really is no hope for you, Poom, none at all."

Poom held his arms out to his sides. "Now what have I said?"

Lawton shook his head and walked off briskly, to catch up with the others. Reaching them he struck up a conversation with Hannock. Realising that Hannock was an honourable man, he chose his words carefully. "Have you served Prince Jared for long, Captain?" he asked.

"We grew up together, been friends all our lives," answered Hannock.

"Ah, so more a labour of love than a sense of duty to one's betters?" Hannock offered no reply, simply continuing to lead his horse along the boggy track that the entire party was now trying to negotiate. "I do hope you'll forgive Poom. He has been a warrior all his life and can be a little abrupt at times."

"Nothing to forgive," said Hannock curtly.

"It's his age you see, getting a bit grumpy lately, what with all the scars and broken bones."

"We all have scars," Hannock replied quietly, inadvertently raising his hand to his eye-patch.

Lawton pointed briefly so as not to offend. "Old war wound?" he asked.

"You could say that," answered Hannock. "Or you could say a lunatic prince-cum-sorcerer, with delusions of grandeur thought it would be a good idea to blow me up!"

"My apologies, Captain, I did not mean to pry into your private affairs."

"There's nothing private about my affairs, Lawton. I'm here for good old fashioned revenge. Karrak took half of my face, tore my body apart and nearly killed me. If not for Jared and that dear sweet grumpy little git, Grubb,

358

I wouldn't be here today. They know why I'm here now, there's no illusion of duty. Find him, and kill him, that's my only agenda," he snapped.

"I do so like a man who knows his own mind, Captain, very pleased to make your acquaintance." The pair shook hands, or paws, or whatever it was that the Gerrowliens had, a hand shape, covered in gold and black fur with razor sharp claws retracted, just as a cat's would be.

A mutual respect had been formed.

"How old, exactly is Poom, if you don't mind me asking," asked Hannock.

"Well if you ask *him*, he'll lie and tell you he's two hundred and sixty."

Hannock started to laugh, "Really?"

"I know, ridiculous isn't it?"

"Just a bit," replied Hannock, "As if?"

"Yes I know, but we humour him… he's actually three hundred and seven." Hannock's mouth fell open, his eyes wide. "Are you alright, Captain?"

***

The wizard's body smashed into the wall. "My Lord, it happened so quickly, we could not prevent it, we tried…" he said, gasping for air before being blasted across the room again.

"Do you realise how difficult it is to arrange for a senior member of the Administration to be left

359

unattended, let alone vulnerable to kidnap?" screamed Karrak.

"My Lord, I beg you, please. I will make this right, just give me a chance…"

"Silence, worm. He's dead, how can you make this right? We both know that necromancy will only return the body, not the mind. His knowledge has been lost and I must start again." Karrak continued in his rage. Raising his hand, he was about to destroy the cowering wizard without hesitation, when Darooq stepped forward.

"My, Lord Karrak. Please forgive my interruption but I must speak with you urgently."

Karrak had never had anyone interrupt him before and was taken aback by the interjection of, what had become, his right hand man, the confusion showing as he turned to face him. "Can't you see I'm busy?" he sneered.

"Indeed, my Lord, but I am afraid this cannot wait," replied Darooq, looking Karrak directly in the eye.

Karrak turned to his victim. Kicking him in the face he snarled. "I'll deal with you later. Lock him up," he said to no one in particular. Two cloaked figures hurried forward and, grabbing the man by the arms, dragged him from the room.

"This had better be good, Darooq," said Karrak.

Darooq gestured toward the doorway that lead to the next room and followed Karrak through it. Once inside, he spoke. "My Lord, I do not think it wise for you to kill one of your loyal followers, especially in front of witnesses."

"Who are you to question me, Darooq, how dare you?" shouted Karrak.

"My Lord, we are few in number as it is. Killing one is harmful enough, but if others begin to fear your wrath if a mistake is made, they may decide not to follow you at all and depart. We need as many as possible. Sooner or later an assault must be made, if you wish to recover the Elixian Soul, and there will be more than a mere handful guarding it. Strength in numbers is the only thing that can ensure your success at its retrieval."

Karrak slumped down on a chair in front of a large desk on which he began to drum his fingers. He thought for a few moments and looked up at Darooq. "So what do you suggest, pat him on the head and say never mind?"

"It's a little late for that, my Lord. But he has been punished. Show leniency in front of the others this time and they will trust in you, but if you insist on killing this man, you risk losing them all."

"And you, Darooq, would you also abandon me?" asked Karrak.

Darooq was no fool. He was a powerful wizard in his own right. He was neither scared nor intimidated by Karrak, but his loyalty toward him was not completely altruistic. He wanted the wealth and power of which Karrak had spoken, and knew that it would only be a matter of time before this egomaniac would bring about his own destruction. Once he was out of the way, Darooq would take the opportunity to seize all that Karrak had so diligently obtained. "No, my Lord. I for one, shall not abandon you, whatever your decision."

This course of events had been the result of a momentary lapse of concentration. The wizard charged with overseeing the incarceration of Derrin, believing his prisoner to be a mindless body, had left him unwatched for just a few minutes. Derrin however, had retained just enough of his faculties to take a knife that had been left nearby, to cut his own throat, thus depriving Karrak the pleasure of questioning him, and recovering the vital information he craved, the location of the Elixian Soul.

***

Xarran, Alexander and Drake entered Emnor's office slightly sheepishly, followed by a relaxed Harley. He himself was used to being summoned at strange hours of the day, understanding that, no matter what his personal goals were, Emnor's requirements would always take precedence. Closing the door gently, they faced the Head of the Administration who was sitting at his desk, fingers interlocked as if waiting for any one of them to speak. An uncomfortable silence ensued until Harley, as usual, took the initiative. "You asked to see us, Master Emnor."

"Indeed I did, Harley, indeed I did. Tell me, how would you all feel about getting out of here for a while, stretch your legs, as it were?" The four friends exchanged glances, unsure as to what their reply should be. "Don't worry, it's not a trick question," said Emnor, his face breaking into the mischievous grin with which Harley had become very familiar.

"Is there a problem, Sir. Have we done something wrong?" asked Harley.

"Oh no, not at all, quite the contrary, dear boy. You've shaken up a lot of wizard's beliefs that we should, under no circumstances, use wands. Furthermore, many believe that I was coerced into using my new staff."

"What's that got to do with us… going out?" asked Drake.

"That's Master Emnor to you," mumbled Harley.

"I mean, Master Emnor… Sir," added Drake.

"Well you see I have a friend who may need a little help in the not too distant future and I believe that we, and I do mean *we*, could be the ones to offer it," said Emnor.

"What kind of help, Master Emnor?" asked Xarran.

"Well, not to put too fine a point on it, magical assistance in a major battle. However, although it seems imminent to me, it may not, to him. But mark my words, your very lives will be in danger should you choose to embark on this adventure."

"Well you can count me in then, do I have to sign anything?"

"Young Master Drake, maybe a little more thought should be given before volunteering," said Emnor.

"Master Emnor, have you met my father? *He's* an adventurer you see, always off discovering things, fighting monsters and the like. He seemed to think that me being a wizard was a bit, you know, girly. Now, if I could combine adventure, as you put it, with magic, that would really put his nose out of joint, so as I said, count me in."

"And if you're killed during said adventure?" asked Emnor.

"He'll be as proud as punch, because I'll have died a hero!" answered Drake with a big smile on his face. It seemed that the 'mad' part of his name really suited him.

The only one that seemed hesitant toward Emnor's proposal was Alexander. He was an only child and, as his father had died when he was very young, voiced his concern that if anything were to happen to him, his mother would struggle to support herself financially.

Assurances were made, not only by his friends, but by Emnor himself, that if anything were to happen to him, his mother would be provided for, for the rest of her days and would want for nothing. "Count me in," he said.

"I'm up for it!" added Xarran, resolutely.

It may have seemed foolish to the untrained eye, to take four very young wizards, the eldest being Harley at the age of twenty-two, into such a dangerous situation. There were many, far senior in years, who thought themselves to be one of the most powerful in the land, but Emnor knew different. These young men were more powerful than they themselves realised and their naïve, humble, if somewhat childish natures, although 'childish' only applied to Drake, would ensure their survival in the most perilous of situations.

Their meeting lasted for many hours as Emnor explained fully, what they were about to face. Once they were dismissed, each member of this secretive band departed Emnor's chambers, under no illusion that this was to be a simple field trip. They continued to meet over the next few days. Plans were made and strategies discussed until each member was positive of his role in their mission, the mission of saving Borell.

So it was, a week later, that in the cold light of dawn, five wizards, cloaked and with cowls pulled over their heads, departed Reiggan Fortress, their mission known only to them.

***

The mouth of the cave was as black as pitch. The companions stared hard, waiting for the slightest of movements from within. The night was still with not a breath of wind, and not so much as a blade of grass twitched.

"I'm telling you…" said Poom, lying flat on his back with his arms folded across his chest, "there's nobody in there."

"That's what he wants you to think," said Hannock pulling his bulky bundle closer to him as he lay prone, still watching the cave.

"I think he may be right, Hannock. We've been here for over an hour and we've neither seen nor heard anything," said Jared.

"I know you want him to be in there, Mr Captain, so you can bash him up a bit, but that doesn't mean he *is* in there," said Lodren.

"Thanks for that, Smiler, now shut your face," said Hannock, becoming a little tetchy.

"Do ye want me to go and have a look, you know, if you're afraid to go yourself?" said Grubb, who knew how to rile Hannock easily.

"You keep out of it, half pint, I've got enough with Corporal Cheerful here without you joining in."

"Ooh, I'm a corporal," said Lodren.

"Now see what you've started."

Faylore could bear it no longer. "The cave is obviously empty. What we need to know is, how long it has been empty, and how long it will remain so."

"I totally agree, Madam. Poom, off you go," said Lawton. In the blink of an eye, Poom was gone. The others watched closely as Poom, travelling so quickly that he barely cast a shadow, disappeared into the cave. Within a second, there were roars and crashing coming from within that caused the rest of them to charge at varying speeds toward the cave. Lodren held his hammer, Jared his sword, Faylore her bow and Grubb had transformed into the four-armed beast, but all were left behind by Lawton, who sprinted ahead. Reaching the cave, they ventured into the pitch blackness, and silence. Suddenly a flame erupted at the far end of the cave and there stood Poom, by himself, perfectly fine. He looked at them in turn for a moment, and then burst into fits of growling laughter. "You should have seen your faces," he said amongst his guffaws, tears dripping off his furry face, "That was brilliant… priceless."

The others however, did not see the funny side. Not even Lawton cracked a smile. "That was in very bad taste, Poom, very bad taste indeed," he said.

"Oh come on. There's no harm in breaking the tension with a bit of fun is there?" said Poom.

"You think it funny do you? Tell me… just how fast are you… *pussy cat*?" Hannock's voice was slow and menacing and the others turned to face him, as, unusually, he was behind them, "…Think you can outrun *this*?" He was pointing a crossbow directly at Poom, but not a standard crossbow. It was the golden crossbow, the crossbow that had put an end to Jared's bewitched mother.

"Put it down, Hannock, there's no need for that. It was just a sick joke, my friend, he doesn't understand," said Jared.

"Maybe he'll understand once a bolt pierces that thick, mangy skull of his," said Hannock.

Poom was unused to being threatened, and was deeply offended at being referred to as a *pussy cat*. He began to growl quietly, his eyes darting from side to side, assessing his chances of dodging the bolt, but uncomfortable as he was with the situation, he was not afraid. He had survived many battles in many wars and had witnessed rage in the eyes of many beings. This time was no different. In previous encounters, admittedly, there had been nobody attempting to mediate, so he chose to stand his ground and remained silent.

"I always believed you had a far better sense of humour than that, Captain Hannock. I remember how you and Prince Jared were always larking about as children, making fun of us barmpots."

The familiar voice came from behind Hannock. Emnor had returned, accompanied by his four faithful followers. The comment seemed to spark a memory in Hannock's mind. He knew Emnor's voice, but still enraged, he did not turn to face him.

"Things change…" he said, "… *people* change."

"Have you changed so much, Hannock? So much that you would shoot an unarmed ally?" asked Emnor.

Looking to the floor, Hannock lowered the crossbow, turned, and exited the cave.

***

The companions and their friends had agreed that it was safe enough to set camp, but at a sensible distance from the cave, making sure that it was still within visual range. The keen eyesight of the Gerrowliens and, of course Faylore, would ensure that any slight movement or flicker of torchlight would not go undetected.

Lodren was overjoyed at the prospect of catering for so many guests and their varying palettes. He pottered around like a mother hen in a bid to provide a sort of, verbal menu, but found himself having to insist as most were too polite to voice a preference toward a particular dish. "Look, it's no trouble at all, have what you like, *how about, why don't you try…*" seemed to be all he said for about twenty minutes.

"Bugger 'em. Just make a pot of stew or somethin' and give 'em some of it. Stop fussin' over 'em, they ain't bothered," suggested Grubb.

"Now, now, Mr Grubb, I don't tell you how to change into a bird or that big thing with four arms do I? So I'll thank you not to interfere with my catering duties."

"Just tryin' to help that's all… catering duties my backside," added Grubb.

Hannock had wandered a short distance away from the camp and could be seen sitting, with his back against a rock, sharpening his sword, again.

"He has such a fire in him, Jared, it could endanger you all," said Emnor.

"He's just, frustrated Emnor. It's taken us weeks to get here, and we're no closer to finding Karrak than we were before. With no visible trail to find, how then are we able to follow?" asked Jared.

"My students and I are able to travel much faster than you and your carts, and I have heard whispers," said Emnor.

"Whispers?"

"Apparently there is a village, Cheadleford, still a fair few days from here."

"There are villages in all directions, Emnor. Why would this one be any different?"

"There are rumours of strange beasts roaming the area, similar to wolves, but deformed, and bigger. Merchants that traded with the villagers are too afraid to go near the place and nobody who lives there has been seen for weeks. It's as if it has been wiped from the land, simply disappeared."

"How do you know, who told you?" asked Jared.

"That is of little importance, Jared. All I know is that it warrants investigation."

"But, Emnor, you and I both know that there are always rumours of monsters and beasts out here in the wilds. Village folk are prone to exaggeration, they've always been the same."

"That is very true, but I've seen these beasts, Jared, so has Faylore, and they belong to Karrak."

Jared looked at Faylore, who had been listening intently to their conversation. If she had thought it to be private she would have moved away, but nothing remained a secret between them. "It may be worse than it seems, my dear Jared," she said, "if there *are* indeed beasts in the area you can almost guarantee that they were formerly the villagers and that Karrak has *transformed* them."

"But that's not possible. He wouldn't, he couldn't, surely?" Jared began to babble.

"I'm afraid he can, and he would. And probably has, Jared," said Emnor.

***

369

"I don't care, I'm not apologising. Stupid one-eyed creep pointed a bloody crossbow at me, just for having a laugh. He should apologise to me. I should just go over there and rip his bloody head off."

"Poom, what would you do if, in battle, somebody blinded me in one eye?" asked Lawton.

"Easy, rip him apart, stick my spear right up his…"

"Alright, I get the idea. What if afterwards, somebody made a joke about it without knowing the whole story?"

"Same again, rip… OH! You mean?"

"Yes."

"And the man he's looking for was the one that…?"

"Yes."

"Bugger."

"Yes, Poom, couldn't have put it better myself."

"But I never made a joke about his eye, I mean, did I?"

"I know that, and you know that, but… is it starting to dawn on you now?" asked Lawton.

"Maybe I should go and apologise."

"I think that's an excellent idea, so glad you thought of it, Poom."

"I'll be back in a while, Lawton, just going to have a look around, you know, check the perimeter."

Their conversation had not been heard by the others. Poom now stretched himself, trying to look inconspicuous as he began strolling, seemingly aimlessly, toward Hannock.

Hannock did not hear his approach and started a little as Poom began to speak. "Looks like the sky will stay clear tonight, stroke of luck I suppose." Hannock glanced at him briefly but gave no response. "So, any idea where he might have gone then, this, sorcerer fellow?" asked Poom.

"Not a clue, but no matter how long it takes, I'll find him," muttered Hannock.

"When you kill him, what do you think, quickly, or nice and slow?" Hannock stared at Poom in amazement at the inappropriate question. "Sorry, I shouldn't pry, not my business. Look, I never meant to offend you earlier, it's just that, well normally it's just Lawton and me. We've been friends for years and he's used to me, we have the same sense of humour you see, but sometimes I open my big mouth when I should keep it shut and he kind of keeps me in line. I still think I'm a cub some days and he tells me to act my age, I'm nearly two hundred and sixty, you see."

On hearing the comment, Hannock couldn't help himself as a huge grin appeared across his face.

"Oh good, you're feeling better, Captain. You're smiling. Are you smiling or are you growling? I can't tell with you people, see, because your faces are... bald."

Eventually, having settled their differences, Hannock and Poom ventured back into camp. They suspected that they had been the topic of conversation during their absence, but both had agreed to ignore any awkward silence or overzealous attempts to include them in inane conversation.

It was agreed that Emnor and '*the boys*', as they were referred to, would go on ahead of them to investigate Cheadleford village as Emnor had suggested. The others would catch up with them as soon as possible, but if there was anything that Emnor deemed of importance he, or one of 'the boys' would travel back to inform them immediately.

"Excuse me, Mr Emnor," said Lodren, "how do you manage to get to and from places so quickly?"

"Relocation spell, Lodren, very easy spell really for us wizards," answered Emnor.

"Easy for you maybe, I nearly ripped my flamin' arm out the socket," muttered Drake.

"I told you to concentrate, Maddleton. Didn't I tell you to concentrate?"

"Yes, Master Emnor, you told me to concentrate, but you didn't tell me I shouldn't hold on to the gate whilst I was doing it, I wasn't ready, Master Emnor… Sir."

"Shut up, Drake, stop moaning," hissed Harley.

"Tell ye what, *I'll* go and have a look. You wizards still have to land on the ground but I can just fly over the place," said Grubb.

"Are you a Vikkery?" asked Xarran.

"How do you know about the Vikkery?" asked Grubb, frowning suspiciously.

"I'm a wizard, I know about lots of things, but I must say I do think the Vikkery are fascinating," said Xarran.

"Well now that you mention it, we are pretty fantastic," said Grubb suddenly looking very smug.

"Don't forget modest and kind-natured, Grubb," said Hannock smiling, but not daring to look Grubb in the eye.

Poom found this hilarious and, doing his best to stifle his laughter for fear of upsetting anyone else, did one of his now, well-known lightning dashes so as to be out of earshot, returning a few minutes later. The discussion continued.

"If there are any sorcerers there, Grubb, they may cast fire spells and you could be killed. No, we shall go first," said Emnor.

"Yeah, 'cause it doesn't matter if we get blown up, there's loads of wizards, they can just send some more," said Drake.

Harley slapped him around the back of the head to shut him up.

"Enough for now I think, time to eat. Who wanted the roast duck?" asked Lodren.

***

Darooq backed into the shadows. Many wizards were moving about the village but it would have been foolish to think that he could blend in with them, and he was no fool. Biding his time, he moved from one building to the next, pausing often as yet another figure passed, just yards in front or behind him. Each time he would watch them closely, hoping for a tell-tale sign. Walking perfectly upright or too quickly would suggest youth, and this was something for which he had no use. He was looking for someone not so spritely or maybe with a stoop, something that would betray advanced age, a senior wizard, one that would have information or knowledge that *may* be useful. To kidnap a youth would no doubt prove fruitless. Then he heard a voice, a voice he recognised from his days spent in Reiggan Fortress, Schnepp, one of the seniors. If anyone held secrets, it would be him, but how to catch him off guard?

Darooq slipped his hand inside his robes and drew from them a dagger. Nothing fancy, bone handled with a plain blade, but razor sharp. Still with his eyes on Schnepp, he crept closer, still secreted in the shadows. He was now only ten feet away and with a final check to make sure the old man was still alone, he raised the dagger and plunged it into his own shoulder. The searing pain shot through him but he held his hand over his mouth until the initial shock passed, before lurching forward.

"Master Schnepp, Master, please, help me," he whispered, holding out his uninjured arm and dropping to his knees as the old man turned around.

"What has happened to you, my dear man?" asked Schnepp, shuffling forward to aid him.

"In the shadows… a man… a knife," breathed Darooq.

"Here, let me help you," offered Schnepp and leaning down, took Darooq by the arm.

Darooq placed his hand against the side of the old man's face. There was a flash, like a tiny lightning bolt that travelled from Darooq's hand to Schnepp's temple, causing the old man to collapse in a crumpled heap beside his attacker. A moment later Darooq once again placed his hand against the old man's face. The pain in his shoulder was distracting and he barely managed to focus before, uttering a few quiet words, the air around them shimmered and they both vanished.

The companions milled about the camp, packing away the last few bits and pieces that were left, Lodren paying special attention to his pots and pans as usual, Hannock checking his one-man armoury, Faylore re-stringing her bow and Grubb attending to his beloved Buster and the rest of the horses.

Lawton and Poom paced back and forth, anxious to begin the journey to Cheadleford. As it was usually just the two of them, they were unused to having to wait around, and it showed.

"Are you ready yet?" asked Poom with a sigh.

"Just a few more minutes, Mr Poom," called Lodren.

"You'll get used to it. It's like waking at dawn, realising there is nothing to do and then sitting on a rock, waiting for dusk," grumbled Grubb.

"Why do they take so long to get ready?" asked Lawton. "We could have been half way there by now."

"Like I said, you'll get used to it. I did."

The band of wizards, having no carts to pack or other such burdens to bear, was ready to depart and Emnor approached Jared, smiling cheerfully. "Well, we're off. Just one thing before we do, I have a gift for you, here you are."

Emnor held out a small, linen-wrapped object and Jared took it, thanking him graciously. Carefully unwrapping it, he gave a slight gasp. "My dear Emnor, it's magnificent. What have I done to warrant such a gift?" Without his knowledge, Jared was holding the Heart of Ziniphar.

"My apprentice and his colleagues here made it for you, it's a simple talisman. Supposed to glow to warn you of danger, so *they* say anyway," said Emnor, pointing toward Harley and the other young wizards.

"But it must be worth a fortune looking at the size of this ruby, Emnor."

"We are wizards, Jared. We don't care about monetary value. Don't make a fuss, you'll only embarrass them, put it on, and *keep* it on," instructed Emnor.

***

Emnor, Harley, Xarran, Alex and Drake made their way toward the cave in order to make a final check on its desertion. Finding it still empty, they continued around the base of the ridge and were soon unable to see the companion's camp.

"Master Emnor, why did you give the Heart to Prince Jared?" asked Harley.

"Trust me, my boy, he will have far greater need of it than any of us ever would," answered Emnor.

"Surely he will not have to face the dangers that we shall, Master, after all, we are going ahead to clear the path for him and the others," continued Harley.

The others were listening and Drake, as usual, saw his chance to join in. "We are wizards, we don't need talismans to protect us. We have our own magical powers remember, Harley?"

"Quite right, Maddleton," said Emnor, "but we shan't be facing Karrak, Prince Jared will."

"How can you be sure of that, Master Emnor?" asked Xarran.

"I just am. We'll leave it at that shall we?"

They knew that this was the end of the discussion. Pressing the Head of the Administration was not something any of them dared to attempt, however amiable a person he was. "This is far enough I think, now, everybody, *concentrate,* that means you, Maddleton."

***

Moments later with a gust of wind that swayed the trees, they appeared on the outskirts of Cheadleford village. Emnor held up his staff and the boys brandished their wands in outstretched hands. It was only just after dawn and, when they had left the companions it was a bright morning with a slight breeze, but here the air was still and there was an unnatural gloom that only seemed to be over the village itself. There was an ominous silence. The village was skirted on three sides by dense forest yet not so much as a solitary bird song could be heard.

"Be on your guard, gentlemen. Follow me," said Emnor, as he took his first few, tentative steps.

The first building they came to gave an indication that what they were about to encounter would not be pleasant, charred across half the width of the facia with blood splashes across the other half, it set the pulses of the younger wizards racing. It was all well and good to be bold and brave when miles away from harm, but now, that safe distance was gone, and the reality of the dangers were now being realised by these young inexperienced wizards.

Surprisingly, or not, the only one that seemed unaffected was Drake. Whether he was brave or simply too stupid to realise the potential danger could have been debated at a later date, but for now, it was just what Emnor needed to inspire courage in the others.

"I'll go this way, Master, you go that. We'll go around the edges first and then start checking inside the remaining buildings…" Drake realised what he had just said and scrunched up his face, not through fear but in realisation that he had, in a way, almost made it sound like an order to the Head of the Administration. "… If you think that's a good idea Master Emnor," he added, not daring to turn and face him.

"I think it's an excellent idea, Maddleton. Harley, go with him, you two, with me."

They met on the other side of the village a few minutes later but neither had anything to report. They checked the buildings one by one, Emnor deciding that this would be best done as a collective. Only one building remained and they approached it warily. It was the inn.

"The Hangman's Noose, that's nice, nothing scary about that is there?" Xarran's question was of course a sarcastic, rhetorical one as he looked around at the others.

"Nothing at all…" replied Alex, not taking his eyes off the door whilst pointing his wand in his quivering hand, "… after you, Xarran."

They entered the inn with as much stealth as possible, listening intently, which was difficult with their hearts beating so loudly in their chests. Ordinarily, Emnor would not have been so cautious, but his concern for the safety of his young charges was in the forefront of his mind.

The bar room was empty, and a thick layer of dust on the bar itself suggested that it had been abandoned for some time. Broken furniture was strewn about and what seemed to be more bloodstains, adorned the floor and in some places, the walls.

"Shall I check the cellar, Master?" whispered Drake, much relieved when Emnor replied.

"No, you stay here, I'll go."

He ventured down the dark, narrow, creaking staircase and now, at the foot, found himself in darkness. Suddenly a gentle light appeared before him, a floating, glowing orb that hovered a few feet in front of him as he made his way across the cellar floor. As he took a step, the orb moved ahead of him like a lantern. There were beer kegs stacked against the far wall and a table had been placed at the side of the room, now with a broken chair leaning against it. There was nothing out of the ordinary in the cellar apart from a large pile of grey rags in the one corner. Emnor prodded at them with the end of his staff. The pile seemed to roll forward and to his horror they unravelled completely. The arms fell to the side and the head hit the floor with a thud as a corpse spilled out onto the floor, eyes still wide open and the throat even wider. Emnor recoiled and tripped on the broken chair. Unable to stop himself he fell backwards and crashed through the rickety table. There was a commotion on the stairs as all four of his students came charging down to his aid, unnecessarily, but they were not to know that. The boys stared, aghast at Emnor's discovery. "Did you know him, Master?" asked Harley.

"Well he has been dead for some time, and the body has begun to decay, but he does seem familiar, maybe…"

"Well whether you do or you don't, Sir, I think we should at least build a pyre and take care of the corpse," suggested Xarran.

"No, we can't. It would alert anyone nearby of our presence. We'll have to bury him," said Emnor.

"Bury him? But that's barbaric, Master, I mean, put him in the ground?"

"Whoever he was, I'm sure he'd understand. It's all for the greater good, Xarran."

On Emnor's instruction, the boys began to dig a shallow grave just outside the village. Drake complained about having to do manual labour.

"If you know of a spell that will allow us to complete the task a little quicker I'm sure we'd all be happy for you to share it with us," suggested Alexander.

"Well I'm sure I could do something," answered Drake.

"I meant without blowing up the remnants of the village," said Alexander.

"Ah, see what you mean, it probably would be a bit on the loud side," admitted Drake.

"Good grief, you were going to blast a hole in the ground. That was your idea, wasn't it?" asked Alexander.

"Might have been," answered Drake pouting slightly.

"Emnor suggests not lighting a fire so that we remain undetected but 'blow 'em up Bill' here wants to announce our presence on a much grander scale. You're unbelievable, Drake," said Xarran.

Emnor had the far more gruesome task of preparing the body for internment and had sent his young charges away before he commenced with his macabre duty. He had seen many corpses in his time, but they were recently deceased and embalmed, not in the early stages of decomposition. He decided to wrap the body as tightly as possible in the robes that, had at first, appeared to be just a pile of rags, whilst showing the deceased the utmost respect. Laying it flat on the floor, he straightened out the legs and pulled gently at the robes, then drew the cowl over its head and finally folded his left arm across the chest. It was only when he began to gingerly bring the right arm across that a glint of light caught the ring on the index finger. Merely interested, he leaned closer, hoping that, if he recognised it, he may gain insight into the man's identity. The light was poor in the cellar and although the glowing orb remained, its fault was that if one approached it, it would move away.

"Forgive me, my dear man, I shall return it in just a few moments," Emnor said quietly as he carefully removed the ring from the dead man's hand.

As Emnor passed through the doorway of the inn he blinked in the daylight, it was gloomy admittedly, but still much brighter than the dank cellar. Harley and his friends had completed their own unpleasant task and, as Emnor had commanded, were waiting just outside.

"Is everything alright, Master. Can we be of any help?" asked Harley.

"Our friend downstairs was wearing a ring. It appears vaguely familiar, but I can't quite place it. Take a look, boys, see if any of you recognise it would you," said Emnor. This was obviously an instruction, not a request.

One by one, they inspected the ring until eventually, only Xarran remained. Taking it from Drake, he let out a gasp. "This belonged to Master Derrin. The man downstairs is Master Derrin," blurted Xarran.

"Are you sure, I mean completely sure, Xarran?" asked Emnor.

"Yes. I commented on it once and he showed it to me more closely. It's a kind of family crest and has been passed down through generations of his family for hundreds of years."

Emnor stroked at his beard nervously and began pacing back and forth, muttering to himself.

"What's wrong, Master?" asked Harley.

"Harley, I need you to go back for the others. I know we don't usually hold with such things, but you must use your powers of relocation to bring them here one by one. Start with the slowest first, probably the nice one, Lodren and then, more importantly, Prince Jared. Don't bother with the Gerrowliens they can make it here in a couple of hours by themselves. Go, *now*," replied Emnor.

***

Harley appeared in a cloud of black smoke. Usually his technique was far more refined and he was a little embarrassed at how amateur his appearance must have seemed to the startled travellers. Crossing the short distance to Lodren, he grabbed him by the wrist.

"Master Emnor needs to see you all, *now*," he said, and in another cloud of black smoke, vanished.

The remaining members exchanged looks of amazement.

"The old fella must be mighty hungry to need Lodren that badly," said Grubb.

"Somehow I don't think he's hungry," said Hannock, reaching for the crossbow.

"I don't think you'll need that, Charles. He'd hardly take Lodren first if they were in the middle of a battle," said Faylore.

"Agreed, he'd have grabbed a warrior, me," said Poom without hesitation.

"Quite right, Poom…" said Lawton "…send the old ones in to die first so the younger ones survive," said Lawton.

"What do you mean, the *old* ones? I'll have you know…" But his protest was cut short as Harley reappeared.

"Lawton, Poom, Master Emnor asks that you head for the village as fast as you can, we'll wait for you there…" he said, "… Prince Jared, you next please."

"What the hell is going on, what's this all about?" asked Hannock, becoming a little agitated.

"Apologies, Captain, orders are orders, no time to explain," and now grabbing Jared by the wrist, Harley disappeared once more.

***

Schnepp opened his eyes. He was bound to a chair in a dark room but was most surprised to find that he was completely alone. A few feet in front of him was a large desk and on the desk an ominous looking wooden box. He stared at it for a few moments until realisation dawned on his face, he had seen it's like before. He pulled at his bindings to no avail, he was a frail old man despite his magical prowess and they remained secure. Closing his eyes in order to concentrate, he began to mutter, hoping to secure his freedom with magic, but this too, proved useless. A faint scratching could be heard from inside the box as Schnepp's fears were now confirmed. *What sort of person would have such a thing in their possession?* It was not long before he had his answer. It seemed as if he had been tied to the chair for hours as he awaited his fate. The pain in his back grew increasingly worse, his brittle bones strapped tightly to the unpadded wood. Then he heard the footsteps heading slowly toward the room. The door opened silently and he saw the silhouette of the huge man standing in the doorway.

"Karrak Dunbar if I'm not mistaken," he said quietly.

"I was, in a previous life, before everything was stolen from me," replied Karrak.

"Nothing was stolen from you, Karrak. Your own petty jealousy robbed you of everything that you regarded as your own, that and your insanity," said Schnepp.

"You would do well not to aggravate me, old man," roared Karrak.

"Why, what else can you do to me, tie me to a chair? Torture me? Just get on with it. I don't wish to spend my last moments of life listening to the ravings of a lunatic."

"Torture you? Oh no, I have a much better idea than mere torture."

384

"You mean the Globbiran spider you have in that box? Is that it? Is that all you have, a spider? Do you have any idea how old I am? The minute that thing latches onto the side of my head I'll probably have a heart attack and if not, I'm sure I won't survive three or four days while it chews away at my brain. I don't have many years left in me anyway, so as I said, get on with it, you'll get nothing from me."

"I could just possess your body, then I'll have all the answers I need," suggested Karrak.

"You have hexes and runes all around this room to prevent the use of magic. You'd have to take me out and then I could use my own magic before you could possess me."

"Not if I were to render you unconscious, old man."

Schnepp began to laugh, "You really are pathetic, Karrak. If it were that simple you would have done it by now and this tedious conversation would not be taking place, which would be a blessing, you're fishing, BOY. These waters are empty, Karrak, the fish aren't biting today, so kill me or let me go. Either one will be a release from your prattling."

Karrak wanted to rip the old wizard apart and it took every fibre of his being to contain his rage. Turning his back on him, he took a deep breath. "Very well, I'm a reasonable man, Master Schnepp. What do you want? What can I offer you in return for one location? That's all I want, one simple location."

"No, Karrak, what you want is the Elixian Soul, do you think me that naïve?"

"Well that might be useful I admit but all I need is the location, its acquisition would be my problem. Come on, Schnepp, I'm going to get it anyway, name your price."

"Your head, on a plate you maniac, now are you going to open that box or not?" shouted Schnepp.

***

The companions had now all been brought to Cheadleford village, apart from Grubb who had insisted that he would not leave Buster or the horses unattended. "Look, just go and do what ye have to do, leave me here, I'll catch up later. Besides, all the food and things are on the wagons and we can't do without those," he protested.

The others, along with Emnor and the boys were now gathered in The Hangman's Noose. A few waves of a wand had repaired enough tables and chairs to accommodate them all, as they sat awaiting whatever dire news Emnor was about to announce. Derrin's rudimentary funeral had taken place during the transportation of the companions, with Lodren taking the initiative of banging a headstone into the ground with a gentle tap of his hammer.

"Derrin was a senior member of the Administration and there is no reasonable explanation as to why he would be here in Cheadleford. I personally, have not seen him for weeks, but if there were something of importance here, I'm sure he would have informed me. That leads me to believe that he was brought here against his will."

"But there's nothing here, Emnor," said Jared.

"Exactly, so no witnesses. This was always a rough village, full of thieves and bandits. Decent folk avoided it and only travelling merchants of dubious character would venture here. Secrets would be easy to keep."

"Karrak's beasts were here, I know that for sure, I can smell them," said Faylore.

"So Karrak was here, Derrin was here and those beasts were here. This is worse than I feared," said Emnor.

The door to the inn opened and closed in a split second, and there stood Lawton and Poom.

"Did we miss anything?" asked Poom.

"Only that they've decided that the sorcerer and his pets have been here. Oh, and they found a dead body," said Lawton.

"How do you know all that?" asked Lodren. "Have you been listening outside?"

Lawton sighed, "Well there's a strange scent in the air of an animal I don't recognise, you said something about the villagers being turned into some kind of beasts so therefore it must be them, that means the sorcerer must have been here. There's a freshly dug grave on the outskirts of the village, it hasn't rained and the ground is dry and grey but the soil on top of the grave is damp and black, so it can only just have been dug. On top of that there's a headstone that's been carved too neatly to have been done with tools so that means magic has been used and on top of it there are some slight cracks as if it has been knocked in with a hammer, that hammer at a guess," and he pointed at Lodren's hammer.

Lodren smiled and clapped his hands. "He's very good isn't he? Do another one," he said.

Lawton was astonished that the Nibby thought that his deductions were some kind of trick.

"As I was saying…" continued Emnor, slightly annoyed at the interruption, "… it looks as if Karrak has taken to kidnapping senior members of the Administration in a bid to acquire information."

"But what information could he hope for? He knows more magic than most of the Administration put together," said Xarran.

"He's not looking for more magic… he's looking for the Elixian Soul!"

The source of the announcement was unexpected. Had Emnor spoken these words it would not have been surprising, but it had been said by *Alexander*. The room fell silent as all eyes turned to face him. The most questioning being those of Emnor. "Tell me, Alexander, what do you know of the Elixian Soul?" asked Emnor.

Alex made light of his comment and gave a nervous laugh. "Only that it's a myth, Master Emnor, you know, like buried treasure stories."

"It's not a myth, Alex, and you know it's not…" said Xarran, "… because you told us that one of the seniors mentioned it to you once, and that *someone*, was Master Derrin."

"Yes, I did say that, but I never believed it. I just thought you might find it a bit of fun. He wouldn't mention something like that if it were real would he, not to me. It was just a laugh, like ghost stories told in dark halls at night, things that go bump in the night, a powerful stone that would bring about the end of the world, it can't be real, can it?"

"What would you say, Alex, if I told you that not only is it real, but that it has been protected by the Administration for centuries in the bowels of Reiggan to prevent it from falling into the wrong hands?" asked Emnor.

"So that's why you warned us that our lives could be in danger? Karrak wants to find the Elixian Soul in order to rule the world!" Harley had at last fitted all pieces of the puzzle together.

"Yes and if my brother does get his hands on the Soul, he will show no mercy. He'll destroy anyone who dares stand in his way," said Jared.

"We'd better kill him quick then, where are you keeping this, *thingy* Soul?" asked Poom.

"Reiggan. We returned it to Reiggan Fortress, the last place he'd think to look," answered Emnor.

"You hope he doesn't..." growled Hannock, reaching for the golden crossbow that now hardly ever left his side "... but I hope he does."

"Well there's nothing we can do right now. We shall stay here overnight whilst we decide what our next steps should be," said Emnor.

"But it's barely midday, Master Emnor. We could cover a lot more ground if we continue immediately," said Xarran.

"And what of Grubb, do we leave him behind? Do we also leave His Royal Highness and his companions? Do you not think that a little selfish?" asked Emnor.

"I could fetch Grubb, there and back in ten minutes, then we could go on ahead," suggested Drake.

"Could you also bring the carts and horses?"

"Yes, if we do it in pairs," replied Drake.

"I'm a bit worried about Mr Grubb, out there all on his own," said Lodren.

"Worried about him!" exclaimed Hannock, "You've witnessed his transformations, Lodren, who would want to mess with that?"

"All the same, Mr Captain, I want to go back and get him, make sure he's safe," replied Lodren, holding his hammer and tapping it against his free hand.

"There are the Hissthaar to consider. They always travel in packs and if they do happen upon Grubb, they will attack," advised Lawton.

"They'd be in for a shock if they did," laughed Hannock.

"Harley, Xarran, return to Grubb and escort him here would you? Let us not take any risks," ordered Emnor.

"I'll go with you, Mr Grubb can be ... *difficult* ... with strangers," said Lodren.

"What? Dear old grumpy Grubb. Are you thinking of the right person, Lodren?" asked Hannock, laughing again.

"He wouldn't be so grumpy if you didn't keep teasing him, Mr Captain," Lodren snapped.

"Oh dear, looks like it's contagious, you've got it now, the curse of the grumps." Hannock it seemed, was back on form. Admittedly his goading of Lodren was uncalled for, but it was good to hear him laughing again.

"I shall accompany you," said Faylore. It was quite obvious to all that this was not a request.

"As you wish, Your Majesty," said Harley with a clumsy bow.

Alexander and Drake stepped forward, it had become obvious that this was a major operation to retrieve Grubb.

"And we'll join you shortly," said Poom, "Still need to stretch my legs and another sprint will do me good."

Lawton looked at Poom with half-closed eyes, "What do you mean *we*?" he asked.

"Oh, alright then, Fatso, you wait here if you like," replied Poom.

"I shall, and don't go too fast will you? Too strong a breeze may dislodge more of your mangy fur."

The pair growled at one another in jest and with a gust of wind, Poom was gone.

***

The two young wizards, along with Lodren and Faylore, appeared just a few yards away from Grubb who, now used to the appearances and vanishings, barely turned a hair.

"What have you come back for now, all that magic making you hungry? Need some food off the cart?" he grumbled.

"No, we're here to help keep you safe, Grubb," said Lodren.

Grubb stopped dead in his tracks and looked about him. The open plains stretched for miles in every direction and there was no movement save the birds in the sky. "From what!?" exclaimed Grubb.

"Well you never know. You might get bitten by a snake or something, then you'd need our help," suggested Lodren.

Grubb shook his lowered head and sighed in disbelief. "Come on, Buster, if we ignore 'em they might bugger off and leave us in peace."

The relocation of the horses and carts had not been as easy as they had first envisaged and, many hours later, they were all gathered in the village. Poom had joined them and, wanting to stretch his legs had spent most of the return journey running in circles around the carts before they were spirited away. Satisfied by his exercise, he now lay flat on the limb of an overhanging tree panting, his tongue hanging from the side of his mouth, looking very pleased with himself.

Not surprisingly, a large campfire had been built at the far end of the main road through the village. Consideration had been given to using one of the buildings as temporary lodgings but none of them could bear the discomfort they felt within, especially when re-entering The Hangman's Noose. They discussed the risk of alerting nearby enemies of their presence before lighting the fire but decided that, if in fact there were any, they would surely have been detected by now.

A huge smile came upon Lodren's face as he saw the firelight and he wasted no time in grabbing for his pots and pans. "Is there any water nearby?" he asked. Lawton pointed at the well located on the other side of the road. "Never even saw it, got a bit excited I suppose," said Lodren and dashed across to it.

***

392

Later that evening, having enjoyed a hearty meal, they all sat around the campfire.

Emnor had spoken with Jared a little earlier and they had decided between them that a formal meeting should be held in order to ascertain what part, if any, each was to play in the continuation of their quest.

"My friends, I thank you all for your participation in what has become a most arduous task so far, but I fear that any who may remain in our company…" began Jared.

"Look we don't need any of your fancy speeches," interrupted Grubb, "What ye want to know is, who's staying and who's going, right? We might be killed, we might be burned, bashed or blown up, right? So who wants to carry on? Raise your hands if you do and bugger off now if you don't."

Jared stared open-mouthed at Grubb who now had his hand in the air as, one by one, the rest of the now large gathering, followed suit.

"Right, that's that out of the way, so what's the plan, Your Highness?" asked Grubb smiling! Grubb… smiling?

"Ever thought of writing speeches for a living, Grubb?" asked Hannock.

"Captain Hannock, Sir… get stuffed," replied Grubb, *still* smiling.

***

The companions, along with the wizards and Gerrowliens, discussed their plans at length with only one objection being raised, by Hannock.

"You know that if he gets his hands on the Soul you won't be able to stop him," he said.

"But we must make sure that he doesn't," stated Emnor.

"No, what you're saying is that you're going to try to stop him. If you can't, you might hesitate if there's only one conclusion, kill him. But I won't hesitate, you need me with you."

Emnor had to resign himself to the fact that Hannock was right. The slightest hesitation could easily result in the death of any one of them. "Very well, I concede. I admit that the last thing I could bring myself to do is to destroy him, but I also admit that his destruction may be our only option," he sighed.

"I could kill him," Alexander said quietly, then, realising that he had said it out loud added, "If one of us was in danger, I mean."

"We leave at dawn, Captain Hannock, make sure to drink at least a pint of water before we depart," said Emnor.

"A pint of water? Why do I need to drink a pint of water?" asked Hannock.

"Just do it, soldier boy, unless you want to arrive looking like our friend there," snapped Drake and pointed at the freshly dug grave.

***

The following morning Drake approached Hannock and thrust a water pitcher toward him. "Drink up," he said.

"Thank you…" said Hannock, then lowering his voice added, "… and the next time you call me soldier boy, I'll take your head off… *boy*."

"If you say so, soldier boy, if you say so," smiled Drake.

The wizards, along with Hannock appeared in the mouth of the cave in which the companions had first met Grubb so long ago.

Confusion swept across Emnor's face as he sniffed the air. "Do you smell that, Hannock?" he asked.

"Smoke, and a lot of it. Not merely a campfire, I suspect," Hannock replied.

"Gentlemen, ready your wands," instructed Emnor.

"Ready your what? What's a *one*?" asked Hannock.

"I'll tell you later, Captain, oh, and it's a wand."

Emnor headed along the trail with Hannock at his side, flanked closely by the others. Rounding the familiar curve they saw the gates of Reiggan Fortress, fully open, smoke billowing from them.

"This is worse than I feared, we are too late," said Emnor.

They hurried forward and on reaching the gates, headed through into what was once the magnificent courtyard. Not one of the marble statues remained intact, parts of the walls were missing and everywhere was charred and black. Hannock raised the golden crossbow in front of him, prepared for the worst.

The boys' mouths fell open as they witnessed the horrific scene. The corpses of many wizards littered the courtyard, some still smouldering having been burned alive, others crushed by falling masonry.

"Try not to look at them, boys, stay on your guard," said Hannock. He had witnessed carnage before and knew that his words were meaningless to them, these were not battle-hardened warriors, just boys.

Emnor half walked, half stumbled across the courtyard. These were his friends, friends he had known for decades and in some cases, centuries. His heart skipped a beat. The secret staircase, *it was open.*

He rushed forward and descended, almost falling in his haste. He paused at the foot seeing that the chamber doors too, were open. He stood in the doorway staring at the pedestal and then at the wall behind it where the body of Schnepp had been pinned with crossbow bolts through his wrists, the words 'my thanks' burned into his chest.

Emnor turned to Hannock.

"He has it. *Karrak has the Elixian Soul... His ascension has begun."*

They must now become…

THE BANE OF KARRAK